Praise for Emma Miller and her novels

"[A] heart-warming romance."
—*RT Book Reviews* on *Courting Ruth*

"There is warmth to the characters that will leave readers looking forward to seeing more."
—*RT Book Reviews* on *A Match for Addy*

"A captivating story."
—*RT Book Reviews* on *Miriam's Heart*

Praise for Debby Giusti and her novels

"The active pace becomes more engaging as the drama intensifies."
—*RT Book Reviews* on *The Agent's Secret Past*

"Plenty of suspense, a captivating mystery and fast pacing make this a great read."
—*RT Book Reviews* on *Protecting Her Child*

"Detailed descriptions and well-developed dialogue create the perfect pace."
—*RT Book Reviews* on *Person of Interest*

Emma Miller lives quietly in her old farmhouse in rural Delaware. Fortunate enough to be born into a family of strong faith, she grew up on a dairy farm surrounded by loving parents, siblings, grandparents, aunts, uncles and cousins. Emma was educated in local schools and once taught in an Amish schoolhouse. When she's not caring for her large family, reading and writing are her favorite pastimes.

Debby Giusti is an award-winning Christian author who met and married her military husband at Fort Knox, Kentucky. Together they traveled the world, raised three wonderful children and have now settled in Atlanta, Georgia, where Debby spins tales of mystery and suspense that touch the heart and soul. Visit Debby online at debbygiusti.com; blog with her at seekerville.blogspot.com and craftieladiesofromance.blogspot.com; and email her at Debby@DebbyGiusti.com.

Courting Ruth
Emma Miller

and

The Agent's Secret Past
Debby Giusti

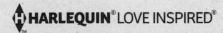

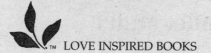 LOVE INSPIRED BOOKS

Recycling programs for this product may not exist in your area.

ISBN-13: 978-0-373-83814-1

Courting Ruth and The Agent's Secret Past

Copyright © 2016 by Harlequin Books S.A.

The publisher acknowledges the copyright holders of the individual works as follows:

Courting Ruth
Copyright © 2010 by Faulkner, Inc. and Judith E. French

The Agent's Secret Past
Copyright © 2014 by Deborah W. Giusti

www.Harlequin.com

Printed in U.S.A.

CONTENTS

COURTING RUTH

Emma Miller

For my great-grandmother Emma, a woman of deep faith, enduring love and legendary might.

May you be blessed by the Lord, my daughter; this
last instance of your loyalty
is better than the first.
—*Ruth* 3:10

Chapter 1

Spring... Kent County, Delaware

Ruth Yoder lifted her skirt and deftly climbed the wooden stile at the back corner of the fence that marked the property line between her family's farm and their nearest neighbor. The sun-warmed boards felt good on the soles of Ruth's bare feet, bringing back sweet memories and making her smile. *Dat's stile, God rest his soul.* How she missed him. The world had always seemed safe when her father was alive. Without him at the head of the table, life was more uncertain.

What *was* certain was that if they didn't hurry, recess would be over, and Mam wouldn't get her lunch. "Come along, Susanna," she called over her shoulder to her sister.

"Come along," Susanna repeated as she scampered

up the stile, clutching their mother's black lunch pail tightly in one chubby hand. Susanna would be eighteen in a few months. She should have been able to carry the lunch across the field to the schoolhouse unaccompanied, but in many ways, she would always be a child.

The English said Susanna had Down syndrome or called her a special-needs person, but Dat had always said that she was one of the Lord's gifts and that they should feel blessed every day that He had entrusted her to their family. Susanna's chubby face and slanting blue eyes might seem odd to strangers, but to Ruth, her dear little face, framed by the halo of frizzy red hair that marked her as one of Jonas Yoder's seven daughters, was beautiful. Susanna's white *Kapp* tied over her unruly bun, her Plain blue dress and white apron were exactly like those that Mam had sewn for Ruth. But Susanna's rosy cheeks, stubby little feet and hands and bubbly personality made her unlike anyone that Ruth had ever known.

Sometimes, to her shame, Ruth secretly felt the tiniest bit of envy for her sister's uncomplicated world. Ruth had to struggle every day to be the kind of person her mother and her church expected. Being a good soul just seemed to come naturally to Susanna. Ever since her sister Johanna had married and moved to her husband's farm down the lane, the responsibility of being the oldest child had settled heavily on Ruth's shoulders. It was that sense of responsibility that had caused her and Mam to have words after breakfast this morning. Not an argument exactly, but a disagreement, and that conversation with her mother made her stomach as heavy as one of Aunt Martha's pecan-raisin pies.

"You're twenty-three out, Ruth," Mam had reminded

her as she'd taken her black bonnet from the hook and tied it over her *Kapp* before starting off for school. "You joined the church when you were nineteen. You've done a woman's job in our house since you were fifteen. It's past time you chose a husband and had your own home."

"But you need me here," she had insisted. "Without Dat, running the farm, taking care of Susanna and teaching school is too much for you. It's better that I remain single and stay with you."

"Fiddle-faddle," Mam had said as she'd gathered her books.

" . . Roofie! You're not listening to me."

"*Ya,* I am." Ruth shook off her reverie and steadied her sister as she descended the steps on the far side of the fence.

"But you're not. Look!" Susanna pointed. Above the trees, in the direction of the school, rose a column of smoke.

"Samuel's probably burning brush."

"But, Roofie." Susanna trotted to keep up with Ruth's longer strides as they followed the narrow path through the oak grove. "I smell smoke."

"Mmm-hmm," Ruth answered absently. Tonight she would apologize to her mother and—

"Fire!" Susanna squealed as they entered the clearing surrounding the one-room schoolhouse. "The school is on fire!"

Ruth's mouth gaped in astonishment. Ahead, clouds of smoke billowed from the front porch and cloakroom of the neat, white schoolhouse. In the field, behind an open shed, Ruth spotted the children engaged in a game of softball. Upwind of the building, no one had smelled the smoke yet.

"Sit down, Susanna," Ruth ordered. "Sit here and guard Mam's lunch."

"But the school—" her sister protested, hopping on one bare foot and then the other.

"Don't move until Mam or I come for you."

Susanna sighed heavily but dropped to the ground. *Thank You, Lord,* Ruth thought. If there was one thing she could depend on, it was that Susanna would always do as she was asked, so at least she wouldn't have to worry about her safety. Closer to the school than the field, Ruth ran toward the burning structure, bare feet pounding the grass, the skirt of her dress tugging at her knees.

As she drew closer, she saw Mam's new student, Irwin Beachy, crawl out from under the porch. His face and shirt were smudged black, and he was holding his hands out awkwardly, as though they'd been burned.

"Irwin? What happened? Are you hurt?" she called to him.

The boy's eyes widened in terror. Without answering, he dashed away toward the woods.

"Irwin!" Ruth shouted. "Come back!"

When the boy vanished in the trees, she turned back to the school. An ugly crackling noise rose and flames rippled between the floorboards of the front porch. Through the open door, she could see tongues of red flame shimmering through the black smoke. The cloakroom seemed engulfed in fire, but the thick inner door that led to the single classroom was securely closed.

Wrapping her apron around her hands to protect them, Ruth grabbed the smoking rope that dangled from the cast-iron bell by the steps. She yanked hard, and the old bell pealed out the alarm. Then she released the rope and darted to the hand water pump that stood in the yard.

By the shouts and cries coming from the ball field, Ruth knew that the children had heard the bell and seen the smoke. By school age, every Amish child knew what to do in case of a fire, and she was certain they would arrive in seconds. She pumped hard on the handle of the water pump, filling the bucket that always sat there, and then ran back to dash the water onto the front wall of the school. Two of the older boys pounded up behind her. Toby Troyer pulled off his shirt and beat at the flames with it. Vernon Beachy grabbed the empty bucket from Ruth's hands and raced back to refill it.

Ruth's mother directed the fire-fighting efforts and instructed the older girls to take the smaller children back to where Susanna waited so that they would be out of danger.

Two of the Beachy boys carried the rain barrel to the other side of the schoolhouse and splashed water against the wall. Other boys used their lunch buckets to carry water. One moment they seemed as if they were winning the battle, but the next moment, flames would shoot up in a new spot. Someone passed her a bucket of water, and Ruth rushed in to throw it on the porch roof. As long as the roof didn't catch fire, the building might be saved. Abruptly, a sensation of heat washed up over her. She glanced down to see that sparks had ignited the hem of her apron.

As she reached down frantically to tear off the smoldering apron, strong hands closed around her waist and lifted her off the ground. Before she could utter a protest, Ruth found herself thrown onto the ground and roughly rolled over and over in the grass. Her bonnet came off, her hairpins came loose, and her hair tumbled down her back.

"Are you trying to kill yourself? Didn't you see your apron on fire?" A stranger with the face of an angel lifted her into his arms, and gazed into her face.

Ruth couldn't catch her breath. All she could do, for a second, was stare into the most beautiful blue eyes she had ever seen. Behind her she heard the shouts of male voices, but she couldn't tear her gaze from the eyes.

"Are you all right?"

She swallowed hard, unable to find her voice, and nodded as she began to cough.

"You scared me half to death," he murmured, still holding her against him, his body as hot against hers as the flames of the fire behind them.

"Is she hurt?" Mam laid a hand on Ruth's arm as her rescuer backed away from the smoking building.

The sound of her mother's voice brought her back to the reality of the situation. "Put me down," she ordered, embarrassed now. "I'm fine."

"Her apron was on fire. Her clothes would have gone up next," he explained, lowering Ruth gently until her bare feet touched the ground.

"It looks like the fire's almost out," Mam said, turning to see Roman and one of the older boys spraying the back wall with fire extinguishers. "Thank goodness they were able to climb in the window and get the extinguishers."

Ruth snatched off her ruined apron and accepted her *Kapp* that Mam handed her. Flustered, she stuffed her loose hair up in the dirty *Kapp,* stabbing the pins she had left into the hastily gathered knot of red hair.

"You sure you're all right?" The beautiful stranger

was beside her again. He cupped a strong hand under her chin, tilted her head up and looked boldly into her face.

Ruth bristled and brushed away his hand. The man staring at her was no angel and entirely too handsome for his own good. He was tall and broad-shouldered, with butter-yellow hair that tumbled over one eye and a dimple on his square chin. He was clean-shaven, she noticed, so he wasn't married, although he was certainly old enough.

She choked and coughed again, more flustered by his familiarity than by the smoke still lingering in her mouth and lungs.

"Eli Lapp." He offered his hand to her the way the English did, but she didn't take it.

Another flush of embarrassment crept across her face.

"And you must be Ruth, Hannah's daughter," he said, letting his hand drop, but still grinning.

Ruth looked to her mother, feeling a betrayal of sorts. Mam knew this Eli? How did he know Mam? How did he know Ruth?

A hint of unease flashed across her mother's face, quickly replaced with her normal calm. "Eli is Roman's sister's son. He's come from Belleville, Pennsylvania, to work for Roman. We met at the chair shop yesterday. Thank the Lord he was close enough to help. You might have been badly burned."

"I didn't need rescuing," she protested. She didn't want to be beholden to this arrogant stranger who made her feel so foolish. "I saw the sparks. I was taking my apron off when he threw me on the grass."

"Nevertheless, I thank God that He sent someone

to watch over you." Mam squeezed her hand. "I don't know what I'd do without you."

Mam turned to face the school. The fire seemed to be out, and the men had set aside the fire extinguishers. "I just don't see how this could have happened. We haven't had a fire in the stove in weeks, and we have no electricity."

"I'd say somebody started it," Eli replied. "That's how this kind of thing usually happens."

Immediately, Ruth thought of Irwin Beachy, who she'd seen running away from the school, but she didn't say anything. Irwin had a reputation for causing trouble. He'd been a thorn in Mam's classroom ever since he'd come from Ohio to live with his cousins after his parents had died. But Irwin could have just been frightened by the fire. It would be wrong to accuse him, especially in front of this Eli.

"It was good you came when you did," Mam said to Roman as he approached. "God must have sent you. If it wasn't for you, we might have lost the school."

"We were delivering a table to Esther Mose. We heard the bell." Roman glanced at Ruth. "Good you thought to ring it." He slapped Eli's shoulder. "And good my nephew saw Ruth's clothes catch fire."

"Glad to be of service." Eli stared boldly at Ruth and she felt heat wash over her again. "I'd hate to see such a pretty face burned."

Ruth felt so self-conscious that she wanted to melt into the grass. "We're thankful God sent you to save the school," she said stiffly.

"No lives were lost and no one was injured," Mam said. "Wood can be replaced." She straightened her shoulders. "It appears we'll be in need of a good carpenter. We're nearly at the end of the school term, and the children can't miss any days, especially those who are graduating."

Eli winked at Ruth. Even with her face smudged with soot and her red hair all in a tangle, she was the prettiest girl he'd ever laid eyes on. She had the cutest little freckled nose and a berry-colored mouth. She wasn't very tall; her head came barely to the top of his shoulder, but she was slim and neatly put together in her modest blue dress. But most of all, he was drawn to her eyes, nutmeg brown with dashes of cinnamon and ginger. "Aren't you a little old to still be in school?" he teased.

"I am not in school," she corrected him. "My mother forgot her dinner bucket, and I came to bring it to her."

He grinned mischievously. Ruth wasn't just pretty, she was saucy. A man didn't come across too many saucy Amish girls where he came from. Mostly, they were quiet and meek. Hannah Yoder's daughter was different, not just a pretty face and a tidy body. She had spirit, and he liked her at once. "If I thought you would bring my lunch, I might forget it, too."

Chapter 2

The hanging oil lamp cast a warm golden light over the Yoder kitchen as Ruth's family prepared for supper that evening. This was her favorite part of the day, and despite the near-tragedy of the fire, she found sweet comfort in the familiar odors of baking bread and the clatter of dishes and silverware.

Dutifully, Ruth helped her sisters carry food to the old trencher table that Dat's great-grandfather had crafted. The kitchen was Plain, spacious and as neat as the starched white *Kapp* Mam wore to Sunday services under her black bonnet.

Ruth was carrying two steaming bowls of corn chowder to the table when she heard a knock on the back door.

"Whoever could that be?" Mam asked.

Anna placed an iron skillet of fresh-baked biscuits on top of the stove. "I'll get it."

Ruth had a strange feeling she knew who the unexpected visitor was, and she hurried to the window over the sink and tugged back the corner of the yellow chintz curtain. The minute she saw him, she dropped the curtain and spun around, leaning against the sink. "Don't answer it!" she called, panic fluttering in her chest.

"Don't answer it?" Anna laughed as she walked toward the back door. "Ruth, what's gotten into you? You hit your head when that boy rolled you around in the grass today?"

Susanna giggled and covered her mouth with a chubby hand. Nothing was said or went on in Susanna's presence that wasn't repeated later to anyone who would listen.

"No, I didn't hit my head," Ruth whispered loudly. She felt silly and shaky at the same time, as if she'd played ring-around-the-rosy too long with her nephew. "It's supper time. Just let him go."

"Him?" Anna raised a blond eyebrow and Susanna giggled again.

Eli heard the sound of feminine voices on the other side of the door and yanked his straw hat off. Then, feeling silly, he dropped it back on his head. What was he doing? He wasn't *courting* the girl; he'd just stopped by after work to check on her. Okay, so it wasn't on his way home, but it *was* the proper thing to do, wasn't it? To check on a girl after she'd nearly caught her clothes on fire?

Eli groaned. Who was he kidding? He knew very well Ruth was fine. She'd made that quite clear at the school yard. He should never have come to the Yoder house. When he had left Belleville, he'd sworn off pretty girls. They were nothing but trouble. Trouble, that was what it was that had led him here tonight, and if he had any sense at all, he'd turn and run before the door opened.

That was the smart thing to do. Eli took a step back, cramming his hat down farther on his head. A smart man would run.

He was just turning away when he heard the doorknob, and he spun back, yanking off his hat again. In his mind, he already saw Ruth, pretty as a picture, smiling up at him, thanking him for rescuing her from certain death today. He smiled as the door opened.

But it wasn't Ruth, and he took a step back in surprise, nearly tripping down the step. Definitely not Ruth. This girl was taller and far rounder and not nearly so gentle on the eyes....

She looked as startled as he felt.

"H-hi." Her round cheeks reddened as she wiped her hands on her apron, a smile rising on the corners of her lips.

He had that kind of effect on girls. They smiled a lot, giggled when they looked at him. "H-hi," he echoed, feeling completely ridiculous. He heard someone whisper loudly from inside.

"Tell him I'm not here."

The girl at the door smiled more broadly, bringing dimples to her cheeks, and she took a step toward him, practically filling the doorway so he couldn't see inside.

Eli took another step back. That had to be Ruth he'd heard. It had sounded like her.

"Bet you're Eli," the girl said, crossing her arms over her plump chest.

He nodded, wishing more with every second that he'd taken that opportunity to run. "Yeah, yeah, I am."

He looked down at his scuffed boots, then up at her again. "I…stopped by on my way home just to see… to make sure Ruth was all right," he stammered, and then started again. "You know, with the fire and all."

"Just on your way home from the chair shop?" She nodded, still smiling. She knew very well his uncle's farm wasn't on his way home.

He didn't know what to say, but that didn't seem to bother her.

"I'm Anna, Ruth's sister." The big girl glanced over her shoulder. "We're just sitting down to supper. Would you like to come in? We've got plenty."

"Anna!" came Ruth's voice from inside, followed by more giggles.

For a second Eli was tempted. The smell of fresh biscuits made his stomach growl. Supper with Ruth would make the day just about perfect.

But she was a pretty girl, and he was supposed to be staying away from pretty girls.

"No. Thank you." He took another step back, making sure he hit the step. "I need to get home. Aunt Fannie will be expecting me. I just wanted to check to be sure she was okay. Ruth." Somehow his hat had gotten in his hand again, and he gestured lamely toward the house.

"She's fine," Anna said sweetly. "She really appreciates you putting the fire out on her apron and saving her from burning to death in front of all the children."

"Anna, please!" Ruth groaned from behind the door.

Eli had to suppress a grin. "Well, good night."

"Good night." Anna waved.

Eli nodded, stuck his hat back on his head, turned and made a hasty retreat before he got himself into any more trouble.

The minute Anna shut the door, Ruth grabbed her arm. "What are you doing inviting him to supper?" she whispered, not wanting Mam to hear her. In the Yoder household, there was always room for another at the table.

"He's very cute," Anna said. "He was just checking on you. He wanted to make sure you were all right." She grabbed the biscuits to put on the table. "I think he likes you. Susanna said she thought he liked you."

Ruth's heart was still fluttering in her chest. The idea of a boy that good-looking liking her was certainly not a possibility. Boys like Eli liked girls like her sister Leah. Beautiful girls. Or they liked exciting girls like Miriam. Ruth knew she was attractive enough, but she was the steady girl, the good girl. She wasn't beautiful or exciting.

"Supper time," Mam called with authority, looking from Anna to Ruth.

Mam never missed a thing, but luckily, she said nothing about Eli being at the door. Ruth didn't want to talk about Eli. Not ever. She just wanted to pretend the whole thing with her apron catching fire had never happened. It was too embarrassing.

"I hope there's enough here," Anna said, when they'd finished silent grace.

"This is plenty, daughter."

"It all looks delicious, Anna," Ruth said, finding her normal voice. Seated here at the table with her family, she could push thoughts of Eli Lapp and all her tumbling emotions out of her head. "But then everything you make is delicious."

Anna smiled, always grateful for a compliment. Cooking seemed to be what she lived for. Ruth cared deeply for Anna, but even a sister's loving eye couldn't deny the truth that Anna's features were as ordinary as oatmeal. Her mouth was too wide, and her round cheeks as rosy as pickled beets. Anna was what Mam called a healthy girl, tall and sturdy with dimpled elbows and wide feet. The truth was, Anna took up twice the room in the buggy as her twin Miriam.

Ruth knew the neighbors whispered that Anna would never marry but would be the daughter to stay home and care for her mother in her old age, but she thought they were wrong. Surely there was a good man somewhere out there who would appreciate Anna for who she was and what she had to offer.

"That was Eli Lapp at the door just wanting to make sure Ruth was all right. He was on his way home from the chair shop." Anna cut her gaze at Ruth.

Miriam nearly choked on her chowder. "That was Eli Lapp from Belleville at the door?" She looked at their mother. "Dorcas said he rides a Harley-Davidson motorcycle. Aunt Martha saw him."

"He's allowed to if he hasn't joined the church yet," Anna offered. "Dinah said he's *rumspringa*. You know those Pennsylvania Amish are a lot more liberal with their young people than our church."

Susanna's eyes widened. "*Rump-spinga?* What's that?"

"*Rumspringa,*" Mam corrected gently. "Some Amish churches allow their teenage boys and girls a few years of freedom to experiment with worldly ways before they commit their lives to God. Anna is right. So long as Eli hasn't yet been baptized, he can do what he wants, within reason."

"*Rumspringa,*" Susanna repeated.

"He's wild is what he is." Miriam's eyes twinkled with mischief. "That's what everyone is saying. Handsome and wild."

Ruth's throat tightened. She was just starting to feel calmer, and now here they were talking about that boy again. It was almost as bad as having him right here at the supper table! Why was Miriam teasing her like this? She knew very well Ruth wasn't interested in Eli Lapp…not in any boy.

"Let us eat before everything is cold." Mam didn't raise her voice, but she didn't have to. All eyes turned to their plates, and for several loud ticks of the mantel clock, there was no sound but the clink of forks and spoons against Mam's blue-and-white ironstone plates and the loud purring of Susanna's tabby cat under the table.

They were just clearing away the dishes when a knock came at the kitchen door. "Who can that be now?" Miriam asked. "Think it's Eli Lapp again?"

Anna and Miriam exchanged glances and giggled. Ruth stepped into the hall, seriously considering marching straight up the stairs to an early bedtime.

"I'll get it." Anna bustled for the door.

"*Ne.* I'll get it." Mam straightened her *Kapp* before answering the door.

When Ruth peeked around the corner, she was relieved to see that it was Samuel Mast, their neighbor.

He plucked at his well-trimmed beard as he stepped into the kitchen. "You're eating. I should have waited."

"*Ne, ne,*" Mam said. "You come in and have coffee and Anna's rhubarb pudding with us. You know you are always welcome. Did Roman say how much the repairs on the school would cost?"

Anna carried a steaming mug of coffee to Dat's place. Since Dat's death, the seat was always reserved for company, and Samuel often filled it.

Ruth thought Samuel was sweet on Mam, but her mother would certainly deny it. Samuel was a God-fearing man with a big farm and a prize herd of milk cows; he was also eight years younger than Mam. Nevertheless, Ruth observed, he came often and stayed late, whenever someone could watch his children for the evening.

Samuel was a widower and Mam a widow. With Dat two years in the grave and Samuel's wife nearly four, it was time they both remarried. Everyone said so. But Ruth didn't believe her mother was ready to take that step, not even for solid and hardworking Samuel.

The trouble was, Ruth thought, Mam couldn't discourage Samuel's visits without hurting his feelings. They all valued his friendship. He was a deacon in their church, not a bishop, as Dat had been, but a respected and good man. Everyone liked him. Ruth liked him, just not as a replacement for her father.

And now Samuel would be here all evening again, delaying Ruth's plans for a serious conversation with Mam about Irwin Beachy running from the fire. She didn't want to make accusations without proof, but she couldn't keep this from her mother. If Irwin *had* started the blaze, something would have to be done. But now there would be no chance to get Mam alone before bedtime. Samuel had settled in Dat's chair, where he would stay until the clock struck eleven and Mam began pulling down the window shades. Talking to her mother about Irwin would have to wait until tomorrow.

Maybe that was a better idea anyway. Ruth was still

flustered. First the incident at the school with that Eli, and then him showing up at their door asking for her. This had been a terrible day, and that wild Pennsylvania boy hadn't made it any better.

Every Friday, three of the Yoder girls took butter, eggs, flowers and seasonal produce to Spence's Auction and Bazaar in Dover, where they rented a table and sold their wares to the English. They would rise early so that they could set up their stand before the first shoppers of the day came to buy food from the Amish Market and prowl through the aisles of antiques, vegetables and yard sale junk. If the girls were lucky, they would sell out before noon.

The income was important to the household. There were items that they needed that Mam's salary couldn't cover. And no matter how tight the budget, each girl who worked was allowed to take a portion of the profit for her marriage savings or to buy something that she wanted. The sisters shared equally with Susanna, who always did her best to help.

Susanna loved the auction. She liked to watch the English tourists and she loved to poke through the dusty tables of glass dogs and plastic toys in the flea market. Today, Susanna had made a real find, an old Amish-style rag doll without a face. The doll had obviously had many adventures. Somewhere she'd lost her *Kapp* and apron, but Ruth promised that she would sew Dolly a new wardrobe and assured her sister that this doll was Plain enough to please even the bishop.

Today had been a slow day. They hadn't sold everything, and it was long past lunchtime. Now it was clouding up in the west, and it looked to Ruth as if they might get an afternoon thunderstorm.

Across the way, Aunt Martha and Cousin Dorcas were already packing up their baked-goods stall. Ruth was just about to suggest to Miriam that they leave when, suddenly, there was a loud rumble.

Heads whipped around as Eli Lapp came roaring down the driveway between the lines of stalls on a battered old motorbike. Ruth almost laughed in spite of herself at the sight of him on the rickety contraption. Even she could see that it was no Harley motorcycle, as Aunt Martha had claimed. It was an ancient motorized scooter, hand-painted in awful shades of yellow, lime and black.

Susanna's mouth opened in a wide *O* as she pointed at the motor scooter. Miriam called out and waved, and to Ruth's horror, the Belleville boy braked his machine right in front of the Yoder stall.

"Hey!" he shouted, over the clatter of the bike. "Ruth, good to see you again."

Ruth's eyes narrowed as she felt a wash of hot blood rise up from her throat to scald her cheeks. Aunt Martha and Dorcas were staring from their stall. Even the English were chuckling and ogling them. Or maybe they were looking at the ugly bike; she couldn't tell.

"Want a ride?" Eli dared, grinning at Ruth.

She was mortified by the attention. Eli Lapp was not only riding a ridiculous motor scooter, he wasn't dressed Plain. He was wearing motorcycle boots, tight Englisher blue jeans and a blue-and-white T-shirt, two sizes too small, that read "Nittany Lions."

"*Ne.* I do not want a ride," she retorted. "Go away."

She thought she spoke with authority, but her voice came out choked and squeaky, and Miriam giggled.

"It's perfectly safe, teacher's girl," he said. "I've even got a helmet." He held up a red one, almost as battered as the bike.

"Ne," Ruth repeated firmly, avoiding eye contact, even though he was staring right at her.

"If you won't, I will," Miriam cried, throwing up both hands.

And before Ruth could utter more than a feeble *"Ne,"* her sister scrambled around the table, hitched up her skirt and apron, and jumped on the back of the scooter.

"I want a ride, too!" Susanna declared, bouncing up and down.

Ruth cut her gaze to Miriam as she watched her boldly wrap her arms around Eli's waist. "Miriam," she ordered, "get off—"

Eli winked at Ruth, and the motorbike took off down the drive, out of the auction and onto the street, leaving her standing there looking foolish and Susanna jumping up and down for joy.

"Oh! Oh!" Susanna clapped her hands. "Did you see Miriam ride?"

"Help me load the rest of our things into the buggy. She'll be back in a minute," Ruth said, a lump in her throat.

She told herself she was upset that Miriam was doing something she shouldn't be, but she knew in her heart of hearts it was that boy again. He was making her feel this way. And she didn't like it. Not one bit.

As Ruth walked to the buggy, trying to look casual, she glanced in her aunt's direction. Aunt Martha had her head close together with Dorcas, and the two were talking excitedly. That was definitely not good. Miriam's poor decision would be all over Kent County by supper time. And there would be no doubt who would be held accountable. Ruth would.

She was the oldest left at home. Susanna and Miriam were her responsibility. They had not been baptized into the church yet, but she had. She should have known better than to let Miriam do something so foolish, so not Plain.

Ruth was just checking the horse's harness when she heard the growl of the motorbike as it grew closer again. Stroking the old mare's broad neck, she turned to see Eli and Miriam riding straight at her. A moment later, her sister was holding three ice-cream cones in the air and trying to get off the scooter without showing too much bare leg. Eli was laughing and talking to her as if they were old friends.

"He bought us ice cream." Miriam licked a big drip of chocolate off her cone and handed the vanilla one to Susanna. "What do you say, Susanna?"

"Danke," Susanna chirped.

"And here's one for you." Miriam had a twinkle in her eye as she held out the ice cream to Ruth. "I know you like strawberry."

"No, thank you," Ruth said stiffly. "I don't want any."

Miriam shoved the cone into her hand. "Don't be such a prune," she whispered. "Eat it. Mam wouldn't want you to waste food."

Ruth glared at Eli as she felt the cold cream run down her fingers.

"I see Miriam got back in one piece," Dorcas called as she hurried across the driveway toward Ruth. "Mam saw her and—"

"Here." Flustered, Ruth handed her cousin the ice-cream cone. "You like ice cream. You eat it."

Eli looked right at Ruth, laughed and roared away on his noisy machine.

Chapter 3

Ruth glanced at Mam and then turned her attention back to Blackie, their driving gelding, and eased him onto the shoulder of the busy road to allow a line of cars to pass. Blackie was a young horse, and Ruth didn't completely trust him yet, not like she did old Molly, so she liked to keep a sharp eye out for traffic.

"So why did you wait so long to tell me about Irwin?" Her mother's soft voice carried easily over the regular clip-clop of Blackie's hooves on the road and the rumble of the buggy wheels. The rain, which had held off all day, was coming down in a spattering of large drops.

Miriam had gone ahead with Anna, Susanna and Johanna and her children to the quilting frolic at Lydia Beachy's house in the big buggy, leaving her and Mam to follow in the smaller courting buggy. Dat had brought this single-seat carriage from Pennsylvania with him twenty-six years ago. It was just the right size for two, perfect for private conversation. Ruth had counted on being able to voice her concerns about Irwin, and she wanted to tell Mam about this afternoon's incident with Eli Lapp and his ridiculous motorbike before anyone else did.

"Ruth?" Mam pressed.

"I meant to, but…" An ominous roll of thunder sounded off to the west, and she flicked the reins to urge Blackie into a trot as she pulled back onto the road. "But Samuel came last night and then there was no chance to talk with you alone and today we were both gone all day."

"I see. Well, Irwin wasn't in school today."

"He wasn't?"

"I asked three of Irwin's cousins why he wasn't there and got three different excuses," Mam said.

Ruth sighed. "I don't want to accuse him. I just thought it was strange that he'd run away like that. I suppose he could have seen the fire and been trying to put it out." She hesitated. "But since Irwin is always making mischief…"

"Losing his whole family in a fire, coming to Delaware to live with people he hardly knows, it's no wonder he acts out." Mam folded her arms in a gesture that meant no nonsense. "I won't judge him until we know the truth, and neither should you."

Ruth didn't want to argue with Mam, but neither was she going to hold her tongue when she had something to say. "He did set Samuel's outhouse on fire last month. He gave Toby a black eye and you sent him home twice from school for fighting this month."

Mam frowned. "The boy has a lot of anger inside. He needs love, not accusations and false judgments."

"But if he makes a habit of playing with matches..."

"Where's your charity? In my experience, the wildest boys turn out to be the most dependable men."

Ruth winced. "You know I don't mean to be unchari-table. I just thought you should know what I saw with my own eyes."

"And rightly so." Mam nodded. "Now that I do know, I'll handle it."

When Ruth didn't comment, Mam continued. "The school can be repaired, but if people start talking about Irwin, the damage to a child's soul may not be so easy to mend."

"You're right, but what if he's a danger to others?"

"Have faith, Ruth. I'll do my part, the Beachys will do theirs, and God will do the rest."

"What will you do?" Her heart went out to the boy, as unlikable as he was, but they had to think of the other children's safety, too. As much as she valued her moth-er's judgment, she had to be satisfied that they weren't taking unnecessary chances to protect Irwin.

"I'll talk to him privately." Mam pursed her mouth. "Last night, Samuel confided that he suspects his twins know something about the fire, something they were afraid to tell."

"What made him think that?"

"Samuel said it wasn't what they said— it was what they *didn't* say." Mam squeezed her hand. "We'll get to the bottom of this. Not to worry."

She glanced at her mother, wanting to believe her, wishing her own faith in others came as easily as it seemed to come to Mam. "You always say that."

"And it's always true, isn't it? Things usually work out for the best."

Her mother smiled at her, and Ruth was struck by how young and pretty she still was at forty-six. Tonight, she was wearing a lavender dress with her black apron, and her black bonnet was tied over her starched white *Kapp*. No one would guess by looking at Mam's waistline that she'd given birth to seven children. "You must have been a beautiful bride, Mam."

"Why, Ruth Yoder, what a thing to say. I hope I was properly Plain. Vanity is not a trait to be encouraged."

Ruth suppressed a smile. Mam might not admit it, but she cared about her appearance. It was Ruth's opinion that on her wedding day, her mother must have been just as beautiful as Leah. Hadn't Dat always said he'd snapped up the prettiest girl in Kent County? "No one could accuse you of *Hochmut,* Mam. You never show a speck of self-pride."

"Not according to your *grossmama*. It took a long time for your dat's mother and family to accept me after we married."

"Because you grew up Mennonite and had to join the Amish Church to marry Dat?" That was something of a family scandal, but once she had joined the church, no one now could ever accuse Mam of not being properly Plain in her demeanor or her faith.

"Maybe, or maybe it was that your dat was her only son."

"And we were all girls."

"God's gifts to us, every one of you." Mam squeezed her hand. "Believe that, Ruth. Your father never blamed me that we had no sons. He always said he got exactly what he prayed for."

Ruth's throat constricted as she turned Blackie onto Norman and Lydia Beachy's long dirt lane behind the Troyer buggy. "I miss Dat."

"And so do I. Every day."

"Does that mean you're not going to marry Samuel?"

Hannah chuckled. "If I were to consider such a thing, wouldn't it be wiser to settle that matter with Samuel first?" She patted Ruth's hand again. "Mind your own mending, daughter."

As Blackie's quick trot drew the buggy toward the house and barn, Ruth realized that she hadn't had time to tell Mam about Miriam's ride on the back of Eli Lapp's motor scooter.

As the buggy neared the rambling two-story farmhouse, Ruth saw several of the Beachy children in the yard taking charge of the guests' horses. As she reined in Blackie, she spotted Irwin coming out from behind a corncrib to take hold of the horse's bridle. "A good evening to you," she called.

Irwin winced and took a firmer grip on Blackie. The horse twitched his ears.

"We missed you at school today, Irwin," Mam said mildly.

He mumbled something, fixing his gaze on his bare feet.

Ruth climbed down out of the buggy and gathered their quilting supplies. "Did you hurt yourself?" she asked, noticing a soiled bandage on the boy's left hand.

"Ne." He tucked his hand behind his back.

"It's all right, dear." Mam smiled at him as she picked up the *Blitzkuchen* Anna had baked. "No need to explain. I'll talk to Lydia about it."

His eyes widened in alarm. "Don't do that, teacher."

"Then we'd best have a private talk. Come in early tomorrow morning."

"But that's Saturday. There's no school on Saturday."

"I need help to move some of the desks around to make room for Roman to do the repairs." She paused. "And, Irwin? Don't be late."

"Be careful with Blackie," Ruth cautioned. "He's easily spooked."

Irwin nodded. "*Ya,* I will." He led the horse a few steps, then glanced back over his shoulder. "You won't say nothin' to Cousin Lydia, will ya?"

"After we have our talk, I'll decide if there's anything Lydia and Norman need to know."

"I don't mean to make trouble." He shrugged. "It just happens."

"Sometimes trouble finds us all," Mam said as she started up the steps to the house. Ruth hurried ahead and opened the door for her.

Inside Lydia's kitchen, Hannah and Ruth greeted several neighbors. From the next room, where everyone had gathered, Ruth could hear the excited buzz of voices as members of the community caught up on the latest news. One of Lydia's girls took their black bonnets and capes, and Lydia turned from the stove to welcome them.

Lydia was a tall, thin, freckle-faced woman with a narrow beak of a nose, a wide mouth and very little chin. "I'm so glad you could all come," she said with genuine warmth, deftly sliding a pan of hot gingerbread onto the counter. Lydia's voice came out flat, evidence of her mid-western upbringing. "After yesterday's fire, I didn't know if you'd feel up to joining us."

Ruth couldn't help noting Lydia's rounded tummy.

Another baby on the way. God was certainly blessing the Beachy family. Lydia was a true inspiration to Ruth. She hadn't hesitated when Irwin's family had been lost, and she had welcomed him into her family.

"It smells wonderful in here," Mam said, glancing around at the pies and cakes set on the table and counters. "You know we wouldn't miss your frolic. The quilt money will help with the school repairs."

Ruth looked around for her sister Johanna. The community quilting project to support the school was her idea. Johanna had sketched antique quilt patterns and carefully chosen the fabrics and colors. Everyone contributed to the cost of the material, and at each quilting night, every woman would sew one or more squares. Later this summer, they would assemble them in a day-long effort.

Ruth wasn't nearly as talented with a needle as Johanna, but she loved the chance to get together with friends and neighbors, especially when they were all working for such a good cause.

Lydia's crowded kitchen, smelling strongly of cinnamon, ginger and pine oil, was pandemonium as always. Both the woodstove and the gas stove were lit, and the room was overwarm. A large, shallow pan of milk, covered with a thin layer of cheesecloth, sat waiting for the cream to rise beside a spotless glass butter churn. On the counter and in the big soapstone sink, the last of the Beachy supper dishes stood, waiting to be washed. Without being asked, Ruth rolled up her sleeves, took down a work apron from a hook and went to the sink.

Four small giggling children, one of them Johanna's three-year-old son Jonah, darted around the long wooden table chasing an orange tabby. The cat leaped to a counter and dashed to safety, barely missing a lemon pie piled high with meringue, and headed for a direct collision with the unprotected pan of milk.

Lydia juggled a pitcher of lemonade in one hand as she snagged the cat with the other. Without hesitation, she then separated two toddlers tugging on the same stuffed toy. "Out," she commanded, shooing the children toward the sitting room. As the last little girl's bonnet strings passed through the doorway, Lydia turned to Mam with a look of despair.

"A long day?" Mam asked.

"I hate to complain, Hannah."

"Complaining is not the same as sharing our woes."

"It's that boy. I'm at my wits' end with Irwin. I try to be patient, but—"

Ruth turned back to the sink full of dishes and tried to give them a little privacy even though her mother and Lydia were only a few feet away.

"I know he's having a hard time adjusting, Lydia," Mam supplied.

"He is. He and our Vernon scrap like cats in a barrel. At twelve, the boy should have some sense, but…"

"He'll come around," Mam soothed.

Lydia lowered her voice. "It's what I tell Norman, but he says we can't trust the boy. I didn't think it would be this hard."

"No one doubts that you and Norman have been good to Irwin."

"We try, but he's late for meals. Remiss in his chores. He let the dairy cows into the orchard twice." Lydia sighed. "I hope we haven't made a mistake in opening our home—"

A baby's wail cut through the murmur of female

voices from the other room. "Is that your little Henry?" Mam asked.

"Go, get off your feet and see to him, Lydia," Ruth said, turning from the sink. "You, too, Mam. I can finish up here." The dishes clean and stacked neatly in a wooden drying rack, she dried her hands on a towel. She was just reaching for the can of coffee when she heard her aunt Martha's strident voice.

"Hannah, here you are." She bustled into the room, letting Lydia pass, but blocking Mam. "I wondered where you were."

Ruth forced a polite greeting. Aunt Martha was more trouble than a headache. According to Dat, his older sister's hair had once been as red as his. Now the wisps of hair showing under her *Kapp* were gray, and the only auburn hairs were two curling ones sprouting on her chin. She was a tall, sparse woman with a thin mouth and a voice that could saw lumber.

"How are the children?" Mam asked. "And Reuben? Is he well?"

"His bad knee is troubling him. He thinks we might have rain all weekend. I left him working on his sermon for Sunday services."

"I'm sure it will be as good as his last service," Ruth said, unable to help herself. Reuben was a good man, but he could be long-winded. *Very* long-winded. In fact, he could speak more and say less than anyone she knew.

Mam threw Ruth a warning look, and Ruth hid a smile.

Aunt Martha glanced around, a sure sign that she was about to launch into one of her reprimands. When she did that, Ruth could never be sure if she was looking to be sure no one was near, or hoping they were.

"I've been wanting to speak to you, Hannah."

She took on a tone Ruth knew well. Mam was in for it. "You were my younger brother's wife, and I have a duty to tell you when I see something not right." Aunt Martha cleared her throat. "You, too, Ruth."

Ruth steeled herself. So she was in for it as well.

Aunt Martha was a faithful member of the church and the community, but she liked to point out the errors of other people, especially Mam's daughters. And too often, she saw a small sin bigger than it actually was.

Ruth wasn't sure if she was in the mood tonight to be too charitable. "Aunt Martha…"

"Quiet, girl. Show some respect for your elders. It's for your own good and your mother's. I don't say this lightly." She sucked in her cheeks in disapproval.

Ruth gritted her teeth. She had to learn to be more patient. Like Mam. She wanted to be more patient; it was just that sometimes Aunt Martha made it difficult.

"And me being the wife of the minister, well, that makes it my duty, as well…" Martha took a deep breath and pointed a plump finger at Mam. "Hannah, your household is out of control." She scowled at Ruth. "And you're partly to blame."

Ruth bit her bottom lip to keep from speaking up. It did no good with Aunt Martha, not when she was like this. It was better just to keep quiet, listen and hope the tirade passed quickly.

"And I'm not the only one to have noticed," Martha went on. "Reuben was just saying to me the other day that it's unseemly for you, Hannah, to be teaching school like an unmarried girl."

"I'm sorry my teaching troubles you," Mam said. "But our school needs a teacher, and I'm qualified."

"The school board and the bishop approved Mam's appointment," Ruth put in. "And her salary helps to support our family."

Martha frowned. "Your mother should have remarried by now. Then it wouldn't be necessary for her to work."

"It's only been two years, Martha. Jonas…"

"Two years and seven months, sister. By custom, it's time you put away your mourning and accepted another husband. If you had a God-fearing man in your house, your girls wouldn't be acting inappropriately."

"Inappropriately?" Mam's brows arched. "How have they behaved inappropriately? Lately?" she clarified, spunk in her voice.

"Today. At Spence's."

"Eli Lapp was there," Ruth explained quickly. "He bought ice cream for Susanna and Miriam."

Aunt Martha eyes widened with great exaggeration. "So this is the first you've heard of it, Hannah? Miriam made a show of herself with that wild Belleville boy. She rode on his motorcycle in front of everyone. With her skirts up and her *Kapp* flying off her head. Her arms were around his waist. I saw it with my own eyes."

"Really?" Mam asked.

Ruth noticed Lydia and Aunt Martha's younger sister, Aunt Alma, peering into the kitchen. Lydia's cheeks took on a rosy hue. "I'm sorry. We didn't mean to—"

"Ne," Mam said. "There's nothing to hide. Martha was telling me that my tomboy daughter was riding behind Roman's nephew on a motorcycle at Spence's today."

"Scooter," Ruth corrected gently, feeling she had to defend her sister, even though she didn't really want to defend Eli. "It wasn't really a motorcycle. It was a motor scooter—"

"Scooter? Cycle? It doesn't matter what the loud English machine is called," Aunt Martha declared. "It's unseemly for a young girl like my niece to make such a spectacle of herself." She glared at Ruth. "Or for her older sister to allow it."

Mam chuckled. "It would be just like Miriam to take a ride on the machine, wouldn't it?" She shook her head. "But it's not so bad, is it? She's not joined the church yet. It's natural for her to dabble with the world…just as *we* did once." A smile tugged at the corners of her mouth as if she knew some secret about Aunt Martha that Ruth and the others didn't.

"It's wrong," Aunt Martha argued, her cheeks turning red. "You've been far too lenient with your daughters."

"Mam is a good mother and a good role model," Ruth said.

"You hold your tongue, young woman," Aunt Martha fussed. "This would never have happened if my brother was alive."

"*Ne.* Probably not," Mam said. "And I agree that a motor scooter is dangerous, especially without a helmet. I'll speak with Miriam about it."

"You don't understand the danger of situations like these," Aunt Martha went on. "Of what people will say. How could you? You weren't born Plain."

"What does Mam being born Mennonite have to do with—"

Mam silenced Ruth with a wave of her hand. Once Mam's temper was set off, she could handle Aunt Martha, and Mam's amusement had definitely faded.

"Martha, you should mind the sharpness of your tongue. I don't think my being born Mennonite has anything to do with my daughter taking a ride on an old motorbike, and I don't think your brother, my husband, would approve of such talk. None of us should be too quick to pass judgment on Eli Lapp. He's *rumspringa* and a visitor among us. How can we condemn what his church and family allows?"

"I suppose you believe Ruth is right, too." Martha planted her hands on her broad hips. "In allowing Miriam to do such a thing."

"Ruth is a sensible girl," Hannah pointed out. "She'd never let her sisters come to harm. I trust her judgment."

"Maybe you shouldn't this time." Aunt Alma, a shorter and paler reflection of Aunt Martha, hustled up to stand beside her sister. "I had a letter just yesterday from our cousin in Belleville about this Lapp boy. It's worse than we first thought."

"Tell them, Alma. I think it's for the best we all know what's what," Aunt Martha prodded.

Aunt Alma needed no further encouragement. "Rumor has it that Eli's family sent him away because he got a girl in the family way and refused to marry her."

Ruth's chest tightened, and she suddenly felt sick to her stomach. She didn't want hear any more, but she couldn't help herself. She couldn't walk away.

"So!" Aunt Martha cried, seeming almost pleased with the awful accusation. "Is that the kind of young man we want to welcome into our community?"

Eli moved deeper into the shadows of the lilac bush that grew outside the Beachys' kitchen window. He could see Ruth standing very still near the sink, a dry-ing towel in her slender hands. There were other women in the room, but Eli paid no attention to them; he saw no one but Ruth. Light from a kerosene lantern illumi-nated the planes of her heart-shaped face and glinted off the strands of red-gold hair that escaped from her *Kapp*. She was a beautiful girl. No, a beautiful woman.

He wished he'd gotten here sooner, wished he'd thought sooner of bringing the hand drill that Roman had promised to loan Norman. If he'd walked faster across the fields, maybe he would have had been in the yard in time to take Ruth's horse when she and her family had arrived. Then he would have had the oppor-tunity to speak a few words with her.

It was obvious that Ruth Yoder didn't think too much of him, which was a new experience for him. Back home, girls and their mothers and their aunties usually liked him a lot, sometimes too much. He supposed it was his bad luck to be born with his dat's features. Too pretty for a man, they'd always called him, too fair of face to be properly Plain. Truth was, Dat's face had got-ten him in plenty of trouble…as it had his son.

This was one time Eli would have liked his looks to be an asset. He'd taken one look at that mane of tum-bled auburn hair in the school yard, and his heart had swelled in his chest, beating as if he'd run a mile. There was something about Ruth Yoder, something about the curve of her lips and her stubborn little chin that got to him in a way no other girl had ever done.

But Ruth Yoder was a religious girl, the kind he'd always steered clear of, the kind of girl he knew would have no interest in him. So why had he walked two miles through the rain tonight to catch sight of her?

As much as he hated to admit it, he knew the answer. He'd been lightning-struck by a red-headed girl with soot on her nose and fire in her eyes.

Chapter 4

More white *Kapps* and curious faces appeared in the archway leading to the sitting room. The women all stared at Ruth, her mother, Aunt Martha and Aunt Alma. Fortunately, Lydia came to the rescue. Bouncing a wailing infant on her shoulder, she pushed through the crowd and raised her strident voice above little Henry's cries. "Shouldn't we get to work on the quilt?"

"Ya," Mam agreed, nodding. "We have much to do." She linked her arm through Aunt Martha's. "Come, sit by me, sister. Your stitches are so neat that I find myself inspired just watching you."

Aunt Martha's beady eyes narrowed in suspicion, but Mam's genuine smile weakened her fortitude. "All right, if you want. I never meant harm, you know, Hannah. We have to look out for each other."

Aunt Alma nodded vigorously. *"Ya,* we must. You are our dear brother's wife."

"It is hard to be a mother," Aunt Martha added. "Harder still to be a mother without the strong guidance of a husband."

Several others agreed and apprehensive expressions gave way to general good humor. Whatever the women had heard would soon make the rounds, but Ruth knew that her mother was liked and appreciated in the community. Mam would not come out the worst in this.

"Ruth, could you pull the kitchen shades for me?"

Johanna, who'd come into the kitchen as the others were filing into the sitting room, winked at Ruth as she crossed to the window to help. "What was that all about?" she whispered. "What's Miriam done now?"

Ruth bit back a chuckle. "I'm in hot water, too. And Mam."

Her sister made a tsk-tsk sound with her tongue and both broke into suppressed giggles. "For shame," Johanna admonished.

"Johanna!" Lydia called from the next room. "We can't start until you assign squares."

"Go on," Ruth urged. "I'll get the shades."

As Johanna left the room, Ruth turned back to the bank of windows that lined the wall, assuring plenty of light in the big kitchen even in winter. No curtains covered the wide glass panes, just spartan white shades. There was nothing to hide, but drawing the shades after dark was a custom strictly held to in the Amish community.

As Ruth reached for the last blind, she noticed movement near Lydia's lilac bushes outside the window. At first, she assumed it must be one of the children. But the figure was too tall and broad-shouldered to be a child. She paused, drawing close to the window for a better look, cupping her hands around her eyes to cut down on the glare reflected from light inside the kitchen.

To her surprise, a man stepped out from behind the lilacs almost directly in front of her. Light from the window shone on his face as he turned toward her, and she realized she was almost nose to nose with Eli Lapp.

Ruth jerked back, heart pounding as though she'd been racing Miriam to the orchard. What was he doing there, spying on the women? Was he some kind of pervert? She grabbed hold of the shade and yanked it down, but not before she caught a glimpse of his expression. He was grinning at her!

Cheeks burning, she marched across the kitchen and flung open the back door. "What are you doing out here?" she demanded.

"Watching you."

"Where are your manners?" She ran her hand over her *Kapp* and then dropped it to her side, once again flustered by him. She'd caught him doing something wrong; why was she the one who felt foolish? "Did your mother never teach you better?" she demanded, trying to cover the awkwardness she felt with anger. "Why would you stare at me through a window?"

"You're pretty when you're cross. Did you know that?"

"You! You are impossible!"

"You should have talked to me when I came to your house," he said, still grinning like a mule. "I just wanted to know if you were all right."

"I'm fine. I told you that at the school. I'm not hurt." She paused to catch her breath. "I thank you for checking on me, but—"

"How many sisters do you have?"

"How many sisters?" she repeated. She felt tongue-tied, awkward. She knew she must be as red as a beet. It wasn't as if she wasn't used to talking to boys. She had lots of friends who were boys: Dan, Charley, even Gideon, but none of them had ever made her so...so not like herself. "Why? Why do you ask me that?"

"Don't you know how many sisters you have? It must be a lot."

There was a broom standing beside the door. She wanted to pick it up and hit him with it. She'd never wanted to cause hurt to anyone before, but this...this Eli Lapp was impossible. She forced herself to speak calmly. "There is my older sister Johanna, the twins, Miriam and Anna. Anna met you at the door—"

"Aha. So you *were* listening. You told her to tell me to go away. You were afraid to talk to me," he said.

"I was not. I was helping my mother put supper on the table. It was not the best time for a guest to arrive uninvited. And now you know I am fine. I have thanked you." She crossed her arms over her chest. "So you can leave me alone."

Eli took a step closer. She could smell some kind of shaving lotion or maybe men's perfume. Who could tell what he would wear? What he might do? But it smelled nice. Manly. "You didn't answer my question."

There he was making her feel dizzy again. "What question?"

"How many sisters you have," he teased. "A teacher's daughter, you should be good with math."

"Don't be ridiculous! I know how many sisters I have. There are seven of us."

"All redheads? I like redheads."

Unconsciously, Ruth tucked a stray curl back under

her *Kapp*. "That is none of your business. I'm going back inside, and you should go...go wherever your affairs take you." She turned away.

"Do they have names, these other sisters? Are they all as pretty as you are?"

She spun back, quickly losing control of her patience again. "There's Johanna, me, Anna, Miriam, Leah, Rebecca and Susanna. And they are all prettier than me."

"I'd have to see that to believe it."

Ruth opened her mouth, then closed it. Not knowing what else to say, she closed the door hard and hurried into the sitting room.

She found a seat between Dinah and Anna and located her own sewing kit. It seemed that everyone there was talking at once. Miriam was passing out squares of cloth, and young and old were busy threading needles.

"Dinah has suggested that we hold the end-of-year school picnic early," Mam said. "She has another idea to help pay for the building repairs."

"We could invite the other Amish churches," Dinah explained, "and have a pie auction for the men. Each unmarried woman will bake her favorite pie and donate it, and the bachelors will bid on them."

"And whoever buys a pie gets to eat lunch with the girl who made it," Johanna explained. "They do it at the Cedar Hill Church in Nebraska where Dinah's cousin lives. And they always make lots of money."

Ruth tried to look interested in the plans, but she couldn't really concentrate. She kept thinking about what Eli had said. He said she was pretty. No one had ever told her she was pretty. Did he mean it? Why did she care?

Then she thought about what Aunt Alma had said

about the letter she'd received. Could it be true? Could Eli have gotten a girl in the family way? Sometimes even Plain youth strayed from Amish beliefs, but such mistakes were rare. She'd never heard of any Plain couple who'd failed to marry if there was a babe coming. If Eli had gotten a girl pregnant, he'd be married now, living in Belleville, wouldn't he?

"Ruth." Dinah nudged her and motioned to Hannah. "Your mam wants something from the carriage."

Ruth looked up.

"That old section of quilt in the black bag," Mam said, "The one with my great-grandmother's sunflower pattern. I think we left it under the buggy seat." She glanced back at Lydia. "It's not in the best of shape, but it's so pretty, I've always kept it."

Ruth nodded and rose, then hesitated. What if Eli Lapp was still out there? She didn't want to see him. Couldn't. Not after the way he'd teased her…not after the way she'd talked to him.

But there was no way to refuse her mother, not without giving her a reason, and right now the idea of that was more frightening than the idea of coming nose to nose with Eli again.

Forcing herself to move, Ruth picked her way through the closely seated women. As she reached the door, she contemplated what she would do if Eli was still standing outside near the kitchen door. Not that she was afraid of him. She'd simply ignore him. He could grin foolishly at her if he wanted to, but if he got no reaction from her, he'd soon leave her alone. The Yoder girls didn't associate with boys like him.

Immediately, a flood of confusion washed through her. Was she as lacking in grace as Aunt Martha? Was she judging Eli and finding him guilty, simply on gossip? What if the whole story was wrong? In her eagerness to share, Aunt Alma didn't always get the details right. What if Eli was innocent of any crime other than riding an ugly motor scooter and coming to Delaware to work in his uncle's chair shop?

And he'd said she was pretty. She smiled, in spite of herself.

Her heartbeat quickened as she opened the back door and descended the wooden kitchen steps to the yard, eyeing the lilac bushes. There was no sign of Eli there. Near the barn, several small boys chased each other in a game of tag, but there was no sign of the Belleville boy there either. If she could just find her horse and the courting buggy in the dark, amid a sea of black buggies, she could grab the quilt square and hurry back into the house.

Irwin stepped out of the corncrib and walked out into the muddy yard. "Looking for your carriage?"

Irwin was very Plain, even for an Amish, so Plain that he stood out among the other boys. His trousers were too high on skinny ankles; the corners of his mouth were red and crusted, and his narrow shoulders sagged with the weight of a man six times his age. He looked as though he could do with a few good meals and a haircut.

Her mother's words about being quick to judge echoed in her ears. Was she judging both Irwin and Eli unfairly? Would she be just like her Aunt Martha in ten years?

"I did like you said," Irwin volunteered. "You said your horse was easy spooked, so I unhitched him and turned him into an empty stall in the barn. Your buggy is in the barn, too."

It was more words than she'd ever heard Irwin offer at one time. And putting Blackie in the barn was a kind thing to do. "Thank you," she said, smiling at him. Maybe Mam was right; maybe there was more to this boy than anyone saw at first glance.

He tilted his head and reverted to his usual soft stammer. "Sure," he said, then walked away.

Raindrops spattered her face and arms as she hurried to the barn. Inside, a single lantern hung from a big cross-beam. Dat's buggy was where Irwin had said it would be, standing alone in the center of the aisle between the box stalls. Blackie raised his head and nickered. Ruth went to him and rubbed his head, noting that a big bucket of fresh water hung from one corner post, and someone had tossed hay into the manger. "Good boy," she murmured.

"Me or him?"

The voice from inside the buggy startled her. Eli Lapp. *Again.*

She sucked in a breath and made an effort to hold back the sharp retort that rose to her lips. "Are you still here?" she asked, her voice far too breathy for either of them to believe she was entirely composed.

He chuckled, a deep sound of amusement that made her stomach flip over. "Maybe I hoped you'd come out here looking for me."

She stared at him. "Why would I do that?"

He grinned. "Tell the truth. You did, didn't you?"

"*Ne.* N-not for you. Mam asked me to fetch something from the carriage."

She hadn't been able to see him clearly in the shadows outside the house, but she could see him now. Eli was wearing Plain clothes tonight, black trousers, blue shirt, straw hat, but he was still *fancy*. He was chewing a piece of hay, and it gave him a rakish look.

Hochmut, she thought. But she couldn't deny that she found him handsome, so handsome that she could feel it in the pit of her stomach. Was this temptation? The kind Uncle Reuben talked about in his sermons sometimes?

"Be a shame to waste a courting buggy," he said. "A Kishacoquillas buggy, if I'm not mistaken." He offered her his hand. "Why don't you come up and tell me about it?"

She tucked her hands behind her back. "I just need the bag from under the seat. There's a piece of an old quilt in it. My sister wanted us to bring it for the pattern." Now she was rambling. She wanted to leave Mam's bag and run back to the house to the safety of the women's chatter.

"Still scared?" He was teasing her again.

"Of what?"

"Me?" He held out his hand seeming to dare her.

She would not get into the buggy with him. It was a bad idea, a decision that could only… But somehow, without realizing how or why, she found herself clasping his hand. It was warm and calloused, a strong hand, and nothing at all like the familiar hands of her sisters.

The next thing she knew, she was perched on the seat beside him.

"See," he said, grinning at her. "I come in peace."

"You…you," she sputtered. "I don't like you one bit."

He laughed. "Oh, yes, you do. Otherwise you wouldn't have come looking for me. Or gotten into the buggy." He looked down. "And you wouldn't still be holding my hand."

Ruth jerked her hand from his, mortified. It wasn't that she meant to let him hold her hand; he just had her so confused.

She fumbled under the seat for Mam's bag. Eli's all-too-warm leg rested innocently against hers, making her vividly aware of his strong body and broad shoulders. He smelled clean and all male. She'd always hated the stench of tobacco that clung to some men, but there was none of that about Eli. His hair and body were fresh, his old high-tops were polished to a shine, and the nails on his big hands were clean and cut straight across.

"I have to go back inside."

"*Ya,* I suppose you do," he agreed. "But it's nice sitting here, don't you think?"

"*Ne.* I don't." It was actually. Her mouth was dry, her heart raced, and her knees felt oddly weak, but the barn did smell good and the rain patting on the tin roof sounded comforting.

And then he took hold of her hand again.

She wanted to pull her hand free. He'd gone too far. She wasn't the type to be so easy with a boy. Especially one she didn't know. A boy with a reputation. She had her good name to think of, her family's. "Let me go, Eli."

He released her immediately. "You haven't asked me about the burns on my hands, the injuries I got by coming to your rescue and saving you from a fiery death." He held out his hands. They were lean hands, a working man's hands.

"See that? And that?" He indicated two tiny blisters

and a faint redness. "I may need to see an English doctor—go to the hospital."

Ruth could hardly hold back a giggle. "That? That's the smallest blister I've ever seen, Eli. You boys in Belleville must be sissies, to make such a fuss about a little burn like that."

"Say it again." He stared intently at her, making her warm all over again.

"What?"

"Eli. Say my name again. I like the way you say it."

Ruth clutched the quilt bag to her chest. "I have to go. I—"

"Ruth?" Irwin pulled open the heavy Dutch door of the barn. "Teacher wants to know what's taking so long."

"Coming." Quickly, she scrambled down, ignoring the offer of assistance from Eli's outstretched hand.

He chuckled and put a finger to his lips. "I won't say a word," he promised. "What happened here in the barn will be our secret."

"We have no secrets," she said and marched stiffly away, trying to salvage some shred of dignity.

If Irwin knew that she hadn't been alone in the buggy, he made no mention of it. She went back to the house. As she neared the sitting-room entrance, she heard Aunt Martha's raised voice.

"She's not getting any younger, Hannah. What was wrong with Bennie Mast, I ask you? Eats a little too hearty, maybe, but a good boy, from a good family. I'm telling you, she's too choosy, your Ruth."

"She's that," Aunt Alma joined in. "And I heard she turned down Alf King, wouldn't even ride home from the singing with him. If she's not careful, she'll miss out on the best catches. She'll end up marrying some Ohio widower twice her age."

Ruth stopped short. Bad enough she'd made a fool of herself in the barn, but now her aunt was holding her up as an old maid, someone who couldn't get a husband. She couldn't believe they were talking about this again. Why wouldn't they understand that she couldn't accept Bennie or Alf or the other boys who'd wanted to drive her home from a young people's singing? Why couldn't she make them see that her duty was to remain at home to take care of Susanna and her mother? That not every woman could or even should have a husband and children of her own? Mam needed her. Her little sister needed her. Her responsibility was to her family.

"Here's your bag, Mam," she said too loudly as she entered the room. "So many buggies in the yard, it took a while to find ours." That wasn't dishonest, was it? Or had her foolishness with Eli Lapp caused her to make up lies as well?

"Look at these colors," Mam said as she took the bag from Ruth. "Barely faded in all these years. And such beautiful needlework. I vow, Johanna, you must have inherited your great-great-grandmother's gift with stitchery."

Ruth settled gratefully into her empty seat and picked up her square of cloth. She would make up for her wasted time in the barn, and she would forget Eli and his inappropriate behavior. It would have been a much easier task if the memory of his hand on hers wasn't so real or if she could forget how nice it had been sitting next to him in the privacy of the big barn. No boy had ever made her feel that way before.

* * *

Hazel Zook's round cheeks and pink laughing mouth rose to haunt Eli, replacing the image of Ruth Yoder's angelic face in his mind. He picked up his pace as he strode back across the wet fields toward his uncle's house. Glimpses of that night flashed in his head. He'd put miles and months between him and Hazel, but it wasn't enough. He just couldn't get her and what had happened off his conscience.

Light rain hit him in the face as he walked, and he wondered if coming to Seven Poplars might have been a mistake. Maybe he should have run farther, gone into the English world and never looked back. He wondered what was keeping him from taking that final step? He was already lost to his own faith. People would never let him forget what had happened back in Belleville.

What was he thinking coming here? Was he going to ruin another woman's life now? Ruth Yoder was a nice girl, a girl from a strict family and church. She deserved respect. And the best thing he could do for her was to stay away. He should never have gone to the Beachys' tonight. Better choices.

He wished things could have been different, that he'd made a better choice that night at the bonfire. He wished he'd done the right thing, but now it was too late. There was no going back and no changing what had happened.

The bishops and the preachers said that God was merciful; they preached it every service. They said you could be forgiven any sin if you truly repented, and maybe that was true. But what they didn't say was how you could forgive yourself.

Chapter 5

The following Monday afternoon, Ruth left Susanna and Anna baking bread to walk to the school. Mam wanted to work on lesson plans after supper, and Ruth had offered to carry her heavy books home for her. It was so rare that Ruth had time alone to think, and it was such a pretty day that she enjoyed having the errand.

Eli Lapp and how to handle him was foremost in her mind. It was clear that he wasn't going to stop following her around until she made him understand that he was wasting his time with her. She needed to explain that it was nothing against him; she had no plans to marry anyone.

Still, she had to admit that she liked being told she was pretty, and that he was both clever and attractive. Vanity, she feared, was one of her sins. After all the talk about her being an old maid, it was nice that someone liked her, but it had to stop. The trouble was, she didn't know what she should say to Eli. How could she tell him to quit courting her when he'd said nothing about wanting her for his girlfriend? What if he laughed at her? What if he told her that she had completely misunderstood, and she was the last girl he would consider as a wife?

And then there was the problem of Irwin. The boy had promised Mam that he'd meet her at the schoolhouse on Saturday, but he hadn't shown up, and she'd had no opportunity to speak to him alone at church. Ruth wondered if Irwin had come to school today and if Mam had been able to question him about the fire.

Eli Lapp hadn't attended the Sunday services, but that hadn't kept him from being the center of attention. Hearing the girls giggling about how handsome he was, or the mothers repeating that Eli was just the sort of boy that Preacher Reuben warned them about, was no help.

"Shepherds of our church must be diligent to protect our lambs," Aunt Martha had warned a group of mothers. "The loose ways of the world threaten our faith."

Ruth wondered if her father would have agreed with Aunt Martha, or would he have made Eli welcome and tried to turn him back to the Plain ways? Ruth hadn't done anything wrong in the barn, but if people knew she'd been alone in the buggy in the barn with Eli, her reputation could be tarnished. For all she knew, Irwin was the kind of person to tell tales, and that worried her. It wasn't necessary to simply avoid wrongdoing, but a Plain person had to avoid the perception of wrongdoing as well.

For an instant, just as Ruth rounded the bend through the trees, she remembered the schoolhouse as she'd seen it the day of the fire, and a knot rose in her throat. So many bad things could have happened. But this time, there was no smoke or the scent of smoke. School was out for the afternoon, but a few of the boys had remained for a game of softball on the grassy field. Samuel Mast's buggy was there, as well as Roman's big team and wagon, the horses standing nose to nose at the hitching rail.

When Ruth entered the schoolroom by the temporary steps, she found Roman, Samuel and her mother deep in conversation about the building repairs. Mam was smiling, and it sounded as though she was getting her wish for more room. The hand-drawn plans spread out on the desk enlarged the main area by the size of the original cloakroom and included a new porch with an inside sink and water faucet.

"Isn't this wonderful?" Mam exclaimed. "We'll be able to add eight more desks and a new cloakroom."

"Will it be done in time for the new school year?" Ruth asked, looking over the drawing.

Roman nodded. "With Eli to help, we'll finish by September."

"So Eli's good with his hands," Samuel observed.

"*Ya*, he's a fine craftsman, that boy."

"You can go on home," Mam urged, resting her hand on Ruth's arm. "We've still got things to discuss here, but there's no need for you to wait for me. If you can take the reading books and the big arithmetic book, I can manage the rest."

Ruth gathered up all the texts, including the oversize cursive writing book, said goodbye, and walked out of the school. She had just started toward the woods when Eli stepped out from behind the shed.

"Don't pop out at people like that," she said. Her cheeks felt as warm as if she'd been standing over a kettle of simmering jam. Just being near him scrambled her wits and made her tongue thick, and she was immediately more annoyed with herself than with him. She was a woman grown and should have more sense.

Worse still, Ruth had the sinking feeling that Eli knew the effect he had on her. "What do you want?" she asked.

"Does a person have to want something or can a person just say hello?"

He had a good point, but she certainly wasn't going to tell him that.

"Where are you going?" he asked.

She moved around him and continued walking. "Home."

In two strides, he caught up with her and scooped the books out of her arms. "These are heavy. Let me drive you in Uncle Roman's wagon."

"I prefer to walk." She tried to retrieve Mam's textbooks, but Eli held fast to them.

"I guess you can take them in the wagon if you want to." Ruth walked away. "Just leave them on our porch."

"I'll walk." He chuckled as he caught up. "You're stubborn, aren't you, Ruth Yoder? Miriam said you were."

All the Yoder girls were a handful. He liked that, and he liked their mother, Hannah. It wasn't often you found a widow teaching school. He thought the whole family was a breath of fresh air, even if Ruth could be as prickly as a green briar vine. He'd never known a girl to be so immune to his charms.

"When did you talk to Miriam? Certainly not at church."

"I'm not much for church. Not lately."

He had stayed away from church services yesterday because he had wanted to make sure he didn't see her. No, that wasn't true. He probably would have stayed away just the same. He didn't feel at ease at a worship service anymore. He couldn't see where he would ever be the type of man God would want. He had considered going, had gone so far as to ask Aunt Fannie to iron his good shirt and trousers, but in the end, he'd just stuffed them back in the drawer and gone off to the Dover Mall on his scooter. Instead of worship, he'd spent his afternoon feeding tokens into a video game box. His father would have been proud of him...a chip off the old ice block.

"I heard you were *rumspringa*. I suppose you like English ways."

"Some. Maybe."

"I suppose you drink beer," she accused.

"*Ne*. I don't drink alcohol. I never have." He never understood why anyone would want to drink a substance that made them angry or foolish or made them act as they never would have sober. He looked into Ruth's warm brown eyes, and for just a second, he saw a flash of compassion.

"I didn't mean to accuse you," she said in a gentler voice. "It's just that I know it goes on. I hear lots of *rumspringa* boys do."

"Girls, too," he admitted. "But not me. When I was eight, my older brother was riding in a car with some guys who were drinking. He was killed in an accident. I never thought it was something I wanted to do." He swallowed hard. Why had he told her that? He rarely felt comfortable sharing his feelings. It wasn't something a man did…not something he did.

She stopped and faced him. "I'm sorry. I didn't know." Her tone was suddenly tender, her voice sweet.

He nodded, too full of emotion to answer for a long moment, then he said, "Free, my brother, was funny, and he used to take me fishing sometimes."

"It's hard to lose someone you love." She started toward home again. "My dat died two years ago. I miss him every day."

Somehow Eli sensed that everything had changed between them. He was walking beside her, and they weren't arguing. They were just talking like friends, talking as though he'd known her his whole life.

"My dat died, too, when I was young. I don't remember much about him, just him laughing and me jumping out of the hayloft into his arms." He hesitated. "Mam never talked about him much."

"Did your mother remarry? My aunts are urging Mam to, but I don't think she's ready."

"My stepfather, Joseph, is my father's second cousin. He married my mother when I was four, but I never thought of him as a father, just Joseph. He already had his own sons. He never liked Free and me much, and he was strict."

Ruth reached down to pluck a wild daisy from an open space beside the path. She brushed the flower petals over her lips and asked, "Is your mother happy with him? Is he a good man?"

"Joseph is a hard worker. He provides for her." He shrugged. "I never asked Mam if she was happy. In my family, you don't talk about private things."

She nodded. "My dat was different than a lot of men I know. He laughed when he was happy, shouted when he was mad and wasn't ashamed to shed a tear when our old collie died. He used to talk to us about everything."

"He must have been a special man. I wish I could have known him," Eli said. Uncle Roman was the closest he'd ever had to a father figure, and because of the distance, he hadn't seen too much of him until he'd been invited to live with them and work at the shop. "I think my uncle Roman is a little like that," he admitted. "It seems like he's a man who talks."

"*Ya*, we all love Roman." She smiled at him with her eyes. "Roman says you're talented with your hands. Your stepfather must have taught you woodworking—"

"*Ne*. My grandfather taught me his trade. I was apprenticed to him after my brother died. Mam had a new baby and I went to live with my grandparents. It was better for Mam that way." He paused for a second. "Enough talk about me." Eli's mood changed swiftly. Their conversation was becoming too intimate, and he wasn't comfortable. He forced a grin. "Why doesn't a girl your age have a steady beau?"

"That's a rude question."

"I just wondered. I mean, you're pretty, smart, and I hear you aren't afraid to make a sharp deal with the English tourists at Spence's."

"Miriam talks too much."

He laughed. "She does talk a lot." Not three days ago, he'd promised himself he wouldn't have anything more to do with Ruth Yoder. And here he was, walking her home with an armload of schoolbooks like some grass-green boy too baby-faced to shave. And saying things he'd never said to another girl.

What had made him tell Ruth about Free? He should have gotten over Free's death a long time ago. Hadn't his grandfather insisted he had gone to a better place, and only a selfish boy would want him back? But that was hard to accept then and still was now. Somehow, he felt he would never get over losing his brother, and that everything had started to go wrong, not when Dat had walked out, but the night Free had gone out joy-riding and never come back.

When they reached the stile at the fence line, Eli dared Ruth to jump and offered to catch her. He didn't mean any harm, but he would have liked to have circled her small waist with his hands and to get close enough to smell the sweet shampoo she used on her hair.

But Ruth was having none of it. She scrambled down the steps and hurried on ahead of him. As they crossed the fence, the closeness between them seemed to evaporate. Now she was just an attractive girl, and he was just a stranger with a bad reputation.

"Oh, no!" Ruth cried. "The cows are out."

Eli looked in the direction she was pointing. A heifer was trotting down the rows of ankle-high corn, snatching mouthfuls of newly sprouted field corn and munching for all she was worth. Ruth snatched off her apron and, waving it, ran toward the wayward animal.

"Shoo! Bossy! Get back!"

Eli placed the stack of books on a dry tuft of grass and dashed after her. Another cow, a black and white one wearing a bell around her neck, was just loping into the cornfield. And behind her, on a plow horse, came Ruth's sister Miriam, riding astride, skirts up around her knees and *Kapp* flying off her head. A Shetland sheepdog ran after them barking.

Since Ruth seemed to have the heifer on the run, Eli turned to cut off another cow. Yet another cow, followed by a calf, appeared on the far side of the field. Eli waved to Miriam and pointed. "I'll get this one!" he shouted. Miriam dug her bare heels into the horse's sides and lumbered after the runaway mother and baby through the corn.

The three of them had rounded up the escapees and were just driving the four animals into the barnyard when Samuel Mast's buggy came up the lane.

"Oh, no," Ruth groaned. She dropped the broken cornstalk she'd been using as a switch and hastily tied on her apron and tucked the worst of the loose strands of flyaway hair under her *Kapp*. "It's Samuel and my mother. We're in trouble now."

Miriam slid down off the horse and shook her lavender skirt over her ankles. "You'd better get away while you can," she whispered to Eli.

Eli glanced from one sister to the other. "Me? What did I do? You were the one on the horse." He pointed to Miriam, then hooked a thumb in Ruth's direction. "And Ruth just helped to catch—"

Miriam wrinkled her nose and tsk-tsked. "I'm telling you, you should go. Hannah Yoder doesn't lose her temper often, but when she does, no one is spared."

Hannah was climbing unaided out of the buggy. She looked at the cows, then back at the three of them, took a book from Samuel and started toward them. Samuel frowned, clicked to his mare and sent her trotting back down the lane in less time than it took Ruth to close the pound gate.

"What is this?" Hannah demanded.

"The cows were in the corn," Eli began. "We were just—"

"Thank you for your help. Come again another day, Eli Lapp," she said, her tone clipped. "I wish to speak to my daughters about their behavior. And it is best if you leave us in private."

He hesitated. "I left your books back in the field. I'll just—"

"Ruth will fetch the books." Hannah's eyes flashed. "You will come for dinner on Sunday. It is not a church Sunday, and I've already invited your uncle Roman and aunt Fannie. Now, you can help best by leaving us."

Eli felt his face flush. "They did nothing wrong."

"It is not your place to decide," Hannah retorted. "Your uncle was looking for you. Best you hurry back to the school. Now."

Eli looked at Ruth, excited at the thought of having Sunday dinner with her, feeling guilty about abandoning her, but Hannah was obviously giving him no choice in either matter. "Sunday, then," he said. "I'll be here Sunday for dinner." Abruptly, he turned on his heel and strode back toward the cornfield and the path that led to the school. Ruth's mother might have the reputation of being a pleasant woman, but now...

Now, he wouldn't want to be on the receiving end of whatever she would have to say to her daughters.

"Mam," Ruth started, as soon as Eli was out of earshot. "It's not Miriam's fault. She was alone here when the cows got loose."

"Not exactly alone," Miriam admitted. "Anna and Susanna are in the house, and Irwin was here."

"Irwin?" Mam demanded. "Irwin? What was he doing here?"

"He came to talk to you. He thought you'd be home from school. He was helping me move the cows from the little pasture into the pound next to the barn, and…" She left her sentence unfinished.

"Where's the boy now?" Mam rested both hands on her hips.

"I told him to go home," Miriam answered.

"Mam, it was an accident that they got out," Ruth said quickly. "She just thought she could get them in quick if she took the horse."

"To have Samuel and that boy see my daughter riding astride a horse, bareback, no shoes, no stockings, like some…some English jockey?"

Mam didn't get loud when she was angry, but her words cut like briars.

"I'm sorry, Mam," Miriam said. "I won't do it again."

"Is this the first time you've ridden the horses?"

Miriam sighed.

"Or the second?"

"Ne."

Ruth reached for her sister's hand. "Mam…don't be angry."

"You be quiet," Mam said. "I'm not speaking to you. I'm speaking to your sister." She folded her arms over her chest. "Isn't it bad enough that I had to listen to your aunt Martha chastise me in front of everyone at the quilting because you rode on Eli Lapp's motorcycle?"

"Mam, that's not fair," Miriam protested. "It was just a ride and an ice-cream cone. And he bought one for Susanna, too. He's nice, Mam. He didn't mean any harm."

"I'm at my wits' end with you, Miriam. You are not a boy. You are a girl, a Plain girl."

Miriam burst into tears and ran toward the house.

"Miriam," Ruth called after her.

"You're almost as much to blame as she is," Mam said, turning on Ruth. "When you saw her on that horse, you should have told her to get down, not encouraged her."

"I'm sorry, Mam." Ruth met her mother's gaze. "You're right. I should have told her to get down the minute I saw her."

Mam sighed, her face softening. "It's only that I want my girls to be good women. Good Plain women."

"I think we are, most of the time," Ruth dared.

To Ruth's surprise Mam smiled faintly. "I think you are, too. Now, come." She headed toward the house. "There are chores to be done and Miriam's dander to be smoothed."

Ruth nodded. She could understand Mam's concern for Miriam's behavior, but she knew her sister, too. Miriam didn't mean to break the rules about riding horses, showing her legs and losing her *Kapp*. She was just high-spirited. Inside, where it mattered most, Miriam's soul was pure and truly Plain.

Hurrying to catch up with Mam, Ruth took hold of her hand. "Please don't be upset with yourself. You were right and we were wrong. You're the best mother in the world," she said and meant every word. "Dat would be so proud of you."

"I hope so," Mam replied. "I worry about raising you girls…if I'm doing right."

"You are," Ruth assured her, but a small shiver of unease made goose bumps raise on her arms. Mam was the wisest woman she knew. If Mam didn't always know the best thing to do, how could she ever hope to make the right choices?

Chapter 6

"I'm not going," Ruth said. "Anna and Miriam and Susanna can go without me." She turned the handle on the butter churn as hard as she could. Already specks of yellow were showing in the thick, rich cream.

"Are your arms tired? I'll help," Anna offered. It was a rainy afternoon, and they were all gathered in the kitchen. Anna was pressing the wrinkles out of her starched *Kapp* as Susanna eagerly slathered generous gobs of marshmallow filling on her still-warm chocolate cookies and pressed them together, forming fat whoopie pies. Miriam's sleeves were rolled up as she scoured the stovetop vigorously, while their mother sat at the table shelling peas.

"You should all go," Mam advised. "Young people should be together and have fun."

Ruth turned the crank harder. The butter was forming into chunks now. If there was one thing she could do, it was make beautiful, sweet butter. She loved the process, feeling the soft, squishy butter in her hands, adding just the right amount of salt and waiting to see if the blocks came out of Mam's wheat-patterned mold in perfect shapes. Not everyone could make good butter. It was the only chore in the kitchen where she could outdo Anna, and she took secret satisfaction in her gift. "I'm getting too old for singings," she said, giving the handle another turn. "It's for the younger girls and boys."

"Nonsense," Mam declared. "Samuel told me that tonight there will be wagons to take you to the homes where there are shut-ins. Your hymns will give them so much pleasure, and you know that God has given you a rare voice."

Ruth unscrewed the lid on the churn and dumped the ball of butter into a clean cloth. "Making butter is messy," she said, trying to change the subject. She did love to sing. Secretly, she wanted to go with the young people, but she was afraid. What if Eli was there? What would she say to him? What would he say to her? She sighed. She was probably making something out of nothing. If Eli was there, he probably wouldn't even notice her with all the other girls there.

"Like life," Mam said.

"What?" Ruth asked.

Mam motioned with her chin. "You said making butter is messy, and I said, 'It's like life.'" She chuckled. "But when everything goes right, you are left with a treasure."

"I wasn't even sure you would let us go to the singing," Ruth said.

"Aren't you afraid we'll do something scandalous again?" Miriam chimed in.

Their mother fixed the two of them with a cool gaze. "I was upset," Mam admitted. "And let my temper get the best of me. I know you are both good girls. It's just that you have a reckless nature, Miriam." Her stern look melted to a smile. "You're too much like me, I fear."

"Like you?" Susanna licked a sticky finger. "You would never ride a horse like a boy and show your legs."

Mam tossed a pea shell at her. "Not only would," she admitted. "Did."

"Mam!" Anna said in astonishment.

Ruth's eyes widened in surprise. "You didn't! Did you?" It was hard to imagine her mother breaking the rules.

"Not even Mennonite girls were allowed to enter the horse race for the Amish boys at the Harrington fair when I was young." Mischief sparked in Mam's eyes. "So I borrowed my cousin's clothing, pinned my braids up under his straw hat, and used his name to enter the race."

"You rode in a boys' race?" Susanna demanded. *"Ne!"*

"I tried. I got as far as the first turn on the track before my hat blew off and my hair tumbled down. Everyone laughed."

"But you won the race, didn't you, Mam?" Ruth said. She was laughing now with the others.

"Tell us," Miriam urged. "You did."

Mam grimaced. "I did not. The boys were so surprised that half of them reined in their horses, and two of the riders crashed into each other. My pony reared up, and I fell off, right in front of the grandstand." She shook her head. "It was years before people stopped teasing me about it."

Susanna's eyes widened in excitement. "Were you in trouble?"

"Big trouble." Mam covered her face with her hands, remembering. She dropped them. "You see, at the time, I was thinking about what I wanted to do instead of what was best for my family or our community. People blamed my parents because I broke the rules."

"It was a bad rule," Miriam said. "Girls should be able to ride in races."

"Maybe," Mam agreed, "but rules are made for a reason. If they are unfair, people should work together to change them. But no one, least of all a silly thirteen-year-old girl, should decide what rules she will follow and what she will ignore. Because I broke the rule, riders or their mounts could have been badly hurt."

"I understand," Ruth said. Then she giggled. "But I would have liked to have seen you dressed up like a boy."

"It probably wasn't as good a disguise as I thought," their mother admitted.

"So Miriam takes after you," Ruth said thoughtfully as she began to squeeze the liquid out of the yellow butter. "And look how well you turned out."

Her mother shook her head. "I work hard every day to be the type of woman I believe God and my community expect. We all have parts of our nature that need constant care, lest, like an unweeded garden, the unpleasant things spring up and choke out the good."

Susanna stuck the last pair of cakes together. "Weeds, Mam? How could you grow weeds?"

"I could," Mam teased. "Right out of my hair, so that I couldn't get my *Kapp* on."

Susanna laughed and they all laughed with her. Then she glanced at Ruth. "I want to ride in the wagon and sing songs. Will you come, Roofie? Please."

Ruth pressed the new butter tightly into the mold. "We'll see," she said. "We'll see." But she knew she would. She knew that she couldn't bear to stay away and miss the evening of fun…and just maybe the chance to see Eli again.

Eli unbuttoned the top button on his good shirt because he felt like his collar was choking him and drained the last of the root beer in his paper cup. Lots of young people from three churches had arrived at the Borntragers' barn for the singing, and the straw wagons were already filling up with chattering girls in starched *Kapps* and aprons. The boys and young men hung back, some playing a loud game of dodgeball, but most just watching to see which girls would climb into which wagon. Every boy wanted to choose his wagon wisely, depending on which girl he was sweet on, and no one wanted to appear too eager to climb on amid all those blue, purple and green dresses.

Eli hadn't wanted to come. What if Ruth Yoder was here? He'd made up his mind that being around her was a mistake. He kept telling himself that the only reason he felt such a strong attraction to her was that he was a long way from home and all his friends. He might have a bad reputation in Belleville, but at least everyone knew him. There, he felt a part of the community. Here, he just stood out.

Maybe he should do what everyone had expected

when he left home, leave and turn Mennonite or even English. He had a trade. He could get work, get a driver's license and buy a car. Other boys and even a few girls he knew had done it. Then he wouldn't have to live by the strict rules of being Amish. He could do anything he wanted.

So why was he here? He'd promised himself when he left his grandfather's house that he would choose his own path. He'd spent half his life in a household where religion dictated every hour of the day. He'd never been whipped, never gone without food or a clean bed, but his grandparents had seen him as a way to make up for his father's mistakes. They were determined that he would live a moral life, that he not leave the church. Sadly, their attitude had done more to turn him against the Amish lifestyle than they could ever imagine. In their quest to save him, his grandparents had dedicated their lives to raising him in a somber house without laughter, where charity was freely given to others, but withheld from their own grandson.

That wasn't to say life in Belleville had been bad. Some things about his growing up had been good. He'd loved the old farm and the stillness of his grandfather's orderly woodshop, the clean scent of the shavings that fell from the lathe, the feel of cherry or walnut or pine taking shape under his fingers. He'd taken pleasure in the carefully cared-for tools and the furniture and cabinets that the shop produced. And he'd found sinful pride in his gift for making a chest of drawers or a table that would last for centuries and only become more beautiful with the years.

Sometimes in the long hours he spent alone in the shop, he had imagined Jesus as a humble carpenter in his own shop. If he had lived in those old times, Eli wondered if he and the Lord might have been able to talk about a particular slab of wood or the patience it took to achieve a hand-rubbed shine on a tabletop. And he wondered if the Lord could have explained why Eli's brother had had to die in a ditch before his life had really begun.

Eli glanced around, feeling more out of place by the second. He shouldn't have come here tonight. He'd only done it to please Aunt Fannie and because he liked to sing. He had a good voice and a good memory for the old hymns in High German. Singing at service and young people's gatherings had always been one outlet that hadn't displeased his grandparents.

"Go," Aunt Fannie had urged him. "Meet the young people. You'll make friends. Go to the singing."

Uncle Roman had shrugged. "Go and take the small buggy," he'd offered. "Maybe you'll find a girl who'll let you drive her home."

Small chance of that. But just in case, he'd curried Uncle Roman's bay gelding until his hide gleamed and polished his hooves with lamp black. He'd washed down the buggy and shined the wheels. And he'd replaced some of the ordinary lights required by law on the back of the buggy with flashing blue bulbs. There wasn't any sense in having the reputation of being wild if you didn't make the most of it.

Singings were supposed to be fun, to be a healthy way for young people to get to know each other, for forming friendships that led to marriage. Tonight's procession would go from house to house. They would remain long enough to sing a selection of hymns and then pile back onto the wagons to go to the next house.

And the rule was, everyone had to switch wagons at each stop. The scramble to get together with the boy or girl you liked, without the adult chaperones catching on, was tricky.

A young man, Mahlon something—Eli didn't know his last name—was the singing leader for the evening. Mahlon shouted out for everyone to climb on the wagons, that it was time to leave. If Eli wasn't going to go, this was his opportunity to slip away without anyone noticing. He'd spoken to a few guys he'd met already, tossed a few balls, had a soda and a doughnut, but no one would notice if he didn't go with the group. He could drive around for an hour or two in his uncle's buggy, and then go home. Aunt Fannie would never know the difference.

Eli was just sidling toward his horse and buggy when he heard a high squeal and spotted Miriam in the lead wagon, tugging on a younger girl's hand. On the ground, giving the plump girl in the blue dress a push up, stood Ruth. Tonight she was in purple. Her *Kapp* was neatly in place, hiding every strand of red hair; her stockings were pressed smooth, her apron was blindingly white and her shoes were shined. The face under the white *Kapp* was so full of life, so beautiful, it made his breath catch in his throat.

A boy took Ruth's hand and helped her up, and the driver clicked to the team. The big Percheron draft horses broke into a trot, and the second team pranced and strained at the reins, eager to follow. Other boys hurried to catch up and leaped on the wagon of their choice, some making quite a show of it.

Eli stood watching. He could just see the back of Ruth's *Kapp* as her wagon rolled away. At the last possible minute, Eli made up his mind. He dashed after the third wagon and hopped on beside a skinny teen in a green dress and black sneakers. She flashed a big smile at him and slid over to make room, patting the seat beside her. Eli gave her a hesitant smile and wondered if this was going to be a long evening.

Ruth was glad she'd given in and come when she saw the smile on old Warren Troyer's face. Warren's mother was ninety and in a wheelchair. She was so crippled up in her body that she seemed no bigger than an eight-year-old child. Her pinched face was as lined as a dried apple, but her eyes gleamed with pleasure, and she clapped her small wrinkled hands with joy. Susanna wiggled with excitement as Mahlon led the group into another song. Willard and Amy had set up a long table with sandwiches, chips, cookies and jugs of apple juice.

Ruth was so glad Mam had urged her to come. Riding the wagons, singing the old songs was as much fun as it had always been. And she had to admit that Mahlon's attention wasn't unwelcome. Even if she didn't want a beau, it was nice that she had someone to talk to besides her girlfriends and sisters.

At each house, the groups had formed into two sections, one of boys and one of girls. Both sounded good tonight, all the male and female voices blending in. A deep, rich male voice behind her made Ruth glance over her shoulder. To her surprise, she saw Eli Lapp standing beside Mahlon. She hadn't expected that Eli, of all people, would know the words to the hymns or would have such a gift for singing. Miriam noticed him, too. Ruth saw her sister smile at him. She would have to make certain that Miriam remained with her when they got back on the wagons and that they picked one that Eli wasn't riding on. Mam had just gotten herself calmed down. It would not do to give Aunt Martha something more to gossip about.

Later, at the refreshment table, Ruth was telling Amy Troyer how good her ham sandwiches were when someone thrust a cup of juice into her hand. When she turned to say thank you, Eli Lapp was grinning down at her. Standing this close to him, she realized just how tall he was. Her fingers closed around the cup.

"Nothing special," Amy said. "Boiled ham and homemade mustard. I can give you the recipe for the mustard if you like."

"Ya," Ruth answered. "Mam would like it."

"Everything is good," Eli agreed. There were lots of pretty girls here tonight, but none of them shone as brightly as Ruth Yoder. He hadn't guessed that she had such a beautiful voice, so sweet that it gave him shivers down his spine.

Mahlon shouted for the young people to gather for a prayer before they got back on the wagons. Ruth and Eli moved off with the others to the porch where the bishop waited. "What wagon are you getting on?" Eli whispered.

The bishop was beginning to offer the prayer.

"Shh," Ruth whispered. She closed her eyes, all too conscious of Eli standing very close on one side of her and Mahlon on the other.

"Have a safe night," the bishop said when he had finished. "Be careful and enjoy yourselves."

Eli leaned down. "Ride with me, Ruth," he said, trying to keep the eagerness out of his voice.

"It's best if I don't. We wouldn't want anyone to get the wrong idea."

Eli stiffened.

Ruth heard Mahlon chuckle.

"She's riding home in my buggy tonight," Mahlon said.

Eli looked into Ruth's eyes, and in the illumination of the carriage lamp, for just a second, she caught a flash of deep disappointment.

And then he turned, uttered a sound of wry amusement and walked away, trying to tell himself that it didn't mean a thing, trying to convince himself that one pretty girl was like another, when all the while he knew better.

"I did not say *'ya'* to riding home with you, Mahlon," Ruth said. "That was an untruth. I have my own buggy, and I have every intention of driving Susanna home in it."

She should have been pleased by Mahlon's attention, but she felt bad for Eli. It had to be hard to come to a new place with new faces. Mahlon could have been nicer to him, at least invited him to join them in the wagon for the next leg of the trip. Mahlon knew very well that he and she were just friends, and he knew her well enough that he understood that she wasn't looking for a husband. "Why don't you take Anna?" she suggested. "She likes you."

"And I like Anna," he said. "I just like you better."

"I haven't changed my mind," she pointed out, looking for Eli in the sea of boys in colored shirts. Blue. His had been blue…the color of his eyes. She didn't see him anywhere.

"Come on, let me drive you home. Anna and Mir-

iam can take your little sister home safely enough."
Mahlon took her hand and pulled her back to the first
wagon. "On to the Millers' place," he told the driver,
then looked back. "Have we got everyone?"

Ruth glanced around, saw Susanna and Anna in the
second wagon and settled back into the straw. The evening had started out so well, but now she was feeling
out of sorts. She wished she could just go home. As the
wagon rolled down the Troyers' driveway, she looked
back for Eli again, but he was still nowhere. To her surprise, she was disappointed. Disappointed she might not
see those blue eyes again tonight.

It was almost ten o'clock by the time the wagons
rolled down the last lane and turned back toward the
Borntragers' farm. A few of the young people were still
singing, but for the most part, there were more giggles
and laughter than adhering to the hymns. Miriam was
on the same wagon with one of her best friends, and
they were teasing Harvey Borntrager, Dinah's fifteen-
year-old brother-in-law. Everyone liked Harvey, but this
was the first time he'd been allowed to go to a singing,
and he had to expect his share of ribbing.

The evening ended on a high note with one of the
other churches inviting all the young people to a day
of fishing and games later in the summer. The chaperones kept close watch to see that no one was left behind
as everyone found their respective buggies or, if they'd
walked to the Borntragers' place, that they found their
own group to go home.

Susanna had fallen asleep on the wagon, and it took
both Ruth and Anna to get her down and into their
buggy. Mahlon, Ruth was pleased to note, had found
another girl to escort home. Ruth was just fastening

the last strap on Blackie's harness when Eli appeared by the horse's head, startling her again. She met his blue-eyed gaze.

"Sure you don't want to ride with me?" he asked.

She swallowed. "I told you that I didn't think it was a good idea," she reminded him.

"Just as well," he said. He reached behind him, caught the hand of a girl standing in the shadows. "So you won't mind if I take Miriam instead?"

"I—*Ne*," she stammered. "I mean, that's not—"

"See you at home!" Miriam called excitedly, leading Eli away.

"Miriam!" Ruth tried to push Blackie's head aside so she could see her sister, but he was being stubborn. "Mam won't like it. You can't—" But once again, she was standing there helpless as her sister dashed off with Eli Lapp. She tried to convince herself as she climbed up on the bench beside the sleeping Susanna that the distress she felt was concern for Miriam, but there was no denying the truth.

Secretly, she wished she was the one sitting beside Eli on the buggy seat.

Chapter 7

On Friday, Roman and Eli began work on the repairs at the Seven Poplars schoolhouse. Samuel had brought his farm wagon to carry away the burnt wood and pieces of foundation, and Hannah had dismissed the older boys to provide additional labor. Anna and Susanna had gone to Spence's Auction with eggs, flowers and strawberries, but Miriam had stayed behind and volunteered to carry all the school desks out into the yard and give them a good cleaning. Mam's older female students were helping. Ruth and her mother divided the remaining children into reading groups and led them away from the building to continue class outside.

Ruth found a spot under an oak tree at the edge of the school yard to spread out blankets. All her students were girls; her mother had taken the boys into the shade on the far side of the ball field. Even here, Ruth found that the loud sounds of hammering and clattering wood drew the children's attention and kept them from giving full attention to their reading lessons.

Surrendering, Ruth asked Verna Beachy to read aloud from a battered copy of *Heidi,* and that seemed to satisfy everyone. Ruth's attention, however, drifted from the story, and she glanced back at the school to see Miriam chatting with Eli as she scrubbed a desk with a wet sponge.

Ruth felt vaguely out of sorts and looked away, then back again. She hadn't spoken to Miriam about her reckless decision to ride home in the buggy with Eli after she'd already been in hot water with Mam over the motor scooter. Although everyone always knew which couples left the singing together, Amish tradition was to give young people privacy by pretending not to notice. Miriam had returned home shortly after Ruth, but Miriam hadn't dropped so much as a hint as to whether she'd enjoyed the secluded time with Eli or how he'd behaved. And Mam, who usually knew everything that went on in the household, seemed to be oblivious. It wasn't like Miriam to be so secretive, but Ruth didn't know how to ask without seeming jealous. Not that she was. Was she?

Ruth didn't know if she was more vexed with her sister or with Eli. Miriam should have better sense. What kind of boy paid attention to one sister and then the other? That wasn't the way things were done here in Kent County. And he was way too forward, to boot.

Usually a boy didn't directly ask a girl to ride home with him from a social. He'd have a friend speak to one of her friends first to see whether the girl was willing. Certainly no one ever courted two girls at the same time. That would be considered fast behavior and would invite a talking-to by Uncle Reuben or the bishop. Belleville was a long way away, but Ruth didn't think customs could be all that different in Eli's home community.

Ruth's thoughts drifted back to the other night. Had Eli been serious when he'd asked her to ride home from the singing with him? She'd refused him. So why was she feeling the green pangs of jealousy?

The unkind thought that Eli might have been using her to get close to Miriam occurred to her. But that didn't make sense. Wasn't Miriam the one who'd first encouraged him by accepting the ride on his ridiculous motorbike at Spence's?

As far as Ruth was concerned, Eli Lapp was causing far too much trouble in Seven Poplars. The best thing Ruth and Miriam could do was stay away from him. But that was going to be hard to do now, what with him working at the school and, worse, coming to dinner.

Ruth couldn't imagine what had possessed Mam to invite him for Sunday dinner. Mam had also asked Irwin, but Mam often asked pupils to her home so that she could give them personal attention. But Eli? How were people to stop talking about Miriam riding his motorbike if Mam invited him to their house? The community would think the two were courting.

Maybe they were....

One of the first-graders climbed into Ruth's lap. Little Rosy was wide-eyed and adorable, enthralled by the tale of Heidi's adventures. Ruth couldn't help cuddling the child. As Ruth gazed around at the circle of innocent faces beneath their white caps, she was struck by the strong bonds of love that bound them all together.

Sweet or naughty, quick or slow, spirited or plodding, Ruth loved each of the girls as if they were her own sisters. It gave her a deep satisfaction to know that these young people were the future of the Amish church and community. They would guard the faith and uphold the traditions she held so dear, and most of them, God willing, would always be part of her life.

Her choice to remain unwed meant never having her own children, never sewing small *Kapps* and aprons, never watching a boy take his first steps into manhood. Ruth thought she was prepared to make that sacrifice, but this afternoon, she felt a deep sorrow at what she would be giving up. In the Amish faith, it was the hereafter that was important, not this earthly existence. But for the briefest space of time, she allowed herself to imagine her own baby in her arms, her own kitchen, and putting a hearty midday meal on the table for a husband.

Ruth's insides knotted as her overactive imagination betrayed her. In her mind, she saw a bearded man filling the kitchen doorway…a man with Eli's blue eyes, his butter-yellow hair and his roguish grin. "Something smells good, Ruth," she could almost hear him say. "Ruth."

She blinked and focused on Verna Beachy's owl-like expression.

"The bell," Verna said.

Rosy squirmed out of Ruth's arms. "School's over," Rosy piped.

Ruth chuckled. "You're right, girls. Go on."

Laughing and chattering to each other, Elvie, Verna, Rosy and the others hurried to gather their lunch boxes and bonnets. Samuel's ten-year-old twins, Peter and Rudy, and the other younger boys were running back to the schoolhouse as well. And almost before Ruth had folded the blankets, the children were scattering: some on push-scooters, a few on in-line skates and others running barefoot across the fields toward home.

Samuel drove the wagonload of burned wood out of the yard. There was still a great deal of hammering and crashing coming from the front of the schoolhouse, but the other men were still working. Mam had gone inside, and Ruth could see her pulling down the window shades.

Ruth started toward the building when she spied Irwin open the door to the girls' outhouse, a squirming snake clutched in his hands. He saw her and quickly tucked the snake behind his back as he let the door swing shut.

"What are you up to now?" Ruth demanded. She'd been wanting to speak to the boy ever since Miriam had told her that she was sure their cows getting out was no accident. Apparently, Miriam had gone to open the water pipes at the base of the windmill and left Irwin to fasten the gate. Miriam believed that he'd deliberately let the animals loose. "What are you doing with that snake?"

"Snake? What snake?"

Ruth saw the reptile drop and slither away. It was a black snake, at least two feet long. She stepped in front of Irwin and looked directly into his eyes. "You were trying to frighten the girls with that snake, weren't you?"

"No, I just…" He shrugged and stared at the ground.

Ruth folded her arms. "You were playing a mean trick. You know you don't belong near the girls' outhouse."

Irwin's prominent ears took on the glow of ripe tomatoes as he tried to bury his chin in his faded shirt.

She gently raised his head so that he had to meet her gaze. "You were making mischief again, weren't you? Just as you did at our house when you let the cows out."

Irwin sniffed and rubbed his nose with the back of a grubby hand.

"Don't you know that our cows could have become sick from eating the corn? Not to mention the damage to the crops. You know how valuable the animals are. Why would you do such a thing?"

He shrugged.

Ruth took a deep breath. Dealing with this child was frustrating. She forced her tone to copy her mother's, authoritarian but soft. "Mam has invited you to Sunday dinner. You *will* be there. Understand?"

Irwin nodded.

"And no more tricks. Not at the school nor at our farm. Or else."

"I won't, I promise," a man's voice said.

Ruth turned around to find a grinning Eli standing behind her. As she turned, Irwin made his escape. He dove under the fence rail and plunged down the path that led through the grove.

"You're no help," Ruth admonished Eli. She told him about the snake in the girls' outhouse.

Eli laughed. "And Irwin pleaded innocent, did he?"

"'Snake, what snake?'" She snickered. "He's impossible. You never know what he'll do next."

"Boys will be boys," he offered, palms up as if that explained it.

"Miriam thinks Irwin deliberately let our cows out.

That's why she yelled at him and sent him home instead of asking him to help round them up."

Eli regarded her, his blue eyes thoughtful. "Roman thinks the kid might need more help than his cousins can give." He shook his head. "Norman and Lydia already have a full plate with their own children."

"But they're all Irwin has," Ruth said. "His parents and sister died in the fire. Where else would he go?"

"I don't know. I've been wondering the same thing." He motioned toward the school. "Wanna come inside and see what we got done today? Back at the shop, Roman and I are working on some built-in cabinets."

She looked up at him, thinking again how tall he was and how sure he sounded of himself when he talked about his skills at building. "They sound nice," she said lamely, debating whether she wanted to inspect the progress. Out here she could breathe, but for some reason, going inside with him didn't seem like all that good an idea.

Miriam came out of the school and waved. "Eli!"

Ruth took a step back, feeling as if a bubble around her and Eli had burst. It had been so nice, just talking, but the moment had passed, and she felt awkward with him again.

Glancing at Miriam, who was practically running to Eli, Ruth wondered if her sister expected her to leave the two of them alone, or should she pretend that she knew nothing about their mutual attraction?

"Mam wants us to go to the chair shop and make a phone call." Miriam reached in her pocket and pulled out a small piece of paper. "We need to make a dentist appointment for Susanna." She smiled at Eli. "Roman said you wouldn't mind driving us down in his buggy."

"Ne," Eli said. "I'll be glad to."

Miriam looked back to Ruth. "Mam wants us to call before the office closes for the afternoon."

Their church didn't allow phones in their homes, but because Roman did business with the English, the bishop had permitted him to have one installed in a small lean-to shed at the side of the chair shop. Any member of the community was free to make calls when they needed to.

Feeling like a third wheel, Ruth looked from one to the other. "No need for me to come," she offered. "I can just—"

Miriam shook her head. "Mam said *both* of us. I have the number."

"I'll go, but you're going to have to make the appointment," Ruth insisted. "You have to learn to do it sometime."

"All right," Miriam agreed. "And afterward, we can walk home."

"No trouble to drive you home," Eli insisted.

"Samuel says the board has approved our pie auction at the picnic," Miriam said as Eli went to get the buggy.

"Good." Ruth studied her sister. Miriam's cheeks were rosy and her eyes sparkling, but she hadn't so much as glanced at Eli as he walked away. Was she trying to hide her feelings for him, or was she just excited about the school frolic?

"I'm going to make a cherry pie with a lattice-top crust." Miriam chatted as they walked toward the wagon. "Have you decided what kind you'll make?"

Ruth groaned. "I don't know." She shook her head. The last time she'd attempted an apple-cranberry pie, her crust was tough and the apples in the center only half baked. "I don't really want to go. Maybe I won't even make—"

"Mam promised that we would all make one." Miriam smiled. "Even Susanna."

Ruth rolled her eyes, and they both giggled.

Eli returned with the horse and buggy and halted the animal so that they could climb in. Miriam scrambled up first, next to Eli. Luckily, the front seat was roomy enough for all three of them.

Roman's horse was a showy dapple-gray, and once they were on the road, Eli passed the leathers to Miriam. Laughing, she urged the horse into a trot. Ruth braced her feet against the boards and enjoyed the feel of the warm breeze against her face.

"Do you like music?" Eli asked.

"I do," Miriam said.

To Ruth's surprise, he reached under the seat and came up with a small boom box that played CDs. He pushed a button and Garth Brooks filled the air, singing a fast song about a rodeo rider and a thunderstorm. It was on the tip of Ruth's tongue to remind Eli that the music wasn't Plain and that Mam wouldn't approve, but she knew that Garth Brooks was one of Miriam's favorites. She had to admit that she liked country tunes herself. *Just this once,* she thought. What harm could it do?

By the time the story-song had ended and another singer, a girl, began a tune about an Appaloosa horse, the three of them were having fun laughing and tapping their feet to the music as they arrived at the chair shop all too soon. Eli clicked off the machine and tucked it back into his hiding spot as Miriam turned the gelding into the parking lot.

The main structure was about forty feet long, made

of concrete block, the front faced with yellow siding. There was a big yard and storage sheds behind the chair shop. Beyond, down a short lane, stood a neat story-and-a-half house where Roman and Fannie lived with their children. Eli's aunt was in the side yard taking clothes off the line. They waved, and she waved back.

Stopping at the chair shop always made Ruth a little sad because it made her think of Dat and the times she'd come to watch him at work here when she was small. But it made her feel good, too, because rent from the building and house made it possible for Mam to provide for her family.

There were three windows along the front of the shop, all with white curtains. The Dutch door in the center was painted blue. On the wide porch two rocking chairs were displayed as examples of the furniture that Roman and Eli made.

Eli jumped out and helped Miriam down. As Ruth scooted over to climb down from the buggy, Eli looked up at her. "If you come inside, I'll show you the cabinets we're making for the school."

Ruth bit down on her lower lip, glanced at Miriam, then back at Eli again. "I should go help Miriam…in case they have any questions at the dentist's office."

"It's okay. You go," Miriam called, turning to go. "I'll be fine."

"She'll be fine," Eli repeated. His expression was bold, almost amused as he met Ruth's gaze.

"All right," Ruth said hesitantly. "I'd like to see them."

He looped the leathers over the hitching rack and returned to offer his hand as she climbed down. Tingles ran up her arm as his strong fingers closed around hers.

Confused, and a little excited, Ruth's heart beat faster as she followed Eli up onto the porch and into the shop. She couldn't deny that she was attracted to him in a way that she'd never been to any other boy.

She should have turned then and gone back to the buggy, but she didn't want to. She wanted Eli to smile at her…wanted him to forget her sister and think only of her.

Roman's oldest son, Tyler, was at the corner desk in the showroom-office, poring over a math book. He grinned up at them and then sighed and applied his pencil to the yellow answer sheet with dogged determination. Eli nodded to him and led Ruth down a hall and into the workshop.

Instantly, she was enveloped in the smells of fresh sawdust, paint stripper, varnish, stain and wax. Racks of tools hung on the wall to her left, and on a wide workbench lay an unfinished, ladder-back chair. In the center of the room stood the carved headboard of an old bed in the process of painstaking restoration.

"These are for the school," Eli said, walking around the headboard to show her a length of cabinets that stood in the far corner. Ruth saw at once that these were not finished in veneer, but fashioned of thick pine boards with sturdy hinges. If there were no more fires, water or insect damage, the cabinets should serve the children well for decades.

Ruth followed him over and stroked a smooth door. "You didn't use plywood."

Eli grinned. "*Ne*. Reuben made a gift of the boards. He said they'd been drying in his grain shed for twenty years just waiting to be put to a good use. The hinges are ones we salvaged from an English job. They were just going to throw them away, so I asked if we could have them."

"Foolish, throwing them away," Ruth agreed. She fingered the nearest hinge. "But it must have been hard work to clean them."

Eli shrugged his broad shoulders. "A little elbow grease and some strong paint remover. Tyler helped."

"Mam will be so pleased." She opened a door and then closed it. "The doors fit perfectly. They don't even squeak," she teased.

"Of course they don't squeak." He laughed. "I've something else to show you. It's out back."

Ruth glanced in the direction of the front of the shop. "I should probably see how Miriam is—"

"Miriam will be fine," Eli insisted. "It's just a phone call. Come on. You'll like this even better than the schoolhouse cabinets."

Curious, Ruth followed him out of the shop across the yard and into a small shed beyond. Here, too, was a workbench and a tool chest. On the bench stood an unfinished chest with a gently rounded top. The piece was fashioned of cherry, about three feet long and no more than twenty-four inches high with bracket feet and a shiny brass lock. But it was the decoration that stunned her. Carved into the front was a strawberry plant, bursting with berries and two little birds, replicas so lifelike that she half expected them to pluck a strawberry and fly away.

"Oh," she gasped, unable to resist running her fingertips over the design. "Eli, you did this?"

His eyes lit with pleasure. "Do you like the wrens?"

She had known they were wrens. The bright eyes, the perky tails, the boldness, they could only be Carolina Wrens. "*Ya,* I do." She hesitated. "Is this for an English customer?"

"*Ne*. For an Amish."

She nibbled at her lower lip. "It is beautiful, *ya,* but I think not Plain."

"My hands form what I see in my mind."

"But we Plain people are not of this world but the one to come."

He nodded. "If God gave me this dream, this skill, maybe He wants me to make use of it."

Ruth shivered, despite the warmth of the shed. "You must guard against the sin of pride, Eli," she chastised, unable to meet his gaze. "You are not so Plain as other men."

"As Mahlon?"

She felt her cheeks grow warm as she looked at him and then away again. The chest was the most beautiful thing she thought she had ever seen, so beautiful that it made a lump in her throat. "He is a sensible…"

Eli chuckled. "You are very serious for such a pretty girl, Ruth. You accuse me of *Hochmut,* but you seem full of pride, as well."

"Me?" Her eyes widened in surprise. This time, she didn't look away from him. "How do I show false pride?"

He shrugged. "Think about it. Doesn't it give you satisfaction that you work so hard to take care of your mother and your sisters? That you've decided to sacrifice your own life to remain on the farm and—"

"Who told you…" She swallowed in an attempt to ease the knot in her throat. She knew who'd been talking about her. Miriam. Again. "You don't understand, Eli. Someone has to—"

"I may not attend church as I should, but I spent my childhood listening to God's word. And one of the sermons I remember my grandfather giving was about martyrs. He said that only the Lord chooses martyrs. Make certain that you really know what God wants of you before you decide on a path, Ruth."

Moisture blurred her vision. Was Eli right? She backed away from him, uncertain as to what to say... to think.

"I'm sorry," he said, taking a step toward her, reaching out with one hand. "I didn't mean to—"

"Ruth!" Miriam came around the corner of the building. "There you are. I got the appointment."

Eli met Ruth's gaze again as he lowered his hand to his side. Miriam looked at one and then the other.

"Come on," Eli said, walking past Ruth and out of the shed. "Let me drive you both home."

"Ne." Ruth's voice sounded strange in her ears. "We will walk. We can cut across the pasture."

Miriam and Eli exchanged glances. Miriam chuckled. "So we walk. I'll see you on Sunday, Eli. At dinner?"

"Ya," he answered, hooking his thumbs in the waistband of his pants. "I'll be there. I wouldn't miss it."

Chapter 8

At noon on Sunday, Ruth watched as Anna welcomed Fannie Byler into the kitchen. Dinner wasn't until one o'clock, but Fannie was Mam's dearest friend, and she'd come early to chat before the meal. Roman, Eli and the children were expected later. "Come in, come in," Anna urged, waving a wooden spoon.

Fannie's wide-brimmed black bonnet framed a plump rosy face with bright blue eyes, a snub nose and a wide smile. "I brought a lemon sponge cake," she said, after they'd all exchanged hugs.

"Wonderful," Mam said. "Anna made pies this morning. And Ruth's just finishing the coleslaw."

Anna placed Fannie's basket on the counter, and Susanna took her bonnet and cape.

"Irwin is coming," Susanna bubbled. "I think he eats a lot. He's a bad boy at school, but Mam told him he had to behave."

"Irwin's coming?" Fannie rolled her eyes.

"Mam often invites her pupils," Ruth explained, with a meaningful glance in Susanna's direction.

Mam put a finger to her lips, and Fannie nodded, catching on.

"Not likely anyone would go hungry at your table, Mam," Anna said, attempting to distract Susanna from sharing Irwin's shortcomings.

"Ne." Susanna turned to Fannie. "I carried pickled beets and applesauce up from the cellar."

Fannie fanned herself, dropped into a rocking chair and gazed with admiration at the kitchen table. Ruth poured coffee for the older women and then returned her attention to the coleslaw.

"Goodness, I'll be glad when my Clara and Alice are a little older," Fannie said, not in the least put out that Mam had cut off her question about Irwin. "These girls of yours are a marvel." She poured a dollop of thick cream into her coffee and stirred in three spoons of honey.

It was always nice to have Fannie and her family at the dinner table. If Ruth could only be as pleased with their other dinner guests. She knew it wasn't her place to question who her mother invited to Sunday dinner, but she didn't trust Irwin, and Eli…

She didn't know where in her head to begin with Eli or what to do with all the emotions he stirred up. He troubled her, with those rumors of his reputation. He just looked like trouble. And gossip or not, there had to be some truth to what Alma had said about him, didn't there? Alma wouldn't just make up such a terrible story, not even about a stranger. And it wasn't just the gossip that made Ruth uncomfortable. There was something more about Eli. It was the way he had made her uncertain about the life decisions she'd made. And then there was the matter of Miriam. She couldn't deny that Eli was exciting, but at the same time, she was afraid that her sister was becoming too attached to him.

Abruptly, she yawned and covered her mouth with the back of her hand. Thinking about that beautiful chest with the carved birds and the fear that Eli had made it for Miriam had kept her awake until after midnight last night. By the light of day, Ruth knew the idea was preposterous, but silly notions did that to you at night sometimes; they made you totally illogical.

"Roofie?" Susanna was standing beside her, a sugar bowl in her hand. "Can I put the sugar in now?"

"Just a minute." Ruth began to stir mayonnaise and lemon juice into the grated slaw. "Now," she said to Susanna.

Susanna carefully carried the sugar bowl back to the table. Watching her, Ruth couldn't help but smile. Susanna was such a sweet soul. Dat had been right. She was a blessing to their family. Eli didn't understand why Ruth had made the decisions she had. God had trusted her family with Susanna, and it was only right that Ruth be here to care for her. It was selfish to consider anything else. Some day, Mam would grow old, and they both would need strong hands to support them.

"It was good of you to ask Eli to dinner," Fannie was saying to Mam. "He's a good boy, no matter what some people say. I'm hoping that if families like yours welcome him, others will."

Mam glanced at Anna. "Could you help Susanna find a clean *Kapp* and apron?"

Since it was just the family this morning, her sisters

had covered their freshly washed hair with kerchiefs, but would need *Kapps* before male company arrived. "I can do it," Ruth offered. "I'm ready, and I finished the slaw."

"Ne." Anna caught Susanna's hand. "Come on, Susanna-banana. I'll braid your hair." Susanna giggled and followed her out of the kitchen.

When Susanna was safely out of earshot, Fannie spoke softly. "I know you've both heard the rumors about Eli, but I wanted you to know I don't believe them. There are things the boy isn't telling us. Roman says he has a good heart."

Ruth tried not to listen, but it was impossible not to hear Mam's reply. "I keep telling Martha and Alma it's wrong to judge Eli without proof."

Fannie sniffed. "That Alma asked me straight out if Eli was shunned in Belleville. He wasn't." She leaned close to Mam and lowered her voice. "Roman thinks the world of his sister Esther, but he thinks she's ill-treated Eli. You know about Eli's real father, don't you?"

Mam shook her head.

"He left the Old Order Amish church. Went to the English." Fannie glanced across the kitchen. Ruth concentrated on prying open a plastic container of sesame seeds.

"You needn't fear to speak in front of Ruth," Mam soothed. "She'd not spread ill about anyone." She chuckled. "Our Susanna is another story. She means no harm, but whatever she hears…"

"Well, it's no secret," Fannie continued. "The way Roman tells it, Eli's father abandoned his family and his faith. He always had an eye for worldly ways. He liked the English women with their legs all bare and their bosoms showing, and they liked him, too. One day, when he was plowing, he just left his team in the field and walked away."

Ruth couldn't contain her curiosity. "He just abandoned his family?"

Fannie nodded. "Too handsome for his own good, some said. They claim Eli is the spitting image of him. The oldest boy favored Esther's side of the family, and she had a soft spot for him. But their father..." Fannie shook her head. "'Course, he died before Roman and I started courting."

"There was a tragedy with Eli's older brother, too, wasn't there?" Mam asked. "Terrible for your sister-in-law."

"And for Eli, I imagine." Ruth sprinkled sesame seeds over the coleslaw. She shivered at the thought of losing one of her sisters.

"It was Eli looking so much like his father that worried Esther," Fannie said. "At least that's what Roman thinks." She added more honey to her coffee. "Roman says Esther never gave the boy a chance to explain his side. You know, concerning that girl who made the accusations. Then, before the matter could be brought to the church, she took off—ran away."

It was on the tip of Ruth's tongue to ask Fannie if Roman had asked Eli himself if it was true about the girl, but she didn't. Maybe she didn't want to know? Maybe because as long as it was just a rumor, Ruth could think Eli might be innocent.

Mam shook her head. "Some English people think that such things never happen to us, but they do. We are all human and all capable of sin. It's what happens after we sin that really matters."

A knock on the door startled Ruth, and she crossed the kitchen to answer it.

"It's too early for Roman," Fannie said. "He..."

Ruth didn't hear the rest of what Fannie was saying. Her attention centered on the tall figure standing on the back porch. It was Eli. She swung open the door, suddenly feeling guilty. Had he heard them talking about him?

He grinned shyly. "Ruth."

"Eli." Her hands nervously found a speck of mayonnaise on her apron.

He stepped into the room. "I came early," he said, stating the obvious.

Eli's yellow hair was damp, his cheeks freshly shaved. He was wearing English jeans and the Nittany Lions T-shirt, and his head was uncovered. No hat at all.

Mam rose from the table where the women had been enjoying their coffee. "Good to see you, Eli."

Eli shook his head. "I meant to say, I came early... to...speak to you," he said, directing his attention to Hannah.

Ruth looked at him. What he'd have to say to Mam, she couldn't imagine. Surely, he didn't have the nerve to ask if he could walk out with Miriam. Not dressed like that. And it was too soon. No one here really knew him. Surely, their mother wouldn't...

"Yes, what is it, Eli?" Ruth's mother didn't seem to notice the English clothes.

Eli straightened and cleared his throat. "They have movies," he began awkwardly. "At the mall."

"Ya," Mam agreed. Her mouth tightened into a thin line, but her eyes twinkled with mischief. "This even I have heard."

Eli shuffled his feet. "Today, they show a…"

Ruth folded her arms over her chest. A movie at the mall? Her gaze darted from her mother back to Eli. He looked so young, so unsure of himself.

"Speak up," Fannie said.

His words came out in a rush. "A decent movie. *Noah and the Ark*. No bad talk or fancy behavior. I saw it. Last night. Roman and I went to be sure…"

Fannie's eyes widened in surprise. "That's where you and Roman went? He never said a word."

Eli extended one hand toward Hannah. "Would you give me permission to take—"

Mam frowned, interrupting. "You want to take my daughter to the mall? On a date?"

"Not a date, exactly. Just to see the movie. A good story, a Bible story. Educational. And full of wonders. The ark that God bade Noah to build, the animals, the great flood that covered the earth."

"Which one?"

Eli's brow furrowed beneath the fringe of yellow-blond hair. "Which one?"

"Which daughter do you wish to take?" Mam demanded, her eyes still twinkling.

"Um." His cheeks grew bright red. "Susanna and Anna, Miriam and Ruth."

"Oh, no," Ruth interrupted. "I'm not—" She fully intended to refuse the invitation but before she could get the words out of her mouth, she suddenly realized that she wanted to go. Desperately. With Eli. The back of her eyelids stung. But Eli had really come to ask Miriam to go to the show with him. He'd just asked about the rest of them when he had lost his nerve. He didn't really want Ruth to go. That was plain to see.

A slow smile spread over Mam's face. "And if Fannie and I wanted to go with you to see this *Noah and the Ark?* Would you take us as well?"

"Ya," Eli answered. "I would. And there would be room."

"On your motorbike?" Mam asked. She was teasing him outright now. Ruth knew it, and a small part of her felt sorry for Eli. Mam had raised his hopes. He looked so eager, and when Mam would tell him Miriam couldn't go, that none of them could go, he would be crushed.

"Ne." He raised his chin and stared back at her boldly. "I hoped you would let them go. I hoped they would want to, so I asked a driver to come with her van. There will be room for anyone who wants to go."

"Susanna would love it," Ruth put in, feeling a trickle of excitement.

"What of my dinner?" Mam asked. "What of my turkey and the ham?"

"There is a show at four o'clock," Eli explained. "We'll have time to eat, drive to the mall, see the movie, have an ice cream and be back before dark."

"I can see that you've thought this out," Mam said. She nibbled her bottom lip, a habit that Ruth and her mother shared. Then, Mam turned and looked straight at her. "What do you think, Ruth? Would your sisters like to see this movie?"

Fannie frowned. "The bishop might not think…"

"But the bishop isn't here. It's Ruth I asked," Mam said.

Ruth's mouth felt dry. "I think," she began. "I think that Miriam has not yet been baptized in the church, nor Susanna. I think the movie might be educational for them."

"And you?" Mam asked. "What do you think about going?"

Ruth couldn't look at her mother or Eli. She wanted to say she didn't want to go, but she couldn't lie. "*Ya,* Mam," Ruth admitted glancing at the floor in front of Eli's boots. "I would like to see the movie, too."

"It's settled then." She nodded. "You may ask my girls, Eli. But I expect them home before dark."

"We will be," he promised. "I'll take good care of them."

"And one more thing," Mam said.

"Anything," Eli said.

"Church is here next week. I would like you to help us make ready. And I would like you to come to the services." She arched one eyebrow.

Eli grimaced. "I'll come because you ask," he said. "But don't blame me if your bishop kicks me out the door."

"He would never," Mam assured firmly. "Bishop Atlee is a fair man and a good shepherd to his flock. You'll be welcome here. You'll be welcome in our church, or I will know the reason why."

Anna, wearing her best Sunday-go-to-meeting dress and bonnet, led the way up the carpeted ramp through the darkened theater and found a seat. Ruth slid in beside her, followed by Susanna, clutching an enormous container of popcorn and so excited that she had the hiccups. Ruth had to admit it had been very thoughtful of Eli to invite Susanna. None of the boys in the neighborhood were unkind to Susanna, but Eli was the first to ask her to go on a date with her sisters.

Miriam sat on Susanna's right, leaving Eli next to the aisle. A few English turned to look and whisper, but then they lost interest and returned to their own conversations. Ruth could see that they were the only Amish in the movie this afternoon, perhaps in the mall. She had expected to be an object of curiosity, but stares always made her feel uneasy. She didn't think of herself as old-fashioned or quaint, simply apart from the larger world. The way she dressed and the way she lived was outward proof of a covenant with God; she didn't think herself better than the English, simply different. And different they were. That was obvious sitting here in the movie theater in a sea of brightly colored tank tops, dangling earrings and sparkly open-toed shoes.

Loud music blared from speakers on the walls, and on the screen, bottles of soda pop, boxes of candy and bags of popcorn danced and bounced. It looked very silly, but Susanna was entranced. She'd never seen a show before. Other than Eli, none of them had. Now that she was here, Ruth was nearly as excited as Susanna She hoped that coming hadn't been wrong. It had always been a secret dream of hers to watch a movie in a real movie theater. There might be consequences next Sunday, but this afternoon, she would see one of the great stories of the Bible come alive.

Miriam was laughing and talking to Eli. They both seemed so much at ease here among the English, something Ruth had always struggled with. Of course, Eli wasn't wearing Plain clothing, but her sister was. Miriam's modest blue dress, black bonnet and apron and black shoes were as Plain as her own. Miriam always embraced new experiences wholeheartedly, and Ruth was certain that when it was the right time to join the church, she would be one of the most faithful. And if Eli and Miriam were to be a couple, he should realize that nothing would divide Miriam from her faith and family.

It wouldn't matter if Eli had done the terrible thing he'd been accused of, if he truly repented and made his peace with God and the church. Sometimes it was hard to forgive and forget bad sins, but forgiveness was an important part of their faith. How could a person expect God to forgive them their sins, if they were unable to forgive others? But Ruth doubted Mam would let this relationship between Miriam and Eli go much further without this serious matter being addressed.

The lights dimmed. A message appeared on the screen asking people to turn off their cell phones. But before that request had died away, Susanna leaned close and whispered that she needed to go to the bathroom. Ruth rolled her eyes. She'd known that giving Susanna a large soda pop was bound to have consequences. "I'll take her," Ruth whispered to Miriam.

When they returned, some sort of cartoon squirrel was scampering off the screen with a cupcake balanced on his head. A pit bull was chasing the squirrel but not having much luck, as the barking dog kept slipping in the strawberry icing. Susanna laughed and wiggled her way past Eli and Miriam back to her seat. Ruth followed. Then the music changed, and a rainbow of lights swirled on the big screen, signaling that the main feature was about to begin.

So entrancing was the story and so real were the characters playing Noah, his wife and their sons, that Ruth could almost, but not quite, forget that it was Mir-

iam, not her, sitting beside Eli. Ruth was trying to concentrate on Noah's conversation with an invisible voice,
when Eli passed Susanna another cup of soda pop. "You
shouldn't give her..." But Susanna was already inhaling the drink. All that popcorn had made her thirsty
all over again.

Eli shifted in his seat. The movie was a good one,
better than the violent one he'd walked out of two weeks
ago. He liked going to the theater. Usually, he sat near
the back, by himself, and tried to understand the English, both on the screen and sitting around him. He and
Hazel had sneaked away one night to see a romantic
comedy. Both of them had been embarrassed by the
loose behavior in the story. They'd stayed to the end,
but he'd felt ashamed of himself as he'd walked out
at the end of the feature. It had been wrong to bring
Hazel there, and he knew it. But she'd wanted to go
and had threatened to go with some of her girlfriends
if he wouldn't take her.

Sometimes...most of the time...he felt as if he were
caught halfway between the Plain life and the English
world. He didn't know if he was completely responsible
for Hazel's disgrace, but there was plenty of guilt to go
around. Maybe she would have gotten into trouble even
if he hadn't taken her to the party that night. He'd never
know, and he'd never be sure if God or Hazel could ever
forgive him. Because of their irresponsibility, a child
had been conceived. Hazel's life, his life and the lives
of their families might never be the same.

Did he have the right to be with another girl? A good
girl like the sisters sitting beside him? Was he making
another mistake, one he would live to regret? If he did

choose the Amish path, would he later change his mind and run, as his father had?

Noah was leading the first pair of animals into the ark when Eli heard Susanna's whisper. This time, it was Miriam who took her hand and offered to escort her to the bathroom. Eli tensed. He swallowed, his mouth suddenly dry. When they returned, he could step out into the aisle and let Susanna and Miriam return to their seats. That was the right thing to do, the sensible thing.

But when the girls returned, Eli did what he'd wanted to do since they arrived; he got up, moved two seats over, and sat next to Ruth. She turned to look at him in surprise, before taking her elbow off the armrest dividing their seats and staring straight ahead at the screen.

Eli couldn't pay attention to the movie anymore. He was too acutely aware of the scent of green apple soap. The seats were very close, and he caught glimpses of Ruth's face in the flash of lightning from the screen. A feeling of protectiveness seeped up from the pit of his stomach. For all her prickly exterior, she was everything a man could ask for in a woman: beautiful, kind, strong-willed, loving. But she was more; Ruth was a true example of the faith. Why couldn't he have met her before he'd taken Hazel to that party? If he had…if he had, everything would be different. His life would be different now.

He locked his fingers together in his lap, and moisture rose along his collarbone. He didn't know what to do; he'd courted girls before, but no one like Ruth. He'd never felt this way about Hazel or Mary or Edith. He'd never worried that one of them might rebuff his attention. Maybe it would be better not to show Ruth how attracted he was to her, rather than make a fool of himself.

Eli glanced back at Miriam. She was leaning forward in her seat, deeply engaged in the movie. Susanna and Anna were both watching the movie screen, eyes wide with wonder. No one was watching him. No one would see him in the dark. Holding his breath, he reached over and covered Ruth's warm hand with his.

Startled, she turned toward him. For a second, her small hand trembled in his, as soft and fragile as a new-hatched chick....

In the dark, he searched her gaze and for just that split second, he felt a connection with her that he had never felt with anyone before. "Ruth."

His voice shattered the moment, and she pulled free. "Eli!" She looked at him and then away.

He felt his face grow hot with embarrassment. "I'm sorry. I didn't—"

"Shh," a woman called from the row behind them.

Anna glanced at Eli, then back at the screen.

Heart thudding against his ribs, Eli gave a sigh and turned back to the gathering storm that threatened to overturn the ark. He felt that way sometimes...lately, a lot of the time. But not tonight. Not tonight, because even though she had snatched her hand from his, she had let him hold it for a second, and he was pretty sure she had enjoyed it as much as he had.

With Ruth beside him here in the dark, peace and a sense of wonder settled over him. Whatever happened, nothing could take away his certainty that, at this moment in time, he was exactly where he should be.

Chapter 9

On Tuesday morning, Ruth and Miriam took freshly picked strawberries, spinach, lettuce, radishes and twelve dozen eggs to Spence's. They rarely went to the auction on Tuesdays, but the strawberries might not keep until Friday's market. Both Anna and Susanna had remained at home to catch up on chores. There was a charity-work sewing bee at Aunt Martha's that night, and the four sisters and Mam would be going after a light supper.

As usual, Miriam drove the horse, and while she chatted merrily, Ruth just listened. What had happened at the movies had troubled her greatly—not only that Eli had attempted to hold her hand, but that she'd almost permitted it. Ruth grimaced. There was no getting around the truth. She had allowed him. It had only been for a few seconds, but she hadn't immediately pushed his hand away, and she couldn't deny that she'd felt a rush of excitement when his warm hand closed around hers.

And Anna had seen it. She hadn't mentioned it, but Ruth wasn't deceived. It simply wasn't Anna's way to intrude on personal matters or to chide her older sister for a serious breach of decorum. Eli's behavior afterward—pretending that nothing had happened and buying them all Boardwalk Fries—only made things worse. Although she normally loved fries, Ruth hadn't been able to eat a bite. It would have choked her.

Eli was the worst sort of flirt. He'd taken Miriam to the movies, sat by her, and then tried to take liberties with another sister. It wasn't right. It just wasn't. Ruth didn't know what was allowed in *his* community, but it wasn't the way things were done *here*. As a baptized woman, Ruth should have known better than to go to the show with him at all. If she'd refused to attend the movie, if she'd protested, Mam might have kept her sisters home as well. But she hadn't. Eli had charmed her into forgetting who and what he was and who and what she was.

Then, to make matters worse, Ruth had been a coward afterward. She hadn't been brave enough to tell Miriam or her mother about the hand-holding incident. Instead, she'd acted as though everything was fine. She'd thanked Eli for taking them to the mall, and she'd told Mam about the movie and how tears had filled her eyes when the dove had returned to Noah with an olive leaf, proving that God's mercy had saved them from the flood. She'd laughed with Susanna about the monkeys riding on the tiger's back and the grumpy water buffalo. And all the time, in her heart, Ruth knew that she'd done something wrong…that she had committed a sin. The sin hadn't been the actual holding of hands, but the jealousy she had felt over Eli's attention to Miriam. And the pleasure she had taken, knowing he had held her hand for an instant, instead of Miriam's.

Ruth felt her face burn with shame. She wished she'd had the opportunity to talk to her mother, but Mam was busy with plans for Saturday's school picnic. They'd had to change the date so that the guests from the other churches could come. It would be a busy week when they added that on top of Sunday church at their house. For the picnic, each family with children in the school would bring food to share, but Mam always made extra dishes as well as treats for the children. There was so much to do this week that she just couldn't trouble Mam with her problems, especially those of her own making.

The traffic light changed; a truck horn blew, and Miriam flicked the leathers over Blackie's back. The horse trotted briskly through the busy intersection. Ahead were the railroad tracks. Spence's was only a few blocks away, and once they reached their stand, they might not get an opportunity to talk in private. Ruth opened her mouth, but before she could get a word out, Miriam asked. "All right. What's the matter? Did you catch Susanna's toothache?"

"What?"

Miriam chuckled. "You're as sour as one of *Grossmama's* pickles this morning."

"Am I?"

"*Ya.* You are." Miriam's brown eyes took on a concerned expression.

Ruth flushed an even brighter shade of red. Had Miriam seen Eli take her hand? Her pulse raced. "I'm not sure what we did Sunday was right."

Miriam laughed. "I thought so. You're feeling guilty about the show, aren't you? I thought it was wonderful. You can't tell me that you didn't have a good time."

"Movies are worldly. Not Plain."

"The story of Noah is from the Bible. I liked it. I'll go see it again, if I can convince Eli to take me."

"That's what I…" Ruth felt awkward. How could she say this? "Miriam, that's what I've been thinking about. I know you like Eli, but I'm afraid he isn't right for you," she blurted. "He…he's fast."

Miriam chuckled as the buggy bumped over the tracks. "He's not fast. He's just different from all the boys we know—the boys we've grown up with, and he's good-looking. That's why you're attracted to him." She glanced at Ruth. "You think he's cute, don't you?"

Ruth swallowed hard. "I'm not attracted to him. But he has a handsome face," she conceded.

"And nice shoulders." Miriam gave her a mischievous look. "Don't tell me you haven't noticed how wide his shoulders are. And he has nice hands."

More than that, Ruth thought. From the crown of his head to the soles of his feet, Eli was perfect. Just seeing him step into a room made her tongue stick to the roof of her mouth and her stomach do cartwheels. But good looks and a beautiful body were not what mattered most in choosing a husband. *For her sister.* What was important was the way a person was inside and if he shared your faith. An Amish marriage was about family and community and living according to God's word.

"Miriam, you're not listening to me. I'm trying to tell you that he may not be an appropriate beau for you."

Miriam laughed. "He's not *my* beau."

"But it looks like he's courting you. People think he is. And Eli isn't serious," Ruth insisted. "You can't trust him."

Miriam didn't say anything. She just kept sitting there with that silly smile on her face.

This wasn't going well at all. As much as Ruth loved Miriam, she could be so annoying, at times. She lowered her gaze, the guilt washing over her again. "There's something I have to tell you."

Another buggy was stopped ahead of them at the next light. Their cousin Dorcas leaned out of the carriage. "Hey," she called.

They waved back. "Do you think Dorcas is going to buy a pie at the market for tomorrow?" Miriam asked. "That might be smart if she wants to share pie with a boy on Saturday. The ones she bakes are even worse than yours." Miriam laughed, tickled with herself.

"I don't want to talk about Dorcas or about pies." Ruth clasped her hands together and hurried to confess what she'd done before she lost her nerve. "Miriam, listen to me. It was wrong, what Eli did," she finished. "He never should have tried to hold my hand when he was there with you."

"He held your hand?" Miriam cried excitedly.

"And I never should have let him. I'm so sorry, Miriam. It was wrong of me, I know, and—"

"That's what you've been so worried about for two days? Because Eli held your hand at the movies?" Miriam guided the horse around a produce truck that was double-parked in the street. Her voice was laced with amusement. "You should have said something. You've upset yourself for nothing. Eli isn't my boyfriend. He doesn't like me that way and I don't like him. I'm glad he held your hand."

"But—"

"When I find a boy I want to be with, I'll let him hold my hand. I might even let him kiss me. Once. After he asks me to be his wife, when I know he's serious. But before I gave him my answer." She looked at Ruth with great sincerity on her pretty face. "What if he's a bad kisser? Would you want a husband who was a bad kisser?"

Ruth was shocked. And relieved. Miriam didn't like Eli. She wasn't interested in him as a beau. "That's not the way to choose a husband, Miriam! You shouldn't be talking...even thinking about kissing."

"I think about kissing a lot," Miriam babbled on, not seeming to realize what a monumental moment this was for Ruth. If Miriam didn't like Eli, if he wasn't interested in Miriam, did that mean—

"What about Uncle Reuben?" Miriam continued with a giggle. "With that beard. It's so long and pointy. What kind of kisser do you think he is?"

"Miriam!"

Her sister grinned. "I'm just teasing you."

"Sometimes I wonder about you."

"Well, it's true. I will kiss my betrothed before we're married, and I won't feel guilty about it."

"Mam would be shocked if she heard you talk like that."

"Would she? For a happy marriage, you have to have love between a man and a woman. Then the tears and the laughter and the making of the children that follow will be right and good."

"I can't believe I misunderstood what was going on

between you and Eli. I was so afraid you'd be upset with me, but you have to admit it would have been wrong to let Eli hold my hand if he was courting you."

"*Ya,* you're right. But if we were *walking out* together, and he would do such a thing, better for me to know before the wedding than after." Miriam guided Blackie off the street onto the gravel lane that ran behind the auction house.

"And you're sure Eli doesn't like you?" Ruth said.

"I think Eli is a special person. But he's not the one for me and I'm not the one for him. I think he's already set his sights on someone else. But that doesn't mean I can't have fun with him."

"People will think—"

"So long as Mam knows I'm doing right, so long as my family knows, I don't care about anyone else. Besides, I'm *rumspringa.* I plan to have some fun." She giggled. "But once I join the church, I'll be as upright as Johanna."

And they both laughed at the thought. Johanna was now the ideal Amish mother and wife, but during her running around, their older sister had given Mam more than one sleepless night and more than one gray hair.

"Do you know what she said yesterday?" Miriam asked. "Johanna. About going to the picture show? She said that if she'd known we were going, she would have brought the baby and Jonah to Mam and come with us."

"Her husband would never have permitted it."

"Maybe not, but you know how headstrong she is." Miriam's eyes sparkled. "She takes after Mam."

"Mam?"

"*Ya,"* Miriam answered. "Johanna told me that when

Mam was a teenager, she used to go to the movies all the time with her English girlfriends."

"Do you think that's why she let us go?"

"Maybe she just wanted us to see for ourselves." Blackie trotted across the lot and came to a halt behind their usual table. "Good boy," Miriam said.

"Then I'm glad I went." Ruth got down from the buggy. "But I wouldn't have wanted to see a show that had shooting or bad language."

"Me, either." Miriam removed Blackie's bridle and slipped a halter over his head before tying him to a tree. They were lucky to have a table in the shade.

Feeling as if a great weight had been lifted off her shoulders, Ruth began to remove the boxes of strawberries. She had no idea how she felt about Eli or the hand-holding, now that she knew she hadn't interfered in Miriam's courting. At least she knew she hadn't hurt her sister. She had only the first tray out when a regular customer stopped and bought two dozen eggs and two quarts of berries. As Ruth counted out the change, she realized that they were short of dollar bills. "I'll go inside to the market," she offered. "As soon as we finish unloading."

"Need some help?"

Ruth turned to see Eli standing behind her.

She glanced at Miriam in confusion. He was the last person she wanted to see today. What should she say to him? She didn't look at him; her hands trembled as she tucked the change into the little cloth pouch they kept it in. "Shouldn't you be at the shop?" she blurted.

"Roman had some refinished furniture to be auctioned off today. I brought it in, and I'll wait to collect his money." Eli pulled eggs from under the buggy seat and carried them to the table.

"Good," Miriam said, plucking the money bag from Ruth's hand. "Since Eli's here to help, I'll go get that change."

"Don't go," Ruth said. "Eli's not..." But her sister was already walking away. Ruth glanced at Eli, and he grinned back at her.

"Guess you're stuck with me."

"I don't need any help." She tried hard not to look into his eyes.

A tattooed woman with long white-blond hair and short shorts waved her hand at Ruth. "Miss! Can I get some service here? Are these local strawberries?"

"Picked this morning," Eli assured her. Flashing a big smile, he grabbed up a plastic bag and went to the table. "You won't find any fresher. Or sweeter. How many quarts would you like?"

A bald man with a little dog on a leash approached the table. Ruth sold him radishes, lettuce and a dozen eggs. Two more customers stopped, and Eli went back to the buggy to bring more strawberries as Ruth waited on them. Business was brisk for ten minutes, and Ruth would have run short of change, but Eli changed a twenty for her with small bills from his pocket.

"Are you thirsty?" he asked when there was a break. "Would you like a soda pop?"

She shook her head. "I'm not thirsty."

He was standing so close that his gaze made her nervous...made her remember when he'd tried to hold her hand. She felt herself blush. "Thank you for your help. I'm sure you have things to do. There's no need for you—"

"I like helping you. I think we make a good pair, don't you? Look, half your berries are gone already. You'll be sold out before noon." He grinned. "Unless you want to stick around and let me buy you lunch."

She shook her head adamantly. "No. Miriam and I have to go home. We have to finish chores and start supper. There's a work bee tonight at Aunt Martha's."

"I know. The men are going. We're repairing Reuben's windmill."

Ruth tried to think of something to say that wouldn't sound stupid but she couldn't think of anything. She straightened the rows of quarts of berries.

Eli leaned against the table and crossed his arms over his chest; he'd pushed up his sleeves so his muscular forearms flexed. "Are you baking a pie for the school picnic?"

"I suppose."

His blue eyes danced with mischief. "Do you make good pies?"

"Not very good," she admitted. She couldn't help smiling. "Awful, as a matter of fact."

An English woman pushing a baby stroller approached. "Are your eggs fresh?" she asked Eli.

"Still warm from the hen," he quipped.

Ruth nibbled her lower lip. How could he talk to the English so easily? She felt a twinge of uneasiness and glanced up to see Aunt Martha glaring at her from her stand across the way.

"How much are your berries?" the woman customer asked, ignoring the sign. "That other stand usually has them cheaper."

"They do sell them cheaper," Eli said. "But ours are larger and haven't been sitting in a refrigerator since last week." He winked at Ruth, completely embarrassing her. But a part of her liked it.

The woman nodded and picked up two quarts.

Most of Aunt Martha's strawberries were still on her table. She wouldn't be pleased if Ruth sold out first. "Maybe I should go and see if Miriam's all right," Ruth suggested when the lady pushed her stroller away, carrying the strawberries.

"I'm sure she's fine. You can't leave me. More people may come, and then it will take both of us. The English, they hate to wait." He pushed his wide-brimmed hat a little higher and smiled at her. "After all, this is your stand. You wouldn't want to leave me to do all the work, would you? Besides, I make a mistake and then they'd be buying from your aunt Martha next time." He rolled his eyes.

Ruth couldn't help herself. She smiled back.

"It took forever, and by the time I got back, Eli and Ruth had sold all the strawberries," Miriam chattered. "Can you believe that?" She dropped the handle of the red wagon. "Your turn, Ruth. This is halfway."

The evening was so nice that Miriam had suggested the five of them walk to Aunt Martha's. The shortest way wasn't by the road but through the apple orchard, down the woods trail and across Uncle Reuben's meadow.

"All them strawberries," Susanna echoed. She was wearing a new robin's-egg-blue dress tonight and was so pleased with herself that she kept hopping from one foot to the other.

"What Miriam's not telling you is that she abandoned me," Ruth teased. With a mock sigh, she picked up the handle of the child's high-sided wagon. She would need to take care not to turn it over in the sandy lane and spill the treats they were bringing to share. As usual, Anna had used her time wisely, and the cookies and molasses doughnuts had already been made when they got home from the sale. The wooden wagon was even heavier to pull this evening because Mam had insisted on bringing three pounds of butter, a gallon of buttermilk and four quarts of strawberries. What Aunt Martha needed with more strawberries, Ruth didn't know, but it was one of those instances when it was easier to go along with Mam than to argue with her.

"Can't you walk faster?" Anna asked. "We'll be late for the prayer."

"Go on ahead," Ruth said. "Aunt Martha will be put out if she has to wait." She didn't mind pulling the wagon. Anna had done all the baking today, and it was a beautiful night for a walk. Birds were singing in the apple trees; frogs were croaking, and the air smelled sweetly of honeysuckle. "If I'm late, I'll just sneak in the back."

"Maybe we should go ahead," Mam agreed. She stopped beneath the spreading branches of an apple tree. "But I have something I need to talk to you about first, girls. It's Irwin. Samuel said that the board members have been getting complaints from parents. Some of the other children are saying Irwin started the fire at the schoolhouse. If anyone brings it up tonight, say nothing that will contribute to the gossip."

"What a terrible thing to accuse him of," Anna exclaimed.

Miriam considered the accusation. "The poor boy is ornery, but setting the school on fire?"

Ruth looked at her sisters, then at Mam. She wished she could tell Miriam and Anna about seeing Irwin running from the school after the fire broke out, but she'd promised Mam not to tell anyone. As time passed, as difficult as it was to believe that the boy would do such a terrible thing, there were no other suspects, and it seemed as though he might be guilty. And if he was, she didn't know what would happen. Someone who started fires was dangerous. She hoped that no one would bring in the English police. No matter how serious, it was better to keep Amish trouble in the community.

"I'm not ready to give up on Irwin," Mam said. "I don't want any of you to, either. I talked to Lydia today and I've arranged for Irwin to come to our place early before school and again in the afternoons to help with the milking and outside chores."

"You want Irwin near our cows?" Miriam asked. "After he let them into the corn?"

"Mam, I don't think—" Anna began.

"It's settled, girls. It will be good to have a man around the farm again." Mam chuckled. "Even a beanpole of a boy, badly in need of fattening up."

"But Miriam and Ruth milk the cows," Susanna said.

"There's plenty of work for all of us," Mam assured her. "And I know I can count on all of you to be kind and make Irwin welcome."

It took a great deal of effort for Ruth to hold her tongue, but she stared at the ground and kept walking slowly as the others hurried on ahead and vanished down the lane.

Of all of her mother's ideas, this one with Irwin had to be the worst. Ruth jerked the wagon over the ruts in the dirt lane. What if the boy started a fire at their place? They'd have to watch him closely, and from what she'd seen of Irwin, he'd be a lot more trouble than he was worth.

The left wheel suddenly sank into the sand and the wagon tilted. Ruth dropped the handle and grabbed the glass jar of buttermilk with one hand and the toppling basket of gingerbread with the other. Strawberries rolled out onto the ground. "Christmas fudge!" she cried.

"What kind of talk is that?" came a voice out of the rows of apple trees to her left.

Ruth knew that voice. She twisted around to see Eli coming toward her out of the trees. "Stop that," she snapped. "Stop what?"

"Sneaking up on me. You keep doing that!"

He laughed. "It looks like you need help, Ruth Yoder. Unless you want me to keep walking and leave you to deal with this all by yourself." He scooped up a strawberry, blew the sand off and popped it into his mouth.

"What are you doing here?" She felt foolish. Again. She was down on her knees trying to rescue Anna's cookies and the gingerbread, both in danger of following the errant berries. "Don't just stand there. Grab something."

Eli took hold of the corner of the wagon and lifted it. The jar of buttermilk, the strawberries and the desserts slid back to safety. Ruth got to her feet and brushed the dirt off her dress. "You're lucky I came when I did," he said. "Otherwise." Eli shrugged. "Gingerbread disaster."

"This isn't the quickest way from Roman's to Aunt Martha's house."

He looked solemn. "It's not? That's funny. Miriam told me to come this way."

"Miriam? Did you think she'd be walking along this lane this evening?"

"I'll never tell." He folded his arms over his chest.

Ruth was almost sure he was teasing her. Had Miriam planned this? It was her idea that they should walk. She took the first turn with the wagon, not sure whether or not she liked the idea that he planned to come this way just so he could bump into her. She had a mind to send him on his way. But the wagon was heavy and they were going the same way. She exhaled. "So long as you're here, you may as well pull the wagon."

"Ya," he agreed. "That might be best." He was laughing at her with his eyes, enjoying getting her goat once again.

She watched him as he grabbed the handle of the wagon. "Why do you do this?"

"What? Come to your rescue all the time?"

She made a sound of exasperation, but it came out lame even to her ears. "Stop teasing me."

"I like teasing you. It's just too easy."

"Fine. Be like that." She turned and started walking down the lane, leaving him to follow with the wagon. Her heart was racing. She felt giddy. And it was all his fault.

"Ruth."

The sound of her name on his lips was as sweet as the mockingbird's song. She glanced back at him.

"Will you walk with me?" He wasn't teasing her now. His tone was sincere. His gaze held hers.

"Why should I?" She was asking herself as much as him.

He stopped and pushed his wide-brimmed hat up, and she found herself looking right into his blue eyes.

"Please," he said.

She felt suddenly breathless. "If you want," she answered softly. "But talk only. No more holding of hands."

"Ne," he said. "Of course not." But he couldn't leave it at that. "Not unless you want to."

"Why should I want to hold your hand?"

"I don't know. I think maybe you wanted me to before."

"I did not."

He laughed, walking beside her. "I don't take you for a liar, Ruth. It's one of the reasons I like you. I would think you would always be honest with people."

How can he know that? she wondered. *I can't even always be honest with myself.* But he was right, she couldn't out-and-out lie. "Okay, maybe I wanted you to, a little. Maybe," she admitted. "But it was a mistake."

"Ya," he agreed. "Probably a mistake, but nice. Very nice."

Chapter 10

Walking beside Ruth felt good to Eli. For all her prickly exterior, there was something so sweet and innocent about her that it made him want to throw his arms in the air and shout for joy. And what he said about thinking she would not lie was true, even if he had been teasing her. What he liked about Ruth was that she wore her faith, not like a crown of thorns, but as a glittering mantle of content. She knew who she was, and she liked the person she was. She believed in herself and God. She didn't have to preach to people. Simply watching her as she followed the righteous path, day after day, made him wish he was the kind of man Ruth would choose to marry.

Since the death of his brother, he'd drifted further and further from the Amish way of life. The incident with Hazel had alienated him even more from his community, and the notion that he'd never be able to find his way back haunted his dreams. Was he too much like his father, as his mother had accused? Was it impossible for him to consider living in the faith he'd been born into?

If he'd taken Hazel to be his wife as everyone had expected, assumed responsibility for her child and formally asked for forgiveness, there would be no question of his future. He could have taken over his grandfather's woodworking shop and made a decent living building sturdy kitchen cabinets, lawn furniture and storage sheds. His community would have embraced him, and in time, the gossip would have faded and his new family would have been accepted.

But, as much as he'd liked Hazel, he hadn't loved her. He hadn't been able to turn his back on the possibility that he'd find a girl he truly loved and marry her. And he hadn't wanted to spend the rest of his life making lawn furniture. He wanted to shape beautiful things out of wood, to bring the images in his head to shape, to make his birds come alive. Selfishly, he'd put his own desires before the needs of the baby and Hazel. And now, things might never be made right.

Eli was afraid he hadn't changed, and he hadn't learned from his mistakes. Proof that he was still acting selfishly was right here in this apple orchard. Instead of involving Ruth in his troubles, he should get on his scooter and drive to the far end of the country, perhaps even to Alaska. He should go where no one knew him and where no Amish had settled. He should find a place where being Plain meant nothing to the English, and Eli Lapp would be just another craftsman who was skilled with wood.

Instead, he was walking through an apple orchard

with the most fascinating woman he'd ever met, a devoted daughter and sister whom he had no chance of winning, someone who would someday marry a God-fearing Plain man. Together, the two of them would raise a family of red-cheeked, happy kids, children who would know who and where they belonged and would never imagine turning English. *Ruth.* Even her name was straight from the pages of the holy book. It was Ruth who sacrificed everything for love. He would never deserve her; he was causing trouble for her just by being near her.

But he couldn't make himself let go.

Eli thought that if he could explain what had happened with Hazel to anyone, he would like it to be Ruth. And he needed to talk to someone about it. It was like a burr in his shoe, always there, always rubbing. He knew Ruth had heard the rumors, and it was unfair to keep the truth from her. But he had to protect Hazel, and dragging her down to excuse his own actions would be a worse sin than what he'd done, wouldn't it? "Eli."

A flood of emotion swelled in his chest. *"Ya?"*

Was it right that he could take such pleasure in hearing her say his name? He was like any other man, English or Amish, but Ruth was special. He'd never felt so happy just to walk with a girl. He remembered how warm and soft her small hand had felt, and how right it had felt, sitting in the semidarkness of the movie theater beside her.

"Are you coming to church tomorrow at our house?" she asked, breaking through his thoughts.

He didn't want to. It would be a mistake. Sitting through the sermon, letting himself believe that there might be hope for him and then having that hope dashed. It would simply hurt too much.

"Are you?" she pressed when he didn't answer.

"I promised your mother, didn't I?" he hedged. Not that it would be of any use. He'd leave the service with the same empty feeling he'd had for years, that he wasn't worthy of God's love…that he didn't belong.

"You should come. Mam will be disappointed if you don't." She turned to look into his eyes. "But you have to want to be there. It's no good if you sit like a lump or let your mind wander. You have to open your heart to the preacher's message."

"What if it's not meant for me?" he asked, revealing more than he wanted to, more than was safe.

"But it is," she insisted. "We have only to believe in our faith, to follow the laws, and we're assured of a place in heaven."

"You, maybe. Being good comes easy for you."

"*Ne.* That's not true." There was a little smile at the corners of her mouth as she looked down at her bare feet. "You don't really know me. I'm selfish and impatient. I judge people too quickly, and…" She sighed. "This list is long. I work at it every day. I really do. But I have failures and doubts. Everyone does. Like with Irwin."

"What's he doing now? More trouble?"

She shook her head. "Mam asked me not to talk about it…but…she wants him to come and help us out on a regular basis. I don't know if it's safe to have him on our farm. When I saw the fire at the schoolhouse…"

He waited, unwilling to press her.

"You can't say anything," she told him, obviously hesitant.

He stopped the wagon. "You know I won't. What is it, Ruth? What's troubling you? What did you see?" She was close enough for him to smell the clean scent of her hair and see the concern in her dark brown eyes.

"He crawled out from under the cloakroom and ran away. And he had burns on his hands."

"You think he started the fire?"

She nodded. "Mam says not to jump to conclusions until we know, but Irwin won't ever tell us if he's guilty. He never admits to doing wrong. I know he's been hurt by losing his family, but what if there had been children inside the classroom? They could have been killed. Setting fires is not just a boy's mischief. It's evil."

Eli let go of the wagon handle and folded his arms over his chest. "Have you asked Irwin what happened?"

Ruth rolled her eyes. "I can't get two words out of him. Samuel's twins may know something, but they aren't talking, either."

"What if I talk to the boys, see what I can find out? Maybe it would be different coming from me, me being a bad boy and all."

He smiled and she smiled back. A smile that lit up his heart.

"I'd appreciate it," Ruth said with a nod. "Mam has a good heart, but…"

"She's a wise woman."

"I'm afraid she's too trusting."

A high-pitched yelp broke the tranquility of the twilight. Eli glanced around, trying to find the source. "Did you hear that?"

"Over there." Ruth pointed toward a hedgerow at the edge of the orchard. "I think it's some kind of animal. Maybe a fox."

The pitiful squeal came again. A thick wall of mulberry bushes and old-growth cedar trees ran along the property line between the Yoder farm and that of Martha and Reuben Coblentz. Eli left the wagon, and as he approached the hedgerow, sparrows flew up out of the wild roses. He crouched down and carefully pushed aside the thorny foliage.

"Be careful," Ruth cautioned. She had followed him, but stayed back. "It might be a sick raccoon. You know they can carry rabies."

Something thrashed in the prickly vines. "What's wrong? Are you hurt?" he murmured and then laughed. "Well, look at this." He thrust his hand into the tangle and pulled out a ragged, burr-encrusted and pitifully thin puppy. "It's a dog," he announced.

Half-healed cuts and patches of dried blood marred the little animal's black-and-white fur. One paw was swollen and the plume of a tail so matted that it was hard to see where briars ended and puppy began. One ragged ear stood up and one hung down, but black button eyes stared at him hopefully and a red tongue licked at his hand. The whine rose to a joyous yip, and the little dog wriggled so hard Eli thought it might pop out of its skin.

"Ach," he said. "You've had a rough time of it, haven't you?"

"Oh, let me see," Ruth cried. "Poor little baby. How did he get here?"

"Probably dumped by the English." Eli stood. "It happened all the time on my grandfather's farm. City people think they can just drop their animals in the country."

"Poor baby. Let me hold him."

"Better not," he cautioned. "He's crawling with fleas."

She uttered a sound of amusement. "Think I'm afraid of a few fleas? Give him to me." She took the puppy from his hands and held it against her. "Sh, sh, hush now, *liebchen*. You're safe now," she crooned. "We'll take care of you."

The puppy began sucking frantically at her fingertips.

"He's hungry."

"Starving, I'd say. He was caught in the briars. He may have been out here for days."

"Poor little thing." She looked up at Eli, her brown eyes sparkling with determination. "I'm going to take him home and feed him."

"He needs a bath, I'd say."

"First some chicken broth and rice, then a bath." She glanced back at the wagon full of goodies. "Can you take those things to Mam? I'll have to miss tonight's work bee. I can't take him with me, and he needs attention now."

"You're willing to miss the frolic to tend to a stray?"

She laughed, heading back toward the path. "It wouldn't be the first time."

"It's too small to be of much use as a farm dog. There must be an animal rescue place in Dover." He followed her. "I could take it there tomorrow if you want."

"Ne." She shook her head. "We found him, Eli. God must want us to take care of him."

He thought about that. He liked animals, but his grandfather had never allowed any animal on the farm that wasn't of use, either for work or meat. Old horses and cows past their prime had gone to the auction, and barn kittens had regularly been disposed of. As a child, he'd shed tears when a favorite was sold off or simply vanished, but he'd learned to accept the way things were.

Ruth's determination to care for this little waif touched him. "If you're going to take the dog home, I could deliver the food and then come back to help—"

"Ne." She shook her head. "It would not look right, both of us missing. People would think that we were together."

He smiled at her in what he hoped was a persuasive way. "But that would be true, wouldn't it? We would be together, taking care of the pup."

"Are you looking for a way to get out of work? Uncle Reuben expects you to do your share." She looked down at the squirming dog in her arms. "I can do this. You just take Mam's contributions to the house."

"You're sure?"

"I'm sure."

"What will your mother say about you bringing him home?" he ventured. He knew what his mother or his grandmother would have said. *The dog wasn't worth saving.*

Ruth smiled up at him and then turned away, headed back toward her farm. "She'll fuss at the cost of the shots and vet bills, but she'll let me keep him. Mam only pretends to be tough. Inside, she's as soft as Susanna's whoopie pie filling." She looked back over her shoulder at him. "Good night, Eli Lapp. See you another day."

"Another day," he murmured to himself. The he grabbed the wagon handle and hurried up the lane. He couldn't wait for another day with Ruth.

* * *

"Women are in the front room," Reuben said, not seeming to care why Eli was pulling the Yoders' wagon. "Just carry that stuff in and leave it on the kitchen counter. Then come back and find a hammer. There's some loose nails on the windmill ladder. You can start by fixing that."

Eli nodded and picked up the gallon jar of buttermilk. It had gathered a little dust but otherwise seemed none the worse for wear. Taking the gingerbread in his free hand, he walked up onto the screened porch and into the kitchen. Every available tabletop and counter seemed to be crammed with food, but he found a spot and slid the buttermilk into the open space.

From the other room, he heard the murmur of chattering women. But as he turned back to fetch the rest of Hannah's things, he caught snatches of conversation coming from the porch.

"…asking for trouble. If my brother was alive, this would never happen." A hand pulled the screened door open.

"But he's not. And I have to do what I think is—" Hannah stopped in mid-sentence and smiled at Eli. "I saw the wagon. Is Ruth inside?"

Eli shook his head. "We found an abandoned puppy in the hedgerow. It was hurt. She took it back to the farm."

"What? A dog?" the older woman said. "I never."

"This is Reuben's Martha," Hannah said, introducing them.

He nodded. "You have the stand across from the Yoders, at Spence's."

Martha sniffed and scowled at him.

"It was good of you to bring the food." Hannah glanced at her sister-in-law. "Susanna picked you some more strawberries. I know you said you wanted to make more jam. Where would you like Eli to put them?"

"In the milk house." Martha pointed. "Over there. There's a cold box, set into the ground." Her mouth tightened into a thin line. "You're late. The men have already started work."

Eli stepped aside to let them pass. Had they been talking about him?

"It's time your Ruth was married, and the next two as well," Martha went on as they walked by. "They come and go as they please."

Eli hurried out onto the porch, eager to get away from the disagreeable woman, but not before he heard her add, "You're treading on thin ice, Hannah. You'll be lucky if you're not reprimanded by the bishop for running such a loose household."

Hannah's soft voice carried through the open window. "You mean well, sister, but you're too quick to judge."

"Are you accusing me of…"

Eli took the porch steps two at a time and let out a breath of relief when he saw Tyler coming across the yard. "Hey," Eli called to him. "Take these cookies inside and the strawberries to the milk house. Reuben is waiting on me."

"Cookies? Sure." Tyler motioned toward the side of the house. "The guys are all over by the windmill."

Eli headed in that direction. He'd take Ruth's wagon home later, once the work was done. Nothing would get him back in Martha's house tonight, or ever again, if he could at all help it. In the distance, he heard male laughter and the sound of hammering. Feeling guilty about the harm he might have done to Ruth's reputation, he quickened his steps.

It was almost eleven when Eli approached Ruth's back porch with the wagon. Only one light was burning up on the second floor, so he tried not to make any more noise than necessary. A few yards from the house stood an old-fashioned, covered well with a winch and bucket and a peaked cedar roof that extended out about three feet. Eli stowed the wagon there. It had clouded up and looked as though it might rain before morning. He didn't want to leave the wooden wagon where it might get wet.

He was still feeling guilty about the confrontation he'd overheard between Hannah and Martha, so he wasn't concentrating on where he was going. As he turned to go, he stumbled over a second bucket in the dark. "Ouch!" he cried.

"Clumsy," came a female voice from the darkness.

He turned and squinted toward the dark house. "Ruth?"

"Did you hurt yourself?" He spotted movement. She was sitting on the porch swing.

"Ne." He had slammed his shoulder into the brick wall surrounding the well, but he was too embarrassed to say so. "I thought you'd turned in."

"Shh. Mam and my sisters are already asleep."

He went to the porch, resting one foot on the first step, but made no move to join her. "How's the dog?"

"Jeremiah. I'm going to call him Jeremiah."

"More name than dog."

She laughed, and she patted the seat beside her on the swing. "Want to see?"

The dog lay curled in her lap, fast asleep.

Knowing he was probably making a big mistake, Eli crossed the porch and sat on the other end of the porch swing. Though old, it was a nice swing. Well built. He wondered if her father had made it. Roman said Jonas Yoder had been a solid craftsman, well respected by both the Amish and English. "I think I might have caused trouble for your mother tonight."

"Aunt Martha?"

"How did you guess?"

Ruth gave the swing a push.

"I don't want to cause trouble for your family."

"Aunt Martha doesn't think Mam should have Irwin working for us. She made such a fuss at the bee that Lydia started to cry."

"So it wasn't me?"

"My cousin Dorcas did tell Mam that you were working at our stand on Tuesday. Luckily, Miriam and I had already told her." Ruth's voice flowed as sweet as honey in the soft darkness of the moist evening air. She held out a towel-wrapped bundle. "I gave him a bath. He smells a lot better."

Eli took the dog awkwardly. "I don't think your uncle likes me much, either."

"Uncle Reuben? He's all right. He takes being a preacher seriously, but he's not mean. And sometimes his sermons are good. Too long, but good. You're lucky. Sunday, we have a guest minister from Virginia. He's visited before, and he doesn't preach nearly as long. And he's funny. He always works jokes in. But you remember the stories he tells from the Bible. His name is David Miller. Do you know him?"

"Ne. At home, we mostly had visitors from Lan-

caster. Bishops and preachers, that is. Regular visitors from all over the country."

"Same here," Ruth said.

The puppy whimpered in his sleep, and Eli petted him. You could feel every bony little rib, but his belly was extended and warm. "He ate good?"

"Mam said I gave him too much, but he was so hungry." She gave the swing another push. "Are you fooling with me, Eli?"

He swallowed. "What?"

"Tell me the truth. I thought you liked Miriam."

"Ne. I mean, I do, but not like that. Not as a girlfriend."

"Oh." Her voice was thoughtful, but he couldn't tell what she was thinking.

"I thought you did," she said.

"It's you I like, Ruth." He watched her in the dark, surprised by his own boldness. He was taking a chance being honest with her, telling her how he felt, but he needed to say it. "Just you."

She didn't answer.

He stroked the sleeping puppy. "A lot. I like you a lot."

"But you always talked to her."

"Miriam's fun. Why shouldn't I talk to her? Besides, *you* wouldn't talk to me."

She was quiet for a minute, and he could tell she was thinking. That was something he liked about Ruth. She was smart. She thought before she spoke, unlike him. It always seemed as if he was saying dumb things.

"You scare me, Eli. I don't know what to think."

"Ya," he agreed. "You scare me, too."

Chapter 11

Eli reached for her hand, but she drew it away.

"Things are too complicated."

"Because of what people say about me?"

She drew in a long breath.

The air was warm. Frogs and insects chirped and buzzed in the soft night. The air smelled of flowers and newly mown grass. Eli felt as though he would fly apart at any second, burst into splinters. He wanted this girl more than anything, more than he'd wanted his mother when she sent him away as a child...more than he wanted to fashion beautiful furniture out of seasoned hardwood. "Ruth."

"Shh, hear me out," she murmured. "You have to understand. I can't be selfish. I have to do what is right."

"Maybe us meeting is right...is what we are supposed to do." She was so near. He felt big and clumsy.

His palm ached to enfold hers. All he wanted was to touch her hand. "I've done things I shouldn't have. But I'd never do anything to hurt you."

"I have to think, to decide what is best." She toyed with the undone string on her *Kapp*. "If I did leave Mam…leave my home…it could only be with a baptized man who shared my faith, who could give his life to God, who could follow our rules. Do you understand?"

"I wish I was as sure of God's will as you are," he admitted.

"I wish you were, too." She rose to her feet. "I have to go in."

"Can I see you again? Can we *walk out* together?"

"I don't know, Eli. I have to pray on it. It's a big step. I've always thought to stay with Mam and Susanna. I can't just change my mind without considering what that would mean." She took a few steps and then turned and reached out for the sleeping puppy. "I'd like to be your friend, no matter what."

He ran a hand through his hair. "I don't know if that's possible, if I could be just…just your friend. Or…" A weight crushed his chest. "Or, if I can ever find the faith you have."

"Pray on it," she advised. "It always helps."

"I'll try."

She cradled the dog in her arms. "Jeremiah is just the right name for him, don't you think?"

He didn't answer, and she slipped into the house, leaving him alone on the porch swing. He sat there for nearly an hour, wishing he could be the man she wanted, wishing she was still here beside him in the soft spring night.

* * *

"You should have been there," Anna said, mounding a deep bowl of flaky pie dough into a ball. "Aunt Martha made such a fuss about Irwin."

"Enough of such talk," Mam warned. "She only means the best for us. Her heart is good." It was late on Friday afternoon, and they had gathered in the kitchen to bake pies and prepare food for the school picnic. Even Johanna had come to help, bringing three-year-old Jonah and the baby.

"You think everyone's heart is good, Mam," Ruth said.

"Amen to that," Miriam agreed. The rest of them laughed.

Mam had received letters from Rebecca and Leah today. Leah's letter was short and funny, but Rebecca had filled them in at great length on all the doings at *Grossmama's* house and in the church and community. It was easy to see why she was a regular contributor to the *Budget*.

"Be careful," Susanna said to Jonah. She was rocking Baby Katie and keeping a watchful eye on Johanna's son as he petted the puppy. "You have to be gentle with him."

"I am," Jonah declared. "I am, isn't I?"

"You are, and I'm proud of you." Johanna beamed at Susanna. "You're so good with both of them," she said. "I wish I had you at my house all the time."

"She has the touch," Anna said, as she tore off a section of dough and dropped it onto a floured board.

Ruth passed her sister a rolling pin. Her own piecrust was as flat and round as she could get it. The dough had already torn twice, and she knew that she'd probably make it worse when she tried to get it into the pie pan. She could make decent biscuits and muffins. Why was pie always a disaster for her? Her crusts were so tough that even Mam teased her that they could patch the holes in the orchard lane with them.

"What's this I hear about someone sitting on our porch swing in the wee hours of the night this week?" Johanna asked. She looked especially sweet today in a lavender dress and white apron. She'd left her shoes on the porch and was barefoot like the rest of them.

"It wasn't someone," Susanna said. "It was Eli. He was on the porch with Roofie and Jeremiah. They were swinging."

"Talking," Ruth corrected. "We were talking."

Anna giggled. "Wouldn't Aunt Martha love to know that? She'd scorch your ears after church." She wiped floured hands on her apron. "Ach! Mam, the pies. Are they burning?"

"I wouldn't be surprised," Mam said. "More chatter than work, I'd say."

Ruth grabbed a towel and used it to shield her hands from the heat as she opened the oven door on the wood-stove and began to remove Miriam's and Mam's pies. "Perfect."

"Don't say that yet," Miriam warned. "You haven't tasted them."

The kitchen door opened, and Irwin stuck his head in. A battered straw hat with an Ohio-style brim hid his pale face. "I got eggs."

Mam waved him in. "Put the eggs on the table. Let me see what you have."

Eyes downcast, Irwin ventured into the warm kitchen and did as he was told. For the past two days, he'd come after school to help with the outside chores, but as far as Ruth was concerned, the boy was lazy. The only thing he'd shown interest in was eating and staring at the new puppy. "Did you clean out the chicken waterers and fill them with fresh water?" she asked. Yesterday he'd forgotten, and she and Miriam had had to do it.

Irwin nodded and nudged Jeremiah with one dirty foot. The trace of a smile skimmed over his thin lips before vanishing behind an expressionless mask. "Can I hold him?"

Ruth blinked as she deposited the last pie safely on the stovetop. Irwin never spoke to Mam unless he was forced to. "Jeremiah's not strong enough to play yet," she said. "Maybe when he's put on some weight and his cuts have healed."

"I know about dogs," Irwin said. "I had me one. Her name was Gretel."

"Where is she?" Susanna asked. "I love dogs."

"Smoke got her."

"Smoke?" Susanna's freckled nose wrinkled. "How did smoke get her?"

"Was it the fire that killed your family?" Ruth asked.

"Yep. Would have got me, too, but I wasn't home that night." He crouched down and stroked the skinny pup. "Gretel was a smart dog. She followed me to school every day. She could sit up and beg and roll over. Better than your dumb dog."

Irwin's thin voice cracked and lower lip quivered.

It was all Ruth could do to keep from weeping. This boy had lost everything in one terrible night, and she'd been less than charitable toward him. He was as damaged inside as Jeremiah was on the outside. No wonder Irwin acted out.

"I think we could use your help in training Jeremiah," Mam said brusquely. "We haven't had a puppy in a long time, and most dogs will learn quicker from a man."

Johanna turned her face away and stifled a giggle. Mam glanced at Ruth, and she understood that her mother was slicing the truth thin to soothe Irwin's pride.

"You may hold Jeremiah, if you are careful," Mam added. "After you've finished with the eggs."

"Wash your hands," Ruth said. "Take these eggs back on the porch and clean them with the vinegar rag. Put the cracked ones aside in the tin bowl, so Miriam can cook them for the pigs. Dry the perfect eggs and put them in the cartons."

"I break stuff," Irwin said. "Maybe somebody else should wash the eggs."

"No," Mam said. "We all learn best by doing. I'm depending on you to do your best. The egg money is important to us. When you're done, you can take care of the puppy. We're busy today, and I think he needs the attention."

"Me want to help Ir'n!" Jonah scrambled to his feet. "Me can wash eggs."

Miriam rolled her eyes. Ruth chuckled as she wondered how many dozen would survive to make it to market next week. "I'm going to watch to see you do it right," Ruth said. She thought Jonah and Jeremiah would be safe from Irwin's mischief, but she was going to keep a sharp eye out for trouble.

"So...you sat on the porch swing with the Belleville boy," Johanna said, when Jonah and Irwin had left the kitchen. "Anything more we should know?"

"Ne," Ruth said, more sharply than she intended.

She didn't want to think about Eli, let alone talk about him in front of Mam and her sisters. She didn't know her own mind yet. "We're just friends."

Anna chuckled. "Where have I heard that before?"

Mam watched through the screen door as the boys washed and dried the eggs. How many were lost, Ruth didn't want to guess, but Jonah seemed none the worse for wear when they returned to the kitchen.

"I can hold Jeremiah now," Irwin said.

"You can," Ruth agreed. "Gently."

"Gentle," Jonah echoed. He stared up at Irwin with all the awe of a small boy for a bigger one. "He little." And then, he repeated, "Jeremiah little."

"I know." Irwin's whining tone belied the gentle expression that came over his face as he cuddled the puppy. Jeremiah squirmed and squeaked as he nestled into the boy's lap. Irwin ran dirty fingertips over a ragged tear in the dog's skin. "Briars got him," he said.

"Yeah. Briars got him," Jonah repeated. He wiggled as close to Irwin as he could, imitating the older boy's stiff posture.

Mam smiled. "Looks like Jeremiah has made a new friend."

"Guess I could help, if you want," Irwin offered. "Take him out to do his business. Dogs like it outside."

"They do indeed," Ruth said. "I think you'll be good for Jeremiah."

"Me, too," Jonah joined in.

Ruth took a glass down from the cupboard and poured a tall glass of cold milk for Irwin and a tin cup, half full, for Jonah. She sliced a hardboiled egg onto a plate, added three fried chicken legs, two buttered biscuits, some cheese wedges and a handful of strawberries. She placed the food on a clean dish towel on an old three-legged milking stool beside the boys. "In case you need something to tide you over until supper."

Jonah nibbled at the cheese and ate a strawberry. Irwin swigged down the rest of the milk in less time than it took Ruth to spread her piecrust in a deep dish and fill it with sour cherries from last August's bounty. From the corner of her eye, Ruth saw Irwin dipping his index finger in the empty glass and letting Jeremiah suck drops of milk. Some of her uneasiness seeped away. Maybe there *was* hope for Irwin Beachy.

"We'll have a light meal tonight," Mam said. "We have that chicken-and-corn soup, chicken sandwiches and fresh salad. Stay for supper, Irwin."

He nodded. "Guess I could."

Anna went to the icebox and took out cold ham, applesauce and a plate of deviled eggs. "If we're having company, I think we'll need more than soup and sandwiches, Mam."

Ruth and Miriam looked at each other. "A lot more," Ruth said, sending them both into fits of giggles. Even Susanna and the boys laughed, although it was clear they hadn't gotten the joke.

Ruth leaned on the counter and glanced around the kitchen at her family. This was where she belonged. This was where she was happiest. It was silly to think of ever leaving home or Mam and Susanna. This was where she was needed most, and it would be selfish to consider anything else, wouldn't it?

She sighed. Making hard choices was part of her faith. She had to do what was right, but how did she know what was right? Why did thoughts of Eli plague her so, and why did she remember every word he'd ever spoken to her? A small lump rose in her throat as she remembered how it had felt when he lifted her in his arms and carried her away from the burning schoolhouse. For an instant, she'd felt safe, safe in a way she hadn't since Dat had passed away.

But thinking of Eli in that way only made dandelion fluff tumble in the pit of her stomach. Moisture gathered in her eyes, and she blinked it away. Eli Lapp was not for her. He was trouble, and the less she had to do with him, the better. She was right; she knew she was right, so why did the clean male scent of him linger in the dark corners of her mind?

Saturday was a perfect spring day for the school picnic; the sun shone, and there was a slight breeze to keep everyone from getting overly warm. All of the parents and most of the relatives and friends who lived in the community turned out, as well as the young people's groups from two other churches.

Before picnic baskets were brought out, there was a volleyball game between the girls and boys. The bonnets won, hands down, because the bishop decreed that all the straw hats would have a handicap. The boys had their ankles tied together with lengths of corn string, so that they were hobbled. It made for many tumbles and even more laughter. After that came an egg and spoon race, adult men against their wives, and then men had been forced to use raw eggs. The losing team, consisting of fathers and grandfathers, would have to serve the children's lunch and clean up afterward.

Roman brought his red cart and driving goats, so that all the small children got rides. There was hymn singing by grades one through three, and a greased pig contest for boys between the ages of four and ten. After a hilarious contest and many near-misses, one of Lydia's children caught the pig and got to keep it, much to the delight of his mother.

"Roast suckling pig for Christmas dinner," she'd shouted. "Yum!" But everyone knew that they wouldn't really eat his pig. Samuel had promised to trade the greased pig, a male, for a young sow. The boy would use that pig to start his own breeding project. If he was diligent, he'd have the start of his own herd and be earning money from the animals by the time he was a teenager.

Throughout the afternoon, Ruth had stayed near Mam, helping to organize the games and prepare for the pie auction. She hadn't taken part in the volleyball because she didn't want to be anywhere near Eli. She'd taken enough teasing from her sisters about sitting in the porch swing with him, and she wasn't about to provide entertainment for the whole community.

Eli, thankfully, realized her reluctance to be seen talking to him and kept his distance, but that didn't keep him from watching her. Her cheeks burned from the intensity of his stare. No matter how busy she was, she couldn't ignore his scrutiny, and Miriam and Johanna had enjoyed every minute of her discomfort.

The day had gone well, but Ruth dreaded what was yet to come. As she'd suspected, her pie-making had been a disaster. She'd made a cherry pie, and when she'd put it in the oven, it had looked respectable. But the cherry filling had bubbled up, the crust had cracked down the middle and burned on the sides. Anna's pies were as perfect as the ones for sale behind the glass cases at Spence's Auction. Mam's pie was beautiful, Miriam's perfectly adequate. Hers was a disaster. And now everyone in the neighborhood would see what a terrible hand she was at baking, and she'd be teased for the next six months—maybe for the rest of her life.

Ruth had been tempted to stay up late and bake a half-dozen pies, hoping that at least one would turn out right, but she'd known better. With luck, no one would bid on her contribution and she could cut it into slices for the children's table. That way, she could discard the burned spots. Kids wouldn't care. They ate anything and didn't know the difference.

The problem was that every unmarried girl between the ages of fifteen and seventy had brought a pie and a picnic lunch that she would have to share with whichever man paid the most for her dessert. Of the older women, there was only Salome Byler and Gret Troyer, both widows and over sixty. Salome's pie was certain to be purchased by her brother Amos, out of pity and to see that no one was poisoned. He was used to her cooking. Salome had outlived three husbands, and Amos claimed that her pies had done in at least two of them. Gret was being courted by her third cousin, Jan Peachy, and Jan was sure to outbid anyone for her strawberry cream delight.

Everyone's eyes would be on her and Dorcas, both single, both old enough for people to whisper that it was time—high time—that they found a husband. Charley might give something for her pie, but Charley was such a tease. If he didn't like it, he'd let everyone know. And he would tease her worst of all. There were a couple of boys in Charley's gang, boys that she'd known all her life, some she even liked. But they'd not bid if Charley bid. And if he did or if he didn't, there was Eli. And who could guess what he would do?

Out of sheer cowardliness, Ruth hid her lunch basket and her pie under the table and covered them both with a spare tablecloth. Then she wandered away from the table, gathered up Johanna's baby girl and edged her way to the back of the crowd, near the buggies. Her stomach clenched and moisture dampened the hairs on the back of her neck. If only Mam and Samuel got so caught up in auctioning off the pies on the table that they'd forget all about hers. She could only hope luck was on her side.

Mam held Dorcas's raisin pie high over her head.

"What are we bid?" Samuel called in his deep auctioneer's voice. "Something in this lunch basket smells awfully good. Is that your mother's roast goose, Dorcas?"

"One dollar!" Charley shouted.

"None of that," Samuel flung back. "This is for the school, and we know your pockets are weighed down with greenbacks. We're starting this bidding at five dollars! Who'll say six?"

Six came and then seven. Amid good-natured catcalls and laughter, the price rose to nine dollars. Samuel brought the hammer down and handed Dorcas's lunch basket to a blushing boy from the north district. Dorcas took the pie, and the two went off amid whistles and hoots to find a place to spread their dinner cloth in the shade.

One after another, the pies went. They fairly flew off the table as money jingled and rustled into Mam's fire-fund tin oatmeal box. Amy's chocolate pie sold for twelve dollars, and then Charley bought Miriam's for fourteen dollars. Samuel claimed a frog in his throat, got the bishop to stand in for him as auctioneer and got a roar of approval when he successfully bid on both Anna's apple-cranberry pie and Mam's honey-pear, paying thirty dollars for the two of them.

"After all this shouting, I'm hungry enough to eat both lunches," Samuel bellowed. Everyone clapped. Last year, Anna's blackberry pie had brought only three dollars, and the boy that won the bid had been thirteen years old. Sharing lunch with her mother and her mother's beau and knowing hers was probably the tastiest pie of all might be a little disappointing to Anna, but she could take pleasure in knowing that she'd brought in so much for the school repairs.

One more pie went to one of Charley's buddies, and when the table was empty, Ruth thought she was home free. But then Mam whispered to Samuel, and he went back and pulled her pitiful cherry pie from its hiding place.

"Ruth Yoder made this one," Samuel said. "We all know what delicious pies those girls bake. Last chance here. Who's going to give me ten dollars for it?" He gave a quick glance at the pie and put it into the lunch basket.

"Fried chicken, coleslaw and potato salad," Johanna called. "Sweet pickles, corn bread and strawberries."

No one offered a bid.

"Ten dollars," Samuel said. "You won't regret it. I've eaten Ruth's fried chicken. And her corn bread is so light, you have to hold it down to eat it." Nothing.

She'd hoped no one would buy her pie. But she hadn't imagined how bad she would feel when there were no bids at all. Dorcas would never let her live it down.

"All right, you high rollers," Samuel said. "Nine dollars. Nine dollars for a pie you'd pay twelve for at Spence's."

"Ruth's was raw last year," Charley said. "How do we know what it tastes like?"

"As if you'd know," his mother chimed in. "You'd eat a dead horse if the buzzards didn't get to it first." That drew more laughter from the onlookers, but no offers for her pie.

Ruth wanted to crawl under the nearest buggy.

"Eight, eight. Who'll give me eight?"

"I will." Eli raised his hand. "But if I die of food poisoning, I'm blaming you, Samuel."

"Eight, eight. We have eight dollars from the young fellow from Belleville. Who'll give me nine?" Samuel chanted. "Nine dollars for fried chicken lunch and cherry pie."

"Might be burned cherry pie," Charley reminded them.

Snickers rippled through the audience.

"Going once," Samuel shouted. "Last chance, boys. I can taste that fried chicken." He lifted the lid on the lunch basket and peered inside. "Looks fine to me. Going twice. Any more takers?" He brought the hammer down with a bang. "Sold to Eli Lapp!"

Eli made his way through to the table and Samuel passed her lunch basket to him.

"Enjoy," Samuel said. "You got a real bargain." He glanced around. "Ruth! Where are you, Ruth? Pass that baby and come get your pie. This young buck has paid his money and wants his dinner."

Reluctantly, Ruth stepped forward.

Eli grinned.

Chapter 12

"I think there's a patch of shade under that old apple tree," Eli said as he took the picnic basket. "This feels heavy." He flashed a grin. "You brought lots of food. Good. I could eat a horse and chase the carriage."

"You might be better off with the horse," she answered. Her cheeks were burning. People were laughing and watching her. Even Susanna was giggling. "I'm not the best pie baker."

"I'll be the judge of that. It's cherry, isn't it?"

"Cherry crisp, more like it," she replied. She followed him, keeping her eyes on his back, trying not to make eye contact with her neighbors. Soon everyone would see just how pitiful a pie Eli had spent his money on. Then they'd all start talking about how it was just as well that she didn't want to marry, because who would want a wife who couldn't make a simple cherry pie?

Families and couples everywhere were spreading cloths to share their lunches. Samuel's twin sons were racing around Mam's basket, and his younger daughter Lori Ann had a thumb in her mouth and was hiding behind his legs. She was a shy little thing who stuttered and suffered from the loss of her mother. Maybe the neighbors were right about it being time for Samuel to put off his mourning and remarry. But why did he have to choose Mam?

Ruth couldn't see her mother accepting Samuel as the new head of the household. It was right that the husband and father assume that place, but Mam had her own way of doing things. They were making out so well that Ruth couldn't imagine Mam or the rest of them adjusting to a new husband's and stepfather's ways. Home wouldn't feel the same.

"How's this?" Eli's question tugged her back into the moment.

"Oh, fine." She would have preferred sitting in the apple orchard alone with Eli, just to escape the stares, but that wasn't an option. She dreaded opening the picnic basket. Everyone would see her poor excuse for a pie and the teasing would start all over again. They'd poke fun at her and at Eli for buying it. She didn't know why she'd let Anna pack it. They should have left it at home or thrown it to the chickens. "I still think you wasted your money," she ventured. "Even if it was a donation for repairing the school."

Eli waited expectantly for her to take out the tablecloth and spread it on the ground. Everyone else was already eating, and if they were too slow, they'd miss the children's sack races later.

"Let's see Ruth's pie!" Charley called from where he

sat on a blanket beside Miriam, only a few feet away. He was already halfway through one of her ham sandwiches. "If it's too tough, you can always use the crust for a wagon wheel."

Eli threw him a look that could have scorched paper.

Ruth kneeled on the tablecloth, shut her eyes and lifted the lid. *What a coward I am,* she thought as she fumbled for the pie. She didn't want to see how ridiculous the burned crust looked, compared to all the pretty pies.

"Careful," Eli warned. "You wouldn't want to drop it."

She glanced down. She had the pie firmly in her hands, but it was all she could do not to gasp for air like a landed fish. *This wasn't her pie!*

This crust was full and golden brown, rising high and dimpled with a pattern of cherries cut into the top, each cut just wide enough to allow the rich red filling inside to bubble up. The edges around the pie were neatly scored, not burned, but perfect and appealing. Ruth could never, in a million years, have made such a beautiful pie.

In an instant, she realized that Anna must have substituted Ruth's ruined pie with one of her own before they left the house. She didn't know when her sister had done it, but it was clear that she had. Had Anna really thought anyone would believe Ruth had made this? But the look on Eli's face answered her question. He was smiling with admiration—at the pie *and* Ruth.

She placed the picture-perfect pie in the center of the checkered tablecloth before glancing across the school yard to see if Anna and her mother were watching. They were talking with Samuel's children, paying her no attention. Now what? Did Ruth just blurt out the truth? It would be dishonest to pretend that she'd baked the pie when she hadn't, but if she came clean now, Charley would make her the butt of his jokes at every gathering for years.

As if thinking about him had drawn him closer, Charley gave a sharp whistle. She looked up to see him standing over her picnic basket. "Would you look at that?" he said, making a show of rubbing his eyes. "Ruth's pie isn't burned this year."

Around her, heads were turning. Dorcas's lunch partner stretched his neck to stare at them.

"You'll be burned if you don't get back here and eat my pie," Miriam said, loud enough for those around her to hear.

Everyone laughed, turning the joke on Charley as he hurried back to his own picnic lunch.

Ruth began removing the sugared peaches and potato salad from the picnic basket, still in a dilemma as to what to say. "Charley's okay," she answered. "He just likes to tease. Isn't he a cousin of yours? Your mother was a Byler, wasn't she?"

"If Charley's a cousin, he must be a fourth or fifth cousin. Not close enough to count. Not when he still has his eye on this pie."

Ruth met his gaze and they both chuckled. Suddenly she felt shy, and she busied herself preparing the feast. He sat, stretching long legs out while she still knelt. "You didn't have to buy my lunch, you know," she said. She'd tell him about the pie when no one was watching them. She unfolded foil-wrapped chicken and passed Eli a plate and several paper napkins.

"Looks like I got the bargain here and the prettiest

girl to share my lunch with." He sprinkled salt and pep-
per on a chicken leg and looked up at her. "No need to
get all red-cheeked and flustered. It's just eating on the
ground. We're not breaking any rules."

"*Ne,* we are not." In spite of her fears, she was having a good time with Eli. He didn't seem like a flirt
or a fast boy today. He felt like someone she'd always
known, someone she could be comfortable spending the
afternoon with whether it was having a picnic lunch or
working on the farm. Still, what she was doing—taking credit for her sister's baking—wasn't honest. She
should explain to him what had happened this instant.
She started to say something, but Eli spoke first.

"This is nice, being here with you. I'm glad I came,
Ruth. And I wouldn't have let anybody else win that
bid if I'd had to go to thirty dollars."

"Thirty dollars? That would be too much," she protested, but tingles of delight ran up her spine to think
that he would do such a thing for her.

"Why not? I earn my wages with my own two hands,
the same as anyone else here. I have no one to support.
Why shouldn't I spend what I like to support the school?
And you," he added. "Mostly you."

Ruth bit off a small piece of chicken and chewed, but
she didn't taste it. Eli made her feel the way she had felt
the day years ago when she'd climbed Aunt Martha's
big oak tree on a dare. From the top branch, she'd been
able to see the farms all around. She was so high that the
cows had looked as small as geese. She'd been so dizzy-
headed that she'd been both thrilled and afraid. She had
stayed there for an hour, too scared to climb down. Yet
it gave her a thrill whenever she remembered it. Sitting
here with Eli as her date was like that. Just looking at

him made her giddy. More than that, Eli didn't talk non-stop like Charley. Eli didn't mind letting her just catch her breath and enjoy the sunshine and the day.

She glanced across the school yard at her mother. Irwin was standing beside Mam. Ruth couldn't hear what they were saying, but Anna handed him a plate of food, and the boy sat down in the grass beside Mam's spread.

Maybe her mother was right about the boy, Ruth thought. Perhaps he was lonely and misunderstood. But as she watched, the minute Mam walked away, Irwin stuck out a foot and tripped ten-year-old Rudy. He fell on his face, smashing his muffin, and Irwin laughed.

Ruth was about to get up when Mam started to give Irwin what for. She didn't need to raise her voice. When Mam was angry, her eyes said it all. A few words from her were worse than any spanking Ruth had ever gotten from Dat.

"Ruth? Are you listening to me?" Eli asked.

She glanced at him. "Irwin just—"

"Samuel and your mother can handle Irwin."

He was right. "I'm sorry. What were you saying?"

Eli's expression was serious. "I want to talk to you about us. You can't pretend that what happened in the movies or the orchard or your porch swing wasn't real."

She looked down at her chicken leg, all too aware of how deeply she'd allowed herself to feel for him.

"I've never felt this way about a girl before," he continued. "And I think you like me."

She sighed and laid the chicken on her napkin. Suddenly, explaining about the pie switch didn't seem all that important. "I *do* like you. It's just more complicated than you make it. Liking you isn't enough."

"Was it wrong of me to come here today? Don't you want me here?"

She looked into his blue eyes. "I do want you here, Eli, but even more, I want you at church tomorrow. Don't disappoint Mam."

"Your mother or you?"

"Both of us," she admitted. Hope rose in her chest and she tried not to let it envelop her. Thinking about Eli…about her and Eli and the future was too much. There were too many obstacles, too much that she was unsure of. She didn't know what she wanted, what God wanted, and what had happened with Eli and that girl.

"I'll try not to. But for today, let's just enjoy the picnic and have fun. Please?"

"All right," she agreed, taking one last look at the pie. She wouldn't ruin the day. She'd make it right tomorrow. She'd tell him she hadn't baked the pie. And if Eli came to services, that might change everything. No matter what he'd done wrong back home, if he was truly repentant, he could find forgiveness, couldn't he? That was the beauty of the faith. God could forgive anything.

Eli held out his plate. "Could I have another chicken leg and some of that potato salad? And maybe some strawberries?"

She laughed and removed two more bowls from the bottom of the basket. "Wait until you see what else is in here," she said. "You might not want to fill up on sweets yet."

"I don't know. My mam always said I had a liking for sweet things."

Ruth blushed, certain he wasn't talking about sliced strawberries.

* * *

Early Monday morning, as soon as the kitchen was readied up, the dishes washed and dried and put away and the floors swept, Ruth hurried out to the garden to pick peas and hoe around the kale, spinach and radishes. Miriam would need her after lunch to help in the fields, but if she hurried, she'd have time to run an important errand.

She needed to go to the chair shop and explain to Eli about the pie. She had asked Anna after breakfast why she hadn't warned her that she exchanged pies, but Anna had only laughed and gone back to skimming cream off a pan of milk and humming the tune from an old hymn. Nothing she said could convince Anna to talk about baking or pies or auctions. Anna was easygoing, but she could be the most stubborn one of all of them.

Eli had kept his word and come to church the day before, but they'd had no time to speak in private. During services, Eli had sat on the men's side of the room, while she had sat with the women. And since the worship was held at their home, she and Mam and her sisters had been extra busy with serving food and welcoming visitors.

The weather had been so good that the young people had set up long tables in the yard, and the communal meal had been held there. Men ate at the first sitting, and there had barely been time to grab a bite herself and help with the children before the second sermon.

The only contact she'd had with Eli had been when she'd handed him a plate of corn bread and filled his glass with cold milk. But that hadn't meant that she was unaware of him. He had been watching her all day, and it had made her self-conscious and fearful that she'd drop a bowl of peas and dumplings on the visiting bishop from Ohio or trip and fall facedown into Aunt Martha's shoofly pie.

After church, there had been visiting and cleanup. Ruth had seen Eli folding tables and chairs and putting them in the special wagon, and she'd seen him helping with the buggies, but all too soon, the day of worship had been over. The family had gone to bed early, tired, but full of peace...all but her. She'd tossed and turned, determined that she had to get the matter of the pie straightened out. Like untangling a knotted ball of yarn, she had to start with one end and work her way through her problems. If she told the truth and cleared her conscience, she might be in a better place to solve the bigger issue of what to do about Eli.

Eli rubbed his fingertips along a chair leg, feeling for rough spots. When he found one, he carefully sanded the maple with the finest grade of sandpaper until the wood was as smooth as glass. He and Roman had been working in the shop since breakfast. Roman had been gluing chair backs and seats together and applying strapping so that they would dry properly, until Aunt Fannie had appeared in the doorway that led to the display area and called to him.

Eli could tell that his aunt had been out of sorts at breakfast this morning, not angry but worried about something. The way she'd glanced at him out of the corner of her eye made him suspect her fuss had to do with him, but he couldn't think of anything he'd done to upset her. Both his aunt and his uncle had seemed pleased that he'd gone to the school picnic and to church with them on Sunday, although neither had commented on it.

Spiritual matters were generally considered too private to discuss, even between family members. If and when he joined the Old Amish Church, it would be his decision, and no matter how much his aunt and uncle might want him to accept the faith, that was between him and God.

Now he couldn't help overhearing as Aunt Fannie said, "This came on Saturday. I thought you should see it first."

His uncle answered her, but his voice was too soft for Eli to hear what he said. Eli knew that it was wrong to eavesdrop, but he was curious. And the only way to avoid hearing would be to put down his work and leave the shop. Then he'd be forced to explain why he'd walked away from a task. Whatever it was that had upset his aunt, it wasn't good. If he'd caused a problem for Roman, he wanted to straighten it out. "*Ne,* it's your house," Aunt Fannie protested.

"It's addressed to Eli. Give it to him."

"Look at it! That's her name, isn't it?"

Eli dropped the sandpaper and stood up, the chair leg still in his hand. He walked toward the front room, but stopped when his uncle walked back into the shop.

"Mail for you." Roman held out a letter. "Fannie should have given it to you Saturday when you got home from the picnic."

Eli took the envelope. In the left corner, a name was printed clearly in blue ink. Hazel had written to him, and the return address was a town in Virginia. Shocked, he looked up at Roman.

The older man's face was creased with concern, but

his gaze held no judgment. "It was wrong of Fannie to keep your mail from you. You'll want to read it in private. The work can wait a few minutes."

Eli nodded. He took the letter outside into the backyard and sat down on a bale of straw. His heart was beating fast. He hadn't thought he'd hear from Hazel. He'd worried about her and wondered how she was, but he hadn't expected this—not after the way they'd parted.

He turned the envelope over in his hand. It couldn't have weighed more than half an ounce, but it felt as heavy as if it were made of cement. Guilt settled over him, and the events of that night at the bonfire came rushing back to haunt him. Catching his lower lip between his teeth, he slowly opened the letter.

There was a page and a half, printed from a computer. Only the signature was handwritten. He read through it twice and sat there for a while trying to decide what to do. He closed his eyes. The sun was warm on his face, and the air smelled of green growing things. From the yard, he heard the bleat of a goat and the flapping sound of clothes drying on a line. Yesterday, when he was listening to the hymns, he'd felt a peace inside. Now he searched for that quiet peace.

After a quarter of an hour, he rose and went to find Roman.

His uncle had returned to strapping the chair parts so that the glue would dry properly. Eli held out the folded pages of the letter.

"Why should I read that?" Roman concentrated on the buckle he was tightening. "It is your business."

"Aunt Fannie is right. I live in your house, and I'm part of your family. You should know what it says.

Please." Eli held it out for him and this time Roman took it.

Eli's uncle went to the bench for his spectacles, blew the sawdust off them, and then wiped them on his blue cotton shirt. He read the letter slowly. When he had finished, he nodded, and handed the letter back. "I see," he said. "And what will you do about this?"

"I don't know. Think about it, I guess."

"And pray," Roman advised. "It's always best."

Eli was cleaning up his work space when Ruth entered by the back door. He turned and surprise showed on his face. He smiled. "Ruth."

"Eli." She glanced around, hoping Roman wasn't here. As she'd walked down the road, she'd thought about what she would say, of just how she would explain the confusion about the pie. Now that she was here with him, she felt just as tongue-tied as ever. Her palms felt damp, and it seemed stuffy in the shop. "I need to talk to you. In private."

"Something I've done wrong?"

She shook her head. "*Ne.* Something I've done wrong."

"Okay." He led her back outside, around the corner of the shop to Fannie's grape arbor. There was a wooden bench there, and he waved her to the seat.

"I'd just as soon stand," she said, feeling more anxious by the moment. She just wanted to get this over with.

He hooked his thumbs into his thin red suspenders and stood arms akimbo, waiting.

Heat flashed under her skin. She stared down at her new black sneakers. She'd been ashamed to walk down the road in bare feet, for fear some English would see her and make fun, but now she felt that that might have been *Hochmut*—that she might have worn the new shoes to show off for Eli. She twisted her hands in her apron. "I wanted to..."

"What is it, Ruth?"

"The pie," she blurted. "It wasn't mine. I didn't bake it. It was Anna's."

He laughed. "Whoever made it, it was good."

She looked up at him. "*Ne,* you don't understand. I let everyone think that it was mine. I took credit for my sister's baking. I deceived—"

"Wicked," he agreed, but he was still shaking with amusement.

"This is serious. Stop laughing at me." She crossed her arms over her chest.

"Do you think I care who made the pie?"

"You should. You paid for it. And if you'd gotten mine—the one I made, you would—"

"Wait. Let me get this straight." He dropped onto the high-backed bench and motioned for her to sit beside him. When she didn't immediately do so, he rolled his eyes. "Sit," he commanded.

Ruth exhaled softly and obeyed, taking care to keep a distance between them. "I didn't mean to take credit for Anna's baking. I made my own pie, but I think Anna switched it."

"So...it wasn't your fault? You didn't know?"

"I knew after we opened the basket. When I saw it. But I didn't say anything. I let you go on believing that it was mine." She lowered her gaze. "I think a part of me wanted you to think I could bake a pie that pretty."

"So now you've come to straighten it all out?"

She nodded.

He turned toward her and caught her hands in his. "All right, you've told me. Your conscience should be clear. Why didn't you tell me right away?"

"I don't know. I was already embarrassed by all the attention. I didn't want Charley to find out. He would have made everything worse."

"And this has worried you since the picnic?"

"I couldn't sleep," she confessed. "I'm an awful pie baker. But I'm an honest person."

"The most honest I've ever known," he said. She tried to pull out of his grasp, but his big hands held hers tightly.

"Don't make fun of me. What I did was wrong."

"Are you sorry?"

"Of course, I am." She looked at him. "Why would I come here to tell you, if I wasn't sorry?"

"And you won't do it again?"

"Never!"

"Then it's over, Ruth. You've nothing more to be ashamed of."

"I don't want you to think bad of me."

"I could never do that." He slid closer to her. "There's something—"

"Ruth!"

Ruth's heart sank as her mother came around the end of the grape arbor.

"What goes on here?" Mam folded her arms over her chest and glared at them. "The two of you have some explaining to do."

Chapter 13

"It's not what you think," Eli said, letting go of Ruth's hand and getting to his feet.

Mam glared at him. "You don't know what I think. My daughters aren't fast girls. You may do things differently in Belleville, but here holding hands is for couples who have publicly stated their intention to marry."

"We weren't..." Ruth began.

"I have eyes to see," Mam said. "Being alone together like this is unseemly." She paused and continued in a softer voice. "You know that there is already talk about you, Eli. It's not fair to Ruth for you to endanger her reputation."

Ruth heard Eli's temper flare. "We weren't doing anything wrong."

Mam looked back toward the shop. "Samuel's buggy is in front. It's best if you come with me, Ruth."

"It's the middle of a school day. Why are you even here?" Ruth demanded. Eli was right. They hadn't done anything wrong. Why did her mother have to assume the worst? And how had she known where to find them? Why was she looking? "Did Anna tell you I was coming to the shop?"

"You mean, am I spying on you?"

Mam's hazel eyes took on the glint of polished pewter, and Ruth's heart sank.

"Why would you think such a thing?" Mam's tone barely masked her hurt feelings. "When have I *ever* spied on you?"

"It's my fault," Eli said. "Don't blame Ruth. There was a misunderstanding and we were talking and…"

Mam silenced him with a raised palm. "Eli, please. It's best if Ruth and I discuss this in private."

"Mam!" she protested. "Don't make more of this than—"

"The children are on their noon break," her mother cut in. "Elmer has an abscessed tooth, and Lydia asked me to call our dentist. I borrowed Samuel's horse and buggy to save time coming to use the phone." Lines at the corners of her eyes deepened. "I didn't know you were here until I arrived and Fannie told me where to find you, thinking I knew you were here."

Eli frowned and gestured. "Great. Now here comes Roman."

Ruth heard the scrape of gravel and turned to see the older man striding down the path, followed by his two yapping rat terriers. She glanced back at Eli and said softly, "I'd best go."

He nodded. "We'll talk later."

"Eli?" Roman brushed sawdust off his worn leather

apron as he approached. "Is there something?" He looked from Eli to Mam as the yipping little dogs darted past him. "Quiet!" he ordered. The brown and white terriers leaped up, stub tails wagging. "Get down, I say. Behave." His cheeks reddened. "Fannie spoils them."

"The dogs are fine." Mam leaned to pet one and then the other. "No treats today," she told the terriers.

"I thought there might be…" Roman tugged at his beard and glanced at Eli "…a problem here."

"Mam came to use the phone," Ruth explained. "I'm riding back to the school with her." She averted her gaze as she hurried past Roman. It was bad enough that Mam had embarrassed her in front of Eli. She didn't want to drag his aunt and uncle into it.

As she walked to the buggy behind her mother, feeling like a chastised child, she felt Eli's gaze on her back. She wanted to turn back, to try to make things right with him, but she didn't. Maybe because she was afraid, afraid of what she might say. What she might not ever be able to say.

The two women disappeared around the side of the chair shop. For a moment, Roman and Eli looked at each other without speaking, and then Eli said, "We were talking and Hannah came along. She didn't think us sitting alone here looked proper. But we needed to talk." He scuffed the ground with his boot. "You know, about things."

One of the terriers nipped playfully at the hem of Roman's black pants, and he shook it off. "Did you tell her about the letter?"

Eli worked his jaw but didn't respond.

"It's right that they should know."

"Hazel wrote to me. It's not a matter to be gossiped about."

"*Ne,* but you need to tell Ruth. If you're familiar enough with each other to sit on the bench alone together, you're familiar enough that she needs to know." He paused. "And around here, what concerns one of us, concerns all." Roman slipped his thumbs under his black suspenders. "Fannie's worked herself up pretty well over it. That letter."

"Did you tell her what Hazel said?" Eli's gaze searched his uncle's face.

"Not my place." Roman was quiet again for a moment and then went on. "If you've a mind to settle here—and you know you're welcome in our home—you need to make peace with your mother. It's the only way to make things right…to think about starting your own family."

Eli understood what he was talking about. If he had any thoughts whatsoever of making a home and a life with Ruth, he needed to tell her what had happened with Hazel. But why should he have to? Why couldn't Ruth take him for the person he was today? Not back then, back there.

"Then there's the matter of the church," Roman said.

Eli tightened his fingers into fists at his sides. "You mean I'd have to join if I want any chance with Ruth."

"It's your choice, joining the church or not. You have to decide for yourself what you want from this world," he said, obviously feeling awkward. "But I wouldn't be telling the truth if I didn't tell you it's what I wish for you…what I've prayed for."

Eli was surprised that his uncle would say these personal things to him. This wasn't the kind of thing Plain people talked about, especially men, and he knew it had to be difficult for his uncle. But Roman had always been a little different. His grandfather had called him weak, but he wasn't. Eli wished he had the inner strength Roman possessed.

"I think you'd find peace," Roman added.

"You don't know how I've struggled over it. I don't know what to do." Eli couldn't look Roman in the eyes any longer. "I'm not certain if I belong in the church or in the outside world. I'm not certain where I belong."

"Hard to know when you've been uprooted the way you were. Kind of like seedlings that have been transplanted. They get confused sometimes, growing one direction, then the other." Roman looked off in the distance. A blue jay cackled. "Your *grand* was a hard man, not just on you, but on himself. I always thought your mother should have kept you at home with her. You'd have gotten used to a stepfather. Joseph would have been fair with you."

Eli shrugged. "Maybe it was best they sent me away. They say I'm like my dat. Maybe I'm his son, more than hers. Headed for a bad end."

Roman grimaced. "I've heard that said, but I don't believe it. I knew your father, Eli. There was a lot of good in him. If he'd lived, I think he would have come back to us...to his family and his faith."

A lump rose in Eli's throat, and he didn't answer, afraid his voice would crack. He wasn't exactly embarrassed by his emotion, but it wasn't something one man shared with another.

"You hear what I'm saying?" Roman's own voice filled with feeling, surprising Eli. "*I knew him.* And I don't see the bad side of him in you." He looked in the direction the two women had gone. "Just be sure you don't take a path that's not yours. And don't take along somebody else with you. You're better than that."

Eli knew he was talking about Ruth. "I care about her. A lot. I'd do nothing to hurt her."

Roman walked away, the dogs trailing him. "Then see you don't."

"Why did you have to say anything about marriage?" Ruth agonized aloud when she and her mother were alone in the buggy. She sat up straight and gripped the leathers in both hands as a pickup truck pulling a boat whizzed past them on the road. "And why did you mention the gossip about him? It's not like you to be uncharitable."

"And it's unlike you to be caught holding hands with a boy in Fannie's grape arbor," Mam returned. "Fannie saw the two of you. What must she think?"

No other traffic was in sight, and Ruth used the break to cross the intersection onto the quieter road that led to the school.

Mam's chin went up, and she planted both black leather shoes together on the floorboard. "There's something you need to know for your own good. Eli had a letter from the girl."

Ruth's stomach turned over. She didn't know what to say.

"You know who I mean," her mother continued. "The girl who accused him."

"A letter from her doesn't mean that Eli's guilty of anything wrong." But it *could* mean that they still cared for each other, Ruth thought. Or it could mean she was trying to start trouble for him again. Now, here in Seven Poplars. "I suppose Fannie told you about the letter."

"She did but not to hurt Eli or you. She wanted to protect you, to keep you from being harmed."

"Fannie's his aunt. She's supposed to—"

"She thought I should know and that you should know. Fannie is a sweet woman. She'd never intentionally spread rumors and the letter wasn't a rumor. It was real. She held it in her hands and read Hazel's name on the envelope before turning it over to Roman, who gave it to Eli."

Moisture clouded Ruth's eyes, but she kept her gaze on the horse and the road ahead. "Do you know what happened to her? The girl? Her church didn't shun her, did they?"

"*Ne,* but Martha says the girl ran away after the baby was born. No one knows where she is. Except Eli, maybe," she added.

"She ran away with an infant?" Compassion flooded Ruth's heart. "I can't imagine. Her family must be so worried."

"She didn't take the baby, an older sister did. The sister and her husband live out west somewhere. They'd been married six years without being blessed with children. Martha said that it was Hazel's idea to let them adopt the infant. The girl said she wasn't ready to be a mother."

Ruth had no answer for that. She couldn't imagine giving birth to a child and not raising it. But considering the circumstances, perhaps the girl's decision had been the right one. No one among the Plain people would hold a baby responsible for the mother's mistake.

"So you see why Fannie thought you should know he'd heard from her." Mam's voice was gentle this time.

But Ruth didn't want soft words. She felt all in turmoil inside: scared, angry. "Eli isn't the type of boy who would get a girl in trouble and not marry her!"

"Ruth, Ruth, Ruth, what's come over you?" Her mother stared at her, obviously not approving of her passionate outburst.

"Nothing. I simply refuse to believe such a thing about Eli."

"So you *do* like him."

"As a friend."

"Sounds to me like *more* than a friend," her mother said, shaking her head. "Daughter, I'm worried about you. You're like an apron on the clothesline, flapping in the wind, one way and then the other."

Ruth pulled hard on the right rein, guiding the gelding off the road and onto the grass shoulder before yanking the horse to a halt. The dapple gray stopped so quickly that the buggy swayed. "What's that supposed to mean?"

"It means that until Eli Lapp came to Seven Poplars, you knew your own mind. You said you knew what you wanted. You told me that you weren't going to marry, that you would remain at home with me and Susanna. The past two weeks, you've lollygagged in the orchard with the boy, sat on the porch swing in the dark with him, and the two of you have been caught holding hands in the grape arbor." She gestured outward with her hand. "Not to mention going to the movie or eating together at the school picnic. You say you're not courting, but it looks like it to me."

Ruth didn't know what to say. How could she explain to Mam that she hadn't intended to do any of those things with Eli? They'd just happened. How could she tell her how giddy he made her feel inside? She swallowed. "I don't believe Eli would ever abandon his child. There must be more to the story."

"Have you asked him?" Mam was angry. She never shouted like Aunt Martha, but the angrier she became, the lower her tone of voice.

Ruth slapped the reins over the horse's back, and the buggy lurched forward. "I wouldn't pry." She glanced at her mother. "Aren't you always telling us not to judge?"

"*Ya,* that I do say. So the Bible tells us. But it also speaks about children respecting their parents."

Ruth nibbled at her lower lip as the horse broke into a trot. "Have I been disrespectful?"

"You just accused me of being uncharitable."

"I didn't mean it, not really. I'm sorry."

Hannah sighed, sitting back on the buggy seat. "You have always been a good daughter, one your father would be proud of. But the time has come for you to make up your mind about what you want and follow that path. You need to think before you act. You need to set a good example for your sisters and the younger girls in the community."

The horse's hooves clicked rhythmically against the road. "We really weren't doing anything wrong in the grape arbor," Ruth said.

"An action doesn't have to be wrong to give the appearance of mischief. What if it hadn't been me who found the two of you, but your uncle Reuben or aunt Martha? Because we're women alone, we have to guard our reputations even more than if your father was alive. Especially since I teach at the school."

"You're right. I didn't think." Shame flooded through Ruth. If people complained, they might think that Mam was at fault for not teaching her daughters proper behavior. The school board could decide not to renew her contract next year. "What do you want me to do, Mam?"

"I don't want you to do something you'll regret for the rest of your life."

"That doesn't answer my question."

"*Ya,* but what I want is not important. You're old enough to make up your own mind what your life will be. You must decide. You aren't like Miriam. You've joined the church."

"I feel awful, Mam. We never argue. I don't want to upset you."

"And I don't mean to be harsh with you, but it's time you act like a grown woman."

There was silence for a moment, except for the clippity-clop of the horse's hooves, before Hannah spoke again. "Look into your heart, daughter. Your path will become clear."

"I want to do what God wants," Ruth said.

"You have only to listen. He will tell you." She pulled a pocket watch from her apron and her expression softened. "Lunch break should be over." She took a black lunch box from under the seat, opened it, retrieving a sandwich. "Have half of this," she offered. "It's your favorite, chicken salad."

Ruth took her section of the sandwich, heading up the lane to the school. "I haven't heard the bell yet," she said between bites.

Mam folded the waxed paper and put it back in the lunch box to use again tomorrow. "I left Elvie in charge of the little ones," she explained. "She might be so busy making eyes at Elmer over her lunch that she didn't notice the time."

Ruth couldn't help smiling. "Elvie and Elmer? She's too young to be thinking of boyfriends yet, isn't she?"

"Elmer is more interested in Eli's motorbike than girls, but Elvie has always liked him, and he could do worse. Her parents are good church members and solid, God-fearing people. Besides, Elvie is the oldest, and she has no brothers. She'll inherit land."

"Don't tell me you're matchmaking your eighth graders."

Mam laughed. "Not me. But Elvie knows her own mind. Mark my words, when he turns eighteen, Elmer will be trailing after Elvie like a fly on jam. And we'll be going to a wedding."

By the time they reached the school yard, Ruth had acknowledged to herself the truth of her indecision. She *had* been vacillating, whipping in the wind, not knowing what direction she was going. It was just that Eli had confused her. The way he made her feel when he was close confused her. He made her doubt her decision to remain unmarried.

But it was clear what Mam thought and wanted. Ruth would pray, but obviously her duty was to her family. Mam was no longer a young woman. She'd reached her mid-forties, and she needed the care and devotion of a daughter.

It would never work out with Eli, anyway, Ruth told herself. He was too handsome for her, too good a catch to really be interested in her. He didn't really want to court her. He was just pursuing her because she'd told him she wasn't interested.

Ruth needed to just let the whole thing go. She wasn't

meant to be a wife. And in time, her deep attraction to Eli would pass. The happiness and well-being of those she loved most must come ahead of any personal desires.

It seemed like the right thing to do, but Ruth's heart felt heavy. Never to marry… It would be a sacrifice, maybe a greater one than she'd ever expected, since Eli came into her life. The heaviness in her chest turned to an ache in the pit of her stomach and spread through her. Resolutely, she pushed back the image of Eli's face and the sound of his voice. She would be strong…she would do what was right…what God wanted.

As she reined the horse into the drive that led alongside the school, Ruth saw that Mam had been right. The students were still at recess that followed lunch, some playing ball, others on the swings, and a few still finishing their lunches. Lydia's Abraham, a gangly nine-year-old, was walking the top rail of the split-rail fence with his lunch bucket balanced on top of his head. Elvie, who was supposed to be in charge, was nowhere in sight.

"See, what did I tell you?" Mam said. "Recess should have been over ten minutes ago."

Eleven-year-old Herman came running around the school, saw the buggy and shouted, "Teacher's back!" As children hurried toward the building from all directions, Abraham lost his footing and tumbled off the fence. The boy rolled and came up on his feet laughing, none the worse for wear. One of his brothers had reached the steps and was ringing the cast-iron bell to signal the start of classes.

Mam got out of the buggy. "I don't see Samuel," she said. "He must have walked home. Can you take the rig back to his barn?"

Ruth nodded. "I'm sorry about what happened."

"Let it be for now. But think on what I said. You have decisions to make."

"I think I already have, Mam. Don't worry. I'd never do anything to shame you or my sisters, I promise."

The entrance to Samuel's lane was only a few hundred yards south of the schoolhouse. Once Mam had her lunch box and notebook, Ruth guided the horse in a circle, preparing to drive out of the yard. But as she turned right, she noticed two boys wrestling on the ground next to the shed. "Hey, you two," she called. "Recess is over. Didn't you hear the bell?"

Irwin scrambled to his feet, grabbed his hat off the grass and shoved something into his pocket. The top button was missing off his shirt, and one suspender hung off his shoulder. Weeds were tangled in his scarecrow hair. The other boy, Samuel's son Peter, had more guilt than dirt on his face, and his shirttail was out, but he seemed to have gotten the best of the tussle.

"Were you two fighting?" Ruth demanded. She got down out of the buggy and walked toward them. "Irwin, what did you put in your pocket?"

Peter's face blushed a deep red, and he looked as though he were about to burst into tears.

Irwin hung his head and stared at his bare feet.

"Well, Irwin, I'm waiting."

"What's wrong?" Mam came up behind her. "Why are you boys out here when everyone else has gone inside?"

"I think they were fighting." Ruth dropped her hands to her hips. "Irwin put something in his pocket, and he won't show me what it is."

"Were you fighting?" her mother asked.

A tear rolled down Peter's cheek. *"Ya,"* he squeaked. "We was."

"I'm ashamed of you both." Ruth looked from one boy to the other. "Peter, what would your father say?"

"There is a better way to solve problems than violence." He mimicked Samuel's deep baritone voice so well that it was all Ruth could do not to smile.

"Your father is right," Mam said. "Fighting is not our way. You both are old enough to know better." She held out her hand. "Irwin? What do you have?"

He took a step backward and reluctantly dug into his pocket and produced a pack of matches.

"Is this what you were fighting over?"

More tears streaked Peter's face as he nodded.

"Are these yours, Irwin?" Mam took them from him. He didn't answer.

"Peter, do you have anything you want to say about this?"

The boy shook his head.

"Very well. Peter, you take your father's horse and buggy home and come right back. Tell him that you will be staying after school today. You will both write, *'There is a better way to solve problems than violence,'* two hundred times in your best cursive. And you will both stay after tomorrow afternoon to scrub the schoolhouse floor, wash the blackboards and the windows. Is that clear?"

"Ya," Peter said.

Irwin nodded.

"I will keep the matches." Mam tucked them into her apron. "If I ever catch either of you with matches again, you *and* your father, Peter—and in your case, Irwin, Lydia and Norman—will answer to the school board.

Now, off with you. Irwin, I hope you remembered your math homework today."

Both boys ran.

Ruth watched the boys go. "Something has to be done about Irwin before someone is seriously hurt."

"Something has to be done all right, but I have a feeling there's more to this than they're telling. You see the look in Peter's eyes? You, of all people, Ruth, know things aren't always what they appear. I'll get to the bottom of this, I promise you."

"I just hope it's not too late. He's on our farm all the time. What if he burns our house down?"

"He isn't going to burn the house down or hurt any of us. He's an unhappy child, and we have to find a way to help him."

"He's a bully. You saw him trip Rudy at the picnic. He's always shoving or—" Ruth sighed in exasperation. "Mam, you're too easy on him. He's a real troublemaker. And he seems to have it out for Samuel's twins. He picks on them the most."

"And why is that, do you suppose?"

Ruth stared at her mother.

"What do Rudy and Peter have that Irwin doesn't?"

"A father, but—"

"A father who adores them." Hannah started across the grass toward the schoolhouse, and Ruth walked with her. "Their own ponies. New shoes and new lunch buckets."

"But Lydia and Norman are good to him. It's Irwin that makes people dislike him," Ruth said.

"He has a good heart, daughter. And if we can find a way to reach it, Irwin will return the love we give him twofold."

"I think you've already given him too many chances."

"Doesn't the Lord do that with us? No matter how many times we fail Him, His love is always there for us. We must try to do as much for Irwin, Ruth. If we can't give him hope and a sense of belonging, he will be as lost to us as his family is to him. And that I couldn't bear, as a teacher or as a mother."

Chapter 14

Morning sales at Spence's were so busy that it was one o'clock by the time Ruth felt she could leave Miriam. She'd made plans to have lunch at the Amish Market with Dorcas and two of their girlfriends, and the girls were waiting impatiently to go. Charley's sister Mary and her cousin Jane had already sold all their cut flowers and herbs and packed their wagon for the trip home.

"Go on." Miriam waved them away. "I'll be fine. John said he'd bring me back a sandwich and lemonade."

Jane whispered something to her cousin, and the two giggled.

"I see how it is," Mary teased. "Miriam wants to get rid of us so she can talk to the cute new vet."

"Dr. Hartman is a friend of the family," Miriam corrected, but Ruth noticed how merrily her sister's eyes twinkled. Mam had called John, who had recently joined his grandfather's large animal practice, to help deliver a calf that spring, and he and Miriam had hit it off. He often stopped to see Miriam at Spence's when he grabbed lunch between appointments.

"Remember, your aunt Martha has her eye on you," Jane warned. "Don't do anything with that Mennonite boy that I wouldn't."

"It's lemonade," Ruth defended. "They just talk horses."

"*Ya.* Horses." Mary rolled her eyes. "You know what they say about those Mennonites. She just better keep her *Kapp* on."

Dorcas laughed, too, although Ruth wasn't certain she got the joke. Dorcas wasn't exactly slow, but neither was she as quick-witted or as daring as Charley's sister or Jane. Ruth often thought that Dorcas acted and, worse, appeared closer to forty than twenty.

It didn't help that Aunt Martha, who made all of Dorcas's clothing, was frugal and not the most skillful seamstress. Dorcas's dresses usually were made over from secondhand ones Aunt Martha acquired when someone passed away. It was a shame, really. Although no one could accuse Dorcas of being anything but Plain, she did have nice eyes.

Mam thought that clothing that fit her niece better would improve her appearance and attitude by leaps and bounds. It might even help Dorcas to find a husband. The truth was, there were always more available young Amish women than marriageable Amish men, and Dorcas's chances were hardly better than Anna's.

Together, the four girls walked past a table laden with dusty glass knickknacks and tattered paperback books.

There were stands selling DVDs and records and even used children's clothing, as well as fruit and vegetables. Tables of toys stood side by side with those lined with belts and wallets. One booth was hung with robelike dresses from the far side of the world. An Amish boy from another church district stood amid the garments, fingering one and talking to the proprietor. He seemed to be attempting to get the man to lower the price, but what the boy would do with the foreign-looking dress, Ruth had no idea.

She liked coming to Spence's, and she enjoyed spending time with Mary, Dorcas and Jane. She was the eldest of the four, but they always had fun together. Even Dorcas rarely whined or fussed when Jane and Mary were a part of the group. The cousins were too upbeat and full of fun to put up with Dorcas's sullen moods.

"So," Jane said, clasping Ruth's hand and smiling up at her. "Tell me. What is Eli like? Have you ridden on his motorbike?"

Mary laughed. "Has he tried to steal a kiss?"

"I don't want to talk about him." Ruth's tone sounded sharper than she'd intended. She didn't want to offend her friends, but Eli wasn't a subject she was willing to discuss right now. Maybe not ever.

Jane must have realized that Eli was a sensitive subject because she quickly turned the jest on her cousin. "Maybe you should ask Mary why she's so interested in kissing." She linked her arm through Mary's. "Charley said she was awfully friendly with that Kentucky boy who's visiting at Silas Troyer's. Charley said she served him three slices of strawberry pie and four cups of coffee at dinner after services on Sunday."

"He needed the coffee after all that ham *you* served him," Mary said. "And he likes pie."

"I'll admit he wasn't hard to look at," Jane said.

"And he was really nice," Mary defended. "Silas said…"

As the girls walked, Ruth's thoughts drifted. She spotted an English woman in her thirties, with the same round face and distinctive eyes as Susanna's. She was carrying a shopping bag of vegetables for an older woman who had to be her mother, and the two were laughing as they walked between the stalls.

Ruth thought about an incident at dinner the night before. Susanna had been carrying a bowl of steaming potato soup to the table and had tumbled and spilled the soup over herself, burning one wrist and her ankle. By the grace of God, her dress, apron and stockings had protected her skin from serious burns, but her wrist had taken the worst of the spill.

Whenever Susanna hurt herself, she dissolved into tears. Luckily, Ruth had been in the room and been able to put her sister's wrist under running water to wash away the hot soup. A little ice and some soothing cream on her ankle had dried Susanna's tears, and they'd been able to eat supper before everything was cold. But the incident had reminded Ruth just how challenged her little sister was. What if she'd burned herself cooking while Mam was at school? What if she accidentally started a fire? Mam couldn't be in two places at once, and once Miriam and Anna married, if Anna could ever find a husband, the burden of caring for Susanna would fall on her mother. Like the woman with Down syndrome Ruth had just seen, Susanna would need supervised care the rest of her life.

Mam must have been thinking the same thing because after the incident the previous night, she'd stopped outside Ruth's bedroom door on the way to bed and hugged her tightly. "You're my rock," Mam had murmured. "I don't know what I would do without you."

"Ruth? Hello, Ruth?" Chuckling, Jane waved a hand in front of her face.

"I'm having black forest ham and cheddar on a sesame roll," Dorcas said. "What about you, Ruth?"

Ruth looked up and realized they had reached the deli in the Amish food market. The clerk on the other side of the counter was waiting impatiently for her sandwich order. Embarrassed, Ruth didn't even look at the menu on the wall. "I'll have the same."

"With root beer?"

Ruth nodded and followed the others to a picnic table in the aisle. There were coolers of cheese and sausages on both sides. The food stalls were crowded with customers and the high-roofed building was noisy. The odors of sizzling scrapple, baking bread and brining pickles filled the air. There was about an even mix of English and Amish here today, but Ruth was too distracted to pay much attention to the antique hunters and shoppers.

She kept thinking about how frightened Susanna had looked the night before and how much she wanted to take her in her arms and kiss away her tears, just as she had when Susanna was small. The further she removed herself from the feelings she'd experienced sitting on that bench with Eli, the clearer it was to her where her loyalties had to lie, and the choice her mother expected her to make. She had promised Mam that she'd always be there for her, and she couldn't let her feelings for a boy, feelings she didn't even know for sure were real, come between her and her family duty.

"Eli Lapp," Dorcas said. She smiled, showing a broken front tooth.

Startled to hear his name while she was thinking about him, Ruth looked across the picnic table at her cousin. "What about him?"

Jane giggled and pointed. "Behind you. It's Eli Lapp. Hello, Eli Lapp."

"Want to have lunch with us, Eli Lapp?" Mary offered, joining in on the joke. She scooted over on the bench to make room for him.

Ruth felt Eli's hand on her shoulder, and for a moment she froze.

"Sorry, I can't," he said kindly to Mary. He looked down at Ruth, his hand still on her shoulder. "I need to talk to you. I went by the house, but Susanna said you—"

"You shouldn't have come here," Ruth stammered, getting up and taking a step back so he couldn't touch her. She just couldn't stand feeling the warmth of his skin against hers. She just couldn't. "This isn't…" She looked around, thinking they should move somewhere more private, but that would only make this harder on both of them.

Mary popped up from the bench. "Oh, I think our sandwiches are ready. I'll get them."

Ruth looked at Eli and then averted her gaze. The lunch area was loud, and the voices buzzed around her. "This isn't the place to talk."

He tried to catch her hand, but she didn't let him. "Then where is? I have to talk to you. I need to—"

"I can't do this," she whispered, interrupting him.

There was a lump in her throat that warned her that she was close to tears. It seemed like everyone was staring at them, English and Amish. "Eli, I'm sorry if I let you think—"

"Ruth." He didn't let her finish, and when she looked into his eyes, he seemed to be pleading with her.

These feelings aren't real, she told herself. *It's infatuation. Nothing more.* "Please don't make this hard," she asked him. "Just go."

"A couple of minutes. That's all I need."

She sat down on the bench and swung her legs under the table. Dorcas was staring at them, hanging on every word. Aunt Martha would know what had transpired between Ruth and Eli by supper. *Good,* Ruth thought. *Then everyone will know and the matter will be settled; there was nothing between her and the boy from Belleville.* "You should go, Eli."

"You won't even let me—"

"*Ne,* Eli." She presented her back to him so she wouldn't see the hurt look in his blue eyes, the pain she could hear in his voice. "You're a nice boy, but we were friends, nothing more. And I think it's better if we don't see each other at all…for a while. So… so people don't think we…"

"So people don't think what? That we like each other? Because we do, Ruth."

"*We* don't." Ruth knotted her fingers together, her hands resting on the table. "Just go."

He stood there for another moment and then turned and stalked way, nearly colliding with Mary, her arms full of sandwiches and sodas.

"Aren't you staying?" she called after him, turning with the tray in her arms.

Eli didn't look back.

* * *

Two days later, after supper, Eli returned to the Yoder farm. His pride was still smarting from what had happened at Spence's right in front of half the people he knew in Seven Poplars, but he wasn't ready to give up yet. Hopefully, Ruth had just been upset about being caught holding hands at the chair shop, and once they talked, everything would be okay between them. Hopefully, they would be better than okay.

Hannah was right. It had been inappropriate for he and Ruth to be holding hands, and he had endangered Ruth's reputation by his actions. He needed to do this right. As soon as Ruth gave her permission, he intended to ask Hannah for permission to court her.

Ruth was in the garden with Anna and Miriam. As he walked up the lane, he saw the three sisters and Irwin Beachy. He knew Ruth saw him, but when he reached the garden gate, she was gone.

"She's in the house," Anna said. He knew by her expression that Ruth had told her she didn't want to talk to him, but he walked to the back porch and knocked just the same.

Hannah answered the door.

"I've come to see Ruth," he said.

Her mother shook her head. "I'm sorry, Eli. She doesn't want to talk to you."

"Is it you or her who doesn't want me here?" He shuffled his feet, feeling like a boy in front of his teacher. "It's important."

Upstairs on the second floor, a window slammed shut. Eli looked up, knowing Ruth had been there looking down at him. He could feel his throat and cheeks flush with heat. Ruth must still be angry with him for getting her in trouble. Why wouldn't she give him a chance to apologize? His gut twisted. Maybe it had been a mistake to come today, but he couldn't help it. He had to see her. He had to make the attempt to set things right between them, and he wouldn't believe that she didn't want to see him…that she didn't feel the same way he did.

"She doesn't want to talk to you. Not today."

Irwin came around the corner of the house with the puppy that Ruth and he had found in the hedgerow. The little dog still looked thin, but its eyes were shining, and a pink tongue flicked Irwin's arm. "He's better," Irwin said, holding it up for Eli to see. "He eats good."

Eli stopped to pet the pup as he came down the steps. Irwin was holding it as carefully as if it were a real baby. "You're gentle with him," Eli said.

"I know about dogs." The boy looked up earnestly. "I had one of my own once."

"And you'll have another if you're not careful," Hannah said, following them out onto the stoop. "I never saw an animal take to a boy more."

Irwin came as close to a smile as Eli had ever seen.

"Irwin's going to train him for us," Hannah explained. "It will be good to have a watchdog around here again."

Eli scuffed his boots in the hard-packed dirt. "Tell Ruth I asked for her, will you?"

"She don't want you here," Irwin announced matter-of-factly. "She said so."

Hannah smiled. "You come again another time, Eli. And we'll talk, just you and me."

"No need if Ruth doesn't want me here," he answered, feeling a dull hollowness in his belly. He couldn't remember crossing their yard, but he was certain that he felt Ruth watching him from the window as he walked down the lane.

Ruth woke just after sunrise on Saturday morning to hear raindrops pattering on her bedroom windows. She raised the shades to find the garden and fields hazy and wet, a perfect day, considering the restless sleep she'd gotten last night. She'd made her decision, and she wasn't about to change her mind. But that didn't keep thoughts of Eli from troubling her dreams and conscience. It broke her heart to hurt him, but if someone had to suffer, better him than Mam and Susanna.

She dressed quickly and made her bed. It was nice being the oldest and having a room to herself since Johanna had married and moved away. She'd always loved this room. With the corner windows, white curtains and the braided rag rug, it was bright and cozy, even on a dreary day. She folded her nightdress and tucked it into a dresser drawer, then did up her hair and covered it with a starched *Kapp*.

With all this rain, Ruth was glad she and Miriam had picked berries before dark. Otherwise, they would have had to do it in the wet, because Mam had asked them to put up strawberry jam this morning. They used a lot of jam through the year and always liked to have extra to share with young couples and those in need in the community. Ruth had decided to put some in fancy jars and add gingham ruffles to the lids for sale to the English. She'd seen small containers of grape jelly going for ridiculous amounts of money at some of the stores in town. Strawberry jam would bring just as much, perhaps more.

They were just finishing breakfast when Ruth heard the sound of wagon wheels on the gravel drive. She went to the window and looked out. It had stopped raining, but the sky was still cloudy and gray. "Looks like Roman," she called back to the kitchen. Eli sat on the wagon seat beside him, but she didn't mention that. As foolish as she knew she was being, she didn't want to say his name because if she did, she'd start to struggle with her feelings for him. Just speaking his name aloud made her as giddy as a fifteen-year-old, and whatever ailed her, there was no sense in making it worse.

"He's coming to repair the milk house floor and start on the bookshelves," Mam explained. "He said he'd be here the next rainy day. Guess that's today."

When Dat had been alive, they'd kept enough milking cows to sell milk to a dairy. Now Mam had gotten it into her head to fix the little building up as a library, so that her neighbors could come and borrow books whenever they liked. Both of her parents had loved to read, and they owned more books than anyone she knew. Susanna was thrilled with the idea because Mam had promised her that she could hold the post of librarian. It would be her job to keep the books safe and return them to the proper section.

"My lib-ary!" Susanna exclaimed, clapping her hands. "Today!"

"That's right, today," Mam agreed, rising from her chair at the table. "A lot to do today, Susanna. Working men have to be fed."

"Have to be fed," Susanna echoed happily.

Eli will probably be building the shelves, Ruth thought, gathering dirty dishes from the table. *Great.* She didn't want to see him today, any more than she had on Tuesday or Thursday. What she needed was to put him completely out of her mind, and that was impossible if he was working in her own barnyard.

The screen door banged, and Irwin came in carrying Jeremiah. "Took him out," Irwin declared. "Did number one, but not two."

Susanna giggled. "He means Jeremiah didn't poo," she explained.

"Samuel's here, too," Irwin said. "To help."

Anna picked up the bread tray and walked to the back door. "Anyone for hot raisin scones and coffee?" she called to the men.

Within five minutes, Samuel, Roman and Eli were at the table. Anna set out scones, a pan of gingerbread and some of last night's biscuits to go with hot coffee and thick cream. Mam was smiling. Ruth knew she missed Dat and liked to watch hungry men eat. Still, it was awkward having Eli in the kitchen and having to avoid speaking or making eye contact.

Ruth noticed Irwin watching from the corner of the kitchen. He'd eaten breakfast with them only a short while before, but Dat had always said that boys needed to be around men so they'd know how to act when they grew up. She went to Irwin, took Jeremiah, and motioned to the table. "You'd best have coffee and a bite as well," she said.

He looked at her with hopeful eyes. "Just ate."

"Help yourself, Irwin. You'll be helping the men today. You'll need your strength."

Anna waved the boy to a chair and poured him a mug of black coffee. Irwin added in cream and enough sugar to bake a cake. He didn't grab, but somehow he managed to acquire a slab of gingerbread, a biscuit and two scones. He didn't speak, but he followed every word the men said, and when Samuel stroked his beard during a lull in the conversation, Irwin copied his gesture.

As soon as the last crumb of food disappeared, the men got to their feet and filed out. Eli was the last to go, and as he stopped by the back door, he glanced back at Ruth. She busied herself with gathering coffee cups and carrying them to the sink. She didn't meet his gaze, and after a few seconds, Eli's shoulders slumped, and he followed the others.

"That was kind of you," Mam said.

Her eyes widened. Did Mam mean ignoring Eli was the right thing to do?

"Thinking of Irwin. I think he grew two inches when he slid up to the table between Roman and Eli. He needs to know he's a part of our community. When that happens, you'll see big changes in him."

"I hope so," Miriam replied. "Because he's not much help at milking or feeding up. I've got to tell him every step and then watch to see he does it."

"He'll come around," Mam said. "I've got a good feeling about him."

"How many chickens shall I kill for dinner?" Anna asked. "If they're all sharing nooning with us, we'll need to start now."

"Three, I think," Mam said. "The jam-making can wait until afternoon. We need to put a meal together for the men. Ruth can do the green beans and potatoes, Miriam can whip up a pan of baked macaroni and cheese, and I'll make some coleslaw."

"I'll get the pickled beets and applesauce from the root cellar," Susanna offered, bouncing up and down. She loved company, and she loved helping.

"I think corn bread," Anna said. "That can go in the oven with the macaroni and cheese, but we'll need more meat. Maybe Miriam can take the horse and buggy, drive to the chair shop and bring back five or six pounds of those thick pork chops we froze last week."

Mam had a big chest freezer, but since they had no electricity on the farm, they kept it at the shop. Ruth saw no conflict in that, but she'd once heard Dat in a serious discussion with Johanna's husband about why electricity was forbidden in their homes but not businesses.

"Our faith instructs us to be apart from the world," Dat had explained. "But since we don't live at our businesses, and telephones, copy machines and electric lights are needed to run a business, they're allowed."

Johanna's husband hadn't agreed. He felt that the bishops were wrong to permit the use of electricity anywhere, so he adamantly disapproved of the use of freezers. But then he could sometimes be a difficult man. Johanna had been a happy bride, but sometimes, Ruth wondered if her sister had found satisfaction in her marriage. Certainly, she didn't laugh or sing as much as she used to before she'd become a wife. Maybe that was the way it was when a woman subjected her will to that of a husband. And maybe her own choice to remain single wouldn't be as much of a sacrifice as it seemed now.

Between the five women, they soon had dinner preparations well in hand and found time to start a big kettle of strawberry jam on the back of the stove. Mam and Anna made their jam the old-fashioned way: an equal amount of crushed fruit and sugar. And they always made certain that some of the fruit was green to add natural pectin. The jam took a little longer to cook, but it used less sugar than if you were using commercial pectin, and Ruth thought the taste was better. Timing and stirring were critical, but by the time the first batch was ready, Ruth had rows of jelly jars out of their boiling water bath and ready for the jam.

Whenever Ruth stepped out on the back porch, she could hear the sound of hammering coming from the milk house. As she worked, Ruth tried not to think about Eli, but she couldn't help it. He was right there in her milk house. Any bookshelves he fashioned would be done with care and careful craftsmanship. And whenever she went to the new library to take a book, she'd lift it from a shelf that he'd made. Would they be properly Plain or, somewhere on the farthest back corner, would there be the carving of a saucy wren?

The clock on the mantel had just chimed twelve-thirty when Ruth went to the steps to ring the dinner bell. Laughing and talking, the men walked up from the milk house.

"What's your mam and Anna got good for dinner?" Samuel asked passing. "Is that macaroni and cheese I'm smelling?"

"*Ya*, it is. Have you seen Irwin?" She searched the wet barnyard with her gaze.

"He went to look for the twins. They walked over a little while ago, after they finished their chores at home," Samuel said. "Don't know where they got to." He and Roman walked up onto the porch as Eli came out of the milk house.

Not seeing Irwin, Ruth called out. "Peter! Rudy! Time to eat!"

Eli looked at her and then glanced away. "Maybe they're in the barn," he said.

"I'll go." She went down the steps and brushed past

him. "You go to the table. You don't want to keep the others from their dinner."

Eli didn't listen to her. He followed her to the barn, and when they reached the door, he put his hand on her arm. "Ruth," he began, "we have to talk. I'm sorry for what happened but—"

"Not now, please," she said. "They're waiting for us in the kitchen."

His jaw tightened as he stepped around her and swung the stable door open.

The moment he opened the door, Ruth knew there was something wrong.

"I smell smoke!" Eli said.

"Irwin!" Ruth shouted, running into the barn with Eli. "Boys, where are you?"

A dozen steps into the shadows proved that it wasn't just the gloom of the day that made the barn so dark. Black smoke curled along the wide boards over her head and made her cough. "Fire!" she cried. "The barn's on fire!"

Chapter 15

"Get help!" Eli waved her back. "Get out of here, Ruth!"

"But the children might be in here! And the horses! I have to get the animals out."

Ahead of them in the box stalls, Blackie and Molly were snorting and stamping in fear. Ruth's hands were icy, her heart hammering against her ribs as she ran for the horses. "Irwin! Rudy! Peter! Where are you?" she screamed. Her last words were lost in a fit of choking.

Eli closed his hand over her shoulder, stopping her. "I'll let the horses out."

"I'm not leaving you." A white barn cat streaked past them, its high-pitched screeching adding to the frantic neighing of the horses.

From the gloom ahead came a frustrated child's cry. The stall door banged open, and a horse reared. Ironclad hooves lashed out, colliding with thick oak planks. Suddenly Blackie loomed out of the smoke, a small boy clinging to his halter.

Eli snatched hold of the child and smacked the horse's rump. Blackie shot forward, lunging toward the open door. "Where's your brother?" Eli demanded, crouching in front of the shirtless little boy.

"Hayloft," Rudy managed amid a torrent of coughing. "With Irwin."

Eli gave him a push. "Run to the house! Get your father and Roman!"

A frantic whinny came from Molly's box stall. The sound chilled Ruth's blood. The old mare had survived a fire years ago before Dat had bought her. She still bore the scars on her rump and one hind leg. The slightest hint of smoke had always frightened her. Now she squealed in terror.

"The mare!" Rudy cried, running for the barn door. "I couldn't open her stall door."

"We'll get her," Ruth promised as she ran for the stall. "Fetch the men. Keep low. It's easier to breathe near the floor." Smoldering stems of hay were drifting down from the open hatchway at the top of the loft ladder, stinging Ruth's face and arms.

"Help!" came a muffled plea from the loft above. "Dat! Help us!"

Eli sprinted for the ladder. "I'll get them. You let the mare out," he shouted to Ruth.

"Wait!" She seized a water bucket standing by Blackie's stall and dashed the contents over Eli, soaking his hair and clothing. "Be careful," she warned. She didn't want him to go up there, to risk his life in the fire, but she knew that there was no stopping him.

Eli started up the ladder, and Ruth ripped off her apron and held it over her mouth and nose as she felt along the front of Blackie's stall until she reached Molly's. The air was better here, and she spoke soothingly to the mare as she undid the latch. It wasn't stuck, but there was a trick to opening it that Rudy didn't know.

"Come on, come on, girl," she urged. Snorting, tossing her head, Molly bumped against Ruth's shoulder, and she caught hold of the halter. "Shh, shh," she murmured as she wrapped her apron around the mare's eyes. Tugging on the halter, she led the frightened animal out the back door and into the paddock.

There was no way to tie the horse, so Ruth unwound the apron and let Molly loose. Taking a deep breath of fresh air, she ducked back into the barn, closing the door behind her. The big door was open at the far end of the passageway, and leaving this one open would create a draft that would only make the fire worse. "Eli!" she cried, hurrying toward the ladder. "Have you found them?"

She could just make out a figure climbing down. Not Eli, too small for Eli. "Peter?"

Coughing. A child's sobs. "I'm...sorry... I didn't mean it."

Ruth yanked the boy off the ladder. He was shirtless, too, and covered in smudges of soot. "Peter? Are you all right?"

A flood of tears followed. Not waiting to make sense of his blubbering, she dragged him toward the front of the barn and pushed him black-faced and weeping into the yard. Choking, Peter fell to his knees and began to retch.

A quick look told her that the boy was more fright-

ened than hurt. Again she returned to the smoky barn
and hollered up the ladder. "Eli! What's happening? Are
you all right? Is Irwin up there?" Was it her imagination, or was the smoke clearing a little?

Eli's face appeared at the hatch opening. "We're all
right. Irwin is with me, and the fire's out."

Almost at the same time, Rudy, Samuel and Roman
came running, carrying buckets of water. Close behind
them were her mother and sisters, all carrying containers of water. Ruth stepped aside and let the men scramble up the ladder to the loft, buckets in hand.

"What happened?" Anna demanded, putting down
a soup pot of water. "Are the children safe?"

"Is Molly out?" Miriam asked. "Blackie's running
loose, but I didn't see Molly. Is she—"

"There's Rudy and Peter. Safe." She pointed at the
twins entering the barn. "Molly's fine," Ruth assured
them. "Irwin is with Eli in the loft."

"Was there a fire?" Susanna asked, her eyes huge
and frightened.

"There was, but it's all out now," Ruth assured her.
"Everything is going to be all right."

"Where's Molly?" Miriam demanded, putting down
her dishpan of soapy water. "She must be scared half
to death."

"Out back." Ruth pointed.

"I'll go talk to her," Susanna said, wanting to help
as always. "I'll tell her everything is all right. She likes
me."

"And I'll catch Blackie before he gets in the road."
Miriam took off.

"What happened?" Mam asked Ruth. "How did the

fire start?" Her voice cracked. "Please don't tell me Irwin…"

"I'm not sure how it started," Ruth answered. "But…" She caught Rudy's arm. "I think this young man can tell us."

Peter began to blubber. "We didn't mean to," he wailed. "We was just…" He turned and dashed for the doorway. "And…and Irwin said…and we…"

"Samuel!" Mam called up to the hayloft. "Is everything—"

"Under control, Hannah." Samuel came down the ladder, empty bucket in his hand.

"Then I think we'd best get to the bottom of this," Mam said. "If Irwin—"

"Ne," Ruth said. "Wait, Mam, until we can talk to the three of them together. I don't think Irwin may be the cause of this, after all." Her pulse was still racing. She wanted to see Eli, to make certain he hadn't been burned, but she sensed that this was the moment to find out exactly what had happened.

"How can you say that, after the school fire?" Anna asked.

"Peter and Rudy, come here," Ruth ordered, as the women gathered outside the barn door. The rain had stopped and the sun was trying to peek from beneath the dark clouds.

"And Samuel's outhouse," Anna continued. "You admitted setting fire to that when you did it."

"I didn't," Irwin protested, coming down the ladder behind Samuel and following the women out into the barnyard.

Mam's eyes narrowed. "But you said you did light the fire at Samuel's. Were you lying then or now?"

Irwin stared at the ground. He was a sight. His hair, face, chest and arms and face were smudged black, his bare feet and trousers filthy. He was shirtless, like the twins. Small, indignant red-rimmed eyes peered out beneath a shock of stringy hair. His eyelashes and brows were singed, his hands blistered. "Set fire to the outhouse," he muttered. "Not the school."

Peter and his brother looked nearly as bad, and tears streaked both round faces. Peter was trying to hide behind his twin. Both were sobbing.

"Hush, both of you," Ruth said. "Now, someone tell us exactly what happened here."

"Matches," Peter blubbered. Rudy nodded.

"Told 'im not to," Irwin said. "They don't listen. Spoilt."

"You two were playing with matches in the loft?" Ruth looked from one boy to the next. "Not Irwin?"

Rudy shook his head. Peter stared at his knees.

"Atch," Mam said softly. "So. The truth at last." She glanced up to meet Ruth's gaze.

"And which one of you started the fire under the schoolhouse?" Ruth demanded.

"Him." Peter pointed at his brother.

"Ne," Rudy protested, pointing at Peter. "Peter did it. He wanted to build a campfire like the Indians in our history book."

Ruth used her dirty apron still balled in her fist to wipe some of the black off Irwin's pinched face. She leaned down to speak to him at eye level. "When I saw you come out from under the porch that day, you weren't the one who had set the fire?"

"Ne."

"But you ran away when I called out to you."

Irwin studied the blister on his left big toe.

Eli walked up behind Ruth. She glanced at him, and when he started to say something, she put a finger up to signal him to wait.

"What were you doing under the school, if you didn't start the fire, Irwin?" Mam asked.

"Chased us," Rudy said.

Peter nodded. "Tried to put out the fire."

"He was mad at us," Rudy added.

"Ya," the other twin said. "Real mad."

"But why didn't you tell the truth?" Ruth raised Irwin's bony chin and looked into his pale eyes. The sadness she read there brought tears to her eyes. "Why did you let us think you were guilty when you weren't?"

Irwin grimaced, refusing to meet her gaze. "Who's gonna believe me?"

"There's more to it than that," Mam said. "You were trying to keep the twins from getting in trouble, weren't you?"

For long seconds, Irwin hesitated. Then his face flushed, and he gave a quick nod. "They're just little kids." He scowled at the twins. "Just kids."

"I can see that you were trying to do the right thing," Mam said. "But you should have told me. Because no one knew, Rudy and Peter got away with playing with matches. And because there were no consequences, they didn't stop, did they, Irwin?"

He exhaled slowly.

"Did they?" Ruth persisted.

"Ne."

"Irwin told us to use our shirts to put out the fire," Rudy said. "But it didn't work. So he threw a canvas tarp on it."

"Too much smoke," Peter explained.

"How did you know they were in the loft?" Miriam asked.

Irwin grimaced again. "Didn't. Bell rang for dinner." He shrugged. "Went to find 'em and smelled smoke."

Samuel crouched and opened his arms. The twins ran into his embrace, and he hugged them tightly. Ruth glanced at Irwin. His lower lip was quivering.

"Did you hear?" Anna asked Samuel.

"Enough to know that these two won't make the same mistake again."

Irwin swallowed hard. "You gonna whip them?"

"Ne," the big man answered, "but maybe they'll wish I had." He stood over his children and looked down on them. "You two go on home and tend to the chores now. We'll talk when I get there."

"What about their dinner?" Mam asked. "I've got all that food ready."

"No need for them to eat with us," Samuel said. "Children don't belong at the table with working men." He turned to Irwin. "But you need to wash up and come to dinner. You've earned your place there."

Irwin's eyes glowed, and he straightened his shoulders.

"He is a big help to us," Mam said. "I've been thinking of asking Reuben and Lydia if he could sleep here— for higher wages, of course. I think we'd all feel better with a man on the place."

"Ya," Samuel agreed. "The Beachys got plenty of hands to help, and I can see how you could come to depend on Irwin."

"If he agrees," Ruth said, looking to Irwin.

Irwin reddened beneath the soot-stained face. "Guess

I could do that," he said. "Too much work here for just you girls."

Roman started toward the house. "Don't know about the rest of you, but I'm starving."

"Come," Mam said, heading for the house. "Come and eat before everything gets cold."

Eli touched Ruth's arm. "Do you have a minute?" he asked her. "I still need to talk to you…"

"Mam needs me," she said, folding her arms over her chest. "This isn't the time." She was so confused. She'd promised herself she'd stay away from Eli, but right now, she wanted nothing more than to wrap her arms around him and hold him so tight she could feel his heart beating next to hers.

"You can't keep doing this to me." Eli watched her, but she wouldn't look up at him. "I don't know what to think."

She let her arms fall to her sides. "Can't we be friends and leave it at that?"

He shook his head. "Not with you, I can't," he said. "Never with you."

She kept her gaze on her muddy bare feet. "I wish things were different."

"Ruth," her mother called from the porch, "are you coming?"

"I have to go," Ruth said.

"Me, too." He nodded in the direction of the lane.

"No." Panic fluttered in her chest. "You have to stay for dinner. If you leave now, Roman and Samuel will wonder why. Everyone will be talking about us again."

"I don't mean now. Tomorrow. I have to go to Pennsylvania, to Belleville tomorrow. That was part of what

I've been trying to tell you. Why I needed to talk to you." She could hear the exasperation in his voice.

"But when are you coming back?"

"I don't know. There are things I have to settle there."

"With that girl?" The second the words came out of her mouth, she regretted them. Her knees felt weak. How had she dared to ask such a question of him? It wasn't her place. She had no ties to Eli Lapp. No right to ask something so personal.

"Ruth!" Miriam shouted.

"I have to go." Ruth looked at the house, then at him. All she could think was that he was going away, that she might never see him again. He didn't deny he was leaving to see the girl. What if he was? What if he was going to patch things up between them…whatever there had been between them? "I'm sorry," she said softly. And she was. For too many things.

"You go on." He sounded tired. Resigned. "I'll wash at the well and be in soon."

She turned away, then back toward Eli. "Thank you for what you did. For saving those boys."

"I didn't save them. Irwin did."

Eli might never admit it, but he was a hero. He'd gone up into a loft that he'd thought was on fire. He hadn't thought of his own safety, only that of the children. "It was a brave thing to do. We all know men who have gone into a fire to save someone and not come out." She smiled at him, proud she knew him, sad that she would never know him better. "You're a good man, Eli Lapp."

"No matter what people say?"

She turned and hurried toward the house.

The days after the near-tragedy in the barn passed swiftly. Late spring was always busy on the farm. In a few days, school would be out, and Mam and Irwin would be at home every day. To her surprise, Ruth had discovered that Irwin, who lacked common sense in dealing with the cows and chickens, had a real feel for gardening. He loved pulling weeds, hoeing and planting vegetables. Not only was he as careful with seeds as Mam, the boy had a knack for laying out perfectly straight rows.

That suited Ruth. Her favorite outside chore was tending the flower beds and cutting fresh bouquets for the house. There were always extra flowers to give away and to sell at the auction. She tried to spend as much time in the yard as she could, mowing and making the annual and perennial beds beautiful, but this year, she didn't feel quite the satisfaction she usually did.

Sweet corn wouldn't be planted for another week or two, but Miriam needed help in preparing the field. Samuel had come with his team of Percherons to do the plowing and disking, and when the moon was right, Miriam would hitch Molly to the planter to sow the seed. This spring Irwin would be another pair of hands, and they needed him badly with Leah and Rebecca still at *Grossmama's*.

Keeping busy from dawn until dusk should have assured Ruth a good night's sleep, but it hadn't turned out that way. She couldn't get Eli out of her head, and every night, when she climbed into bed, thoughts of him kept her awake. She went over and over what they'd said to each other the day of the fire and wished she'd said something different, though what, she didn't know. They couldn't be together for too many reasons, but she wished she could have said something to keep him from walking away, looking so sad. Ruth was surprised how much she missed Eli, missed talking to him, seeing him, seeing his handsome smirk. She missed him, and as one week turned into two, she began to wonder if he would ever return to Seven Poplars or if he really was gone for good. Not that she could blame him. Why would he come back?

When Eli had been in Seven Poplars, he'd caused her trouble, but having him away felt even worse. What was wrong with her? Why was she pining over this boy? She'd made her decision, and she had to learn to live with it.

So Ruth tried to keep busy and tried to work hard, thinking hard work would sweep all the feelings tumbling inside her out the door. Or at least under the rug. Today, there would be no time for moping. She, Mam and her sisters were going to Johanna's house to help her clean for an upcoming church service. With three-year-old Jonah and baby Katie, Johanna could use the help. Her husband, Wilmer, had gone with a vanload of mourners to Indiana to the funeral of a great-uncle and would be away for four days. No one said anything out loud, but Ruth and all her sisters, including Johanna, seemed to be relieved he was gone for a few days.

For an Amish man, Wilmer didn't like farming much, and he was not much help with the small property he and Johanna rented from an English man. Johanna took care of the sheep, the beehives and the hundred baby turkeys. She milked two dairy goats and raised game birds for sale to restaurants in the city. And cared for her two children, and put her husband's meals on the table, and washed her family's clothes and did all the work in the house. Wilmer worked in construction, and when he came home after a day's work, he retreated to his workshop or the parlor where he spent evenings reading and writing letters to his relatives.

Wilmer, Johanna said, put in long hours and was a good provider, but he didn't like to hear crying babies or trip over toys. He'd been a serious man when Johanna married him, and in the four years since their wedding, he'd become almost morose.

But Johanna was Johanna, always full of hope and energy. Nothing daunted her, and she looked forward to readying her house for church services with all the excitement of a once-a-year trip to Rehoboth Beach. Johanna loved company, and she loved the company of her mother and sisters most of all. Today would be a wonderful day. They were taking three huge picnic baskets of food, and the housework, shared between them, would go as easy as whipped cream on one of Anna's pumpkin pies.

The morning flew by in a flurry of soapsuds, buckets of ammonia and warm water for scrubbing windows, and the flutter of fresh-washed laundry and rugs hanging on the line. It was a beautiful day, sunny with a cool breeze, and no one minded the heavy work, least of all Ruth. Johanna had a new letter from Leah and Rebecca and kept them in stitches of laughter as she related the newest adventures their sisters had suffered in caring for *Grossmama* and Aunt Ida. The best news of the letter was that Leah was coming home for a visit next month. She'd found another family who had engaged a driver to come to Dover for a wedding, and they'd promised to bring her along.

After a shared midday meal accompanied by warm chatter and laughter, Mam and her sisters all found quiet spots to rest for an hour before tackling the yard work.

Ruth took little Katie up to her bedroom to rock her to sleep. She untied the baby's *Kapp* ribbons and was just about to lay her down for her nap when Mam came into the room.

"She's asleep then." Mam smiled down at the baby. She was chubby and healthy, her mop of dark curls the image of her father's. Jonah, in contrast, had hair as red as Dat's, a feature that Wilmer didn't approve of.

"Johanna's blessed," Ruth whispered. She placed Katie on her back and covered her with a red-and-blue quilt Johanna had designed and stitched before the baby was born. For a moment she stood looking down at the old-fashioned cradle their father had brought from his family home in Pennsylvania. A sweet longing made her sigh with regret...her sisters' babes were the only ones her arms would ever hold.

"She is blessed, as we all are," Mam said, still looking down at her grandbaby.

Together they tiptoed out of the room, and Ruth pulled the bedroom door closed behind them. She was about to descend the stairs to the first floor when Mam touched her arm and motioned her to sit on the top step beside her.

"I need to talk to you."

Ruth sat down, suddenly apprehensive.

"I'm worried about you," her mother said. "You seem so sad lately. Does it have to do with Eli going away?"

Ruth shot her a startled look.

"You think I haven't noticed? Or Anna or Miriam? They were talking to Johanna about it after you brought the baby up." She tucked a stray curl under Ruth's *Kapp* as she had so often when Ruth was a child. "Maybe it is time you start spending less time at home and more time with other young people. If Eli isn't the one for you, there are other men who would make fine husbands."

Ruth stared at her mother in disbelief. "I don't understand. You agreed that I should stay single, stay on the farm to help you with Susanna. Now you're saying I should be finding a husband?"

Hannah looked equally surprised. "Ruth Yoder! When did I ever say you should stay at home?"

Ruth's stomach tightened. She felt as if she was falling. A mistake…a terrible mistake. "In…the buggy. After you caught Eli and me together in the grape arbor." She went on more quickly than before, as if, if she said it, it would be true. "You said I had to set a good example for my sisters and the younger girls in our community. That I had to do what was right."

For a moment Hannah stared at Ruth. "My darling daughter, how did this happen? How did I not make it clear to you what I was saying?" Hannah cupped Ruth's face in between her soft hands. "I wasn't telling you I wanted you to stay home with me. That was my way of telling you it was okay to go, to be with Eli if you wanted. My point was, though, that you had to do it the right way. In marriage, in the church. Not playing games or behaving foolishly."

"But you told me about the letter." Ruth caught her mother's hand and squeezed it. "I value your wisdom, Mam. You were right about Irwin and I was wrong. If you think Eli is an unsuitable match…"

"I was trying to help you think independently and not to listen to what other people said or thought. I told you about the letter so you would have all the facts. I expected you to go to Eli and ask him about the letter."

"Dat wouldn't approve of him, would he?"

Mam sighed. "Probably not, but you aren't like your father. You're like me. When I left my family to marry your father, when I changed my faith for him, it was because he was the one man in the world that my heart told me would bring me true happiness. He brought me my beautiful children and he brought me to God. I want nothing less for you, Ruth."

"Not all marriages can be like that."

"*Ne.* Look at Johanna's. Or Lydia's. They are couples who make marriage work, who take joy in their children and in following God's path. But you need more, my precious one. What if God sent you this Eli Lapp from Belleville? You talk of following God's will. Have you considered that maybe our Lord sent him to you so that you could lead Eli back to His grace?"

Ruth couldn't hold back the tears. Soon she was sobbing, and her mother was holding her as she wept. "It's too late," she managed between bouts of crying. "Too late. I think… I think he wanted to…to ask me if he could court me, but I… I wouldn't even talk to him. He even tried to tell me why he was going to Belleville. But I turned him away, and now he's gone back to that girl…and… I've lost him forever."

Mam pushed back Ruth's cap and kissed the crown of her head. "That might very well be Eli's choice. And if it is, then this isn't the path you are meant to follow. God will never abandon you, my child. He was with me when I lost your father and He is with me every moment of every day."

"But…if I've thrown away my only chance at love…"

Mam rocked her in her arms, her tears falling on Ruth's cheek. "Whatever happens, you will be stronger and wiser for it. But nothing will convince me that your true path is to remain unwed. If not this wild boy, Eli Lapp, then another, I don't know. But what I do know is that you, Ruth, are a woman meant to love and be loved."

Chapter 16

The sixteenth of June dawned hot and hazy, and Ruth awakened with a stirring of hope in her heart. It was her birthday. The sadness she'd felt at losing Eli remained with her, but she pushed it to the far corner of her mind, determined not to spoil the day for her family by pining for what could not be.

Tonight there would be a birthday celebration dinner. They'd invited Samuel and his children and, of course, Irwin, and Johanna and her family would be there. Leah had been able to remain with them longer than she'd expected before she had to return to Ohio, so having her there for dinner would be a special treat. Ruth's one wish was that Rebecca could have been with them, too, but it would still be a fun evening.

The family had never exchanged expensive gifts on birthdays, as the English did, but Ruth was sure that

Anna would bake a coconut cake, and Mam would surprise her with some special treat. More important, when they gathered together to share the meal, Ruth would feel the love and joy of being part of something precious.

Deciding to pick flowers for the breakfast table, Ruth walked down to the orchard with the puppy, Jeremiah, following her. She laughed at the little dog's antics as he sniffed at the scent of a rabbit, leaped to chase a toad and barked furiously at an angry wren that objected to them near her nest in an apple tree. Ruth took her time in the warm sunshine, picking fat black-eyed Susans and delicate Queen Anne's lace. Just as she started back to the house, she heard the sound of a horse and buggy coming up the lane.

Scooping up the puppy, Ruth hurried to see who it was. She couldn't imagine who would be there before breakfast. As she came around the corncrib, she suddenly felt as though she'd tumbled off the top rung of the windmill ladder. Climbing out of a neat new black buggy was Eli. He saw her and smiled, and her knees went weak.

"Ruth."

She opened her mouth to say his name, but she was too breathless to speak. She swallowed, trying to say something, anything, but she could only stare at him, clutching the puppy and the flowers to her chest.

How handsome he was in his black leather boots, blue trousers, powder-blue shirt, navy suspenders and straw hat. He looked so... *Plain.*

"You're back." It was a silly thing to say.

"I'm back." He grinned, then the smile faded, and he looked so serious. "I've missed you."

His eyes were bluer than she remembered. "Gone some time, you were," she managed.

"Ya." He seemed suddenly shy, unsure of himself.

"Busy up there in Belleville, I suppose." She was aware of just how silly those words sounded as soon as they tumbled out of her mouth. She must look a sight, barefooted and *Kapp* askew. She put Jeremiah down, and the puppy barked and spun and ran to bark some more at Eli.

"Hey, puppy." He bent and petted the squirming animal. "He's putting on weight. He looks better."

"If Irwin keeps feeding him, he'll be as fat as a pig." She watched the puppy wiggle with pleasure as Eli rubbed his belly. Silence stretched between them.

"It's early, you're about," she said finally.

"Ya." He stood up, slipping his hands into his pockets, looking at her, then the puppy, then her again. "I thought so, but I... I thought you were an early riser."

She felt her cheeks grow warm. Why was he looking at her so intently? Did she have dirt on her nose? She shifted the flowers from one hand to the other. "I am," she admitted.

Again, they were quiet.

"Those for me?" he asked after a moment.

"Ne." She looked up and then laughed, and he laughed.

It felt good.

There were so many things Ruth wanted to say to Eli. Needed to say. Only she didn't know where to start. Finally she just plunged in. "Roman didn't know if you were coming back or if he should look for someone else to help in the chair shop."

Eli nodded. "I guess he should. I wanted to..." He

took a deep breath. "I came early, Ruth, because I wanted to see you without anybody else around."

She felt a sinking feeling in her stomach. He must have decided to stay in Belleville for good, and he'd come to tell her. She nibbled at her lower lip. She didn't want to hear him say it. "Your family is well?" she said, stalling. "Your mother?"

"Good. She's good. And my stepfather and little brother are good."

"Good," she echoed, not sure what to say next. If he was going back to Belleville, was there any point in saying anything? All she would do was embarrass herself, maybe him.

He took a step toward her. "I know you don't want to talk to me, but I didn't want to go away for good without saying goodbye."

Hot tears stung the back of her eyelids. When she'd seen him in her yard, she'd thought for just a second that maybe there was a chance that she hadn't ruined everything, but now...

"I have something for you. Fannie said today was your birthday, so I hope you'll accept it. I made it for you." He walked to the back of the buggy.

She followed him.

He raised the canvas on the back and lifted out the beautiful cherry box with the round top and the carved wrens that he'd shown her so proudly once before. "It's a bride's chest," he explained. "Remember it?"

"Of course I remember it. It's the most beautiful thing I've ever seen." She set the flowers down on the back of the buggy, unable to take her eyes off the piece of furniture. "But...but I'm not getting married."

She wasn't getting married, not ever. But she wanted

the chest. The finish gleamed in the sunlight, and she couldn't keep her hands off it. She stooped to stroke the smooth wood. "It's not meant for me. You should save it for your intended."

His gaze met hers across the bride's chest with such force that she felt light-headed.

"You will marry," he said. "When the right man comes along, the man who's good enough to deserve you."

"It's a treasure," she said. "And the little birds…" She tried to find the right words. "It's a gift the Lord has given you, to make something so beautiful."

"Not as beautiful as you are to me this moment."

Her breath caught in her throat, and a single tear spilled down her cheek. She looked down. Stood up. "You shouldn't say things like that."

"Why not? It's true. I've never met anyone like you before, Ruth, and I never will again. I'd never give this to another woman." He caught her hand and squeezed it and let go. "It was meant for you. It always was, even before I knew you." He took a breath. "I love you, Ruth. That's why it has to be yours."

She lifted her gaze. "Then why are you going away?" she demanded, suddenly angry. "Are you marrying that Belleville girl? That Hazel?"

He stared at her in astonishment. "*Ne!* Why would you think that?"

"Because you went back to Belleville. Because… I thought…" Confused, she broke off. Behind her, she heard the kitchen screen door bang. Someone had come out on the porch, but she didn't care. "You *aren't* marrying her?"

"I'm not marrying anyone. It was you I wanted, only

you. And if I can't have you, then…then, I have to leave Seven Poplars."

More tears followed the first, and she dashed them away with the back of her hand. She had to say it, she *had* to. Even if nothing would ever come of it. Even if it was too late. Only she didn't know how to tell him she loved him. "But what if I…what if I care for you, too?"

She reached for his hand and clung to it as if she were drowning and he was the only hope she had of living. "Oh, Eli, I've been such a fool. I thought I shouldn't marry anyone." Once she started, the words gushed from her mouth. "I thought it was God's will that I stay with Mam and Susanna and then you came along and I felt differently, but then there was the gossip and then…but then…"

"Wait, go back," he said. "You…you care for me? The way I care for you?"

She looked into his eyes, his face a blur through her tears. "So much it hurts. Only I made such a mess of things."

"Are you saying your mother might give her permission?" Eli asked incredulously. "That she'd let you marry me? If…you wanted to?"

She held his gaze. "She only wants what's best for me. She'd give her blessing if you joined the church. I know she would if you could put the world behind you and your past and be happy being Plain."

"And you would marry me? In spite of all the gossip—"

"I realized I don't care about that. I only care about you. But I'm Amish. I can't live in the English world, and I can't marry a man who didn't share my faith."

He glanced around. "Is there someplace we can sit down?"

"This way." She led him around the house to a bench near the garden gate. Wild roses grew up the trellis behind them, and the newly mown grass was as soft as a carpet under her bare feet. Shyly, she sat on the edge of the seat and tugged him down to sit beside her. "No grape arbor here," she teased. "We're in plain view. We're respectable."

"But I'm holding your hand," he reminded her.

She smiled at him. "Nearly respectable." Excitement bubbled up inside her, and she trembled with joy. Were they really sitting here talking about marriage? Could her world really have tumbled upside down like this so quickly? So beautifully? "Would you consider it? Would you come to church with me? Become a part of it again?"

He raised her hand and kissed her knuckles. "Too late for that. I already joined the church. I went back to Belleville to mend the trouble with my mother, with my family, and while I was there, I talked with our bishop. I met with him many evenings, and he answered a lot of questions that troubled me. He made me look at things differently. *You* made me look at things differently." He grinned. "So last Sunday, I joined the Amish Church."

She touched one navy-blue suspender. "So that's why no red ones?"

"Ne." He laughed. "I sold the red ones with my motor scooter and bought the horse."

She laughed with him. "Not with the money you got from that old motorbike, you didn't. Or did you buy a blind horse?"

"He's a fine horse, strong and smart. Wait until you

see how fast he can trot. And this buggy was a gift from my stepfather, Joseph. He said that I never had my proper portion from my dat. He's a good man, and he is the right husband for my mother. I've never seen her so content."

"I'm glad. And I'm glad you have such a wonderful bishop, that he could lead you to God."

"He is a good shepherd," Eli said, "but it was your mother that opened my eyes more than anyone."

"Mam?"

"Ya. Your mother and Roman and Samuel and you and your sisters." His eyes glowed with emotion. "For many years, I wasn't sure that I belonged in God's grace, or that He wanted me there. But I watched your family and community bring Irwin into your home and love him, despite his faults. It wasn't until I got back to Belleville and had time to think that I realized what I had witnessed here. If there was a place for Irwin in the Plain world, I realized maybe there was one for me."

"There will always be a place for you here, Eli. In our community. In our home."

"So does that mean you'll let me court you?"

"If you'll forgive me for being so stupid and stubborn, for thinking that I knew best what God wanted. You warned me not to be a martyr, to listen to God, and you were right."

"Will you accept my bride's chest?"

"Only if you'll ask me to marry you. Officially." Her heart was so full of joy that she didn't care how forward she was being—that she'd practically proposed to him, instead of the other way round.

"You'd have me, even when you don't know the truth about Hazel and me?"

"I know you, Eli, and I know you'd never do anything dishonorable. You might make a mistake. We all do because we're human. But you'd never desert the mother of your child."

"You're right, I wouldn't." He started to reach into his pocket. "I have a letter from her, a letter that will explain everything."

"I don't need to see your letter," she protested, stilling his hand with hers. "I believe in you."

"But I should have told you the truth as soon as I knew I had feelings for you, and I should have told my mother before I ever left Belleville the first time." He looked away, then back at her. "Will you listen now?"

"If you want to tell me, of course I'll listen."

He took her hand again. "Hazel was my friend, and we went to some parties together, but she was like a sister to me. I was never her boyfriend. Not ever. I knew she liked an English fellow, and I knew she was secretly seeing him."

"You don't have to tell me these things," Ruth said, her heart already going out to Hazel, the girl she had secretly disliked because of the hold she had on Eli. The hold Ruth thought she had on Eli.

"I do need to tell you. It's important that there be no secrets between us."

Ruth nodded and Eli continued. "I took Hazel to a bonfire one night, at Edgar Peachy's farm. There were English there, and she left the party with someone. I tried to stop her but, Ruth, I didn't try hard enough. She was having trouble at home, you know, following the rules…being who her parents wanted her to be. Hazel was always different. She loved school and she wanted to be part of the bigger world. But that night, she'd argued with her father. She wasn't thinking clearly."

Eli sighed, but he didn't look away from her. "I blame myself for what happened. If I had stopped her, if I'd taken her home when I should have, instead of letting her go with that Englisher, maybe it would never have happened."

"Maybe it would have anyway," Ruth suggested softly. "If not that night, another."

"Maybe," he conceded. "But she was so scared when she found out she was going to have a baby. She tried to talk to her boyfriend, but he wouldn't have anything to do with her after that night. So she asked me to marry her so that no one would know what she had done. I liked her a lot, but I didn't love her. I told her I would help her. I would give her child my name, but only if we told the truth first. I couldn't lie about that to her family or mine."

"But, Eli." Ruth brushed her hand over his shoulder. "She told everyone you were the father. And they believed her."

"They did. I got angry, and I let her face her trouble alone. In the end, she gave the baby to her sister, and she left."

"Did you know where she went?"

"Not until I got the letter at Uncle Roman's. Her English boyfriend didn't want to take responsibility for the baby, but his family helped her with money. She's going to go to college to be a nurse. She was writing to me to tell me she is all right and that she was sorry for everything."

"Why didn't you tell your family what really happened?"

"I tried at the time, but they wouldn't listen. You are the only one who didn't judge me."

"Maybe I did, in the beginning." She smiled at him. "Because of those red suspenders and that awful motor scooter. You are a wild boy, Eli Lapp."

"*Was* a wild boy." He leaned close and brushed his lips against hers. "Marry me, Ruth Yoder, and keep me on the path of Godliness. Keep me Plain."

Ruth closed her eyes and savored a second kiss. She was so full of love and joy that she thought she would burst. "Oh, Eli," she began, but then she stopped when she heard Susanna squeal. She opened her eyes to see her little sister scrambling out from behind the rosebushes to run toward the house—her chubby feet bare, her bonnet strings flying.

"Mam! Mam! Roofie's kissing Eli!" Susanna shouted. "Come quick, Mam! Roofie's getting married!"

Chapter 17

For a moment, Ruth sat beside Eli in sweet silence, gazing into his blue eyes, holding his hand tightly. She wanted him to kiss her again, but her heart was pounding so hard that she thought maybe she'd had enough kissing for the moment.

Upstairs, Anna pushed up a bedroom window. "What's going on?" she called. "Why is Susanna—" She broke off when she saw them together, hand in hand. "I'll be right down!"

"I suppose we'd better speak to your mother," Eli said, "before we cause another scandal...to ask her blessing on our marriage."

"*Ya,*" Ruth agreed and giggled with sheer joy. "We wouldn't want to give Aunt Martha even more reason to gossip about us." She was so happy at this moment that she thought she might take off like a dandelion puff and float away.

"Do you want to do it now, or should I, you know, make an appointment or something to speak with her?"

She laughed at that thought. "I don't know. That depends on how soon you want to marry," she teased. "If you mean years from now—"

"I'd marry you today if I could!" Eli caught her around the waist and lifted her up. "I can't believe I'm so lucky," he said, "to come down from the Kishaco-quillas Valley and find you." He lowered her bare feet to the ground and kissed her mouth with such tenderness and passion that tears sprang to her eyes. "Marry me today."

"I can't marry you today!" She laughed, breathless, playfully pushing on his broad chest. "But maybe you should speak to Mam today before there's more kissing."

"Speak to me about what?" Mam demanded, coming around the corner of the house with Susanna tugging on her hand. But Mam's eyes sparkled with mischief, and Ruth knew she really wasn't angry. "Eli, do you have an explanation for kissing my daughter in front of her mother and little sister?"

"Sisters," cried Miriam and Anna together as they joined them.

Irwin was the last to appear, the little terrier in his arms. "All of us," he echoed.

Eli slipped an arm around Ruth's shoulder and pulled her close beside him. The smell of her and the softness of her skin was so sweet that it made him almost giddy. "We're going to be married," he declared more boldly. "Ruth and me. In the church."

"But you have to be Amish," Irwin said sternly. "You can't marry our Ruth if you aren't Plain."

Mam dried her hands on her apron and folded her arms. "Irwin's right. So what do you have to say to that, Eli? Can you be properly Amish? Can you accept our faith and live by it every day?"

"Eli has already joined the church in Belleville. He's one of us now." Ruth looked up at him with such love in her eyes that he felt ten feet tall.

"Can you be a loving husband to Ruth?" Hannah asked. "In good times and bad?"

Miriam's chin firmed. "He'd better be."

"Or we'll know the reason why," Anna added.

"I will," Eli said. "I give you my word." He held out his hand to Irwin. "I would like your blessing, too, since you're the man of the house."

Irwin's ears turned fire red beneath his straw hat, but he took the offered hand and shook it. "I'll hold you to it," he said.

"I want to be part of this family," Eli announced to them all, still holding Ruth in his arm. "I want to be the kind of man Jonas was and a son to you, Hannah, as well as a true brother to the rest of you."

"And I promise you that God will always come first in our home," Ruth said, clinging to him for all she was worth.

"Then you have our blessing," Hannah said.

"Ya," Susanna jumped up and down, clapping her hands. "And now I will have a big brother for sure!"

"And I will have a husband," Ruth said.

"The happiest husband in the world," Eli answered.

Ruth smiled up at him, her eyes shining. *"Ya,* and the happiest wife."

* * * * *

THE AGENT'S SECRET PAST

Debby Giusti

In memory of Ginger Leary
A dear friend who loved books
and always encouraged me to keep writing.

Then he said to them all, Whoever wants to be my disciple must deny themselves and take up their cross daily and follow me. For whoever wants to save their life will lose it, but whoever loses their life for me will save it.

—*Luke* 9:23 24

Prologue

Eight years earlier

The moon peered down between dark, billowing clouds and cast the Amish farmhouse in shadows. Rebecca Miller stepped from her car onto the one-lane, dirt road she knew so well and shivered in the frosty night air.

Leaving two years earlier had sealed her fate. She would not be welcomed nor accepted back unless—and until—she asked forgiveness. Something she could never do.

If only her father had believed her. Perhaps then, she would have remained in Harmony, Alabama, and spent the rest of her life wrapped in the familiar embrace of the Amish way.

Instead she had created a new future for herself in the military. Seemingly a drastic shift from the peace-loving community of her childhood, but then too many ignored what Rebecca knew so well. Evil existed even among the Amish.

After driving straight through from Fort Campbell, Kentucky, her legs were stiff and her shoulders tense.

Cautiously she climbed the front steps, her breath clouding the air. She shivered, anticipating her father's icy stare and quick rejection.

Her sister's words replayed in her memory. *I fear for my life.*

Rebecca tapped ever so lightly on the unlatched door. An even more chilling shiver snaked up her spine.

"Katie," she whispered, pushing the door open.

An acrid stench wafted past her before she saw her father and the dark circle of blood pooling on the wooden floor beneath his chest. The cloying scent of copper clogged her throat and sent a jab of fear deep into her heart.

"Datt?" Without thought, she slipped back to her Amish past.

He lay on the hand-hewn floorboards his bearded face pale and drawn, life ebbing from his glassy eyes. Trying to assess which of the many stab wounds to stanch, Becca dropped to her knees and touched his outstretched hand.

Her father's eyes widened ever so slightly.

"Who was it?" she whispered, knowing even before he answered.

"Ja-Jacob," he stammered, ignoring the ban that forbid him from speaking to his daughter.

A shuffle sounded overhead.

Rebecca's breath hitched. "He's here?"

"Yah."

An unseen sword pierced her soul, the pain so intense she gasped for air. "Katie?"

He pointed to the pantry. "Go," he demanded, with a flick of his hand.

Recalling the times she and her younger sister had playfully hidden in the adjoining alcove, Becca hastened toward the pantry and inched the door open.

Her heart stopped.

Katie sat slumped against the wall, eyes open, face contorted in terror. Blood spilled from the gaping wound that sliced through her gut.

"No!" she moaned ever so softly.

Rebecca bit her fisted hand, unable to see anything except her sister's lifeless gaze. Guilt overwhelmed her. If she hadn't left, Katie would still be alive.

Footsteps sounded on the stairs and warned of his approach. Rebecca scurried back to the kitchen. Her father's head lay slack against his arm. She leaned down to touch his neck, feeling nothing except his soft flesh and prickly beard.

No pulse. No life.

A floorboard groaned on the landing. Close. Too close.

"Goodbye, *Datt*," she whispered.

Rebecca opened the door and slipped into the darkness. Once at her car, she glanced back.

Jacob appeared in the farmhouse doorway.

She could see the outline of his face, his beard, his lips snarling as he stared into the night.

"Who's there?" His eyes found her in the shadows.

He raised his fist in the air. "You cannot run from me, Rebecca. I will find you. When I do, you will die."

Chapter 1

Eight years later

*R*un *faster!*

He was behind her, gaining speed.

The raspy pull of air in and out of his lungs grew louder, signaling his approach.

At any moment, she expected his work-worn hand to grab her shoulder and send her crashing onto the asphalt roadway.

How had he found her?

For the last eight years, she'd been stationed overseas. Three deployments to the Middle East, a twenty-four-month tour in Korea and a three-year assignment in Germany, all far from Harmony, Alabama, and her past.

She smelled his stench, an evil mix of hay and sweat.

"Becca," he whispered in her ear.

She gasped for air, woke from her nightmare, clawed at the sheets and blinked her eyes open, searching the darkness of her bachelor officer's quarters.

Sitting up in bed, she threw the covers aside and stepped onto the floor, the tiles cool to her bare feet. She shook her head in an attempt to scatter the dream that came too often.

She was at Fort Rickman, Georgia, not the Amish community where she had grown up.

Reality check. She had run away from Jacob Yoder eight years earlier. Supposedly he had died later that night after killing her father and sister.

Unnerved by the nightmare, Becca grabbed her holstered, service weapon off the nightstand and stumbled into the hallway on her way to the kitchen. She needed to hydrate her body and clear her mind. If only she could wash the memories away.

She placed the gun, which had been her almost constant companion for the last eight years, next to her purse on the kitchen table and opened the cabinet over the sink in search of a glass. A sickening smell, like rotten eggs, hit her full force.

Pinpricks of fear needled the nape of her neck.

She glanced at the gas cooking range. The burners were off. The flame on the pilot lights glowed crimson in the dark.

The smell was intense, overpowering, deadly.

Run!

She reached for her Glock and slipped her handbag over her shoulder as she raced through the living area to the back door. Fingers trembling, she fumbled at the lock, dead bolt and chain, her progress slowed by the protective safeguards she had put in place. For too long, she had tried to distance herself from Jacob, fearing he was still alive.

Her pulse pounded in her ear, like a ticking time bomb ready to explode. She had to escape before—

The door opened. She ran into the night, inhaling the pure, sweet air that filled her lungs.

In the distance beyond the common green space stood the older BOQ apartments. Even at this late hour a few lights glowed in the windows.

She glanced back at the newly built quad she'd moved into ten days earlier. The only occupant thus far.

Digging into her purse, she traded her gun for her cell and speed dialed the Criminal Investigation Division on post, where she worked. The noncommissioned officer on duty answered on the second ring.

"This is Special Agent Rebecca Miller. Notify the fire department and military police of a gas leak in the new BOQ quad on Eisenhower Drive. Tell them the only occupant has cleared the premises."

Before she could disconnect, the sound of unleashed fury rocked her world. The explosion lit the sky and mushroomed into a giant ball of fire.

The force of the blast pushed against her. She took a step back to keep her balance.

Her ears rang. Her eyes blurred.

She blinked against the brightness.

A surge of heat warmed her for an instant as it blew past, replaced with frigid winter air that penetrated her bones.

Jet-black smoke billowed from the windows of the bedroom where she had been asleep just moments earlier. The terrifying dream had saved her life.

Flames licked at the building's wood facade and devoured the decorative trim. "No," she gasped as the growing inferno turned night into day.

Sirens sounded in the distance. A trail of flashing lights signaled their approach. Fire trucks, followed by military police cars, raced into the parking area and screeched to a stop. Men in turnout gear spilled from the trucks. With swift, sure motions, they connected hoses to nearby hydrants and trained the heavy streams of water on the blaze while maintenance personnel hastened to cut off the gas supply that fueled the fire.

Footfalls pounded on the ground behind her. Becca turned at the sound, ready to defend herself again.

"Are you okay?" Colby Voss.

"How—how did you get here?" Instantly, she regretted the foolish question. No doubt, her fellow CID agent lived in the older BOQs on Sheridan Road, just across the open field.

"Are you hurt?" His eyes roamed her body as if searching for an injury or burn.

With her throat unexpectedly dry, she shook her head and raised her hand to reassure him. Her inability to find her voice caused an additional tangle of concern to wrap around her.

A pressure filled her chest. She clamped down on her jaw to ward off the wave of nausea that swirled around her. She didn't want to appear weak.

Especially not to a guy with inquiring eyes.

For the past eight years, no one had climbed her wall of defense. No one until Special Agent Colby Voss had sauntered into her cubicle ten days earlier to welcome her to Fort Rickman.

So much for maintaining her cool. Although right

now she felt completely drained and unable to maintain anything, let alone her composure.

"What happened?" he asked, his eyes flicking between her and the firemen battling the blaze.

She wiped her hand across her forehead and pulled in another breath of cold night air. "I—I smelled gas. My stove was off. There must have been a leak someplace in the system."

"You were awake?"

A good question, but one she didn't want to answer. She had never told anyone about the reoccurring dreams.

"Just barely. I went into the kitchen for a glass of water and realized there was a leak."

"Good job getting outside."

She didn't need his praise or affirmation. Not tonight. Not when he was standing way too close and adding more anxiety to her already questionable stability.

Turning to stare at the raging inferno, she sucked in another mouthful of air and tried to calm her out-of-control pulse.

"It happened in the empty apartment next door," she said, convinced the gas had seeped into her kitchen from the neighboring unit. "Probably an accidental leak."

Had it been accidental?

Or was something else or someone else involved?

Her stomach tightened.

Surely not someone from her past.

Colby wanted to put his arm around Becca and quiet the fear that flashed from her eyes. He would have done exactly that, if not for the keep-out sign she wore around her heart, which he'd noticed the moment she reported for duty at CID Headquarters.

He had refused to be put off when they'd first met, especially since he had been the new CID agent two months earlier when he transferred from Fort Hood, Texas. He could read her body language and kept his welcome to a firm handshake and nod of his head, knowing all too well about self-sufficient women who didn't want or need a man in their lives.

Becca appeared to be a by-the-book type of agent who kept to herself. Not that he had been staring at her pretty face or green eyes with their flecks of gold. Eyes that she averted whenever he glanced her way.

That elusive shift of attention made him wonder if there wasn't something she wanted to hide. Perhaps he was reading more into what was only her nervous attempt to remain aloof, yet his gut feelings were usually right, and he kept thinking she had something buried beneath her neat and trim facade.

Two military police officers hustled toward them. Colby recognized the taller of the two as Gary Flanders, a put-together sergeant with an interest in joining the CID.

"Hey, sir, you know anything about what happened?"

Before Colby could answer, Becca drew in a deep breath and steeled her jaw with determination. "It was an explosion, Sergeant, in my BOQ."

Flanders pulled a notepad and mechanical pencil from his pocket while his partner stood to the side. "Can I get your name, ma'am?"

"Special Agent Becca Miller. I'm with the CID."

"You were the only resident in the new building?"

"That's correct. I arrived on post ten days ago and

signed for the bottom apartment on the left. The one on the bottom right, as well as the two second-story apartments, were unoccupied."

"What happened?" the MP asked.

"I—I went into the kitchen for a glass of water and noticed a strong gas smell. Realizing the danger, I exited the building."

"Did you see anyone outside?"

She shook her head. "No one."

Wind blew across the clearing and ruffled the pages of the sergeant's notebook. He hunched his shoulders against the cold and glanced at her lightweight flannel pants and T-shirt. "The temperature's dropping, ma'am. Would you like to take shelter in one of the squad cars?"

"I'm fine, Sergeant."

Colby knew better.

Dressed as she was coupled with the plummeting temperature and the shock of seeing her BOQ in flames had to have an adverse effect on her. Even in the half-light, her face was noticeably pale and drawn.

He glanced down at her bare feet.

Time to make a command decision. "My BOQ is just across the clearing. We can continue to talk there."

He shrugged out of the thick fleece he'd grabbed on his way outside and slipped it over her shoulders.

She shook her head. "That's not necessary."

"Maybe not, but humor me."

Their eyes locked for a long moment.

Colby wanted to shake his head at her obstinacy. Someone needed to inform Ms. Miller that taking healthy measures to protect herself wasn't a sign of weakness.

What did she have to prove?

He took her arm.

She glanced down at his hand and then raised her gaze. "Really, I'm okay."

"Maybe, but the temperature is in the forties. You're not dressed for the cold. Neither am I."

He turned to the MP. "Sergeant, I'm in apartment 103, the first door on the left, should anyone need to question either Special Agent Miller or me."

"Yes, sir."

Colby motioned Becca forward and was somewhat surprised when she followed his lead. As tough as she had tried to be over the past few days, he had expected opposition. Not that he wasn't relieved.

Shock was a nasty complication that often went unnoticed. From the knit of her brow and the ever-so-slight slump to her usually ramrod-straight spine, Becca had been affected by the middle-of-the-night attack.

Who wouldn't be? To go from a near sleep to a race for your life could try the best of men—or women.

Glancing over his shoulder, he took in the seeming chaos as the on-post fire company worked to control the inferno that resisted their attempts at containment. The military police, post engineer, fire marshal and fire chief would survey the damage and photograph anything suspect. As much as Colby would have liked to check the property himself, someone needed to get Becca inside and out of the cold.

Tomorrow, the fire marshal and his entourage would sift through the rubble in hopes of uncovering the cause. More than likely, an accidental malfunction from a leak in a gas line or a faulty pilot light coupled with some type of spark.

At the far side of the grassy knoll Becca stopped and glanced over her shoulder at the blaze.

Colby heard the sharp intake of air as she shook her head.

"Was it Jacob?" she whispered.

He leaned closer, not sure if he had heard correctly.

"What did you say, Becca?"

Her eyes widened as if she had forgotten he was there.

So much for making a positive, first impression. Something his sisters would have teased him about mercilessly, if they found out.

Which they wouldn't.

"Did you say 'Jacob'?" he asked.

She shook her head. "I didn't say anything."

But she had. A man's name. Did she associate Jacob—whoever he was—with the explosion?

If so, Colby would keep watch in hopes she would eventually reveal more information. Maybe then he'd know what secrets she kept hidden behind her hauntingly hooded eyes and tantalizing reticence.

Chapter 2

Becca hesitated for a moment before she stepped into Colby's BOQ and flicked her gaze over the leather couch and matching chair bathed in soft light from a floor lamp. A newspaper and stack of fitness magazines were arranged on the coffee table next to a collection of framed photos. She moved closer, her eyes drawn to a picture of a group of girls standing around a much younger Colby in uniform. The family resemblance couldn't be ignored.

"These must be your sisters?" she said.

"All five of them." She could hear the smile in his voice as he headed for the kitchen. "They insisted on a picture before I deployed to Afghanistan the first time."

A bittersweet moment for sure. Pride for their brother was tempered by the reality that he might not come home from war. Photos were something tangible to hold on to when all else was gone.

Graven images, the Amish called them. Her father had railed when she and Katie had come home with a snapshot a friend from town had taken of both of them. Her father had torn the picture into tiny pieces that Becca had tried to glue together later that night after he had gone to bed. If only she had that picture now. Instead, she had to rely on memories that faded with time.

"How do you take your coffee?" Colby called from the other room.

"With a little milk, if you've got it."

"Creamer okay?"

"Perfect."

A biography of General George S. Patton sat on a side table along with a number of training manuals. Military plaques and memorabilia hung on the wall next to citations for an army commendation medal, a meritorious service metal and two bronze stars. Impressive to say the least.

Not only was Colby good-looking but also competent, although she'd realized that the day they'd met. He'd been focused on business and not with making idle chitchat, for which she'd been grateful. Coming into a new unit was stressful. Having to keep up a flow of chatter made it even more so.

Turning, she noticed an open laptop on a desk in the corner. A plasma screen TV and two bookcases, stacked with three-ringed binders, filled the corner of the room and balanced the rather stark but comfortable furnishings. She approved of his uncluttered decorating style. Her own preference leaned to basic needs with few extras, which probably stemmed from her upbringing.

She accepted the coffee Colby offered and wrapped

her hands around the mug, thankful for the warmth of the thick stoneware. After taking a sip, she gazed through the window at her own quarters visible in the distance. The once-sizable structure was now only a shell of steel support beams and charred debris.

Her hold baggage, containing the majority of her household items, wasn't due to arrive from Germany for another two weeks. The fire had destroyed only what she had brought in her luggage. All of which could be replaced.

"These might help." She turned to find Colby holding out a pair of heavy socks.

"Thank you." Accepting the offering, she quickly settled into a nearby chair and slipped the thick woolen coverings over her bare feet. "I didn't realize I was so cold."

"You were bordering on shock, which worried me."

"I appreciate your concern and the coffee." She smiled. Yet her attempt to remain upbeat was only halfhearted. The reality of what had happened tonight clamped down on her shoulders and wouldn't let go.

"Give me a minute to thaw out, then I'll head back to my BOQ," she told him.

"You won't be able to salvage anything tonight, Becca."

"Except the clothes that are still in my car." She laughed at her own foolishness. "I stopped at the commissary after work and lugged the groceries inside when I got home, but I failed to go back for the laundry I had picked up earlier. My gym bag's also in the trunk along with a pair of running shoes."

"What about your weapon?"

She ran her fingers over the purse still strapped to her shoulder. "I grabbed my Glock and purse before I ran. CID badge, military ID card, car keys. Everything I need is inside."

"Sounds as if you were expecting trouble."

Colby's comment struck too close to home.

When she didn't respond, he raised his brow expectantly.

Becca stood, needing to distance herself from his penetrating gaze. She walked into the kitchen and placed her mug in the sink.

"I'll drive you to your car," he said when she returned to the living room.

"Thanks, but I can walk."

"Not in this weather." He glanced at her feet. "I've got a pair of slippers that should fit you. They were a gift from my grandmother, but they're too small for me. The leather soles will protect your feet until you get the gym shoes from your car. You'll also need a jacket."

He disappeared down the hallway and returned with sweatpants and a hooded sweatshirt she pulled over her flannel pajamas. The slippers were roomy but warm.

"Maybe the fleece will be enough," she said, regarding the bulky coat he offered.

He shook his head. "You need more insulation if we're going to be outdoors for any length of time."

"What about you?"

"I'll wear my Gore-Tex. It's with my training gear in the back bedroom."

She shrugged into the jacket that smelled like sandalwood and lime and waited as Colby located his military outerwear and car keys.

Although she appreciated Colby's help, she needed

to keep up her guard. No matter how nice or how good-looking he was, she didn't want anyone to complicate her life.

Her gaze returned to the window and the smoldering ruins beyond. Involuntarily, she shivered, regretting her youthful infatuation with Jacob Yoder when the Amish drifter had first stumbled into her life. How eagerly she had given her heart to him, not knowing he had taken up with an older woman—an infirmed Amish widow whose farm he coveted.

Bitter tears had stung Becca's eyes when she'd learned of their marriage. Even more difficult was her father's insistence that Becca help Jacob's sickly wife with housekeeping chores.

Jacob paid her father nicely for her services, and her needy *datt* turned a blind eye to what Jacob really wanted.

Her stomach soured, recalling when Jacob had lured her to the barn. She'd fought him off and narrowly escaped. Knowing her father would never believe her own innocence, she had run away from Jacob, her father and her Amish roots.

Two years later, her sister's phone call forced Becca to return home, but she arrived too late to save Katie or her *datt*.

With a heavy heart, Becca turned from the window, hoping to distance herself from the niggling concern that too often hovered close at hand.

Jacob was dead.

The case was closed.

But if that were true, then why did some inner voice keep warning her that Jacob Yoder was still alive?

* * *

Acrid smoke hung in the air around Becca's BOQ as Colby parked his green Chevy near her Honda and waited as she slipped on her shoes and shrugged off his suggestion to stay in the car. Worried though he was about her well-being, he admired her determination to get to the bottom of what had caused the explosion.

Together they crossed the street to where Sergeant Flanders stood next to his squad car.

"What's the latest?" Colby asked, raising his voice over the drone of the fire engines.

"We haven't been able to get close to the building, sir, but we've done a preliminary search of the surrounding wooded area and plan to retrace our steps after daylight. The post maintenance company has been called as well as the fire marshal, staff duty officer and post engineer. General Cameron was notified."

Becca stared over her shoulder at a second residence still under construction on the next street. "Has anyone searched the other building?"

"Not yet, ma'am."

She nodded to Colby. "Let's check it out."

Stopping at his car, Colby grabbed a Maglite from the trunk and handed a spare to Becca. "We might need these."

Flashlights in hand, they hustled across a narrow strip of green space and cautiously rounded the front of the structure. A utility van sat at the far end of the parking lot. The side panel decal read Peachtree Construction.

"Why would someone leave their truck in an isolated parking lot overnight?" Becca gave voice to what Colby was thinking.

"Time to have a look-see." He shone his flashlight through the windshield. A ladder and tools were visible in the rear. An insulated coffee mug sat upfront in the console cup holder.

The doors were locked.

Becca raised her cell and relayed the Fulton County tag number to CID Headquarters. "Run the plates. Find out who the truck belongs to and get me an after-duty hours contact number for the company."

After disconnecting, she and Colby entered the second building through an open doorway. Their flashlights illuminated inner walls that were framed but lacked drywall.

Colby pointed to his left. "You go that way. I'll head right." Neither of them spoke as they made their way through the maze of two by fours. The only sounds within the building were their muffled footfalls on the concrete-slab floor and the wind that blew through the open doorway.

They met up at the far end of the structure. A rustle caused them to turn their lights on a rodent scurrying for shelter.

"That's one culprit we don't need to follow." Colby chuckled and then flexed his shoulders, hoping to ease the growing tension in his neck.

"I keep thinking that abandoned maintenance van might be important," Becca said as they exited the building and retraced their steps to the fire scene.

Sergeant Flanders looked up as they neared. "Find anything?"

"One of the construction vans," she said. "We're running the plates and getting a phone number for the company. Probably an Atlanta-based firm that landed the building contract."

"Any sign of the driver?" he asked.

Colby shook his head. "We searched the building. It's clean."

"Maybe the guy caught a ride home with a buddy."

The fire chief hustled toward them. He was tall with serious eyes that stared at them from under his helmet. "The fire's contained. I'll have some of my guys keep watch throughout the night. We don't want any hot embers to rekindle. One of my men is checking out something he saw in the unoccupied apartment on the bottom floor."

The chief's tone caused Colby's gut to tighten. He sensed the entire investigation was about to change.

A younger man in full turnout gear approached the chief. "There's a problem, sir. We found a body in the rubble."

Colby turned to look at Becca. This time she didn't avert her gaze. Instead she stared back at him.

"Was it Jacob?" she had whispered earlier.

Did the dead victim have anything to do with Becca?

"Hurry up and wait" was a standing joke in the army, although there was nothing funny about waiting for the medical examiner to arrive on site. After inspecting the body, he scheduled an autopsy for the following afternoon.

Crime-scene tape surrounded Becca's quarters. A name tag found on the victim identified him as the project manager for Peachtree Construction Company.

At this point, foul play couldn't be ruled out, but the most likely explanation was an accidental gas leak. Either the project manager had entered the unoccupied apartment suspecting a problem or had caused a malfunction once he was inside.

Becca kept thinking of what could have happened had she not awakened. Dark thoughts she had no reason to mention. Certainly not to Special Agent Voss, who hadn't left her side since the explosion.

His presence played havoc with her internal calm. She needed space and a few moments to compose her tired and confused mind. The reoccurring dream of running from Jacob Yoder continued to haunt her. She sighed in an attempt to distance herself from the memory.

"Something wrong?" Colby asked.

Becca shook her head.

"You need some rest."

"I'm fine." A statement she had uttered too many times tonight. She wasn't used to having someone underfoot, although she did appreciate his concern.

"The chief reserved a room for you at the Lodge, Becca. It's time you headed there."

Special Agent in Charge Craig Wilson had arrived onsite shortly after Arnold's body had been uncovered. The CID commander now stood talking to the post provost marshal and Special Agents Jamison Steele and Brody Goodman.

Wilson was a tall African-American with broad shoulders and an innate ability to hone in on pertinent information that often solved a case. The high regard with which he was held in the entire CID was one of the reasons Becca had accepted the Georgia assignment. She could learn much under his direction.

Tonight she feared her credibility had been compromised. Wilson kept telling her to get out of the cold, yet he hadn't mentioned the temperature to Colby nor to the other CID personnel on scene.

Maybe it was the oversize coat she wore and the baggy sweatpants that made her seem needy. Something she never wanted to be.

Wilson slapped the provost marshal's back and nodded to Jamison and Brody before he walked purposefully toward where Becca stood.

"I've assigned Brody the lead on the death investigation."

She nodded. "Yes, sir."

"You were the only occupant of the BOQ, Becca. Any chance the explosion was targeted at you?"

"I'm not sure, sir."

"Has there been something in the past, a person who's given you trouble, someone who threatened to do you harm?"

"There was an incident in my youth, sir, but that person died some years ago."

Wilson rubbed his jaw. "It might be prudent to run down anyone you've arrested in the past few years, especially those who were incarcerated. Let's ensure you can account for anyone who might have a grudge to bear."

"Yes, sir."

The chief glanced at Colby. "Becca's new to post and doesn't know the surrounding area. Look into the explosion, Colby, and ensure it doesn't have anything to do with her past."

"I can handle it, sir," Becca objected.

Wilson's eyes narrowed. "Of course you can, but this might get personal. I want Colby to watch your back."

"But, sir   "

"Time for all of us to call it a night," Wilson said before she could state her objection. "The military police will guard the building. The crime-scene folks plan to go over the area as soon as the fire marshal gives them the okay. In spite of the investigation, General Cameron wants every available unit on post to participate in the half marathon tomorrow." He paused and stared at Colby. "You signed up to represent the CID?"

Colby nodded. "Yes, sir. Becca did, as well."

Wilson turned to her. "No need for you to run, if you don't feel up to it."

"I'm fine, sir."

"Then I'll see you both after the race."

As Wilson headed to his car, Colby touched Becca's arm. "There's nothing more we can do tonight. I'll drive you to the Lodge."

She shook her head, frustrated at being coddled by not only Colby but also the chief. "Thanks, but I can drive myself. Besides I'll need my car in the morning."

The half marathon had been organized as a way to foster good relations between the town and military community, one of a series of events scheduled for the upcoming year that had the post commanding general's full support.

Colby smiled. "The least I can do is follow you home."

She shook her head. "Really, it's not necessary."

Either the tone of her voice or her narrowed gaze caused him to take a step back.

He raised his hands, palms out, and shrugged. "Of course, you're fine. I'll talk to you tomorrow."

Colby turned and headed to his car, leaving her

standing in the parking lot. Hot tears burned her eyes, but she blinked them back and fisted her hands. For some reason, she hadn't wanted him to leave.

Chapter 3

*O*nly a little farther!

Becca pushed harder, her focus on the finish line. One more hill to climb to complete the 13.1K run, her first competition since she had arrived at Fort Rickman.

The cheers of the people lining the streets melded into a single roar that accompanied her up the incline. At the crest of the hill, she sucked air into her lungs, appreciating her body's response to the need for more oxygen.

The finish line lay fifty yards ahead.

Her time was good. Not good enough to win, but nothing to be ashamed of, either.

One last sprint. She kept her eyes on the goal. The Freemont running club official said something over the loudspeaker. Probably her number.

Her footfalls pounded the pavement.

Left, right, left, right...
Inhale, exhale. Inhale, exhale.
Everything faded into a blur.
Push. Harder. Faster.

She broke across the finish. Cheers erupted around her. Her body relaxed, and her pace slowed. She loped through a roped-off chute that would take her to one of the running club volunteers.

"Rebecca."

Someone from the sidelines called her name. A deep voice she knew too well. Fear tightened her spine.

She whipped her head to the right, the direction from which the voice had sounded, and stared into the crowd, searching for a face she would never forget. The face of a man—no, a monster—who had destroyed everything and everyone she had ever loved.

She scanned the bystanders—wives with babes in arms, parents and grandparents waving at their favorite runners, shopkeepers and community leaders support-ing the town's first attempt to host the sporting event.

Surely her ears were playing tricks on her.

She would never forget the deep, almost soothing quality of his voice that persuaded even those most de-termined not to succumb to his diabolical charm.

Evil packed in a handsome face and muscular body.

Goose bumps pimpled her flesh. Despite the exer-tion, she shivered.

Someone shoved a plastic cup into her hand. "Water?" the guy asked.

She switched her gaze to the man and his out-stretched hand. An older gentleman with kindly eyes.

Not Jacob.

"Great run," the man offering water enthused.

Nodding her appreciation, she took the cup and headed farther along the narrowing chute, still studying the crowd, unable to abandon her search.

She had heard Jacob's voice.

A high school volunteer checked the clipboard in his hand and marked off her number.

He pointed her toward the refreshment area. "Sports drinks are available at the table ahead. Burgers and dogs are on the grill when you feel like eating."

She downed the water, tossed the glass in a nearby trash receptacle and slipped through the crowd of those who had already finished the run.

"Good run." Another voice, one she also recognized.

She turned to see Colby approaching her, his angular face still flushed. His group had started ahead of hers.

"With so many runners, I didn't think I'd see you this morning." His smile was warm, but his eyes were serious as if he were searching her face for some sign of weakness. He'd worn the same intense expression last night when he'd found her on the knoll immediately after the explosion.

"No reason to pass up a good race," she offered, hoping he wouldn't push for details.

"You were pretty worn out last night. You should have slept in."

She reached for another cup of water on a nearby table. "I could say the same for you."

He nodded. "You're right, but no reason to pass up a race."

She smiled in spite of herself. "You heard Chief Wilson last night," she offered as further reason for participating today. "He wanted everyone to support the event."

Once again, she flicked her gaze to the crowd. "Did you hear anything new from the fire marshal?"

"Only that he'll check the site this morning. The Atlanta construction company provided the name of the project manager. Ralph Arnold."

"The truck belonged to him?"

Colby nodded. "The Freemont chief of police asked for a court order to search the trailer he rented in town. They expect it to be signed by noon. I'll head that way later this morning"

"Give me the address. I'll meet you there."

"No reason to take two cars." He glanced at his watch. "I'll pick you up at the Lodge, say at eleven o'clock. We can stop by your old BOQ first and still arrive at Arnold's place ahead of the local police."

Glancing at her watch, she nodded. "That works for me."

Becca needed to buy a few items she'd lost in the fire, including a pair of flats to wear with the civilian clothes worn by the CID, instead of a military uniform.

Maybe Colby was right. She was pushing too hard, but it was the only way she knew how to operate. Move forward. Don't look back. Don't think of what could have been. Don't allow anyone to get too close.

Then she glanced at Colby, seeing again that questioning lift of his brow. She would have to be extra careful to guard her past when he was around. For some reason, he seemed to sense the disquiet she carried in her heart.

After saying a quick goodbye, she turned toward the crowd, hoping her abruptness signaled her desire to be alone.

Coming back may have been a mistake.

Supposedly Jacob was dead and buried.

But Colby Voss was very much alive, and although the two men were polar opposites, they both posed a danger.

Jacob did because of the memories that tangled her dreams and impacted her life. Colby Voss was a danger in a completely different way, but she needed to guard against his charisma and his show of concern for her, just the same.

As she made her way through the crowd, her focus shifted back to Jacob.

He was dead.

She hoped.

Colby pulled to a stop at the red light, thinking of the warning signs that had flashed through his mind since he'd met Becca. If only she would lower her guard around him just a bit. Case in point, last night when she'd refused his offer to follow her to the Lodge.

Stubborn pride is what he called it, although not to her face. In truth, it was possibly her dislike of appearing weak or fear of revealing too much about herself. Now that Wilson had tasked them to investigate the explosion's tie-in with her past, Colby hoped to find a way to work with her and not against her.

Frustrated though he had been last night, he had hung back until she left the BOQ parking lot and had followed her to the Lodge. He'd made sure she arrived at the transient billets safe and sound and watched as she scurried inside. Lights came on in an upstairs room, and he'd seen her at the window before she closed the drapes.

Relieved to know she was safe, he'd driven home.

Sleep had eluded him, and he'd spent a great portion of the night focused on Becca Miller and her determination to take care of herself.

Strong women were a challenge, to say the least.

He'd made that mistake once before and still carried the scars. Not physical, but painful nonetheless.

Foolish of him to have thought Ellen would change when they were both deployed in Afghanistan. Her independence and desire to go it alone had forced him to transfer to another forward operating base.

A mistake that haunted him still.

No matter how hard he worked to move on, the reality of what had happened was never far below the surface.

Meeting Becca had brought those memories to light again. Unresolved issues, his sister called them, but then she knew him too well. As much as he treasured their close sibling relationship, he didn't appreciate her uncanny ability to recognize his struggle.

Surely Becca Miller couldn't sense the undercurrent of his life. He prided himself on his outward control and on being a law enforcement officer who got the job done.

Turning into the Lodge parking area this morning, he saw Becca standing in front of the building. She glanced impatiently at her watch.

He checked the dashboard clock. One minute past eleven. Did she think he was late?

Pulling to a stop, he reached across the passenger seat and opened the far door from the inside. Equal footing was what she wanted, which he would give her. Becca was a fellow army investigator. End of story.

So then why did he breathe in the flowery scent of

her shampoo and take a second deep breath as if to ensure what he smelled was real and not his imagination?

He reached forward to help her click the seat belt in place. Their hands touched, sending a ripple of electricity up his arm. Nothing about Becca was his imagination. She was tall and slender, lean in a fit way but not too skinny, with a graceful neck and shoulder-length brown hair streaked with auburn.

She turned and greeted him, but his focus honed in on her green eyes, tired but bright.

"Did you get something to eat?" he asked.

"A couple power bars."

"You want some coffee. Maybe a burger at the drive-through?"

"Only if you do."

"I ate earlier at the race." Not that he couldn't eat again, but they were on a tight schedule, and he didn't want the Freemont police to arrive at the project manager's trailer ahead of them.

"Dental records should come in later today to officially ID Ralph Arnold's body," he told her as he pulled onto the main road and headed to her former BOQ.

"Have they contacted the next of kin?"

"A wife who lives in Marietta, just north of Atlanta. She talked to her husband yesterday evening. He was working late and had hoped to finish sometime before midnight and then drive home for the weekend."

"Now he's dead." Becca tsked. "I feel for the wife. Did they have kids?"

"Two boys."

"Growing up without a father will be tough."

Colby had to agree. "The question we need to answer is what was he doing in the vacant apartment?"

The fire marshal and two MPs were searching Becca's BOQ when they pulled into the quad parking lot.

"Find anything?" Colby asked after he and Becca had introduced themselves and flashed their identification.

"Nothing yet, but watch your step." The marshal pointed to the burned rubble covering the floor. "No way of telling if Mr. Arnold caused the problem or tried to fix what was amiss when he arrived."

"Wouldn't he have called in a gas leak and notified the fire department?" Colby asked.

"More than likely," the fire marshal said. "And if he'd used his cell when he was inside, a spark from his phone could have caused the explosion."

The marshal was a slender guy with bushy eyebrows. He glanced at Becca over the top of his glasses.

"After you smelled gas, Special Agent Miller, you told the MP last night that you exited through the rear of the building." He pursed his lips for a long moment. "Why didn't you use the front door?"

"My first thought was to get out. The back door was closer."

"Then you called CID Headquarters instead of 911?" the marshal pressed.

She nodded. "The number was programmed on my phone. I knew the person on duty could and would notify both the fire department and the military police immediately. Emergency operators ask questions that can delay the process."

The marshal raised his bushy brows. "We have an excellent emergency response system at Fort Rickman."

"That's good to know. I'll use it next time."

As if satisfied with her response, the marshal walked

through the gaping hole between the two apartments and headed into the adjoining kitchen. Becca and Colby followed him into the living area of the unoccupied unit.

The stench of smoke and burned plastic hung in the air. Becca coughed to clear her lungs. Bending down, she brushed some debris aside.

Colby edged closer. "What did you find?"

"Glass shards."

"An overhead light fixture perhaps," he mused.

"Maybe, but most lights are opaque or frosted." She glanced at an opening in the nearby wall. "Guess what used to be here?"

Colby stepped back to view the entire room and realized where she was headed. "The front door."

"That's right. Flanked by panes of clear glass."

Colby knew the significance of finding the glass within the house. "If the panes had blown with the explosion, the shards would be outside the footprint of the structure."

"But they're inside," she said, her face drawn. "The shattered glass makes me think someone else was in the apartment. Someone who had broken one of the glass panes to gain entry into the apartment before the explosion."

"Ralph Arnold had a key to the unit." Colby glanced again at where the front door had been. "If Arnold noticed the broken window, he may have entered the unit to determine what had happened and inadvertently surprised the intruder."

"And was killed for that reason," Becca added. "Then the perpetrator turned on the gas. The explosion covered up any evidence he left behind."

"Evidence and a dead body. But if that's the case, then why was the perpetrator here in the first place?"

Becca didn't want to share her suspicions with Colby. She wasn't ready to discuss her past and the man she had run from years ago.

Had Jacob Yoder found her? If so, he'd entered the vacant apartment earlier in the day and had holed up until she came home from work and eventually headed to bed.

The project manager had surprised Jacob, but Arnold wasn't the target of last night's explosion.

Becca was.

Chapter 4

Becca was eager to find something—anything—to refute her theory about being the target of last night's explosion. If only she could uncover incriminating evidence in the project manager's trailer that would point to his involvement in an illegal operation. Drug smuggling, embezzlement, even human trafficking. Bottom line, she needed a motive for his death that would draw attention away from her.

She and Colby arrived at the trailer and were joined by two officers from the Freemont Police Department. Wearing vinyl gloves, they searched all the logical places where a perpetrator would hide anything he didn't want the police to find.

When their search proved futile, Becca turned to more ingenious hiding spots, but even then she found nothing that seemed questionable.

If she couldn't uncover evidence relevant to a crime, her initial assumption about Jacob Yoder being alive might prove true, which made her even more determined to keep looking.

After searching Arnold's bedroom, she pounded her fist against the wall.

"Take it easy, Becca," Colby cautioned from the hallway.

Undeterred by his comment, she tapped again. "Hear that hollow sound? It could be a secret hiding compartment."

Brody ran his fingers over the walls and stood close enough for her to notice his aftershave. She took a step back, needing to keep her focus on the search instead of his strong hands and the heady scent that wafted around her.

Eventually, he shook his head. "The wall's secure. No cubby holes. No secret hiding spots. Let's keep looking."

He was right, of course, yet she was frustrated by the fruitless search as well as her less than professional response to Colby's nearness. She moved into the living area, forcing her thoughts back to the case. Nothing could be ruled out at his point, but even the idea of a drug deal gone south seemed remote.

The trailer had been in pristine condition when they first arrived. Neat and tidy with a number of scrapbooks containing pictures of Mr. Arnold receiving awards from his superiors. Religious books were stacked on the coffee table, as well as a scattering of pictures of his wife and kids, all of which indicated that he was a salt-of-the-earth type of guy. A well-worn Bible lay on the couch as if he'd read scripture before he had left for work.

More than likely, Arnold's death was a wrong-place, wrong-time incident. Making his rounds last night, he had seen the broken windowpane and entered the BOQ to check it out, never expecting the perpetrator to be inside. Instead he should have called the military police on post and asked them to investigate.

As Colby drove them back to post, Becca kept her eyes on the road ahead instead of on him. She was becoming much too interested in Colby, and instead, she needed to come up with a logical reason for the initial break-in. She quickly narrowed it down to two options. Either the killer entered the empty BOQ because he wanted a place to hole up overnight, or he was there to do her harm.

"You're quiet." Colby broke the silence. "Want to share what you're thinking?"

Exactly what she didn't want to do.

She tried to act nonchalant. "Just wondering about the killer."

"Anyone giving you a hard time recently?" He flicked a sideways glance her way. "We make enemies in this business. Wilson said as much last night. Is there someone who has a beef with you? Someone you sent to prison and now he's out? Even an old boyfriend who wasn't happy when you dumped him?"

"No old boyfriend."

Colby nodded as if relieved, which made her smile.

"That's one down," he said. "Anyone grumbling about being set up or complaining you pushed too hard?"

"Probably everyone I've arrested."

"Do you remember anyone who was more vocal than the rest, more agitated, more out to seek revenge?"

She shook her head. "No one comes to mind."

"You're sure?"

"Yes, I'm sure." She straightened her skirt, still frustrated with her own response to his nearness. "You sound as if I'm under interrogation."

"Of course not. It's just—" He tapped the steering wheel. "I get this feeling you're holding something back. Is there anything you're not telling me that might have relevance to this investigation?"

If only she could tell him about Jacob, but an investigation depended on facts and not some pie-in-the-sky suspicion that a buried killer could come back to life.

Becca had worked hard to get to this point in her career and still walked a tight rope to fit in with a predominantly male work group. She didn't need to spout nonsensical supposition.

"As we both know," she offered, hoping it would ease the tension between them. "The simplest explanation is often the one that proves true. The guy who broke in probably needed a place to hole up overnight. He could have been cold and tried to light the stove to keep warm. If the pilot light was out, the gas could have filled the apartment and caused the explosion."

Colby glanced at her. "And this homeless guy seeks refuge on an army post complete with gate checks and 24/7 security?"

"I admit it doesn't sound likely." He was right. Security was tight on Fort Rickman. If the project manager hadn't seen the broken window, the military police would have.

"You want to hear my theory?" he asked.

She licked her lips, not knowing what to expect. "Okay."

"The perp was interested in you, Becca."

She held up her hand. "That's ridiculous."

"I beg to differ. It's the most plausible explanation." He hesitated and then added, "Anything in your past that could play into the explosion?"

He wouldn't let up, and she couldn't chance what would happen if he knew the truth. "Not that I know of."

"You were fearful last night when the fire was raging, and when we were walking to my BOQ you mentioned some guy's name."

"I don't remember saying anything specific. Besides, my new home was going up in flames. It wasn't that I was fearful, Colby. I was relieved to have gotten out alive."

He nodded. "My oldest sister—her name's Gloria—claims I survived Afghanistan because of her prayers and God's mercy. He must have been watching over you last night."

Thoughts of her own sister made her eyes burn with unexpected tears. She turned her gaze to the side window, not wanting Colby to notice.

His hand reached for hers. "Did I say something wrong?"

For a guy, he had a keen knack of sensing her emotional struggle. Plus, his touch was reassuring, yet she didn't want to seem like an emotional female. In truth, a lot had happened and if she added fatigue to the mix, she could almost forgive herself for appearing weak.

"My…my sister died eight years ago. I keep thinking I've worked through my grief, then something happens and it rushes back again."

"Look, I'm sorry. I didn't mean to make you cry."

"You didn't do anything wrong, and I'm glad Gloria prayed for you." She offered him a weak smile, hoping her face wasn't blotched and her nose beet red from the tears.

"My father always said I was headstrong, but my sister, Katie, claimed I just needed prayer to keep me in line. In hindsight, it was probably wanderlust that got me in trouble at home and made the military seem a natural way of life."

"You transferred to Fort Rickman from Germany?"

She nodded, relieved the conversation had moved to neutral ground. "I asked to work for Chief Wilson. There was an opening, and I got my first choice of assignments."

"Which means your record is excellent or you wouldn't have been selected for the job."

"Maybe it was my sister's prayers finally coming to fruition."

He smiled and squeezed her hand again, a reassuring gesture, she told herself, that any friend would offer.

They rode in silence for a few minutes before he asked, "Did you meet Dawson Timmons when he stopped by the office last week?"

She remembered both him and his wife. "Nice guy. His wife Lillie was equally so. They invited me to the barbecue at his farm."

"Just about everyone in CID Headquarters will be there."

"It was kind of them to include me."

"They're good folks. I served with Dawson at Fort Hood. He transferred here and met Lillie. Now he's out of the army, owns a farm and is living the good life."

"A soldier turned farmer." Becca smiled. "His wife must have changed his mind about law enforcement."

"Actually, he claims to love working the soil." Colby thought for a moment before asking, "Why don't I pick you up tomorrow? We can drive there together. That way you won't have to worry about getting directions."

"Dawson drew a map for me when he was in the office. Between that and my GPS, it shouldn't be difficult to find."

"Call me if you change your mind."

Becca didn't believe in mixing business with her social life. No reason to give folks anything to talk about, especially when she already seemed much too affected by the special agent.

The Lodge appeared on the left. Colby turned into the parking lot. "Did you get the memo about Monday and Tuesday being training holidays?"

"I did." Becca opened the passenger door and stepped onto the sidewalk. "We'll probably be working on the investigation both days. Thanks for the ride."

She waved goodbye and waited until Colby drove away before she dug in her purse for her phone and hurried to her car. Once behind the wheel, she called the former sheriff in Harmony, Alabama.

"McDougal," a raspy voice answered.

"Sir, you may not remember me. I grew up in the Amish community. Now I'm with the Criminal Investigation Division at Fort Rickman, Georgia. There's been a crime on post that may be related to my father and sister's murders."

"Rebecca Mueller, is that you?"

"Yes, sir. Although I go by Becca Miller now."

"What can I do for you?"

"I'm driving to Harmony this afternoon and should be there in a couple hours. I'd like to talk to you about the case."

"I retired and don't have access to any of the old files, although I'd be happy to see you."

She glanced at her watch. "I need to stop by Elizabeth Konig's house first. It might be late afternoon before I get to your place."

"Do you mind telling me what you want to discuss?"

"Whether Jacob Yoder could still be alive."

Colby left the Lodge parking area and turned onto the main road irritated with himself. Once again, he thought of Becca's flushed cheeks and eyes brimming with tears. Grief was insidious, like a sly fox that doesn't want to be seen, until something flushes the animal into the open. His sister had a way of bringing his own pain to light by often saying the one thing that reminded him too much of Ellen.

Death was so…

He hunted for the right word.

Final.

He'd learned that the hard way. Evidently, Becca still had more to learn. From now on, he'd try to be more sensitive to her feelings.

At least, they'd talked openly about her security. Colby planned to keep revisiting the subject until he was convinced she realized the danger she might be in.

A good CID agent had a list of enemies. Becca was no different. Yet she hadn't been forthright about any investigation or arrests that ended badly. Call it his sixth sense, but he distinctly felt she was holding something back.

Jacob? He had heard her mention the name last night, yet she'd denied it.

While searching the trailer today, she'd been like a coon dog hot on the prey's trail. Only they had uncovered nothing of interest, not even a shred of evidence that would raise suspicion. Brody Goodman, one of the other special agents, had checked into Arnold's past. The man's record was lily-white. No arrests. No trouble with the law. Not even a traffic violation. He served as a deacon in his church and was voted favorite coach of his son's Little League.

Yet Becca had insisted if they looked long enough, something would be uncovered, and when they returned to post empty-handed, she'd seemed withdrawn and mildly agitated. Perhaps she had hoped Arnold would be found culpable to take the heat off her. The project manager might have stumbled upon the perp, but Arnold wasn't the reason the guy had been hiding in the BOQ in the first place. Seemed logical that he'd been there because of Becca. Which Colby had mentioned, and she had tried to refute.

He pulled to a stop at an intersection and thought back to her clipped speech and guarded eyes. Becca was an unknown entity. She had transferred from an overseas assignment and had never served previously with any of the Fort Rickman special agents. As much as Colby wanted to believe she was competent, she could be involved in something suspect.

The light changed. He picked up his cell and tapped in the number for CID Headquarters. Sergeant Raynard Otis answered. "Ray, put me through to the boss."

Once Wilson came on the line, Colby filled him in on the clean search of Arnold's trailer. "Sir, I'm concerned Special Agent Miller may have been the targeted victim of the explosion as you mentioned last night."

"Have you discussed your suspicions with her?"

"She's quick to discard the idea, which makes me concerned about her personal safety."

"I wanted her to work with you, Colby. Is that a problem?"

"Ah, no, sir."

"I realize this puts you in a difficult position. Especially if she's unwilling to realize she might be in danger. Keep tabs on her as best you can until we have a better picture of what happened last night. From the short time she's been with us, it's evident she guards her privacy. Make sure her self-sufficiency doesn't get her into trouble. Do you understand what I'm saying?"

"Yes, sir."

Colby disconnected and made a U-turn when the light changed. Wilson was right. He'd put Colby in a difficult position. Keep Becca safe when Becca didn't think she was in danger. Worse than that, she probably didn't want him around.

Approaching the Lodge, he noticed her silver Honda turn out of the parking lot, heading toward the main gate. Could be a long day if she was like his sisters and planned to spend time shopping.

Colby hadn't expected to play bodyguard to another CID agent. A waste of taxpayer money, in his opinion, but Wilson was in charge so he would comply.

Just so Becca didn't spot the tail.

Leaving post, she increased her speed and took a road that bypassed Freemont. He glanced down at his gas gauge relieved that he'd filled up at the Post Exchange gas station two days ago. Settling into his seat, he hung back a number of car lengths and accelerated to keep up with her. At the speed she was driving, Becca seemed determined to get somewhere fast.

Maybe she wasn't heading for the mall after all.

Colby programmed a selection of music CDs that filled the Chevy with country songs about lost loves and broken hearts. He sang along and tapped his hand against the steering wheel in time to the music.

Becca seemed oblivious to his tail, which concerned him. She should have been more observant. Wilson had been right. She needed someone to watch her back. Colby planned to do exactly that.

Nearly two hours passed before she slowed her speed. A road sign welcomed them to Harmony, Alabama. Becca drove to the center of town, turned onto a side road and braked to a stop in front of a small one-story ranch.

Colby pulled to the curb in front of a neighbor's house on the opposite side of the street. Turning off the ignition, he scooted down in the seat and watched Becca scurry along the sidewalk to the modest home. She glanced over her shoulder before she knocked.

He slumped down farther. The last thing Colby wanted was for Becca to realize she was under surveillance.

Chapter 5

Memories of riding to town in her *datt's* buggy flooded over Becca as she stood on Elizabeth Konig's front porch. The locals were used to the Amish way, but visitors and tourists, who came to town specifically to see the plain folks, frequently pointed and stared. Even at a very young age, Becca knew the Amish were different from the English.

In summer, she and her sister would romp barefoot through the tall grass and giggle at night when their father thought they were asleep. Instead they whiled away the hours, talking about their dreams for the future. Katie had wanted to marry and raise a family. Becca's aspirations included world travel. Too often, her dreams leapfrogged from one destination to another, each far beyond anything an Amish girl from Harmony could ever hope to experience.

Now, wrapped in the warmth of those bygone moments, Becca knocked on the front door and glanced beyond the well-manicured lawn to the grove of tall pecan trees that surrounded the property. A thick stand of pines clustered beyond the pecan grove and provided privacy, in spite of the in-town location.

Twenty years older than Becca, Elizabeth Konig had wanted more to life than staying on her father's farm or marrying one of the local Amish boys. She and Becca had that in common.

As a young woman, Elizabeth had left the Amish community and had taken a job in a local fabric store in town. An expert with needle and thread, she was soon teaching classes and making extra money with her sewing. She rented a small apartment in the basement of the shop where she worked and eventually inherited both the store and the owner's nearby home when her spinster boss passed away.

Not only was Elizabeth an accomplished seamstress, but she was also a gifted student and went on to graduate college by taking night classes.

Typically, Amish education ended at the eighth grade, but Becca's mother wanted more for her girls. Her dying wish had been for Elizabeth to homeschool her daughters. To his credit and out of deference to his deceased wife, her father had allowed Becca and Katie to continue their studies, and each girl had eventually earned her high school diploma.

When Becca had run away from Jacob the first time, she turned to Elizabeth for support. A friend as well as teacher, Elizabeth had driven Becca to the recruiting office in a neighboring town and had supported her decision to join the military, which had provided not only a livelihood but also a way for Becca to leave Harmony.

Three years later, Katie had called Becca from the seamstress's house. After her sister's murder, Becca had run back to Elizabeth. With the older woman's encouragement and support, Becca had notified the sheriff of the horrendous slaughter that had occurred at the Mueller farm, and Elizabeth had stayed with Becca during the interrogations that ensued.

Filled with gratitude for the pivotal role Elizabeth had played in her life, Becca smiled when she heard her dear friend's lyrical voice from inside the house.

A sense of homecoming stirred deep within Becca, and tears filled her eyes when the door opened.

"Oh, Rebecca, you've come home."

"Yah, Elizabeth. *Webishtew?* How are you?"

"Better now that you are here." The older woman wrapped her in a heartfelt embrace filled with love and welcome.

"You have grown even more beautiful." The older woman's eyes were damp when she pulled back to stare at Becca.

"You make me blush, Elizabeth."

"It is not prideful if I say it, Becca. Now come in," she insisted, opening the door even wider. "I just made a pot of tea. You must tell me what you are doing in Harmony."

The small living room and adjoining dining area were as meticulously cared for as when Becca had been there eight years earlier.

"Your store is doing well?" she asked as Elizabeth poured the tea.

"Well enough that I have ladies who help me. I usually go in twice a week to catch up."

"And you're happy?" Becca accepted the cup Elizabeth offered.

"Is that the question that troubles you after all these years?"

"There are other things I want to discuss, but first let's enjoy our tea."

The older woman placed the sugar bowl and spoon on the table in front of Becca. She relaxed in a chintz-covered chair, feeling at peace in the familiar surroundings. Even Elizabeth's motherly scrutiny brought comfort.

The older woman arranged a large slice of homemade pound cake on a delicate China plate and topped it with strawberry preserves. "Eat. You are too thin."

Becca laughed as she accepted the cake, enjoying the rich buttery taste mixed with the tart berries. As the two women sipped their tea, Becca shared highlights of her overseas journey before she got to the reason for her visit.

"I'm sorry I didn't write, Elizabeth. When I left after Katie and *Datt* died, I… I needed to leave everything behind."

Elizabeth took a sip from her cup. "You were running away from your past, but you are back now. That's what matters."

"Also…" Becca had to be careful how she broached the subject. "I was worried about your safety. I feared my letters could put you in danger."

"But how could that be?"

"Have you heard anything of Jacob Yoder?"

Elizabeth's eyes widened. "Why would I? He died years ago as you know."

"I believe the sheriff may have been wrong in identifying the body as Jacob's."

The older woman made a clucking sound as she patted Becca's hand. "You were never satisfied with life as it was and always searched for something more. You must accept what Chief McDougal told you and not fear the past."

"I survived what happened, Elizabeth. The past has no hold on me. What I fear is that Jacob is alive." Becca explained about the explosion and hearing his all-too-familiar voice at the Freemont race.

"Accidents happen even with modern gas appliances," Elizabeth insisted. "And surely the voice you heard belonged to someone else."

Becca had hoped Elizabeth would side with her, but inwardly, she knew her theory about the burial mix-up was hard to grasp, even for such a dear friend.

"I'm going to talk to those who live near the Yoder farm," Becca said. "Someone might have information."

"They will not be open with their welcome."

"I know that all too well." Becca had left the community and severed ties with her past. She would not be accepted back unless she repented and asked forgiveness for leaving the Amish way of life. Neither of which she planned to do.

After finishing the tea, Becca stood and hugged her friend once again. "There are so few people with whom I can openly talk about the past, Elizabeth. Thank you for listening."

"You are like family, Becca. Come back often."

Outside, the winter sun hung low in the sky. Becca

raised her hand to shield the glare from her eyes. With her gaze averted, she almost ran headfirst into someone leaning against her car.

Looking up, she gasped. "Colby?"

A swirl of emotion rose up within her. Confusion. Frustration. Anger. "What are you doing here?" she demanded.

She glanced around and spied his car parked across the street on the next block. Her eyes widened. "You followed me here."

"I wanted to help," he offered.

She squared her shoulders and shoved her jaw forward with determination. "I don't need your help, if it includes secrecy and duplicity."

"What you need is to realize you're in danger," he countered, sounding as frustrated as she felt. "Traipsing all over the countryside isn't smart, especially if someone's after you. You didn't know I was behind you because you were so focused on driving here that you failed to notice my tail. That means someone wishing to do you harm could have followed you, as well."

She stared at him, weighing what he had just said. Her anger dissipated somewhat as she realized he was right. Had she been so centered on seeing Elizabeth that she hadn't thought of her own personal safety?

Silence settled between them for a long moment before Colby asked, "Do you mind shedding a little light on why you're here?"

When she didn't respond, he stepped closer. "Come on, Becca. We're both interested in finding out what happened on post. What aren't you telling me that might have bearing on the explosion and murder?"

She shook her head, still not willing to reveal anything to Colby. "My past doesn't play into the investigation."

"You're parsing words."

Which she was, but she didn't know if she could trust him. She never talked about growing up Amish to anyone in the military. Not that she told untruths. Rather, she provided information only on a need-to-know basis.

Becca stared into his eyes, expecting agitation or anger. Instead she was touched by the depth of concern and strength of compassion she saw.

Confrontation would be easier to handle.

Jacob Yoder scared her, but being defenseless around Colby Voss scared her, as well.

"When do you plan to drive back to Fort Rickman?" Colby asked, hoping she would reply at least to that one question.

She dropped her hands. Her guard seemed to slip at the same time.

"Later this evening," she said, all the while trying to step around him.

He moved in front of her, blocking her way.

"Colby, please."

"Please what, Becca? Please don't interfere? We've had a murder on post, and the killer may have been stalking you. I need answers to questions you aren't willing to talk about, like what he was doing in the quadruplex last night, and why you came here and what you hoped to find. I thought we were working together."

She stared at him long and hard as if determined to elude his questions, yet he wouldn't be brushed aside.

Nor would he stop staring into her pretty but confused green eyes. She eventually blinked, which seemed to open the dam that had held her in check. Her lips quivered. She wrapped her arms around her waist and blinked back tears that made him want to reach for her.

"My sister was murdered eight years ago. So was my father." The words tumbled out as if of their own volition.

Colby kept his expression passive. Inside he felt like she'd punched him in the gut. He hadn't seen that coming.

"Jacob Yoder, the man who killed them, died in a house fire that same night." Becca spoke rapidly as if she needed to pour out the information before she had second thoughts. "His wife also succumbed to the blaze. The local sheriff called it a murder-suicide and closed the case."

"Which you thought needed to remain open?"

"I'm not sure the body they found in the burned rubble was the killer's."

Colby didn't want to stop the flow of information or deflate her determination of getting at the truth, but chances were good that the body was who the old sheriff said it was. Errors happened, but logic made him wonder if Becca was digging up something that had been buried for a reason.

"What about dental records?" he asked, hoping to gently expose the fallacy in her supposition.

She shook her head. "None were available."

"DNA?"

"It wasn't done."

"An autopsy?"

"Both bodies were buried without a medical examination."

Becca bit her lower lip and stared at him intently.

She was waiting for a response. He didn't want to provide false hope at this point and decided posing another question might be the safest tactic.

"If the body wasn't that of the killer, whose was it, Becca?"

"That's what I need to determine and why I plan to talk to Jacob's neighbors."

Colby glanced at the row of small homes lining the quiet residential street. "Townspeople who live nearby?"

"Folks from the country."

Horses' hooves clip-clopped over the pavement. Becca turned at the sound. A young girl, not more than twelve or thirteen sat in the seat of a buggy next to an older bearded man.

"There's something you need to know." Becca pointed to the Amish lass. "That young girl? When I look at her, I see myself. In those days, I was Rebecca Mueller. I lived on a farm with my father and sister, Katie. I rode in a buggy, Colby, because I grew up Amish."

Becca couldn't stop talking.

For too many years, she had bottled up the past and ignored her early life. Now that she had revealed the truth to Colby, she wanted him to understand the way her life had been.

Colby took her arm and hurried her along the sidewalk toward where he had parked his car. All the while, she continued to fill him in on her father and sister, their farm, their poverty. She stopped when he opened the passenger door.

"Get in, Becca. If you're determined to visit Jacob's neighbors, then I'm driving. I don't want you on some back road all by yourself. Especially if Jacob is alive. We'll return for your car later."

A sense of relief swept over her. "Then you believe me?"

"I don't know what to believe at this point. But I know you see a connection between what happened to your family and the explosion at Fort Rickman. We're working together so I'm in this with you."

At least Colby was being honest, which she appreciated. Plus, he was willing to consider her theory about Jacob. Having a second investigator reviewing her father and sister's deaths as well as the farmhouse fire that had claimed two lives would be beneficial. Maybe Colby would pick up something she had overlooked.

Something else took hold as Becca directed him out of town and along a narrow road that headed into the country. A sense of connection. She had been alone for so long. Having Colby at her side meant she could share the workload as well as the anxiousness that frequently welled up within her when she dealt with a death case.

Her father had talked about his own anxiety after her mother had died. Too often he grumbled at having no one with whom to share the load, the work, the worry about the farm or what he often referred to as his *cross*. Simon of Cyrene had helped Christ, her father had frequently groused, but he had no one.

Becca had been hard-pressed to find a comparison between her father's situation and the Lord's, yet she couldn't escape the sense of guilt he seemed willing to place on her shoulders. The guilt of her not doing enough or being strong enough or being born the wrong gender had turned into a constant litany around the Mueller house.

Now that she had shared some of her past with Colby, that crush of guilt eased. He was a good man with a finely honed sense of right and wrong and a desire to keep her safe, which she appreciated.

Becca had never wanted a man's protection, no doubt due to her own history with her father and Jacob. She'd always taken care of herself, but ever since she'd met Colby, she'd felt an inner tug to give up some of her insistence on control.

At times, the feeling scared her, but at the moment, she was overcome with relief.

"Will the neighbors want to talk?" Colby asked as they drove into the country.

"I'm not sure. They'll remember I left them eight years ago, in spite of what happened to my father and sister."

Cresting a hill, a patchwork of farms appeared in the distance along with a line of cars that passed them as they headed deeper into Amish country.

"Things have changed," Becca said as a minivan and two four-door sedans sped past. "This area used to be peaceful and isolated. Looks like tourists enamored with the plain life are flocking here now."

Colby hadn't expected traffic this far from town.

"What happened to your family's place?" he asked.

"I've held on to it. The house isn't much and the little bit of land my father owned was unproductive. A local developer was interested in buying the property, but I was getting ready to deploy and never replied to his request."

Becca pointed to the upcoming intersection.

"Turn right at the next road and stop at the first farmhouse. The Hershberger property adjoins Yoder's farm. Sarah Hershberger was an old friend. I'm hoping she'll talk to me today."

A woman stood at the side of the two-story structure, hanging laundry on a clothesline. Seeing the car pull into her drive, she scurried toward her house as if eager to get inside.

Becca called to her as she and Colby stepped from the car. The Amish woman was as tall as Becca and pretty in a homespun way with her long dress, apron and bonnet. She glanced at Colby with some sense of hesitancy as Becca motioned him forward.

Once Becca had made the introductions, Sarah flicked her gaze to the nearby road and motioned them toward her home. "You must come inside. I'm not sure who might be watching."

"You're worried?" he asked.

"It would be better if others don't see me talking to Rebecca. She left the community and turned her back on the Amish way. I accepted her decision. Some do not."

Yet, Sarah was ushering them into her house.

The main room was large with a long, hardwood table and benches that appeared hand hewn.

She pulled the curtains closed before she pointed to the table. "Sit. Please. Do you wish something to drink?"

Becca held up her hand. "We just need to ask you a few questions."

Sarah tugged at the edge of her apron and scooted onto the bench across from them. "What is it you need to know?"

"Jacob Yoder," Becca said.

Sarah studied her friend with serious eyes. "What are you asking, Rebecca?"

"I'm asking if you've seen him."

"The sheriff would know. You should talk to him."

"He'll tell me Jacob is dead," Becca insisted. "I need the truth."

"The truth is not always easy to tell." Sarah licked her lips. "The day before your father and Katie were killed... The day before the Yoder house burned, someone knocked at our door."

"Go on," Becca encouraged.

Colby's pulse kicked up a notch, realizing the importance of what she was about to share.

"A man asked for Jacob," Sarah continued. "I told him he had the wrong house. He said he was Ezekiel Yoder. Jacob's brother."

Colby leaned closer. "Did you see Ezekiel after the fire?"

"No."

"You're sure it was Jacob's brother?"

"That's who he said he was. I would not make this up."

"Of course not." Becca patted her old friend's hand and kept her voice neutral. "Did anyone else know about Jacob's brother?"

The Amish woman shrugged. "I do not know. No one has mentioned him."

"What about Jacob?" Colby asked.

Sarah wiped her hand across the smooth surface of the polished table as if brushing aside crumbs. "I—I thought I saw Jacob."

"Where?"

"Here. I had washed my husband's work clothes and had them hanging on the line outside."

"As you did today?" Colby asked.

She nodded. "*Yah.* I peered from my window and saw someone grab a shirt and trousers off the clothesline. He glanced up before he ran away, but I do not think he saw me through the glass."

"You told no one?" Becca said.

"I feared Jacob would come back."

"So you recognized the man?" Colby asked. "It was Jacob Yoder?"

Sarah nodded, her eyes wide. "It was Jacob."

"Could it have been Ezekiel instead?" he pressed.

"No."

"How can you be sure?"

Sarah glanced at Becca. "You know Jacob. He is handsome. Remember how you said he made you feel when he looked at you."

Becca's cheeks flushed. She glanced at Colby and then back at Sarah. "Are you sure Jacob stole the clothing?"

"I am sure."

"Did you think he might harm you?" Colby asked.

"*Yah,* I was afraid. I knew about Katie's death. Becca's father, too. Everyone was worried."

"Did you tell the police?"

"I told no one."

"Your husband?" Becca asked.

Sarah shook her head. "I feared for Samuel's safety. He does not know."

"Yet you're telling us this now?"

"Because you were one of us, Rebecca. You will find him."

Becca glanced at Colby. The look of determination on her face told him more than any words could. Jacob Yoder was probably alive, just as she had believed all along. If he had his sights set on Becca, Colby would have to be extra vigilant in order to keep her safe.

Chapter 6

"You're sure it was Jacob Yoder?" Colby asked Frank McDougal, when they were sitting in the living room of his spacious home. The former Harmony sheriff had welcomed Becca and Colby into the three-story stucco with detached garage that made Colby wonder about the pay scale for an Alabama sheriff.

"Yes, I'm sure." McDougal nodded emphatically. "Yoder's body was burned in the house fire, but we were still able to make a visual identification. His wife had become infirmed over the last few years of her life and died in her bed. We ID'd her, as well."

"Was an autopsy performed on either victim?" Becca asked.

McDougal glanced at Colby and shrugged. "We're a small town, far from the big city, but we still do things by the book. However, this time an autopsy wasn't warranted."

Irritated by McDougal's excuses, Colby asked, "Were you aware Jacob Yoder had a brother who was seen in the area just a day prior to the fire?"

The retired cop's gaze narrowed. "It's been eight years. Who told you about a brother?"

"A witness who saw him the day before Jacob died."

A muscle in McDougal's jaw twitched. He leaned in closer. "Where was this witness eight years ago?"

"Did you question the neighbors?" Becca asked.

"I talked to Samuel Hershberger."

"What did he say?"

"That he didn't know who started the fire."

"You suspected arson?" Colby asked.

"We suspected an overturned oil lamp."

Too bad he hadn't talked to Samuel's wife. Colby didn't share the witness's name. If Becca wanted to mention Sarah, she could make that call.

The current sheriff would need to know, but there was something about McDougal's insistence he had identified Jacob that made Colby question if the local law enforcement hadn't cut corners. Claiming Jacob Yoder had died in the house fire solved McDougal's need to close the double-murder case. The former sheriff had been ready to retire. Wrapping up the investigation quickly would have made his last days on the job that much easier.

"Ezekiel Yoder was the same height and build as Jacob," Becca said with determination as if unwilling to cut McDougal any slack. "We'll check with the sheriff's office next to see if there are any records of Ezekiel being seen in the last eight years. I'm sure we won't find anything because you buried him."

She pushed her chair away from the table and stood. "Let me know if you remember anything else, sir."

McDougal frowned. "The case is closed, Rebecca."

"It'll reopen when I arrest Jacob Yoder for killing a man at Fort Rickman, Georgia. The army will want to know who's buried in the Amish cemetery under a tombstone marked with Yoder's name. Be prepared to answer that question because I'll be back." She glanced at Colby. "We'll both be back."

Colby stood, his chest swelling with pride at Becca's assertiveness in dealing with the former sheriff. He followed her to his car.

"Good police work in there," he said as she slid past him into the passenger seat

"Thanks, but if McDougal had done his job eight years ago, we wouldn't have this problem today. Back then, everything happened too fast. Even I knew that, but I was too grief stricken to ask questions."

She glanced at the sheriff's home. "McDougal was wrong then. He's still wrong."

Colby climbed behind the wheel and inserted the key in the ignition. "You were justified in coming back to Harmony, Becca."

"I needed you in there, Colby. McDougal still considers me a kid from the past. You provided a bigger threat to him."

"Seems you're the one who got his attention." He reached for her hand and wove his fingers through hers to show his support.

"Where to now?" he asked.

"The sheriff's office downtown. It's not far. Head to the main square and then take a left."

Disappointed to learn Lewis Stone, the current sheriff, was out of the office when they arrived, Becca and Colby left their business cards and asked for him to call them once he returned. On the way outside, Colby spotted a sandwich shop at the end of the block.

"Hungry?" he asked.

"Starving."

"Let's grab some chow." They each devoured a burger and fries before hurrying back to Colby's car.

"Elizabeth's house next?" he asked once they buckled their seat belts.

"If you don't mind. I need to pick up my Honda."

Becca stared at the road ahead as Colby drove toward the town square and thought back to the emotional charge he'd felt when they'd both reached for the ketchup at the diner. Just as earlier, he had wrapped his fingers through hers, which caused Becca's cheeks to turn pink and her eyes to widen.

Now he wondered if he had made a mistake.

He needed to stay in control when dealing with Special Agent Miller. They were two professionals, working together. Partners. Yet when he was with her, he felt like their relationship could grow into something more significant.

Once past the square, Colby turned onto the street where Elizabeth lived and parked across from Becca's car.

Opening the passenger door, she smiled back at him. "Elizabeth may want me to come inside for a few minutes."

"I'll wait. I don't want you to be alone if Jacob is on the loose. Besides I'm in no hurry to get to Fort Rickman."

She didn't object, which confirmed that their relationship had improved over the last few hours.

"Give me a few minutes to say goodbye, and then we can be on our way."

Becca knocked on her friend's door, then knocked again with more intensity.

Elizabeth had planned to be home for the rest of the afternoon, but when the door remained closed, Colby stepped to the pavement. Becca glanced back at him for a split second and then turned the knob and peered through the doorway.

"Elizabeth, it's Becca."

Colby hustled toward the house and followed her inside. Silence greeted them.

"Maybe she's in the backyard?" Colby glanced into a large room where a full-size quilt was stretched over a wooden frame. The colors were flamboyant jewel tones accentuated with lush pinks and purples that didn't seem in keeping with someone who had been raised Amish.

Becca pointed through the large bay window to the backyard and drive. "Her car's parked in the rear."

"She could have walked to town, or she might be visiting a neighbor," Colby offered, hoping to calm the anxiety that flashed from Becca's eyes.

"You're probably right." She pulled a notepad and pen from her purse. "I'll leave a note in the kitchen, by the sink. She'll see it there."

Becca stepped into the kitchen.

The paper and pen dropped to the floor. Dread settled over Colby's shoulders. He knew before he entered the room what she'd found.

"I'm so sorry," he murmured as he crossed to where

Becca stood, staring down at the older woman—no doubt Elizabeth—sprawled on the tile. The woman's mouth hung open as if she was still screaming at the attacker who had cut her throat and taken her life.

Becca's world spun out of control. She clamped down on her jaw and tried to stem the hot tears that stung her eyes.

"It...it was Jacob," she stammered. Her voice broke. She wrapped her hands around her waist unable to pull her eyes away from her friend's face frozen in fear and disbelief.

Tears flooded her eyes, and she gasped with gut-wrenching sorrow that swept over her like a giant tidal wave.

Colby pulled her close and rubbed his hand over her shoulder, trying to comfort her. With the other, he gripped his cell and called 911. After providing the victim's name and address, he added, "Notify the sheriff that it's a homicide. We need law enforcement on site ASAP."

"Jacob saw my car in front of the house," Becca told Colby once he disconnected. "He probably forced his way in after I left. He was looking for me."

"You can't be sure what happened."

"He followed me from Fort Rickman."

"I was behind you, Becca. I would have noticed him."

She looked at Colby with pain-filled eyes. "Then he followed you."

"I didn't see anyone," he said too quickly. "Besides, Jacob might not be the killer."

She shook her head. "It's him. He's determined to take everyone from me."

Becca wiped her hands over her cheeks and struggled to remain strong. "Elizabeth took me in when I didn't have any place to go. She…she encouraged me to join the military and leave the area. Had I stayed in town, Jacob would have come after me, but she saved me from him then. If only I could have saved her today."

Sirens sounded in the distance. The keening wail cut through the afternoon chill. Becca stared down at Elizabeth's body and the blood that pooled on the kitchen floor. Bending down, she noticed skin under the woman's nails. Her friend had fought back, which meant Jacob would bear visible signs of the attack.

"Thank you for that, Elizabeth." Becca's voice was a whisper. "We'll catch him. I promise."

Colby put his arm around her waist and ushered her toward the foyer. "Let's go outside. We don't want to disturb the crime scene, and we can't do anything for Elizabeth now."

Becca followed him onto the lawn where they flagged down the first patrol car as it rounded the corner. Two additional black-and-whites followed, along with an ambulance.

They showed their identification to the first cop on scene. Colby gave him a quick rundown of what they had found before the officer hustled into the house along with two other cops and the paramedics. One officer remained with Becca and Colby, taking down the information they provided.

Across the street, an old woman peered from the window of her small, one-story, frame home.

"You talk to the cops," Becca told Colby. "I want to question the inquisitive neighbor."

She hurried across the street. A frail woman with gray hair and pale blue eyes opened the door.

Becca flashed her ID and gave her name. "There's nothing to fear, ma'am. We've got lots of law enforcement officers on-site."

"I knew something bad had happened," the woman said.

"How's that?"

"I saw a man that looked suspicious earlier today. My daughter called and I talked to her on the phone for a few minutes. When I hung up and glanced outside again, his car was pulling away from the curb. There was a woman in the passenger seat."

"Could you identify either the driver or the passenger?"

The old woman shook her head. "My eyes aren't the best these days, but there's a car out front that looks identical to the one I saw earlier."

Becca stared at the line-up of vehicles, police and civilian. "Which one?"

"The green sedan."

"Did anyone else stop by Elizabeth's house today?" Becca asked.

"No one else that I saw. Only the people who left in the green car."

Becca's heart sank. The neighbor wasn't going to provide information they needed to apprehend the killer. The car she pointed out had a Fort Rickman decal on the windshield. The older woman had seen a man and woman earlier, but that couple had been Becca and Colby.

Glancing at the police personnel scurrying across

Elizabeth's lawn, Becca knew Jacob Yoder had struck again.

She wanted to bring him to justice, but she had no idea where Jacob was or what he was planning to do next.

Lewis Stone, Harmony's current sheriff, arrived on scene some twenty minutes after the first patrol car. He was mid-forties and wore the same brown uniform as the other men, but four silver stars gleamed from his shirt lapels.

Lewis apologized for being away from his desk earlier when Colby and Becca had stopped by his office. Having grown up in Harmony, he remembered the Mueller murders and listened intently when Becca told him about Ezekiel Yoder and voiced her suspicion that Jacob Yoder was still alive.

"I'll quiz Frank McDougal and see what he can tell me," the sheriff assured her.

Becca relaxed her stance ever so slightly, no doubt relieved to finally have a person in law enforcement who believed her story.

"Sarah Hershberger met Jacob's brother," Colby explained to the sheriff. "You might want to talk to her. From what she said, the two brothers were similar in stature and appearance."

"I'll check with Sarah as well as McDougal. As I recall, that was his last case before retirement."

By nine that night, both Colby and Becca knew they could do nothing more in Harmony. They said goodbye to Lewis and then climbed into their respective cars and headed to Fort Rickman.

The back road to the interstate was a twisty two-lane

that loomed dark and foreboding. Becca had a heavy foot on the gas pedal. Colby followed close behind and flicked his gaze to the narrow shoulder on each side of the paved lanes as well as the stretches of wooded acreage beyond.

They hadn't seen any cars since they'd left Harmony, which underscored the remoteness of the area. Colby was anxious to cross the state line and be back in Georgia.

A road sign warned of an approaching curve. Becca decelerated slightly. Instinctively, he tapped the brake, relieved when his car responded. For a second, he lost sight of her car as she entered a second hairpin turn.

Rounding the curve, Colby saw her vehicle in the middle of the road. He tramped on the brake and screeched to a stop. A tall pine had fallen across the roadway, blocking their progress.

Becca was out of her car before he could caution her to be careful. Stepping onto the pavement, Colby glanced into the dense forest on each side of the road, his internal warning system on high alert.

The sky was clear, the wind calm. No reason for a fallen tree. He unbuttoned the safety on his holster. A sense of foreboding ran up his spine and made him stare even harder into the dark recesses of the night.

"Watch out, Becca," he said as she approached the fallen tree and then turned to face him. "We'll have to move the log off the road."

Inadvertently, she stepped into the arc of illumination from her car's headlights.

Colby's shoulders tensed. "You're exposed, Becca. Get away from the light."

He moved toward her. She stepped aside, but not fast enough.

A shot rang out.

For half a heartbeat, Becca froze.

Colby lunged and shoved her to the pavement. Two more shots pummeled the log. A third pinged against her open driver's door.

A car engine whined in the distance. Tires screeched along a narrow path that paralleled the newer two-lane.

"It was a trap," he said, his tone sharp. "You could have been killed."

She nodded. "I wasn't thinking."

At least, she hadn't been hurt.

"Let's wait a couple minutes before we make any sudden moves just in case someone's hunkered down in the woods."

He listened, but heard only the wind in the pines and the croak of the tree frogs. Satisfied the assailant had left in the car with the squealing tires, Colby scooted off Becca.

"Sorry," he said, hearing her groan.

"Not a problem," she mumbled.

"Keep low while I check out the area." He rose to his knees and stared into the shadowed underbrush.

Her head popped up. "I'm coming with you."

"Becca, please."

"Don't try to baby me, Colby."

"Baby you? I'm trying to keep you alive."

"I can take care of myself."

"Oh, yeah?"

What would have happened if she'd been driving home alone? He visualized Becca's bullet-ridden body bleeding on the pavement just as Elizabeth's lifeblood had darkened her kitchen floor.

Without giving voice to that thought, he hurried back to Becca's car and killed the engine and lights. After grabbing a Maglite from his trunk, he moved forward. Before he could object, Becca was beside him.

Reaching the narrow side road, he shined his light on the pavement and quickly found the black skid marks. Deep tire impressions were visible in the mud where the attacker had more than likely awaited their arrival.

Colby snapped a photo of the tread marks with his phone. "Let's hope forensics can ID the type of tire."

Becca pulled out her phone and snapped her own photos before she called the Harmony sheriff's office and relayed the information to Lewis Stone.

Disconnecting, she glanced at Colby. "Lewis said he'll be here in thirty minutes. Let's put out flares to warn approaching motorists."

Colby flashed his Maglite over the fallen tree trunk. Saw marks were visible. This wasn't a tree that had dropped across the road of its own accord, but a road-block that had been purposefully set.

A weight settled on Colby's shoulders. Becca hadn't mentioned Jacob's name, but both of them knew he was the most likely suspect.

So far he had failed to harm her, but he would try again.

Chapter 7

"Hello, sir." Becca greeted Chief Wilson the next day on the sidewalk leading to the Timmonses' newly built home. A circular drive stretched from the rural road to the two-story brick colonial. Shutters framed the expansive windows that offered views into the main room where a number of guests had already gathered.

After the late night in Alabama, Becca didn't feel like being social, but Dawson and Lillie Timmons had been kind enough to include her and the least she could do was attend the barbecue.

"I appreciate you calling and updating me last night," the chief said as they climbed the stairs to the front porch. "As I mentioned, I'm sorry about your friend who died."

"Thank you, sir. Lewis Stone, the Harmony sheriff, promised to keep us in the loop on both the murder investigation and any information they uncover from the sight of the felled tree."

"You mentioned the Amish man who killed your family members had supposedly been buried some years ago."

"That's right. Jacob Yoder."

"Did Stone think Yoder could still be alive?"

"He didn't offer an opinion one way or the other, but he plans to talk to the former sheriff who identified the body prior to burial."

Wilson pursed his lips. "Special Agent Goodman is looking into a contracting situation that might have bearing on the BOQ explosion. I want him to investigate that lead, while you and Colby follow this one. We'll work both issues until more concrete evidence is revealed." He hesitated. "You didn't see anyone who looked like this Amish man, did you, Becca?"

"No, sir." She wouldn't mention hearing his voice at the end of the Freemont half marathon. Wilson wanted proof and not a name called out in the midst of a cheering crowd of running enthusiasts.

"Let me know if you hear back from Sheriff Stone."

"Will do, sir."

Dawson Timmons, a beefy blond with twinkling eyes, opened the door before either she or the chief could knock. The two men shook hands. The former special agent invited them inside and smiled when Becca handed him a bouquet of flowers she had purchased at the florist earlier in the morning.

"These are for your wife."

"Lillie loves flowers. Thanks, Becca." He directed them along a hallway. "Follow the chatter. Lillie's in the kitchen. I'm sure she'll want to put the bouquet in water."

Becca trailed Wilson into a large great room where a number of CID personnel were gathered around a small table filled with a sampling of appetizers. A few wives stood to the side and smiled at Becca. The men made room for the chief around the table where the conversation turned to the upcoming Braves baseball season.

From what she could overhear, the women were discussing their children and the local school system. Just like at all parties, the men and women divided into two groups.

Today, Becca couldn't focus on anything except the very real possibility that Jacob Yoder was still alive, which wasn't appropriate conversation for this afternoon gathering. Not feeling part of either group, she grabbed a chip off a nearby table to cover the awkwardness of standing alone in a roomful of people.

"Try the artichoke dip." Colby appeared at her side.

"It looks good." She smiled.

Colby had a knack for showing up when she felt most vulnerable. In the past, she hadn't appreciated his timeliness. That wasn't the case today.

Following his lead, she scooped a large dollop of dip onto a chip and took a bite, appreciating the rich mix of flavors.

"How are you?" His gaze was filled with concern.

"A little tired, but fine otherwise."

"Long night."

"For both of us." She thought of Elizabeth and her throat tightened.

As if sensing her upset, Colby pointed through the sliding glass doors to the expansive deck that stretched along the back of the house. "Drinks are in the cooler outside. May I get you something?"

"Bottled water, if they have it. Otherwise a soda."

He squeezed her arm before he headed to the deck. Returning, he carried two waters, which he opened then handed one to her.

"Are you always so thoughtful?" she asked.

"My sisters claim they trained me well." His smiled revealed their close relationship. "In reality, I'm just a sensitive guy." He winked, sending a ripple of warmth to circle her heart.

"An officer and a gentleman, right?" Becca repeated the army phrase.

His smile grew even wider. "Always."

Her cheeks burned, and she took a long drink of the chilled water. Cognitively she knew Colby was laying on the charm, but she enjoyed the slight shift in their relationship, especially since they were away from the office and at a social event. Fatigue probably helped to weaken her defenses. Or perhaps after what they had experienced together yesterday, she was feeling more at ease with Colby at her side.

Even without his sisters' stamp of approval, she knew he was a good guy who she could trust. Although with his rugged good looks and outgoing personality, he probably had a string of women trying to catch his eye.

Somewhat unsettled by the thought, she reached for another chip, needing to hide the confusion attacking her midsection. Maybe Colby was already spoken for at this point in his life. Some petite blonde who didn't carry a gun or look over her shoulder whenever she got out of a car.

"You know everyone, don't you?" He glanced around the room, seemingly oblivious to her internal struggle.

She followed his gaze, hoping to refocus her attention on the invited guests. She knew the CID personnel and had met most of the wives at the post-wide Hail and Farewell when she had first arrived at the fort.

An older woman appeared from the kitchen and placed a tray of stuffed mushrooms on the table.

Colby leaned closer, which sent Becca into a momentary tailspin as she inhaled a lemon-lime scent that was totally masculine.

"That's Lillie's mom." He lowered his voice so only she could hear. "Her dad's helping in the kitchen. I'll introduce you."

Knowing close proximity to Colby could be dangerous, at least to her mental well-being, Becca kept space between them as they walked through the dining room and into the kitchen beyond, relieved to be doing something other than breathing in his yummy aftershave.

They found Lillie standing behind a granite-topped island in the kitchen, wearing a wide smile and a flowered dress. She wiped her hands on a cloth and then scurried forward to give Becca a hug. "The flowers are lovely. You shouldn't have."

"It's the least I could do."

"I want you to meet my parents." Lillie introduced the Beaumonts, who were just as Colby had said, caring folks whose words of welcome put Becca at ease.

Seeing how they hovered around their daughter caused a tug at Becca's heart for what had never been part of her own life. As much as Becca needed to forgive the past, she couldn't let go of the bad decisions her father had made concerning his children as well as the pain of his rejection. If only he had believed her when she had told him about Jacob's desire to have his way with her. Becca had fought off Jacob's advances, without the help of her *datt,* who had ignored the danger and provided her with no other recourse than to flee. Regrettably, Katie had been left behind to suffer the consequences of Jacob's anger that led to her death two years later. Now Elizabeth was another casualty.

"The grill's hot." Entering the kitchen, Dawson flashed an endearing smile at his pretty wife whose expression reflected the love between them, causing another tug at Becca's heart.

He lifted the roasting pan filled with ribs off the counter, then pointed to a second pan and nodded to Colby. "Lillie cooked the ribs in the oven, but they still need barbecue sauce and a good searing on the grill. Mind giving me a hand?"

"Not a problem." Grabbing the second pan of ribs, Colby followed Dawson through the back door that led to the deck.

"Do you need help?" Becca asked Lillie once the men had left the room.

Mrs. Beaumont smiled warmly and placed a large bowl of potato salad into Becca's outstretched hands. "This needs to go on the dining room table."

Becca did as Mrs. Beaumont asked and returned to the kitchen, thankful to be of service.

"How was the race yesterday?" Lillie pulled a bowl of colorful congealed gelatin salad from the refrigerator.

"You were there?" Becca asked over her shoulder as she headed back to the table with the gelatin.

Lillie shook her head. "Dawson and I were getting

things ready here, but we saw your photo in the local paper."

Becca tucked a stray strand of hair behind her ear. "I—I wasn't aware anyone took my picture."

"The photo was taken last week when you were signing up to run." Lillie shuffled through the papers on a nearby desk. "Here it is."

The photo showed Becca at the Freemont City Hall, filling out the race forms.

"You might be able to get additional copies from the newspaper office downtown if you want to mail them to family," Lillie suggested.

"One copy is all I need." Becca didn't have any other family members, but she was concerned that someone had seen the photo. Someone from her past. Someone she had been hiding from for eight years.

Colby entered the kitchen, carrying the now-empty roasting pans. "Dawson needs a plate for the ribs."

Lillie handed him a serving platter. "Remind him I like them good and done."

"I'll pass that on." Colby laughed. "But I might need Becca to back me up."

"Go ahead." Lillie motioned both of them outside. "The table's ready. We're just waiting for the meat."

The weather was almost like spring when they stepped outside, though dark clouds hovered in the distance. Becca inhaled deeply, lifting her face to the warmth, glad to have a few minutes to enjoy the sunshine.

The rolling pastures brought back memories of the fields on her father's farm, although his acreage had never been productive, and he had bemoaned the ground on more than one occasion. He had also lamented that his girls had not been the sons he wanted and needed to manage the farm.

A number of people stood near the grill and watched Dawson flip the ribs, basting both sides. The fire sizzled, and the scent of tangy barbecue sauce and roasted meat filled the air.

Becca turned her attention to the winding country road in the distance. Her gaze narrowed as she spied something unusual for this part of Georgia. The muscles in her neck tightened, and her heart skittered in her chest. On the rise of a far hill, a horse-drawn buggy clip-clopped along the horizon.

"What you looking at?" Colby came up behind her.

Caught off guard by his nearness, she shook her head. "Nothing in particular. Just enjoying the idyllic setting."

He inhaled deeply. "The sunshine feels good, although we might have rain before long." He pointed to the dark clouds.

A flurry of activity at the grill caused him to turn. He touched her arm. "Dawson's taking the ribs inside."

"I'll be right there."

She glanced again at the horse-drawn buggy and shivered, not from the cool breeze that had picked up in the last few minutes, but from what the buggy signified. If the Amish had moved into this area of Georgia, someone could be part of that new community. A man she had never wanted to see again. Jacob Yoder.

If he had seen her photo in the paper, he could have make inquiries about the location of where she lived. Surprised by Ralph Arnold once he had broken in the unoccupied apartment, Jacob could have rigged the explosion that had claimed the project manager's life.

Becca had been so careful for so long, but coming back to the South could have placed her in Jacob's path. Two people had died and attempts had been made on her own life. She needed to find Jacob, and the buggy might provide a clue to his whereabouts.

"I want to thank all of you for being with us today," Dawson said when Becca joined the guests inside. "I also want to ask God's blessing on the food."

Colby stared at Becca from the other side of the circle. Not wanting to reveal the mix of emotions welling up within her, she lowered her head and folded her hands while Dawson gave thanks for the food they were about to eat, for the military and CID and for all those in uniform who served. At the conclusion of his prayer, everyone joined in a heartfelt "Amen."

Dawson pointed them toward the dining room. "Ladies and gentlemen, please grab a plate and get some chow."

The people filed through the line and headed for the more casual but comfortable family room where they sat around two long folding tables.

Lillie handed out additional napkins to wipe the barbecue sauce from their sticky fingers. "Delicious," many said as they enjoyed the meaty ribs.

Chief Wilson sat back once he had finished eating and chuckled when Dawson took his empty plate. "I never knew you had culinary skills when you were with the CID."

"It's Lillie, sir. She taught me everything I know." He glanced at his wife across the room and winked. She responded with a fetching smile that wasn't lost on Becca.

From the hint of longing that flashed momentarily

across Colby's face, he too had noticed the intimate exchange.

"Thanks for inviting us here today," the chief said. "It's nice to be in the country."

He pointed toward the deck. "I'm not sure how many of you saw the horse and buggy on that distant farm road when Dawson was taking the ribs off the grill."

"I heard there's a new Amish community in the area," one of the men mentioned.

Wilson nodded in agreement. "As you know, the commanding general is committed to working with the Freemont community. To further that goal, he's interested in hosting a farmers' market and craft fair. His wife is spearheading a taskforce of folks to organize the first event to be held in the field beside the Fort Rickman museum. Mrs. Cameron asked us to work with the military police to provide security. I'll need someone from the CID to represent us on the committee. If anyone's interested, let me know."

"Sir, do you have any idea how many families are in the community and where they came from?" Becca asked.

"I should have more information in the next day or so. I'll let you know what I find out."

"Thank you, sir."

Lillie excused herself to prepare the dessert. Becca followed her to the kitchen with her empty plate in hand.

"Did you save room for red velvet cake?" Lillie opened the freezer and pulled out a container of ice cream. A large cake with cream-cheese icing sat on the counter.

"I'm too full from the wonderful meal. Thank you for a delightful afternoon."

"Do you have to get back to post?" Dawson asked as he entered the kitchen.

"I'm afraid so. Everything was lovely. I appreciate you including me."

Becca left through the kitchen door and hurried to her car. Instead of returning to Fort Rickman, she planned to head in the direction the buggy had gone earlier, hoping the road would lead to the Amish community.

If Jacob Yoder were still alive, would it be too much of a coincidence to have him living close to Freemont and neighboring Fort Rickman?

Becca had spent eight years hiding out in foreign countries to elude his wrath, but she wouldn't live her life looking over her shoulder any longer. From now on, she would take back the life he had ruined.

Glancing at the Timmonses' home, she thought of Colby and his desire to help her. He'd supported her when she found Elizabeth's body and had shoved her out of the line of fire later that night. They were supposed to be working together, but leaving without him seemed the best option. She didn't want him to get involved.

Then she thought of his strong arms and steady gaze and the way her heart fluttered when she smelled his aftershave. Was she making a mistake by excluding him today?

When Becca didn't return to the family room, Colby excused himself and headed for the kitchen where he found Lillie arranging ice cream and cake on desert dishes. Her mother stood at a nearby counter and poured cream into a small pitcher, which she placed next to a sugar bowl on a large serving tray.

"Dessert's almost ready," Lillie said as she rinsed his dinner plate in the sink.

"I'll have to pass, although it looks delicious." He glanced around the kitchen. "I thought Becca Miller was with you."

"She left a few minutes ago."

Colby thanked Lillie and then stretched out his hand to Dawson before he hastened from the house. Had mention of the Amish community upset Becca?

Focused on picking up her trail, he opened his car door and sighed with relief when he saw her sitting in the passenger seat.

She smiled coyly. "I knew you'd follow me so I decided if we're a team, we'd better stick together."

Slipping behind the wheel, he clicked on his seat belt. "Good decision. We'll come back for your car later. Right now, I presume you want to go to the new Amish community."

"Seems we're thinking alike."

As he pulled out of the driveway, Colby knew they'd overcome a huge hurdle. Becca had realized they could work together. If Jacob Yoder was still alive, she'd need backup and another set of eyes to keep her safe. Hopefully, she'd want him around for other reasons, as well. Becca had gotten to him, but in a good way, and Colby wanted to be the person she needed most of all.

Chapter 8

The road Becca and Colby followed eventually spilled into an area dotted with farms on both sides. As Colby drove, she stared out the window, thinking back to house raisings in Harmony, when neighbors gathered to help new families get started.

Hard work was an Amish trait, which her father hadn't inherited. Instead, he bemoaned the lack of sons, causing Becca to overcompensate and try to do the manual labor as well as maintain the house. No matter how hard she tried, she could never do enough to please him. When he had ordered her to accept Jacob Yoder's offer to keep house for his sickly wife, Becca had hoped things would change. Regrettably, they had only gotten worse.

In the distance, she spied a number of buggies parked beside a farmhouse and a newly built barn.

"What's going on?" Colby asked.

"Looks like a barn raising. Everyone comes together to help."

"That's a great way to share the load."

"As a child, I loved gathering for such an event," Becca reminisced. "After the work was done, the children were allowed to romp outdoors while the adults visited."

Colby's eyes twinkled as he glanced at her. "I know you were cute in your long skirt and apron."

"I was too tall and much too thin. *Gangly* would be the best word to describe me. My mother said I'd eventually grow into my body, although she didn't live long enough to see me through that awkward stage."

"You probably tried to fill your mother's shoes."

"And didn't succeed. My father said I was the cross he had to bear."

"That's tough on a kid." Colby shrugged. "On anyone."

"He was never a happy man, but his temperament changed after my mother died. He'd injured his back some years earlier and was besieged with pain. Plus, the farm work was more than we could handle. Katie and I helped, but in his opinion, we never did enough."

They passed the farmhouse with the buggies in the front yard and continued on, studying the homes that dotted the sides of the road. The farms were not large by *English* standards, but each provided ample acreage for the crops and livestock needed to feed a family and cover the cost of necessities as well as the mortgage and taxes for the land.

"I don't want to give you the wrong opinion, Colby. The Amish way is not easy, but it has its own rewards."

"I can see that. In fact, while Dawson was grilling, he talked about the satisfaction of working the land and providing for his family. There's something to say about the simple lifestyle. In fact, the Amish way reminds me of the military with its adherence to rules and high moral code. Too few people hold on to virtue these days. That's something to say for both the military and the Amish."

Regrettably, Jacob Yoder and her father were exceptions to the rule.

Running out of farmland as they approached an intersection, Becca said, "Turn left onto that dirt road. It looks like there's a farm tucked behind that thicket of trees."

Just as she suspected, the thick crop of hardwoods eventually opened into a clearing. A farmhouse, not as large or as well cared for as some of the others, sat in the open space, surrounded by pastures and a small creek. A few head of cattle grazed in a nearby meadow oblivious to the newcomers who pulled into the drive to turn around.

The absence of power and telephone lines confirmed Becca's hunch of this being an Amish home. The house's need for paint brought back other memories from her past.

A barn sat at the side of the property. The door hung on one hinge and flapped in the wind. Dogs barked in the distance.

Becca shivered as she studied the landscape.

"Cold?" Colby asked.

"I'm fine."

He stared at her for a long moment. "You look pale. Is something wrong?"

She shook her head and wrapped her arms around her waist. Another gust of wind forced the barn door to fly back with a bang.

Colby glanced at the darkening sky. "Those clouds look threatening. The farmer's probably at the barn raising. I'd better secure the barn door before the downpour hits."

"I'll go with you."

Becca stepped from the car and inhaled the damp air that signaled the approaching rain. She studied the landscape. Nothing moved, other than the wind through the trees. Even the dogs were silent.

Placing her purse strap around her neck, she felt the weight of her weapon holstered inside. No matter how peaceful the setting, Jacob Yoder could be nearby.

Flicking her gaze over the house and surrounding area, she walked with Colby toward the barn, taking care to silence her footfalls in the winter grass.

As she neared the corner of the house, the dogs started to bark again. She turned to see the chain-link pen that kept them bound, and let out a deep sigh of relief. The dogs—both Doberman pinschers—had jaws large enough to take off her hand. She shivered, then hurried to join Colby.

Glancing into the barn's dim interior, she saw something that shouldn't have been on an Amish farm.

A late-model Crown Victoria, metallic blue in color.

She stooped to examine the tires, thick with red clay. The car had been stuck in the mud recently.

Pulling her phone from her purse, she snapped photos of the tires and the tread marks on the barn's dirt floor. She also photographed the front grill and trunk that lacked plates.

Pointing to the house, she said, "Let's see if anyone's home. I want to find out more about the car." Specifically, she wanted to know who owned the Crown Vic and whether it had been driven to Alabama the day before. The lack of plates brought other questions to mind.

Colby closed and latched the barn and followed Becca to the house. She knocked repeatedly. When no one answered, they returned to the car and drove back the way they came.

Approaching the farmhouse with the newly built barn, Colby pulled to the side of the road.

As if oblivious to the darkening sky, children frolicked on the lawn while the adults chatted nearby. Just as at Dawson's house, the men and women stood in separate groups. A few folks glanced their way and then returned to their conversations.

A man helped a woman into their buggy. After taking his seat, he slapped the reins and the horses stared down the drive. Becca and Colby stepped from the car and held up their identification.

The man hesitated as if weighing whether to stop.

Becca raised her voice. "I'm with the Criminal Investigation Division at Fort Rickman." She pointed to Colby and introduced him before she continued. "You folks know a man named Jacob Yoder? He's six-two, black hair, brown eyes with a small scar on his left cheek."

The Amish man shook his head.

"He's in his mid-thirties," she pressed. "Formerly, he lived in Harmony, Alabama."

"I cannot help you."

She thought of Elizabeth. "He could have scratches to his face and hands."

"I have not seen such a man."

"Do you know who lives in the last farm on the left? Two Dobermans are caged behind the house? A blue Crown Vic is parked in the barn?"

The bearded man shook his head again. "This does not sound like an Amish family." Raising the reins, he clucked his tongue to signal the horses. The buggy creaked forward.

Becca watched it jostle along the road, regretting the Amish need to remain separate from the world and less than forthright with the *English*. Privacy was part of the Amish way, a way that would hinder their investigation.

She turned her gaze back to the hillside. An older woman, her gray hair caught up in a *kapp* bonnet, left the house. She stopped and stared at Becca for a long moment before she joined the other women.

Fat drops of rain began to fall. The people scurried for shelter. Some folks ran for the barn while others grabbed their children and hoisted them into their rigs before climbing in themselves.

Becca and Colby returned to his car and wiped the rain from their faces before he pulled back onto the road. Becca glanced over her shoulder and watched the buggies head in the opposite direction. If only someone had information about a man from her past who wanted to do her harm.

Was Jacob hiding out among the Amish?

Chapter 9

Becca was besieged with dreams of Amish buggies and shots being fired at her in the darkness. A strange, wizened woman, wearing a white *kapp,* sat behind the wheel of a Ford Crown Victoria and accelerated straight toward her.

She woke Monday morning in a cold sweat and glanced at her weapon on the nightstand.

Pulling herself upright, Becca dangled her feet over the side of the mattress and listened expectantly.

A *rap-tap-tap* sounded in the stillness.

She grabbed her Glock and tiptoed to the door.

"Becca, it's Colby." His voice was a whisper, but easy enough to recognize.

"What do you want?"

"To talk."

"Now?" She glanced at the bedside clock. Five in the morning was too early to play nice.

"Yes, now."

She moved aside the straight-back chair she'd shimmied under the door knob as an extra barrier and turned the dead bolt. Inching the door open, she kept the chain guard in place and peered with one eye through the small slit. "What's going on?"

He held up his hands. "Trust me, Becca. I've got a good reason for being here."

"Then start talking."

"I searched the archived newspaper reports of your father's and sister's deaths and found information about Jacob Yoder. He grew up in Pinecraft, Florida, an area in Sarasota. His brother did, as well."

"What's that got to do with me?"

"I'm driving there today. Wilson gave me the go-ahead. I told him you'd probably want to go, as well."

"How long will it take?"

"Five hours to get there. We'll spend the night and head back tomorrow."

She stared at Colby for a long moment, weighing her options. Stay on post or find out information about the Yoder brothers?

"Give me ten minutes. I'll meet you in the lobby."

She closed the door and stood for a moment, waiting to hear Colby's footfalls as he headed downstairs.

Spending two days with the special agent might put her in an awkward position. She and Colby both needed to understand the rules. They were investigating two murders that could tie in with four additional deaths.

Becca was interested. Who in law enforcement wouldn't be? But spending all that time with Colby could be a problem, if he didn't see her as a special agent doing her job and nothing more.

Then she realized the problem wasn't with Colby. It was with her.

Colby checked his watch when he heard footsteps coming down the stairs in the Lodge. Becca appeared wearing a flowing skirt and matching sweater set and lightweight jacket. She'd pulled her hair back from her face and carried a small overnight bag along with her purse.

"You dressed and packed in nine minutes? I'm impressed." He smiled.

"I've done it in less time."

The woman never cut herself any slack.

He reached for her overnight bag and was surprised when she let him carry it for her. Another step in the right direction.

"My car's out front." He motioned her toward the door, which he opened.

The chilly morning greeted them. Becca slipped into the passenger seat while he placed her bag in the trunk. Rounding the car, he climbed behind the wheel, noting the flowery scent that hung in the air. The Amish-girl-turned-cop wore nice perfume. That tiny glimpse into the real Becca behind the reticent facade made him smile.

He handed her a map. "We'll pick up Interstate 75 and drive south to Sarasota. At that point, I may need help with directions."

"What about GPS?"

He patted his console. "Tucked away in case I ever need it. Call me old-fashioned, but I still prefer maps."

"Thank you, Uncle Sam."

"Pardon?" He raised his brow unsure of what she meant.

"We work with maps in the army. No wonder you're more comfortable using them."

"Right." He pulled out of the parking lot and increased his speed when they left post. Once they were on the interstate, he mentioned Pinecraft.

"Did you hear about the area growing up?" he asked.

She laughed ruefully. "Never. We were just trying to survive. Vacations weren't even considered." She paused for a moment and looked out the window. "I often wondered what the ocean looked like. A farm girl from Alabama, especially coming for such a limited environment…"

She shrugged. "I never thought I'd get beyond Harmony. The army expanded my horizons. I did a lot of traveling when I was stationed in Europe. My first trip was to the Mediterranean for a week-long tour run by Morale Support."

"You traveled alone?"

"With someone else in law enforcement."

Colby shifted in his seat, wondering about her European traveling companion. "Some guy you dated?" The question slipped out unexpectedly.

"A woman who worked with the military police. She was a quiet type, and we got along."

Although relieved that she hadn't traveled with a boyfriend, Colby could imagine the number of guys who tried to catch Becca's eye. Who wouldn't? She was pretty in an unassuming way.

"The ocean was always my favorite destination," she continued, seemingly oblivious to his musings about her possible boyfriends. "I loved seeing everything. Rome, Venice, the Black Forest in Germany. Each was unique and special in its own way."

"Nice you took the opportunity to travel."

"You didn't?"

"I've been in Afghanistan on four deployments. Never got to Europe."

"But you've traveled in the U.S."

He nodded. "And spent lots of time at the beach. My sisters love the water."

She smiled. "No one's married yet?"

"My sisters are too independent."

"Sounds as if you don't approve."

"Hardly. The problem comes when they try to tell *me* what to do."

Becca's laughter filled the car with a lightness he hadn't felt in a long time.

"I'm the second from the eldest. My older sister is the only one who pushes the issue." He smiled, thinking of Gloria. "She wants me to settle down."

"Yet she's still single."

"There was a guy. She was head over heels in love with him. We all thought the feeling was mutual. They planned the wedding. The invitations were sent. The gifts had started to arrive. He texted her two days before the ceremony saying he'd found someone else."

Becca turned to look at Colby. "He sounds like a louse."

"I thought as much, but what could I tell her?"

"Now she's protecting her heart," Becca said.

"Exactly. There's a nice guy who keeps hanging around, but I don't think he'll wait much longer."

"You've talked to her?"

"As much as I can. After a point, she closed the door. Better to pull back a bit on the brotherly advice so the door remains open. I've learned to pick my battles."

"She's lucky to have you." There was sincerity in Becca's voice.

"The feeling's mutual, but I worry about her. I don't want her to throw away something good because of fear."

Becca nodded. "Fear can hold anyone back."

He glanced at her, thinking of the fear he'd seen in her eyes the night of the fire. She'd mentioned Jacob. At least now, he knew she had suspected Jacob Yoder right from the start.

Glancing down, Becca picked at the sleeve of her jacket. "My sister and I were close. Katie was two years younger and everything I wasn't. She had a gentle spirit that made her seem vulnerable. That worried me. I wanted her to be a little tougher and stand up for herself."

"You can't blame yourself."

"I blame myself for leaving. It was easier to escape than to change the way things were."

She tugged at her hair. "My father forced Katie to take my place working at the Yoder home after I left. Jacob paid well. Too well. My father didn't understand his dark motives."

Glancing out the window, she sighed. "Maybe he didn't want to see. I had trouble getting away from Jacob. My sister wasn't as strong as I was, so I can only imagine what happened."

"Not all men are self-serving, Becca."

"I know that."

Did she? Or was she too hung up on the past?

She eased her head back on the seat and stared out the window as if to close the door on their conversation. Colby tapped on the cruise control. Traffic was steady with a long string of trucks heading south. He needed to focus on the road and not the attractive woman sitting next to him.

They would have time later to talk about her past and Jacob Yoder and whether Becca was still hanging on to the hurt. Right now, he'd give her space to be in her own world. Hopefully, once they arrived in Pinecraft, they'd find information about Jacob and his brother. If Ezekiel was still alive, they'd be back at the beginning of the investigation with no leads to follow.

Jacob Yoder was a long shot, but his was the only name they had to go on.

Besides, Becca seemed sure he was still alive. And after everything that had happened, Colby had to agree.

Chapter 10

Colby didn't mind the drive, and the hours flew by along with the miles. Becca remained quiet for most of the trip, but the silence was comfortable as if borne from familiarity. At one point, her head drooped against her shoulder, and he realized she was asleep.

The frown lines he saw too often were replaced with a peaceful beauty he found endearing. Becca didn't flaunt flashy good looks, but she had a sweet aura that called to him.

Of course, he had also seen the anxiety and concern written too clearly on her face when she talked about a killer on the loose. Maybe Colby was drawn to the vulnerability she would never admit to having.

His sisters claimed he was overprotective. They laughed when he became too concerned about their well-being or questioned them too extensively about who they were dating and where they were going. He'd learned from his father, and now that Colby was older, he shared the male guardian role along with his dad.

Thinking back to Afghanistan and Ellen, he shook his head ever so slightly. Her self-sufficiency had butted heads with his need to keep her safe. She'd been adamant about not wanting his help. In hindsight, he realized his pride had gotten in the way and caused him to walk away from her when she'd needed him most.

He sighed as if trying to release the painful memory.

"Is there a problem?" Becca asked, her voice thick with sleep.

He turned and smiled at the look of concern she wore so openly. "I woke you. Sorry."

"I must have drifted off."

She glanced at the surrounding traffic, and the city that sprawled out in every direction from the freeway. "If this is Sarasota, I did more than doze."

"You fell asleep after we got gas in Wildwood."

"I should have been checking the map."

"It's been an easy drive," he assured her. "Our exit is just ahead."

The winter sun shone through the windows and warmed the car. Becca slipped out of her coat.

"Ready for air-conditioning?" Colby asked with a smile.

"Actually, I'm fine, although fresh air might be nice." She cracked the window on her side and inhaled deeply. "Do I smell salt water or am I imagining we're not far from the Gulf?"

"About six or seven miles," Colby said. "We can head there later today, after we check out Pinecraft. I thought we'd stop at one of the diners and ask a few questions first. From what I've read, the area is a melting pot for Amish and Mennonite folks from around the country. They seem to let down some barriers when they're on vacation."

"Meaning they'll share information."

"That's what I'm hoping."

Colby exited the freeway and ended up on the east-west thoroughfare. Passing Oak View Drive on the left, they took the next major right into a community of small bungalows and a scattering of shops. Mobile homes were nestled in between modest cinder-block homes where palm trees and flowering shrubs added color and texture to the eclectic neighborhood.

Three-wheeled bicycles were parked in front of a restaurant that served Pennsylvania Dutch cooking. A sign in the window read, *"Schmeckt mir gut."*

"Loosely translated it means the food tastes good," Becca told him.

"Looks like the crowd agrees." Colby pointed to the clusters of people milling around in the parking lot.

A number of the men were dressed in denim overalls and straw hats. Others wore white shirts and dark trousers held up with suspenders. The majority of men had beards that partially covered their weatherworn faces.

The women wore simple dresses and sturdy shoes. Some had white bonnets and aprons. Others piled their hair in large buns at the back of their neck. The loose strands blew around their faces in the gentle breeze.

"Let's get lunch and see if anyone remembers the Yoder family." Colby pulled into a vacant parking space and stepped from the car.

After the long drive, Colby wondered if coming to Pinecraft had been a good idea. He glanced at Becca.

Once again, her face was marked with worry. If only the trip would provide information they needed about Jacob Yoder and his brother. Maybe then she could forget the past and move on with her future.

Becca opened the car door and hesitated a moment, eying an unleashed dog nearby. Waiting until the mutt passed by, she turned to find Colby watching her.

Shifting away from his gaze, she studied the gathering of plain folks, whose friendly chatter and laughter seemed infectious. For a fleeting moment, Becca longed to recapture the essence of her youth. The simple dresses and open faces, all fresh and natural, tugged at the memories she held in the deep recesses of her heart.

A young woman, standing with a number of teens, reminded her of Katie, with her trim body and warm smile.

Becca waved to the small child in an older woman's arms. The toddler giggled and then hid his face against his mother's neck.

Colby touched her arm. He leaned toward her, close enough that she could smell his aftershave. "Too many memories?"

She shook her head. "I'm fine." But she wasn't. She was struck again with the pain of loss. Katie had been such a sweet soul. She should have married well and had a houseful of children of her own. Instead, she had been murdered. All the possibilities of what could have been had ended that terrible night Jacob Yoder forced his way into their home.

If only Becca could have arrived earlier. She could have saved Katie or sent her scurrying into the night away from danger.

Instead Jacob had found her sister, hiding in the pantry.

"Becca." Colby's voice was laced with concern.

She pulled in a ragged breath and focused on the wooden walkway leading to the restaurant. "We'd better get a table before everyone realizes it's lunchtime."

A young woman in a light blue dress and apron showed them to a booth by the window. For a long moment, they watched the flow of traffic on the main road and the influx of people who biked or walked toward the restaurant.

"I would never expect so many Amish to gather here," Becca said. "In Harmony, the Amish kept to themselves. Here it seems they mix with everyone."

"The information I read said many of the folks bus to Pinecraft each year. They rent homes in the area and make friends with people from all over the country."

"They seem so opposite from the closed communities farther north." She thought of her own hesitancy to reveal the truth about Jacob Yoder years ago until he'd become such a threat that she had to tell her father.

What would have happened, if she'd been forthright and gotten help from the local authorities? Would Mc-Dougal have listened to an Amish girl who claimed a married man had tried to touch her?

Naive as she had been back then, she would have choked on the words and would never have been able to describe how he had lured her to the barn and forced her down onto the hay and tried to have his way with her.

So many people didn't understand why she had run away from Harmony. She wasn't running away from the Amish way of life per se. She was running away from Jacob.

He had warned her when she first went to work for him that she could never run away. He would find her. Which is exactly what he had done.

"A penny for your thoughts," Colby said from across the table.

Becca shook her head. "Sorry, I was thinking back to Harmony."

"You'll feel better after you eat."

They both studied the expansive menu.

"I'll have the chicken with homemade noodles, mashed potatoes and gravy," Becca told the waitress when she returned to take their order.

"Meat loaf with the same sides." He looked at Becca. "Iced tea?"

"Please."

The waitress, a middle-aged woman with rosy cheeks, brought two glasses of tea and a basket of freshly baked rolls still warm from the oven.

"I may go into carb overload," Becca said as she placed a plump roll on her bread plate.

Colby did the same, and before he reached for the butter, he noted a family sitting at the next table. The four young children sat still as the parents bowed their heads and offered a blessing over the food they were about to eat.

"My father leads the grace at our house," Colby shared. The memory brought a warm spot to his heart. He'd forsaken prayer since his first deployment. Somehow thanking God hadn't seemed necessary in a war zone, which in retrospect was the most obvious place to include God.

Colby had survived four tours and too many close

calls to count. He joked that his mom and dad and sisters' prayers had brought him home safe and sound from each deployment, yet he himself had given the Lord only the scantest attention in all that time. Dawson's prayer yesterday had seem fitting, and here, in this family-style restaurant, the need to invoke the Lord seemed fitting, as well.

"I don't suppose you'd want to offer a blessing?" he asked Becca.

She shook her head. "Go ahead. You lead."

So much for trying to pass the buck. He cleared his throat and lowered his gaze. "Father God, thank You for our safe journey this morning and for the warm welcome at this restaurant. We ask Your blessing on the food we are about to eat and on those who prepared it. Lead us to information about the Yoder brothers and keep us safe as we do our job." He glanced up, seeing her bowed head and closed eyes.

"Amen," they murmured in unison.

As if she had been waiting for the conclusion of their blessing, the waitress appeared almost immediately with their plates.

Colby's mouth watered at the savory aroma and the huge servings. "Do you cook like this?" he asked Becca.

She shook her head and stared at her plate. "I should have asked for a child's portion."

The food was as delicious as it was bountiful, and they both ate with relish.

"My mother makes a mean meat loaf, but nothing this good," Colby said as he reached for his tea.

"Which you shouldn't mention when you call home."

He laughed. "I know when to be tactful."

She paused, a forkful of mashed potatoes halfway to her mouth. "You're very considerate, Colby."

Considerate? He'd take that as a compliment, although he hoped she saw other attributes in him as well, which he continued to mull over as he finished eating.

At the conclusion of the meal, he sighed with contentment. "My father says a man works better with a full stomach."

Becca laughed. "I'm not sure that applies to women."

She opened her purse, but Colby held up his hand. "I've got the check."

He motioned to the waitress who hurried to the table.

"You enjoyed the food?" she asked, reaching for his plate.

"We did. Thank you." He eyed her name tag. "Miriam, we're trying to locate the Yoder family. They had two sons Ezekiel and Jacob. Both would be in their mid-thirties by now."

"They live in Pinecraft?"

"Years ago they did. Jacob went north to Alabama at some point. I'm not sure what happened to Ezekiel."

The waitress nodded. "I'll check with the other staff, but I do not know the family of which you speak, although Yoder is a common name. There's a Yoder's restaurant in the area, but they do not have sons those ages."

When the waitress left the table, Becca said to Colby, "We need to find an older person who might remember the Yoders we're looking for."

He gazed through the window at a nearby vegetable market and convenience store. "Let's keep asking until we find someone who does remember."

The waitress returned shaking her head. "Everyone

who works here has only come to the area in the last
ten years or so. There was an older family named Yoder
that moved north some time ago."

"Did they have sons?"

"Three girls."

Colby paid the check, and both he and Becca thanked
the waitress for her help. After leaving the restaurant,
they hurried across the parking lot to the marketplace.

An Amish man in his thirties greeted them with a
warm smile. "May I help you?"

After explaining their need for information, he shook
his head. "I knew a Yoder family in Ohio, but no one
by that name in the local area." He pointed to one of the
side streets. "Hershel Trotter and his wife have lived
in Pinecraft for many years and rent rooms on the next
street over. They might be of help."

Leaving their car, Colby and Becca walked to the
house the clerk in the market had described. A small
sign in the front yard read Rooms for Rent.

The sound of voices drew them to the backyard. Four
couples—the men in denim overalls and women in simple dresses—stood around two shuffleboard courts. A
hefty man, mid-fifties with gray hair and an equally
gray beard, shoved his puck down the court. His lie
was good, and he received shouts of encouragement
from the others.

One of the men turned as Becca and Colby approached.

"Good day." Becca nodded to the man and his wife.
She glanced at the other couples who had halted their
revelry and were peering with questioning eyes at the
special agents.

Colby let Becca take the lead, knowing her Amish roots would put her in better stead.

After introducing herself and Colby, she held up her CID identification. "We're searching for information about a family that lived in Pinecraft fifteen to twenty years ago by the name of Yoder."

The man eyed them with skepticism and shook his head. "Yoder is a common name."

"Jacob and Ezekiel were the sons," Becca offered.

"Perhaps Herschel knows them."

As if having heard his name mentioned, a man—no doubt, Herschel—stuck his head out the back door. *"Wiegates?"*

One of the men pointed to Becca and Colby. "These people are looking for someone named Yoder who lived here years ago."

"Abram Yoder?" Herschel asked as he stepped onto the back stoop.

"We only know the names of the Yoder sons," Becca said. "Jacob and Ezekiel."

"Yah, that would be Abram Yoder's family."

"Where is Abram now?" Colby asked.

"With the Lord. He moved north and died some years ago."

"Do you have information about his family?"

"Abram was a quiet man who kept to himself."

If only Mr. Trotter would be more forthcoming.

Colby stepped closer. "Sir, do you know anyone who might have information about the sons?"

Trotter rubbed his beard and stared into the sky. "Sally Schrock would know."

"Where can we find her?" Becca's voice was peppered with a dash of irritation. Colby raised his brow ever so slightly, encouraging her to keep her cool. They didn't need to antagonize Mr. Trotter, especially when he seemed willing to share information.

Trotter pointed to a small house sitting on the corner. "Sally's home is there, but today she went with her son and daughter-in-law to Siesta Key. They fish or walk along the sand, and she sits and watches the people."

Colby groaned internally. "How far away would that be?"

The big man pursed his lips and shrugged. "Too far to go by bike."

"I have a car."

"Then you will have no problem." Trotter pointed west. "Siesta Beach is eight miles away on the Gulf. Follow the signs along the highway."

"Where will we find Sally?"

"Sitting under a large orange beach umbrella."

"She's Amish?" Becca asked.

"Sally is a friend of the Amish and Mennonite communities, but she's *English*."

Colby and Becca offered their thanks and headed back to the car, encouraged by having a name and a possible contact who might know about the Yoder brothers. In spite of the afternoon traffic, they soon arrived at the beach.

Colby parked in the lot provided and sat for a long moment as Becca took in the view of the peaceful inlet on the far western side of the city. The white sandy beach eased into crystal-blue water that stretched to the horizon. Gulls circled overhead, and an occasional pelican glided over the waves seemingly oblivious to the scattering of people on the shore.

"Such a beautiful spot." Becca inhaled deeply. "The air's clean, fresher than anything I've ever smelled."

"You sound like my sisters."

"Is that a bad thing?"

He regarded her sweet face, feeling a strong desire to draw her close. In truth Becca didn't remind him of his sisters. She reminded him of all that was good in life. Unable to stop himself, he reached for a lock of her hair.

She turned to face him, her gaze full of question.

"I'm glad you transferred to Georgia, Becca. Meeting you has helped me put some of the pieces of my past in better focus."

"Is that a good thing, Colby?" Her voice low and full of emotion.

He touched her cheek. "Why wouldn't it be?"

"I've spent eight years running from my past."

"I'll help you find Jacob."

She smiled. "Let's see if we can find Sally first."

Pulling back, Colby realized, once again, that he needed to be cautious around Becca and not reveal the mix of feelings that welled up within him whenever they were together.

He pointed toward the beach. "Notice the orange beach umbrella."

Becca nodded. "Looks like we've found her. Let's hope she'll lead us to at least one of the Yoder brothers."

Sally Schrock was petite and wrinkled with bright pink lipstick and rosy cheeks, not from the sun but from makeup. Her flamboyant beach cover-up and painted nails didn't match the Amish and Mennonite profile of the other folks they'd met in Pinecraft, but if what Trotter had told them was true, she knew the people and fit in with the vacating tourists.

"Mr. Trotter said we'd find you here," Becca mentioned once she had introduced herself and Colby.

A couple of rods and reels were stuck in the sand. An insulated cooler sat nearby. Sally pointed to two empty beach chairs.

"The fish aren't biting today. My daughter and son-in-law are taking a long walk. You might as well sit down and tell me what you need to know."

Without delving into what had happened at Fort Rickman or in Harmony, Becca recounted their trip south and desire to learn more about Jacob and Ezekiel Yoder.

"They were good boys," Sally said with a nod of her bleached hair. "They worked hard and obeyed their mother, although Mrs. Yoder was a hard taskmaster."

"Mrs. Yoder?" Colby shifted forward in his chair.

"That's right. Her husband left her when the boys were young. She ran the business and kept the boys on a tight schedule. They were helping her at an early age and worked far harder than I thought was acceptable."

Sally shrugged her slender shoulders. "In those days, we didn't have the Department of Children and Family Services to call."

"Was abuse involved?" Becca asked.

"Not overt. But the boys were never allowed to play with the other children. They attended public school, but she frequently kept them home from school to help out, especially in the winter snowbird season."

"Didn't the school realize what was happening?"

"I called the principal a few times. She said if the

boys were not physically hurt there was nothing she could do."

"What type of business did Mrs. Yoder have?"

"A bakery and coffee shop. Not too large, but she had a lot of return customers. She kept her staff at a minimum, and as the boys grew they took on more of the workload."

"Did you know the boys?"

"Only from the bakery. Ezekiel was younger than Jacob. Both of them left town years ago."

"And Mrs. Yoder?" Becca asked.

"That's the sad part. She opened the bakery each morning at five. The boys would follow a short while later after they did their chores at home."

Becca looked at Colby as if anticipating what Sally would say next.

"One winter morning there was a terrible explosion. My house was blocks away, and I thought it was either an earthquake or a bomb. Then I heard the sirens from the fire department and paramedics."

Sally shook her head, her eyes filled with regret. "Mrs. Yoder was trapped in the bakery and didn't survive."

"Did they determine the cause?"

"A gas leak. When Mrs. Yoder turned on the stove, the place blew. Her customers were devastated. The boys were less obvious with their grieving. They moved in with a neighbor family for a while and eventually headed north."

"What about Jacob?" Becca asked. "Do you know where he went?"

Sally shook her head. "He left Pinecraft before his brother and never came back. The neighbor said losing his mother was too much for Jacob to bear. Evidently he'd loved her, although I don't see how he could have endured her hateful words and cruel verbal attacks."

"Did he ever strike back at her?"

The older woman shook her head. "He was quiet around her as if he didn't want to draw her attention, but…"

"What, Sally?"

"I saw him look at her sometimes when he didn't know I was watching. He'd narrow his gaze and fist his hands. Both boys ran from her when she went into a rage. I'm sure they suffered when she found them. Since Jacob was older, I often wondered if he didn't try to protect his brother."

"And took the blows for both of them?" Becca asked.

Sally shrugged. "That's what I always thought. Jacob never shed a tear at her funeral, but I couldn't blame him as vengeful as that woman had been."

"Did you ever see Jacob again?"

"Never."

"What about the neighbors who took them in?"

"They left town some years back."

"And Ezekiel? Can you provide a description of him?"

Sally nodded. "Both boys were similar in height and build. Same dark hair. Ezekiel wasn't as handsome, and the difference was noticeable."

"Did people mistake one brother for the other," Becca asked.

"Never."

Chapter 11

After leaving the beach, Becca and Colby stopped at the local police department and talked to a few of the officers who remembered the explosion that had claimed Mrs. Yoder's life. According to their recollection, the blast had been accidental and caused by a faulty stove.

Both special agents left business cards with contact information and asked the officers to call them if they recalled any additional information.

"We'll have to stop overnight along the way," Colby told Becca once they were back on the interstate, heading north to Georgia.

She raised her cell phone. "I'll call ahead and see if I can find accommodations."

Becca reserved two rooms at the Florida Rest Motel about ninety miles outside of Sarasota. When they checked in, she was given a ground-floor room at the side of the complex. Colby parked nearby and ensured she was inside before he climbed the stairs to his own room. Once he stashed his overnight bag, he retraced his steps and knocked on her door.

"It's Colby." He tapped again.

When she failed to answer, he glanced at the parking lot and the densely wooded area beyond. Surely nothing had happened in such a short time. He knocked again and then hustled along the sidewalk to the front of the motel. Entering the lobby, he let out a sigh of relief.

Becca was talking to the man behind the check-in counter. "Breakfast is at 6:00 a.m., ma'am. It's served here in the café." He pointed to a room filled with small tables.

She thanked the clerk and turned toward the door. Her brow lifted, and a lopsided smile tugged at her lips when she spied Colby. "Is something wrong?"

He shook his head a little too quickly and tried to calm his racing heart. "No, of course not. Just checking out the facilities."

"The workout room is down the hall. The motel offers a continental breakfast that starts at six. What time do you want to get started in the morning? I'd like thirty minutes in the gym, if we have time."

"Sure, no problem. Just call me when you're ready to leave." He hesitated then added, "Working out on the treadmill might be a good idea. Shall we meet up at five-thirty for PT?"

"Perfect." She patted his arm and walked around him. "See you in the morning."

"May I help you, sir?" the clerk asked.

"Coffee for my room?"

"Certainly." He reached under the counter and pulled out two sealed foil packets. "Anything else, sir?"

"A place to grab some food?"

"There's fast food out the door and to the left. For more formal dining, you'll have to drive about five miles."

"Fast food works. Thanks."

He exited the lobby and walked around the perimeter of the motel, scouting out the entire complex. One of the first tenets of military readiness was to know the terrain. The motel was a square structure surrounded on all sides by a parking lot. Beyond the pavement in the rear, he spied a field of orange trees. A single-lane dirt road allowed access for farm vehicles.

He stared long and hard into the falling darkness. Satisfied no one was lying in wait, he walked across the parking lot to the small restaurant. After ordering two combo burgers with fries and drinks and a chicken sandwich, he hurried back to the motel, bypassed the stairway to the second floor and stopped outside Becca's door.

"It's Colby," he said as he knocked.

The curtain pulled back, and she peered out the window.

He lifted the bag of food. "I brought chow."

The lock turned and the door opened.

"I thought you might be hungry," he said to Becca, who stood in the doorway.

Her eyes danced from the bag to his face and to the bag again. "Actually, food sounds great. Come in."

He placed the bag on the round table by the window and settled into one of the two barrel chairs. "Burger and fries or a chicken sandwich?"

"The burger works for me, but what about you?"

"I ordered two, just in case. I'll save the chicken for dessert."

She smiled and opened the disposable container he handed her. "As much as I ate at lunch, I shouldn't be hungry."

He lowered his head in prayer.

"Oh, sorry." She dropped her hands to her lap and glanced down. Both of them looked up a few seconds later. She smiled apologetically. "I've gotten out of the habit."

He nodded, understanding. "I was just following Dawson's lead yesterday. He got me thinking about where God was in my life." Colby took a bite of the burger and grabbed a handful of fries.

"And?" she asked, once he came up for air.

He raised his brow. "Pardon?"

"And where is God in your life?"

He pointed toward the ceiling. "Up there someplace." With a laugh, he added, "I don't mean the second floor. He's reigning over the world, taking care of business."

She tilted her head, her eyes inquiring. "Are we part of His business?"

"What do you think?"

She took a sip of her drink before she answered. "I used to think God cared. That what I did was important to Him. Then I grew up and things got more complicated. My struggle with my own *datt* influenced the way I thought about God the Father."

She wiped a few crumbs off the table. "Seems when I turned my back on one, I turned my back on the other as well. Since then I've been on my own."

"But you still believe in God?" he asked.

"I know He's out there." She extended her hand and then pointed at the ceiling just as Colby had done. "Maybe I should say 'up there' as you mentioned, but He's busy with big issues that are more important than my life."

"Is that what your father told you?"

She tilted her head and stared at him. "Why do you ask?"

"Just something that came to mind. Maybe it's the tone you use when you talk about your dad. I got the idea he was a strict authoritarian. When he said something you were expected to obey."

"He said I shouldn't tax God's patience and should accept my life as it was."

"Evidently, he wasn't a touchy-feely type of guy."

She smiled at his sarcasm. "To say the least."

"The way I see it—" Colby wiped his mouth and then dropped the napkin in his lap "—Christ is always ready to help us through the hard times, but we have to ask for His help. We need to invite Him into our lives because of free will. The choice is ours to accept His help or reject it."

Becca frowned. "Are there only two options?"

"Far as I can figure, that's it. If you're not inviting Him into your life, then you've got a keep-out sign on your soul. Because of free will, He won't barge in."

"Which way are you going?"

"I'm ready to open the door I closed in Afghanistan."

She watched him with questioning eyes as if waiting for Colby to reveal more. No reason to mention Ellen— an independent woman who had stolen his heart and then discarded it because of her own need for independence. Better to keep the past in the past.

Thankfully, Becca didn't press the point.

She finished the burger and threw the cardboard container in the trash. Colby tidied his side of the table.

"You didn't eat the chicken sandwich," she said when he stood.

"I'll save it for later."

She reached for her purse. "How much do I owe you?"

"Not a problem." At times Becca seemed as independent as Ellen. Maybe more so.

She pulled out a twenty and handed it to him. "You bought lunch today. I'll spring for dinner."

"Keep your money."

Evidently what he had been feeling about their relationship was lost on Becca. She considered him just another special agent with whom she was assigned to work. Why had he thought a deeper bond had developed between them, something more personal, more intimate?

Frustrated, he threw the bag in the trash.

"What about the chicken sandwich?" she asked.

"I'm not hungry anymore." He reached for the door. "Call me when you're ready to leave in the morning."

Colby flexed his muscles and inhaled a lungful of cool night air when he left her room, relieved to be away from the confused look that had wrapped around her pretty face.

She didn't have a clue about the way he felt, although at the present moment, he was as mixed-up as she looked. On the one hand, he knew Becca was a fellow agent and their relationship needed to be professional and not personal.

The problem remained that, for all her determination, Becca had a vulnerability that touched him to the core. In his family, women were cherished, including his five sisters who drove him crazy when they ganged up on him.

His father adored their mother. She was a strong woman, yet she allowed her husband to care for her in a million small ways that showed his love.

Colby had learned from his dad through observation, but also from the man-to-man talks they'd had on a regular basis since he'd been old enough to realize he was outnumbered by girls in the Voss family.

So why couldn't he buy Becca a burger, insignificant though that might be?

He sighed and shook his head. Time for a reality check. Shove the emotion aside and get back to the job at hand.

His elbow grazed against the weapon on his hip. He stopped at the stairwell and glanced around the parking area, feeling an immediate sense of unease. The last of his frustration dissipated, replaced by an alertness that signaled danger.

A few cars drove along the main road in front of the motel. He glanced at the grove of orange trees behind the lodging. Sweeping his gaze forward, he searched the dark, wooded area, looking for movement. He tilted his head and listened for the sound of footsteps or the crunch of broken glass and breathed in deeply, checking for smoke or anything out of the norm that could be the reason for his internal agitation.

Once again, he walked the perimeter of the motel,

especially aware of the thick wooded areas, and stopped frequently to listen and stare into the night.

The overhead lights on the fast-food restaurant flicked off. A lone clerk, visible through the large glass windows, grabbed his jacket and left through a side door. The kid checked the lock before hurrying to his car.

Colby watched him pull onto the main highway, heading south. The hum of his engine eventually died, leaving only the sound of cicadas and tree frogs to fill the void.

Convinced his internal alert system was being too sensitive in this peaceful, rural setting, Colby returned to the stairwell. He glanced quickly at Becca's door and the glow of light behind the pulled curtains, before he climbed to the second floor and entered his own room. He opened the drapes and stood in the darkness, staring down at the parking lot below.

What had caused his warning signal to go on high alert? Was it being with Becca this evening and getting upset about her need to pull her own weight that had made him tilt off center?

Or was danger lurking outside? Something or someone waiting for Colby to lower his guard?

Becca may think she could take care of herself, but if Jacob Yoder or someone else planned to harm her, she needed to be careful and cautious, which was exactly why Colby planned to remain vigilant throughout the night.

Becca sat on her bed fully clothed and checked the local news on her smart phone. Two men had been shot in a nearby town after trying to rob a convenience store.

The owner kept a gun under the counter and, to his credit, had been able to defend himself and his store.

Squinting from the glare of light, she clicked off the bedside lamp to better view the touch screen on her phone. Although the room was dark, she could see the outline of her own service revolver on the nightstand and remembered back to the first gun-safety classes she'd had in basic training. In spite of her pacifist upbringing, learning to shoot and maintain her weapon had brought peace of mind, knowing if Jacob found her, she could protect herself.

Yet the weapon had offered little protection from the gas explosion. What had prompted her to go into the kitchen for a glass of water? Had God been watching out for her?

With her history, the Lord's involvement seemed unlikely, yet wasn't that what Colby had been trying to say? God was always ready to intervene, when and if we turned to Him in our need. Had she called out to God that night, even subconsciously, and asked His help?

The thought of what could have happened made her stomach tighten. She glanced at the closed motel drapes and the locked door. Strong as she tried to be, she had to be aware of her surroundings at all times.

She didn't have the luxury of relying on someone else to keep her safe. Maybe because she had never had anyone who stepped into that protective role, which Colby seemed so willing to take on.

Yet, she couldn't rely on him. If she did, she might let down her guard, and that could prove deadly.

Better to ensure she kept a barrier up between them. She shook her head and sighed, regretting the reality of her life and wishing that she and Colby could have met under different circumstances.

For a moment she lost herself, thinking of his dark eyes and square jaw and the strength of his arms when he'd saved her life in Alabama. She remembered the masculine scent of his aftershave and the way his breath had fanned her neck.

Memories of his closeness weren't helping her stay strong. In fact, they were confusing her even more. Determined to get her mind off Colby, she dropped her legs to the side of the bed. Time to change into her sweats and call it a night. Morning would come too early.

Before she could place her phone on the nearby table, a shuffle sounded on the walkway outside her room.

A footstep perhaps?

Her heart pounded a warning. She tilted her head toward the window and waited for the sound to come again.

There it was.

A footfall as if someone was walking ever so quietly toward her room.

She freed her weapon from its holster. With the phone in her other hand, she slowly and deliberately moved to the opposite side of the room and stood with her back to the wall and her gun aimed at the door.

Again she listened.

A twig snapped near the window.

Too close.

She tapped Colby's number into her cell. As soon as she hit Send, a barrage of gunfire broke the silence. The window exploded and shards of glass showered over the bed where she had sat moments earlier.

Becca flattened herself against the wall. Bullets cut through the bedding and mattress.

A pause—not more than a second or two—before another stream of shots ate through the motel door. Wood fragments flew in the air like confetti. A sharp chip cut into her cheek.

Her ears roared from the explosive bursts.

As quick as it started, it was over. Footfalls pounded the pavement, running away from the motel.

She threw open the shattered door.

A dark form sprinted across the parking lot toward the densely forested area beyond. "Halt!" she screamed, her weapon aimed at the fleeing shooter.

A car turned into the parking lot, blocking her line of fire.

"Stop," she yelled at the driver and held up her hand. "Stay in your car."

She raced around the vehicle and chased after the assailant, pushing her legs to go faster.

He turned and looked back.

She couldn't see his face in the darkness, but she saw a flash from his weapon.

A lightning bolt of fire grazed her left arm.

Gasping at the pain, she nearly stumbled.

The guy was tall with broad shoulders.

Jacob?

He ran toward the woods.

She stopped, raised her weapon and fired. One shot. Then another.

He slipped between the trees.

Footsteps sounded behind her.

She glanced over her shoulder.

Colby.

"He went into the woods," she called to him. "Circle to the right. We'll block his exit."

Becca ran until she came to a roadway. In the distance, a car turned onto the main highway.

She plugged 911 into her phone and notified the operator to contact the local police to be on the lookout for a car headed south.

"A dark sedan. No, I can't identify the make or model." She gasped, needing to catch her breath. "I'm at the Florida Rest Motel. The attacker fired repeatedly into my motel room."

Colby approached her. "Did we lose him?"

"He drove off." She pointed to the road then gave her name and room number to the operator.

"What happened?" Colby asked when she disconnected.

She filled him in with halting breaths.

Colby reached tenderly for her arm. "You're hit."

"It's not bad. A graze. That's all."

"You could have been killed."

Becca paused, realizing what he had said was true. "But I'm okay." She needed to reassure him as well as herself. "I heard sounds outside my room and grabbed my weapon. Before I could open my door, the window shattered."

He stepped closer and touched her cheek. "Your face is bleeding."

"From a sliver of wood."

Sirens sounded in the distance.

Colby's voice caught. "I wanted to keep you safe, but I wasn't there when you needed me."

She could have used his help, and maybe together, they would have captured Jacob. But what she needed to hear more than anything was the tenderness in Colby's voice. She'd been hiding from Jacob for too long and not allowing anyone to get close. All that had changed when she transferred to Fort Rickman and met Colby.

He'd been the first man to break through her defenses. Being with him made her realize there was more to life than living in constant fear.

She couldn't tell him the truth. Instead, she tried to shove her armor back in place, only the adrenaline rush ended just that quickly, sapping her energy and leaving her shaking and gasping for air.

A lump filled her throat. Colby was right. She could have been killed.

He opened his arms, and she collapsed into his embrace. Tears burned her eyes.

"Shhh," he soothed.

Wrapped in the cocoon of his protectiveness, she let Colby lead her through the darkness. She inhaled the manly smell of him and heard his heart beating in his chest. His strength buoyed her weakness, and more than anything, she wanted to hold on to him and never let him go.

He kissed her forehead and sent a volley of emotion rambling through her. As much as she tried to ignore the longing, she wanted him to kiss her lips and pull her even more tightly into his embrace.

The bright strobe lights of the law enforcement vehicle captured both of them as they stepped into the glare of light.

Becca straightened and swiped her hand across her cheeks. As much as she wanted to stay wrapped in Colby's embrace she needed to be realistic. This was her fight and her family that needed to be avenged.

She couldn't rely on Colby to always help her. If Jacob came after her again, she'd do what she should have done years ago, and that was to confront Jacob face-to-face.

Colby couldn't get past the memory of holding Becca in his arms. Feeling her mold into his embrace had sent an explosion of sensations through his body. Even now, he was having trouble getting his emotions under control.

Seeing her hurt had nearly torn him in two. The EMTs had quickly assured him both injuries were superficial and would heal without complication, however he still stood close, with a watchful eye, as they cleaned the cut on her face and bandaged her arm.

"The paramedic said you need to take it easy for the next twenty-four hours," he told Becca when the medical team returned to their vehicle.

"I'll rest while you drive us home," she assured him.

After they provided information to the local law enforcement, Colby checked them out of the motel and helped her into the car.

"Shall I adjust the seat belt?" he asked.

She smiled sweetly and patted his hand. "Thank you for your concern, but I'm more worried about you having to drive back to Georgia after the stressful night."

With fewer cars on the road at this time of night, the miles passed quickly. Becca stared at the flickering lights and rested her head against the seat.

"Where'd he go, Colby?" she mused.

"Jacob?" Colby flicked his gaze at her.

She nodded.

"He went back to wherever he's been holed up all these years, like a fox in his lair."

"Eight years." She shook her head. "There's no record of his whereabouts. I've checked repeatedly and could never find any thread that led back to him. He must have lived off the land or off the good-heartedness of the Amish since he didn't leave a social security trail. No credit cards or phone or cell phone records to confirm he was alive during all that time. Tracking him down could be impossible, unless—"

She picked up her phone and touched a number of apps.

"What are you looking for?" Colby asked.

"The locations of other Amish communities."

"You can't access all of them, Becca. They're spread out around the country."

"But I can focus on the ones closest to Alabama and Georgia."

"You can't call them or send a text." Colby stated the obvious, but he was trying to be realistic.

"I'll call law enforcement in nearby municipalities and small towns and inquire about crime in the area, especially fires or gas explosions that led to loss of life."

Colby realized where she was going. "And any widows who may have been hoodwinked by an Amish drifter."

"Exactly. Jacob came to Harmony from somewhere. He posed as a drifter who hired out to the widow he eventually married. That's probably the way he's been operating all this time and keeping under the radar. He hits on some unassuming older woman who needs help and then bilks her out of her money or land or both."

"Did you know the woman he married in Harmony?"

Becca nodded. "Mary was a nice lady but rather sickly. Her husband had died of a heart attack. Both her house and land fell into disrepair. Other men in the community helped out when they could, but they had their own farms to tend. Everyone feared she'd lose her property, although a real estate agent claimed a buyer was interested."

"Was Jacob part of the community at that time?"

"He showed up soon thereafter. Easy enough for him to see there was a problem with the neglected farm." Becca brushed a strand of hair back from her face. "He'd done the same thing at our farm. In fact, that's how I met him. He knocked at the door looking for work."

"Because your home needed repair?"

She nodded. "Although that's an understatement. My father would have loved having Jacob's help, but he didn't have money for any hired hands. *Datt* offered him lodging in the barn, which he accepted for a few weeks. Before long, he was helping the widow. Eventually, he proposed and moved in with her."

"Jacob was younger than Mary?" Colby asked.

"Much younger, but even with the Amish such things happen. Jacob had a way of charming people, including the elders. They were happy the widow was being cared for."

"Did Jacob know about the offer on the land?"

"I'm not sure. I never heard him mention selling the farm."

"When did you start working for him?"

"Not long after he and Mary had married. Her heath had declined. Jacob needed help with the house so he contacted my father. Much as I didn't want to work for Jacob, my *datt* insisted."

"What was Jacob like?" Colby asked.

"He could turn on a dime. He had seemed nice when I first met him, but he changed. Or perhaps he had been hiding his true self all along. I soon noticed how he treated his wife when he didn't think I was watching."

"Did you mention your concerns to your father?"

"Not at first. I knew he would say the problem was with me and not Jacob. That's exactly what happened when I finally told him how worried I was about Mary's health."

"Worried in what way?"

"She kept growing weaker. I suspected Jacob was giving her something to hasten her debilitation."

"Poison?"

Becca sighed. "Perhaps. I had no proof, but he wouldn't allow her to see a doctor, and she often grew more agitated when he was around. I never saw any signs of physical abuse, but I overheard him belittle her on more than one occasion."

"Was that the reason you finally talked to your dad?"

Becca rubbed her forehead and didn't speak for a long moment.

"Do you feel okay?" he asked.

"A headache, that's all."

"You need to rest, Becca. Too much has happened. You should talk to Wilson. Tell him to take you off the case. He'll understand."

She shook her head. "I'm the perfect person to go after Jacob. I know what he looks like, the sound of his voice. He can walk in both the *English* world and the plain without being questioned, yet an Amish community is the perfect place for him to hide out because the people stick to themselves and don't mix with the locals in nearby towns. He's hidden with their help for too long."

"Just as long as we work together, Becca."

"I called you tonight, Colby, when I heard someone outside my room. You didn't answer."

She was right. He had seen the record of her call on his smart phone, but he hadn't heard it ring because he'd been on the far side of the building rechecking the perimeter of the motel as a security precaution.

What he had heard was the gunfire, but he'd arrived at Becca's room too late. Seeing the broken window and battered door had sent his heart to his throat until he'd spied her running into the woods.

He had wanted to keep Becca safe, but he hadn't been there in time.

He wouldn't let it happen again. He was committed to protecting Becca and bringing Jacob Yoder to justice.

Chapter 12

Becca and Colby arrived on post in time for her to grab a few hours of sleep before her alarm went off the next morning. The night before, Colby had insisted on escorting her inside and then checked her room before he finally said good-night.

She could get used to having Colby around. Not that she couldn't handle things on her own, but an extra set of eyes working an investigation was nice, especially on a difficult case. Besides, bouncing ideas back and forth helped her sort through the fragments of information they had already gleaned.

Something else was nice about Colby. He had a funny way of touching her arm when he was concerned about her well-being. She tried to ignore the warmth that flowed though her whenever he was near and instead blamed her fluctuating internal temperature on the weather. But southern Georgia's temps were hovering around forty degrees at night with daytime highs in the mid-fifties.

The truth was that Colby's closeness affected her internal thermostat because she was attracted to the handsome agent. Although she knew better than to allow attraction to get in the way of an investigation, she couldn't help herself. At least Colby didn't realize the effect he had on her. She needed to keep her emotions in check as long as possible. Colby was her partner professionally, but not in any other way.

End of story.

In spite of the post-wide training holiday, a number of folks were at their desks when she entered CID Headquarters that morning.

Raynard Otis saluted and then offered her a welcoming smile. "How's it going, Agent Miller?" he asked when she stopped in front of his desk.

"You should be home relaxing, Ray. Didn't you get the memo about the training holiday?"

"Yes, ma'am, and no, ma'am. I read the memo, but where else would I want to be this morning?" He shrugged. His mocha face stretched into a wide grin. "Everyone else came to work today. We've got a major investigation plus other time-sensitive directives that I need to take over to post headquarters. By the way, Chief Wilson said you might be interested in working on the farmers' market task force the general's wife is leading."

Becca held up her hand and shook her head. "Not until we get to the bottom of this current investigation. Is the chief in his office?"

"No, ma'am. I expect he'll arrive shortly."

Becca stopped momentarily at the coffeepot to pour a cup before heading to her office. A bare desk greeted her. No flowers. No plants. No photos of family. Just a computer and a stack of manila folders.

Nice and neat, the way she liked her life to be.

Except things had suddenly gotten complicated.

Logging in to her computer, she quickly produced a list of Amish communities and corresponding law enforcement agencies in the nearby towns. She printed off two copies.

Becca heard Colby's voice before she saw him. He greeted Kay and took the same path she had earlier to the break room and the coffeepot. In spite of the caffeine, he looked tired when he entered her cubicle some minutes later.

"Long time no see." His dark eyes twinkled, and his lips pulled into a smile.

"Did you sleep at all?" she asked.

"A few hours. And you?"

"The same."

"How's the arm?" he asked.

She glanced down at the bandage. "It's fine."

"You always say you're fine. Sometimes I wish you'd let me in on your life."

She stared at him for a long moment. "Okay." Her right hand rubbed across the bandage. "It's sore, but no significant pain."

He nodded. "That's better. Now let's talk to the chief."

"He's not here yet. I checked on the way in."

Colby pointed to her computer. "I can contact some of those law enforcement agencies near Amish communities, if you've got a list handy."

"I'd appreciate the help." She handed a copy of the list to Colby. "If you work from the top down, I'll start at the bottom."

"You know where to find me." He took the printout she offered and waved as he left her cubicle.

The work was slow and frustrating. Becca's optimism plummeted as one after another of the law enforcement agencies had little or no information about crime within the Amish communities, especially nothing about widows dying in explosions or house fires.

Becca rubbed her neck to stave off stiffness from wedging the phone between her shoulder and ear for too long and was glad for the interruption when Colby tapped his knuckles on the wall to her cubicle and peered inside.

"The chief arrived a few minutes ago. Brody is debriefing him now about Arnold. We're scheduled next."

"Let me make one more phone call."

He nodded. "See you in ten minutes."

She plugged in the next number on her list and asked to speak to the chief of police of a small town in Eastern Tennessee once someone answered.

"This is Chief O'Brian." A deep voice.

She pulled the phone closer to her ear.

"Chief, this is Special Agent Becca Miller. I'm with the U.S. Army Criminal Investigation Division at Fort Rickman, Georgia."

"Thanks for your service, and God bless the military. What can I do for you, Agent Miller?"

She provided a brief but accurate description of what had happened in Harmony eight years ago and the need to determine where Jacob Yoder had been living since that time. "We think he may have killed one of our construction contractors on post."

The chief clucked his tongue while Becca waited, hoping for some small bit of information that could help her track down Jacob.

"I don't recall anyone named Yoder," the chief replied. "We did have a guy, about two years ago, by the name of Lapp. Jacob Lapp. Sounds like a similar M.O."

"How's that?"

"Lapp appeared one day and starts helping one of the Amish widows with a farm in need of a man to run it. They marry, her health declines and she dies some months later. No one was suspicious until he wiped out her bank account and skipped town before we could bring him in for questioning."

"Do you happen to have a description?"

"Give me a minute to find the file."

Becca tapped her fingers on her desk.

"Here you go." The cop's voice. "Lapp was six-two. Dark hair. Small scar on his left cheek."

Becca wanted to clap her hands with glee. "That sounds like my perp. When was the last time you saw him?"

"The day of his wife's funeral. He hasn't been seen since then."

She thanked the man, disconnected and with smooth strokes wrote the information on a tablet of paper. She pushed her chair back and hurried to find Colby.

"I've got something." She held up the pad.

"Tell me as we head to the chief's office."

"A chief of police in eastern Tennessee has seen our guy. Same type of deal. An Amish widow. Fail-

ing health. She died and Jacob—this time going by
the name Jacob Lapp—walked away with her money."

"How long ago did she die?"

"Two years."

"That doesn't prove it was Yoder, Becca."

"The description fits."

"A big Amish guy with dark hair. How many men
could fill that description?"

Colby was right, but it was the only lead they'd had
so far, and Becca wasn't ready to dismiss the information as insignificant. If Lapp was Yoder, then Jacob
was still alive.

In spite of her earlier euphoria, she knew that without an eyewitness or fingerprints or DNA nothing could
establish that the two men were the same. Even a photo
would be a plus. But all Becca knew was a man named
Lapp had lost his wife and moved on with the money
that was rightfully his through marriage.

No crime. No evidence. No proof she could place
on Wilson's desk. She'd be better off to keep the information to herself until she had something more significant to report.

She needed to make a good impression on Wilson,
but at this point, she didn't know where she stood.
Working with Colby added another complication to a
very difficult case.

Colby tapped on the chief's door. "Sir, do you have
a minute?"

Wilson glanced at his watch and then motioned for
Colby and Becca to enter. "I have to be at the commanding general's office in twenty minutes. What do
you have?"

"A possible suspect in the Arnold murder, sir."
Aware of the time constraint, Colby gave the chief a
brief overview of what they'd learned about Jacob and
his brother and concluded with mention of the shooting at the motel.

"Did you receive medical treatment when you returned to post, Becca?" Wilson asked.

She shook her head. "It wasn't necessary, sir. The
Florida EMTs cleaned and bandaged the wound last
night. It's a superficial graze and should heal without
additional medical attention."

"You might want to go on sick call and see if the doc
thinks an antibiotic would be helpful. I don't want an
infection to set it."

"I'll watch for any warning signs."

Wilson seemed satisfied. He pursed his lips and steepled his fingers, elbows perched on his desk. "I have a
problem considering Jacob Yoder as the attacker last
night or the person who murdered Arnold. From what
you said, Yoder was killed in a house fire in Harmony."
The chief pushed back in his chair and spread his hands
across his desk. "I don't see how he could have committed this crime."

Colby had thought the same thing himself early on.
Now, after everything that had happened, he believed
Jacob was a very likely suspect.

"Sir, Becca believes the man killed in the house fire
was Yoder's brother," Colby offered. "The two men
were of similar stature and appearance. A mistaken
identification seems probable."

Wilson looked at Becca. "Does the Harmony sheriff
share your suspicions?"

She shook her head. "I don't think so, sir."

"Was DNA testing done before interment?"

"No, sir."

"Are they willing to exhume the body to make a more definitive identification?"

"Not that I know of."

He glanced at Colby, then back at Becca. "I'm more prone to consider the Macon connection as significant in this investigation. Brody came across the owner of a small company whose bid on the housing contract for the new BOQs wasn't accepted. He's had some brushes with the law and has been known to retaliate when his company's offer wasn't accepted. He sent one competitor to the hospital with broken ribs and a cracked jaw. Brody can fill you in."

"Yes, sir."

"If you turn up any concrete evidence that Jacob Yoder is alive, let me know, and we can reevaluate. As it stands now, going after a dead man seems a waste of time and effort."

"What about the shooting last night, sir?" Becca pressed.

"Anyone have a grudge against you?"

"Yes, sir. Jacob Yoder."

Wilson steeled his jaw. From all appearances, he didn't like her rather flip response. "Maybe you should back off a bit, Agent Miller."

Becca frowned. "I'm not sure what you mean, sir."

"What I mean is stay on post and keep a low profile. I want you to handle the security for the farmers' market and craft fair. I've submitted your name to Mrs. Cameron."

"But—"

The chief cut her off and pointed to Colby. "Let

Agent Voss do the legwork on the investigation. You can help him here in the office. I don't want you placed in danger. The CID was short-staffed for too long. Now that I've got a few new faces in the office, I want to keep everyone healthy and productive."

He opened a folder. "Do you know anyone named Brad Nicholson?"

She hesitated as if trying to place the name. "No one comes to mind, sir."

"He's the Macon contractor. I just wanted to ensure both sides of the investigation aren't looking at the same person."

"Sir, Jacob Yoder killed my father and sister. He vowed to kill me."

Wilson's eyes narrowed. "That's significant for sure. But the fact that Yoder is dead seems to close that part of the investigation. Do you understand, Becca?"

"Yes, sir."

Only the look on her face told Colby that she didn't understand nor did she go along with the chief's assessment of the situation or his guidance about her staying out of the line of fire. From what he already knew about Becca, staying at the office wasn't how she wanted to handle this investigation.

Would she obey Wilson's directives. Or would she continue to look for a dead man that she feared was very much alive?

Becca wanted to pound her fist against her desk. She was frustrated with Wilson. Had he even listened to what she told him?

Her father hadn't listened when she revealed the truth about Jacob. Now Wilson was focusing on other clues and missing the very real killer that Becca knew was in the local area.

The chief might think she'd be safe on post, but Jacob seemed able to slip through on-post security with ease. The man needed to be flushed out of hiding, which meant finding him before he found her. Becca wouldn't let him get away. Not this time.

"Come with me," she said to Colby once he entered her cubical.

"You heard the chief, Becca. He wants you to stay on post. Don't go hunting for trouble."

"He's sending Brody on a wild-goose chase. That Macon contractor sounds like a puffed-up marshmallow compared to Jacob."

"Wilson's thinking of your own good, Becca."

"What about the next widow Jacob targets? He's got devious methods that have worked for him in the past. Why wouldn't he be hiding in plain sight in the nearby community? We need to find out who lives in that house in the clearing."

Colby nodded. "I agree, but—"

"Then we're on the same page. By the way, I sent the photos of the car in the barn to forensics, along with the photo of the marks we saw on the side of the road after the shooting in Alabama." She picked up her phone and opened the photo file. "Look at these tire tracks."

He studied the photo, then pulled out his own phone and clicked on his file. He put the photo of the tracks he'd taken in Alabama next to the tracks Becca had photographed in the barn.

"The clarity isn't sharp enough, but both tracks could have been made by the same tires."

She nodded. "And the same vehicle. Let's take a little ride into the country."

"Becca," Colby warned.

"We're not investigating. We're merely seeing the countryside."

"Wilson told you to stay put."

"And before that, he said for us to work together. You told me we're partners."

"Things have changed since then."

She took a step back and raised her hands. "Whatever, but I'm driving to the Lodge."

"Somehow I get the feeling you'll make a detour."

She smiled. "A detour to Amish country. Come with me, Colby. Otherwise, I'll be forced to go alone."

"You're doing this against Wilson's request."

"A request," Becca restated for emphasis. "That's exactly right. The chief didn't order me to stop investigating. Rather, he encouraged me to remain safe. If you're with me, I will be safe. Besides, I'm worried about the people who live in that run-down house where we saw the car. I couldn't endure knowing my lack of action caused someone else harm."

She grabbed her keys and purse and turned toward the door. "What do you say, partner?"

Colby shook his head and sighed with frustration. "We're in this together, Becca, but you need to follow my lead. Don't do anything foolish or bold. Wilson doesn't want you hurt, and neither do I."

"Don't worry. The last thing I want is to be injured or incapacitated when I finally confront Jacob Yoder."

Colby and Becca passed the turnoff to Dawson and Lillie's house and continued on along a narrow road that eventually led to an area of Amish farmhouses. Just as before, Colby was struck by the charm of the simple life. No cars in the driveways or power and phone lines littering the landscape. Not a television dish or porch light in sight.

The land was beautiful even in its winter pause. Barren trees swayed in the wind that stirred from the west, and a flock of birds flew overhead, searching for a place to land.

Colby turned up the heat and glanced at Becca. "You should have worn a coat."

"I'm fine."

"How's the arm and don't tell me it's fine, too."

She smiled, but her eyes looked tired. "Actually, it's aching."

"You need some pain meds."

"I'll take an ibuprofen when I get back to the Lodge."

"You need to go on sick call in the morning."

She nodded. "Maybe you're right."

They were definitely making progress.

"Although," she added, "I hate to seem like a weakling."

"You're not. Wouldn't you tell me the same thing if I had taken a hit?"

"You probably wouldn't listen, either."

He laughed. "You mean we're both cut from the same cloth?"

"Both CID. Both focused on getting the job done. Both type A." She paused. "Except you're the extrovert."

"And you?"

Her slender shoulders rose for a moment. "I'm usually more comfortable hanging out with myself."

She pointed to an intersection. "There's the turn."

The road wove through a dense cluster of trees before it spilled into the clearing. Colby pulled to the side of the road and killed the engine.

He studied the farmhouse. It needed a new coat of paint as if the original job had been done with a cheap product that failed to seal the wood. Curtains covered the windows. The sun peering through the cloud cover painted the house in an eerie light that was both uninviting and cold.

"We can't search without a warrant," he cautioned.

"No, but we can knock on the door and talk to whoever answers." They climbed the front steps, taking care not to trip on the loose plank.

Becca rapped boldly on the door. When no one answered, she called in a loud voice, "Is anyone home? My name's Becca Miller. I'm with the Criminal Investigation Division on Fort Rickman. I'd like to ask you a few questions."

Again she knocked, but the door remained closed.

She glanced at Colby, tilted her head and listened for any sound coming from inside the house.

"Let's check the barn," she suggested.

Colby kept glancing back at the house, feeling an ominous tightness in his shoulders as if someone was watching from behind the closed curtains.

Becca tugged on the barn door and peered inside. "The car's gone."

The two Dobermans appeared on the rise of a hill in the distance. They were huge creatures with sleek coats and mammoth jowls.

Becca gasped.

"Back up nice and easy," Colby cautioned.

They backtracked, their eyes locked on the dogs.

Twenty feet from the car, the animals lunged forward as if on command. Their legs flew down the hillside. Their barks of protest set the hair on Colby's neck on end.

"Get in the car, Becca." He opened the door. She slipped past him.

The dogs were closing in. They bared their teeth and raced forward.

Colby slammed her door and rounded the car. He slipped behind the wheel and pulled the driver's door closed just in time. The dogs circled the car and barked ferociously. Becca shivered.

"We're safe," he said in hopes of calming her as well as his own rapid heartbeat.

He loved dogs, but not as vicious attack animals. Who owned the Dobermans? And had someone commanded them to attack?

Looking up at the window, he caught sight of a face peering around the curtain.

The Amish were a quiet people who kept to themselves, peace-loving and gentle. The vicious dogs didn't seem in keeping with their way of life. Neither did the Crown Vic they'd seen earlier in the barn.

They'd come back, but next time they'd have a search warrant so they could find whoever was hiding inside.

Chapter 13

Becca didn't have time for a coffee klatch with the general's wife and the other folks on the committee to plan the first farmers' market and craft fair at Fort Rickman. She did, however, want to meet the bishop, who was the appointed head of the Amish community.

The following morning, Becca donned a skirt and sweater with a jacket pulled over her shoulders, and hoped she'd be suitably dressed for the meeting at Quarters One, home to every commanding general since the post was built in the 1930s.

Before the army had purchased the land, the expansive farmhouse and surrounding property had belonged to a Georgia farmer. Since then, the rambling structure had undergone a number of renovations. Painted white with large wraparound porches and a gazebo in the front yard, the home was comfortable but elegant in a simple way and befitting the commander and his wife.

Mrs. Cameron was a sweet, Southern belle who hailed from Savannah. Her accent had softened over the years of following her military husband around the world, but a trace of the South remained and seemed evident as she invited Becca into the spacious foyer.

"I'm so glad you'll be able to help us with the planning, Special Agent Miller."

"It's Becca, ma'am. Thank you for inviting me into your home."

The older woman, wearing a pretty floral dress, pointed down a hallway. "Everyone is in the family room. I had the aide build a fire, since there's a chill in the air this morning. Help yourself to coffee or tea and pastries."

"Thank you, ma'am."

A number of people from post headquarters had already arrived and were chatting among themselves when she stepped into the airy room. Decorated with aqua-and-lime-green accents, the splashes of color against the eggshell walls and neutral couches gave the room a casual feel. The logs burning in the fireplace added warmth and a homey touch that Becca found inviting.

Groupings of flowers and books and large ceramic decorative plates added to the cozy ambiance, despite the formal wainscot paneling and massive floor-to-ceiling windows.

Becca poured a cup of coffee and sat in a small chair in the corner. A middle-aged woman perched on a nearby couch stretched out her hand. "I'm Lois Simmons."

The chief of staff's wife. Becca recognized the last

name and accepted the handshake. "Nice to meet you, ma'am. I'm with the CID on post."

"We haven't met before?"

"No, ma'am. I just transferred here from Germany."

"We lived in Heidelberg some years ago." The woman's eager smile revealed her appreciation of the foreign country. "I keep telling Bob we need to get assigned there again."

"It is a beautiful place."

"With wonderful people. Where were you stationed?"

"Garmisch."

"In Bavaria." Mrs. Simmons eagerly chatted about the various trips she and her husband had taken to the Black Forest and surrounding areas. "Were you there for the Passion Play in Oberammergau?"

"Unfortunately no." The three-hour performance was held every ten years and had been ongoing since 1634 in thanksgiving for God's protection over the small town during the plague.

The chief of staff's wife patted her chest with emotion. Her eyes brimmed with tears. "The reenactment of Christ's Passion touched me deeply, especially when He was forced to carry his cross."

Becca knew about crosses, but she rarely thought about the cross Christ carried. Had she strayed so far from her faith?

Mrs. Cameron stepped into the room escorting a man, plain of dress, with a full beard. He held a hat in one hand and a small notebook and pencil in the other.

"Everyone, I'd like to introduce Bishop Isaac Zimmerman, from the Amish community. He's graciously agreed to meet with us and plan the upcoming farmers' market and craft fair that we're so excited about hosting."

She pulled up a chair and placed it on the other side of Becca.

"May I get you coffee and a pastry?" Mrs. Cameron asked the bishop.

"Thank you, yes." He smiled agreeably at the other guests. "I am pleased to join you today."

The general's wife proved to be a good facilitator, and the plans for the market and craft fair were finalized in less than two hours. Those who attended represented various organizations on post. Each group volunteered responsibility for a certain aspect of the event.

Morale Support promised a sound system for the commanding general's welcoming remarks. The post band would provide music, and the children's choirs from the Main Post Chapel would sing at various times throughout the morning.

"I'm glad Special Agent Miller could be with us today," Mrs. Cameron said, nearing the conclusion of the meeting. "Becca, you and your folks will provide security?"

"Yes, ma'am."

The bishop shook his head as if somewhat concerned. "I do not expect trouble. Do you?"

"Not at all, sir." Mrs. Cameron quickly stepped in to reassure the bishop. "But when we have so many people in an area, we like to have security on hand as a precaution. Regrettably problems sometimes occur even in the best of situations."

After a final wrap-up, Mrs. Cameron thanked the committee members for taking part in the planning task force.

As the other folks headed toward the front door, Becca stepped closer to the bishop who had placed his coffee cup and saucer on the small side table.

"Sir, I drove through the Amish community and noticed a house that sits along one of the side roads. It's surrounded by rather dense forest that opens into a clearing. The house is in need of repair, which is not in keeping with the other homes. There's a barn to the left of the main house and a hill behind. The person has two dogs, both Doberman pinschers."

The bishop nodded. "I know of this house."

"Who lives there, sir? Is it someone in your community?"

"An older woman. Fannie Lehman. Her husband died some months ago when a tree fell on him."

Just as had happened in Alabama. "I'm sorry about her loss."

The bishop nodded. "*Gott* gives life and takes it away."

"I'm sure Mrs. Lehman finds it hard to manage her land. Does she have someone to help her?"

"Why does this cause you concern?"

"I'm looking for a man who may be hiding out among the Amish. His name is Jacob Yoder. He's six-two with dark hair and a scar on his left cheek."

"I do not know this man." The bishop reached for his hat. "Besides, the Amish are peace-loving people. We do not deal with violence."

"Yet sometimes it finds you."

His eyes narrowed and his gnarly fingers gripped the brim of his hat. "You mentioned security and now you tell me of an Amish man who hides from the law. I will not take part in anything that brings discord or strife to my people. Even if we have agreed to the market, we must maintain our way of life first. You understand, *yah*?"

A subtle warning, but one Becca understood. If she disrupted the Amish way of life, the bishop would draw back from his agreement with Fort Rickman to hold the market and craft fairs.

Mrs. Cameron stepped toward them. She glanced first at the bishop and then at Becca. "Is something wrong?"

Becca remained silent, waiting to hear what the bishop would say.

"I was discussing the Amish way with Miss Miller and our love for the peaceful life."

"Military personnel are tasked with ensuring the peace, Bishop," Becca answered. "But we know that evil people do evil things."

Turning to the general's wife, she said, "Thank you, ma'am, for the coffee. I'll see myself out."

Becca left the house frustrated by the bishop's stubborn determination to see things only his way. He didn't realize that if Jacob Yoder were in the area, the Amish could be in danger, no matter how peace-loving they were.

She climbed into her car and called Colby. "The meeting ended, and I'm headed back to CID Headquarters. Did Wilson okay the request for a search warrant?"

Colby pulled in a stiff breath. "He was hesitant and wanted to run the request past General Cameron."

Heaviness settled over Becca's shoulders as she recalled the bishop's comment. "I can guess what the general said."

"Nothing is to interfere with our good relationship with the Amish. Evidently Mrs. Cameron has been interested in getting this organized for months. The bishop was the negative force. He's only recently changed his mind."

"But what if Jacob Yoder is hiding out at the house?"

"Wilson considers that a big what-if, but to his credit, he contacted the Freemont chief of police and asked him to increase surveillance in the area. The county sheriff will provide additional backup, although without a photograph of Jacob, law enforcement doesn't know who they're looking for."

"Did you mention the scar on his cheek?"

"A lot of people have scars, Becca."

"The name of the woman who lives in the run-down house is Lehman. Fannie Lehman. Her husband died accidently a few months ago. He was killed by a fallen tree."

"Sounds familiar," Colby said.

The door to the commanding general's house opened and the bishop walked outside.

"Gotta go, Colby. I'll see you back at headquarters."

The bishop nodded goodbye to Mrs. Cameron and walked toward his buggy.

Becca stepped from her car and approached the rig.

"Bishop, I'm sorry if I caused you concern inside. I want the Amish to maintain their way of life, but there is a man I fear may cause problems. He lived in an Amish community near Harmony, Alabama. Some years ago, he killed my father and sister. He may be in this area now."

The bishop's gaze softened. "You carry great pain, and for this I am sorry, but I do not know of the man you mentioned."

"Mrs. Lehman is living alone and vulnerable. Would you ensure no one has moved in to help her? Someone who might have ulterior motives."

The bishop hesitated for a long moment and then nodded. "I will speak to her."

"Thank you, sir."

"But Ms. Miller, you mentioned an Amish community in Alabama. Your father and sister, they were plain?"

She nodded, feeling her eyes sting under his gentle scrutiny.

"And you were, as well?" he asked.

"*Yah.*"

The bishop nodded ever so slightly. "This man, this Jacob Yoder, he caused you to flee the Amish and find safety with the *English?*"

"I was safe for eight years, but he's found me, Bishop. Now I must stop him."

"He is not Amish if he deals in violence. I will ask *Gott* to protect you so this Jacob Yoder cannot hurt you again."

He nodded farewell and climbed into the buggy, the squeak of the carriage and the slap of the reins against the horses' haunches all too familiar. The bishop clicked his tongue, and the horses stepped forward, the creak of the wheels over the pavement sounding in the morning calm.

"Remember, Becca," the bishop called back to her from the carriage. "*Gott* loves you."

"The county sheriff said he'll have his deputies patrol the Amish area," Colby said once Becca arrived back at CID Headquarters. "But he doesn't expect to find anything suspect."

"Is the Freemont chief of police interested in getting a search warrant?"

"Negative. Nor is the sheriff."

"Why not?"

"Because Jacob Yoder is dead. At least, that's what everyone believes. Don Palmer, the current chief of the local Freemont P.D., called Harmony and talked to Lewis Stone. He's sympathetic, but not willing to exhume the body."

"Which doesn't make sense."

"I called him. According to Lewis, he needs to match DNA from the exhumed remains with a DNA sample from Yoder or his brother, which he doesn't have."

Becca held up her hand. "You mean Stone needs something from Yoder's past that contains his DNA?"

"That's the problem. We don't have any leads on the brother, and everything in Yoder's house burned to the ground."

"Is that the only thing stopping him from exhuming the body?"

"Sounds like it."

Becca nodded. "Then we'll have to dig up a sample of Jacob's DNA."

"You mean another trip to Harmony?"

She nodded. "We can go this afternoon."

"Only if you agree to the following conditions, Becca. We work together and you don't hold anything else back from me."

"I promise. Cross my heart."

As much as he wanted to ask what she had on Jacob,

Colby knew Becca's reticence and decided not to press for more details. Everything would be revealed in time.

Right now, he wanted to ensure she didn't go racing off across the countryside on her own. Becca's enthusiasm to find Jacob often conflicted with her need to be cautious and vigilant.

Another concern niggled at Colby. If she had DNA evidence that led back to Jacob Yoder, there could be other secrets Becca was keeping from him, as well.

Chapter 14

Becca sat in the passenger seat next to Colby and watched the countryside roll by as they drove back to Harmony and the Amish community. An afternoon meeting with the military police about post security had kept them tied up at the office longer than they had expected. The only plus was that Becca had been able to coordinate help for the upcoming farmers' market and craft fair following the meeting.

The traffic getting off post at the close of the workday had added to their delay. Road construction as well as a fender bender held them up even longer.

Becca glanced at the sun, low in the sky. The optimism she had felt earlier plummeted. Returning home would be hard enough in daylight. The approaching darkness made her chest tighten. The last time she had been in the house had been the middle of the night to find her sister and father slaughtered by an evil man who still wreaked havoc in too many lives.

As much as she needed to stop Jacob, she was anxious about returning to her past both figuratively and literally.

"You're quiet this evening," Colby finally said, as if aware of how deep within herself she had gone.

"You know how introverts are," she said with a half smile she didn't feel.

"Thinking about your family?"

She nodded. "And that night. Jacob had told Katie he would come after her if she tried to flee. She had struggled to keep him at a distance, but as Mary became more and more infirmed, Jacob became more brazen."

Becca tapped her fingers on the console.

"Katie feared something would happen. She called me from Elizabeth's house." Becca's throat tightened as she heard Katie's frantic voice echo in her mind. "She said she needed me. Katie thought I could protect her and stand up to Jacob."

"You were stationed at Fort Campbell?"

"That's right. I left as fast as I could and drove nonstop for five hours. When I arrived, I found my father on the floor, the life ebbing from him. Katie had been killed in the pantry."

Looking into the darkness ahead, Becca relived the horror of that night. "I heard footsteps upstairs and knew Jacob was still in the house."

She thought again of the heavy footfalls on the stairwell as Jacob descended to the main floor. "I raced outside. Jacob stepped onto the porch and searched the night. He…"

She hesitated, unable to enter again into that moment

when they had connected, his gaze finding her in the darkness. His face had contorted with rage. "He raised his hand in anger and screamed that if I ran from him, he would find me and kill me."

"You eluded him for a number of years."

"Only because I asked for assignments in Europe. I came back for a few weeks of temporary duty here and there." She pushed a strand of hair away from her face. "I... I was always looking over my shoulder, thinking Jacob was closing in on me. Even in Europe, I'd thought I'd see him in the distance. Of course, it wasn't him. It was my mind playing tricks on me."

She touched the window. "I ran out of options and talked myself into believing that he had died in the fire. The job opened at Fort Rickman. I knew Chief Wilson was a strong leader and thought the assignment would be good for my career."

They rode for a few miles before Colby asked, "When you learned Jacob's house had burned and his body was supposedly found inside, did you believe the news or did you suspect he was still alive right from the start?"

"I wanted to believe he had died. Elizabeth had invited me to stay with her. Sheriff McDougal came to her house to question me. He seemed sympathetic and knew I was struggling."

"Did you tell him your suspicions that Jacob was still alive?"

"Not at first, because I wanted to believe he was dead."

"Sounds as if something changed your mind."

She nodded. "I went for a run a few days later. Of course, I was still in shock, still grieving."

Colby reached for her hand. His touch offered support and a connection that had grown stronger in the last couple days. He was more than a partner. Much more.

"Jacob followed me." She shook her head. "I should rephrase that—*someone* followed me. I headed along one of the trails that led into the country. There's a small pond. Moms take their children there to feed the ducks and geese."

"But that day was different?"

Becca nodded. "Dark clouds had formed, and the wind picked up strength. I knew the rain would start soon, but I wanted to circle the pond before I returned to town."

She tugged at her hair with her free hand. "I heard someone call my name."

"It was Jacob?"

"I never saw him, but I recognized his voice." Again her slender shoulders rose. "At least, I thought it was his voice. Rain fell in fat drops that stung my face and mixed with my tears. I ran as fast as I could, but the wind was against me, and the wet ground was slick. I—I kept looking over my shoulders."

"But you didn't see him?"

"No, but I sensed his presence. I told the sheriff. He told me to see a shrink and get some meds."

"Did you?"

"Of course not. I didn't need medication to know what I had heard. As soon as the bodies were interred, I drove back to Fort Campbell and put in for the CID. I needed to have the knowledge and strength and wherewithal to protect myself."

Colby squeezed her hand. "We'll find him, Becca."

She smiled ever so slightly. Much as she wanted Colby's help, she knew this fight was her own and too many had died already. She didn't want to pull him down with her. How could she endure if something happened to Colby because of her?

In the end, she'd have to confront Jacob. She had started the terrible spiral of events that had led to her sister and father being murdered and now even Elizabeth had been a victim of Jacob's crazed wrath.

Jacob was her problem. She'd started it, and she planned to finish it. She'd find Jacob and bring him to justice if it was the last thing she ever did.

Although relieved that Becca had shared some of what had happened long ago, Colby's heart tightened hearing the pain in her voice as she talked about Katie.

Thinking of his own sisters made her regret even more significant. The creep who had jilted his oldest sister, Gloria, was on his list of most heinous individuals.

His sister's broken heart had been hard enough to bear. He didn't want to think about any physical harm befalling her.

Plus, Becca had lost her father. Not that they seemed to have had the best relationship, but he was still her parent, and she had a strong sense of duty to family. Becca had wanted, and needed, her dad's attention and affection. He'd ignored her on that level and instead had made her feel less than important.

Colby thought of the future, wishing his tomorrows would include Becca. Maybe some kids. He'd make sure they knew how much they were wanted and loved. Of course, he'd also ensure they were well mannered and respected authority, but every child needed love and affirmation.

He glanced at Becca. Her head rested against the back of the seat. He wasn't sure if she was sleeping, but he wouldn't do anything to wake her if she were.

Growing up must have been tough, always feeling she didn't measure up. Becca was a beautiful person inside and out, and Colby wanted to tell her how special she was and how important she was to him. She filled his thoughts and made their time together bright. He wanted to tell her a lot of things, which would have to wait until after the investigation.

Right now, he had to help her go back to her past. She carried a lot of pain that needed to be healed.

He knew the internal struggle guilt could cause. If only he hadn't transferred to another forward operating base, Ellen might still be alive. He'd left base earlier that same day. No one expected the mortar attack. He learned later that Ellen had been preoccupied with a report she needed to finish and had hesitated seeking shelter. He'd always been there before to push her to the safety of the bunker in time. Her delay had proved deadly when the second mortar hit.

Ellen had severed their relationship and probably would have ignored his help even if he hadn't left base, yet he still felt responsible for her death. The fact that he hadn't been there to protect her was a wound he wondered if he'd ever be able to heal. That's why protecting Becca was so important.

He glanced at her again. Becca's eyes were closed and her breath shallow. He and Becca both had holes in their hearts that needed to be filled. He wanted to help her. Maybe in helping her, he'd fix his own hurt. Or maybe he would never be able to forgive himself and redeem his past.

Either way, he wanted Becca to heal.

Please, Lord.

He pursed his lips. Did God listen to him anymore, or had He given up on Colby ever coming back to the fold?

Becca had mentioned having to carry a cross. She had her cross. Colby had his, as well.

If only he could help her.

If only he could help himself.

If only God would help both of them.

Chapter 15

The house sat dark against the night sky. Becca had closed her eyes earlier and rested during the drive to Harmony, but she still felt the heavy weight of fatigue, probably brought on by the stress of returning home.

Seeing the house, the memories rushed upon her like the heat from the explosion on post. The unlatched door, the shadowed darkness of the room, her father's butchered body lying on the floor.

She climbed from the car, inhaling the cold, damp air and shivered. Colby placed his arm around her shoulders. She leaned into him, appreciating his warmth. He pulled her closer as if knowing the struggle raging inside her.

At this moment, she needed Colby more than she had ever needed anyone. He sensed that need and pulled her fully into his embrace.

A flicker of moonlight broke between the clouds and bathed them both in light. Colby hesitated and then slowly lowered his lips to hers. She clung to him like a lifeline, wanting to remain forever in his arms. The pain of her past eased momentarily, replaced with a hope for the future, something she had never allowed herself to consider since she had run away from Jacob.

Finding the inner courage to move forward, she pulled back ever so slightly. Colby's voice was husky with emotion when he spoke.

"We don't have to do this now," he told her. "We can come back another time."

She shook her head. "No. I won't run away again. Plus I want the body exhumed as soon as possible to prove it isn't Jacob."

"Without a chain of custody, I doubt whatever DNA sample you have will hold up in a court of law."

"Maybe not, but at least I'll know the truth."

"Whenever you're ready," Colby said, his support reassuring.

An owl hooted from the trees.

Becca squared her shoulders and nodded. "Let's go."

Arm in arm they climbed the steps to the porch, testing each one before placing their weight on the rotten boards. Two of the supporting braces were broken, causing the wooden planks to sag at an angle.

Colby remained at her side, encouraging her to go on. "Don't think about the past," he cautioned. "Stay in the present. Don't look back."

He switched on his Maglite and opened the door. Becca stepped inside, her gaze drawn to the spot where her father had died. A wide stain from his pooled blood still darkened the floorboards.

Colby rubbed his free hand over her arm. "Where do we go now?"

"Upstairs." She motioned him toward the narrow stairwell.

The old house creaked with each step.

Slowly and deliberately, she climbed to the second floor. Colby's footfalls followed behind her. The steady pull of air in and out of his lungs assured her of his presence.

I'm not alone. Colby's with me. This is now.

The dank and musty smell of the old house drew her back in time. For an instant, she was again the defiant youth. Too strong-willed, her father had often said.

How many nights had she retreated to her bedroom dreaming of what her life could be? In those days, she had believed in love and happiness and goodness. Perhaps it had been a way to escape the reality of her existence.

Her father's room sat on the left. She walked past without glancing through the doorway. What did she need to see?

Instead, she was drawn to the open door at the end of the hall. Hesitating for a moment at the threshold, she pulled in a deep breath and stepped into the tiny room, smaller than she had remembered. Her gaze flicked over the single bed and faded quilt. In the corner, mouse droppings were evidence of the tiny creatures that lived here now.

Using both her hands, she pushed the bed aside and shooed away the thick cobwebs as she dropped to her knees. "Shine the light on the floor."

Colby angled the Maglite over where she knelt.

She ran the tips of her fingers across the floorboards, searching for the uneven plank.

Why couldn't she find it?

She pushed the bed farther from the wall and expanded her search until her hand snagged against a sharp sliver of wood. She pulled back.

Colby leaned closer. "What's wrong, honey?"

Becca shook her head. "A splinter, that's all."

Focused on the uneven plank, she dug at the wood. It failed to budge.

"Let me try." Colby handed her the flashlight and knelt beside her on the floor. He picked at the irregular edge and was finally able to pry the plank loose. Using two hands, he eased the board free.

Becca aimed the light into space under the flooring. *Empty!*

She moaned ever so quietly and turned to Colby as if he'd known what she had expected to find. "It's not here."

He took the flashlight from her hand and angled it farther into the hollowed-out area until something metallic reflected in the darkness.

Her treasure box.

Relief swept over her. She clawed at the small container jammed in the back of the cubbyhole. Her fingers eased it forward until she could lift it free.

Her heart pounded in her chest, just as had often happened as a girl when she removed the tin box to look at her precious keepsakes.

Tonight was no different with the steady thump of her pulse and an overwhelming need to glance over her shoulder to ensure she was alone.

Only she wasn't alone tonight. Colby was kneeling

next to her. His presence brought a sense of security and dispelled the darkness that surrounded her youth. She leaned into him, feeling his strength.

He rubbed his hand over her shoulder and waited patiently as she stared at the tin, not quite ready to expose the past.

The bond between them had grown even stronger this evening. She smiled, remembering his kiss and the concern and understanding that was so evident in his gaze.

Colby seemed to care about her in a special way just as she was beginning to realize the depth of her feelings for him. Tonight she was all too aware of his willingness to enter into the pain of her past, yet when she opened the box, he would know what she had always wanted to remain hidden.

She closed her eyes for a long moment before she removed the lid. Glancing down, she saw the bits and pieces of her childhood, so seemingly insignificant, yet each an important facet of her life.

A pretty rock that sparkled like gold. *Fool's gold,* her father called it, but special to a child who had nothing and wanted something of her own. A tiny fossil that opened her mind to the vastness of creation and what had been millenniums ago. A fake pearl necklace she found along the roadway. The clasp was broken and had, no doubt, dropped unnoticed from some woman's neck. Becca had often draped the pearls around her own, knowing her father would call it an abomination if he ever saw her wearing jewelry.

"Your necklace?" Colby asked.

"Something I found and shouldn't have kept."

"What about the fossil and speckled rock?"

"They reminded me of the beauty of God's creation." She smiled ruefully. "I was a romantic as a youth."

He touched her cheek, and she turned to face him. "But no longer?"

Regret tugged at her heart. "I learned too quickly about the reality of life."

He nodded slowly. "Seeing the darkness of the world at too young an age can be painful."

She rested her head on his shoulder, grateful for his presence, before she removed the other items from the box and lay them aside. An envelope sat at the bottom, brittle as parchment and almost as yellow.

Colby angled the light. "Is this what you came to find?"

She nodded. Years ago, she had used a knife to open the envelope, leaving the sealed flap intact. Slowly, she withdrew the note written in script with broad strokes by a black pen.

Meet me tonight at the covered bridge.
Yours affectionately, Jacob Yoder

How could she have been so gullible, so naive, so unaware of how a man could break a young girl's heart? Jacob had never showed up that night, nor the next or the one following. Instead he had turned his charms on the widow Mary.

Becca hadn't seen him again until she was forced to care for the woman Jacob, by that time, had married. Thrown together again, he had hoped to take up where they had left off. At least, Becca had learned from her earlier mistake.

Jacob, on the other hand, didn't understand why

Becca shunned his advances. How could he think she would succumb to his desires when he'd rejected her to marry another?

She still couldn't forgive her youthful infatuation with the handsome stranger who had whispered words that filled her mind with the possibilities of a life together. Her innocent flirting and inability to see the consequences of her actions had led to so much pain, so many deaths. She had to stop Jacob so what she had started long ago could finally end.

Colby called Lewis Stone on the way back to town. "Special Agent Becca Miller and I are heading to your office. We have Jacob Yoder's DNA on an envelope he licked some years ago."

"I'll meet you there," the sheriff said.

Going home had weighed Becca down. Colby saw it in the hesitation in her step and the slump of her shoulders. Surely the memories of the night she had found her father and sister must be affecting her in addition to knowing that Jacob could be nearby.

She had been barely eighteen. How easy for an older man to tease a young, impressionable woman reared in the closed environment of an Amish community.

Jacob hadn't thought of Becca's feelings. More than likely he wanted to control every situation, never weighing how his actions could impact the young woman.

Lights from town appeared in the distance. Colby drove toward the main square and passed the turnoff to Elizabeth's house. Becca glanced out the window at the side street of modest homes.

Her heart must be breaking as she thought of the woman who had assisted her in escaping Jacob's control. A woman who was eventually killed by the very man she had helped Becca elude.

Colby turned left at the square. The sheriff's office sat on the corner. He pulled into the parking area and rounded the car to help Becca with the door.

"Do you want to stay in the car and let me handle this?"

She shook her head. "It's my story to tell, Colby, but thank you for trying to protect me."

With the evidence bag in hand, they stepped into the glare of overhead fluorescent lights. Lewis met them in the hallway. They shook hands, and he ushered them into his office and invited them to sit.

"Tell me what you've got," he said, settling into the swivel chair behind his desk.

Becca placed the paper bag in front of the sheriff. "A sealed note Jacob Yoder gave me approximately ten years ago. Forensics will be able to uncover his DNA from the saliva on the flap of the envelope."

"There's no chain of custody," Lewis pointed out.

"I'm aware the evidence won't be admissible in court."

She moved forward in the chair and glanced at Colby, as if for support. "I…" She shook her head. "We want the body that was found in the Yoder farmhouse exhumed and DNA testing done. My suspicion is that it wasn't Jacob Yoder, but rather his brother, Ezekiel."

"Did Jacob kill his brother?" the sheriff asked.

"At this point, I don't know, but I'd also like his wife Mary's body exhumed and testing to be done for any trace of a poisonous substance."

"He killed her?"

Becca nodded. "I think he was slowly poisoning his wife, which led to her declining health."

Colby filled the chief in on the similar case in Tennessee. "We can't be sure, but the man fit Jacob's description, including a scar on his left cheek, and there seems to be a pattern."

Lewis stared at both of them for a long moment. Colby couldn't determine which direction the sheriff was leaning toward.

Finally he grabbed a pencil and sheet of paper from his desk drawer. "Give me the name of the police department you talked to up north. I'll contact them and include that information in my request for both bodies to be exhumed."

Lewis copied the information Colby provided and then said, "You realize the DNA testing will take time."

Becca nodded. "But you'll start the process, which is what I want."

"I can't guarantee that I'll get the go-ahead on this, but there seem to be enough unanswered questions to warrant an exhumation."

"Thank you." Both agents stood.

"Becca, watch your back," Lewis cautioned. "If what you've told me is true, Jacob will stop at nothing to complete the job he started long ago."

Colby knew the chief was right, but hearing the danger expressed aloud cast a pall on both of them as they drove back to Fort Rickman.

Had Jacob killed Becca's father and sister to get at her? If so, just as Lewis had mentioned, Jacob would stop at nothing to finish the job he had started years earlier.

Chapter 16

After a fitful night's sleep, Becca woke to reveille as the bugle call sounded over a loudspeaker on the nearby parade field. She quickly dressed for the new day and arrived at work just as a company of soldiers passed in formation. The singsong rhythm of their Jody calls floated through the crisp morning air.

Entering CID headquarters, she returned Sergeant Raynard Otis's salute. His welcoming smile provided a positive lift from the darkness of last night.

"Do you ever go home, Ray?" she asked.

"Yes, ma'am. But I like to beat the boss to work and you know Chief Wilson is an early bird."

"Is he in his office now?"

"Roger that, ma'am." Ray checked his watch. "The chief arrived fifteen minutes ago, which was ten minutes after I logged on to my computer."

"Anyone with him?"

"Not that I know of. You want me to let him know you're headed his way?"

"Thanks, but I need to pull some information together first."

Ray pointed over his shoulder. "Coffee's hot, ma'am. I brought doughnuts. Help yourself."

"I'll forego the sugar, but coffee is just what I need. Thanks, Ray."

After pouring a cup, she logged in to her computer and pulled up the list of Amish communities she had compiled. There were a few more towns in Kentucky she wanted to contact before she started looking at Ohio and Pennsylvania. Those states were heavily populated with Amish and would take longer to process.

The first two calls she made provided no information. The third police department said they were tied up with change of shift and would call her back after 8:00 a.m.

Disconnecting, she smiled, hearing Colby greet Sergeant Otis. She met Colby at the coffeepot and held out her cup for a refill.

"Kind of late getting to work this morning, aren't you, Voss?" she teased.

He laughed as he filled her mug. "A little friendly office competition, eh, Miller?"

"Just thinking about the early bird and the worm."

"I'm definitely the worm this morning."

She raised her brow. "Rough night?"

"Just wondering when we'll make progress with this investigation."

She stirred creamer into her coffee and then took a

sip. "I'm calling a few more police departments in Kentucky. Then I'd like to talk to the chief."

"Remember what he told you, Becca?"

"How could I forget? Stay in the office and let you do the legwork."

Colby nodded. "That's it. I should talk to him."

"I want to be there."

"Just let me take the lead. We need to know if that disgruntled contractor from Macon has turned into someone of interest."

"Shall we mention that the Yoder gravesite may be exhumed?"

Colby returned the coffee carafe to the stand. "Let's wait until we have the go-ahead from Harmony."

"That works for me. I'll let you know if the phone calls pay off this morning."

Two hours later, Colby poked his head into her cubicle. "Anything yet?"

"I'm waiting for a return call."

Before he could reply, her phone rang.

She raised the receiver. "Criminal Investigation Division, Fort Rickman, Georgia, Special Agent Miller."

"This is Wanda at Post Transportation."

Becca pushed the phone closer to her ear. "Has my shipment from Germany arrived on post?"

"We tried to contact you yesterday at your BOQ."

"Didn't you hear about the explosion? My BOQ was destroyed. You should have called my cell."

Colby rolled his eyes. Transportation Departments were known for their less-than-stellar customer service.

"Your landline is the only number listed on the paperwork," Wanda said over the phone. "I tracked you down through the post locator."

Becca remembered specifically providing both her land and mobile numbers, but she didn't want to argue with a clerk who was just trying to do her job. "Do you have information about my shipment, Wanda?"

"It's scheduled to be delivered this afternoon."

"Today?"

"Yes, ma'am. At two o'clock. I've got your address as Eisenhower Avenue."

"That's my old BOQ. The one that was destroyed."

"Sorry to hear that, ma'am. Where shall we deliver your shipment?"

"Ah…" She looked at Colby for help. "I need to check with the housing department. Someone in your office told me it would be two more weeks before my things arrived."

"Yes, ma'am. But if we don't have a point of delivery, we'll be forced to unload the truck at the warehouse and reschedule delivery at a later time. We're currently backlogged seven days."

"Give me through the lunch hour to come up with something. Again, I'm sorry for any confusion this may have caused."

Becca hung up and grabbed her purse. "I need a BOQ. Can you talk to Wilson alone?"

"Roger that. Let me know where you end up." He grabbed her arm. "By the way, there's an empty set of quarters on my street."

"That sounds like a solution to my housing problems." She squeezed his hand. "Thanks, Colby."

She hurried to the post housing office and waited far too long for a clerk to process the three people ahead of her.

By the time her name was called, it was almost one

o'clock. She quickly explained the situation and decided to accept the quarters near Colby, sight unseen. After filling out the necessary forms, she grabbed the keys and called transportation on the way out the door. She gave them the delivery address, relieved that she would arrive at her new home just minutes ahead of the moving van.

The two-bedroom apartment was clean and in fairly good shape. She could see Colby's place from her backyard, which made her outlook even brighter. Being stationed at Fort Rickman would be a positive experience after all.

Colby gave her the space she needed and didn't ask too many questions. He hadn't demanded details about the note from Jacob Yoder, which she appreciated, yet they were dealing with a murder investigation. Eventually he would need to know all the information surrounding the case. Information she didn't want to reveal.

She'd ignored logic years ago and reacted with her heart, which had cost her dearly and claimed the lives of her father and sister. As much as she wanted to be open with Colby, she had to be careful. She couldn't make another deadly mistake.

Colby made a quick stop after work and then headed to his BOQ eager to see Becca and find out whether her shipment had arrived. He'd called her cell a number of times, but she hadn't answered, and the phone had gone to voice mail.

If the shipment had arrived, she was probably busy unpacking. The process could take days. Knowing Becca, she would push hard to get settled as soon as possible.

The moving van was just leaving when Colby pulled into the parking lot. He headed to the previously empty apartment and smiled when Becca opened the door.

"Welcome to the neighborhood." He held up a paper bag. "I stopped for food on the way home. Teriyaki chicken and lo mein. I thought you might want to take a break for dinner. I can help you unpack if you'd prefer to eat later."

She inhaled the rich aroma and sighed with pleasure. "Chinese sounds great. I missed lunch, and I'm starving. You must have read my mind."

"Any damage to your things?"

"The usual nicks and scratches, but nothing that can't be repaired."

She motioned him inside and gave him a quick hug in greeting before she pointed to the living room. "The coffee table is the only uncluttered space."

"The Wok provided paper plates and plastic utensils. I told them to pack extra napkins."

She laughed. "You were thinking like a true soldier. I've got colas and water in the fridge. Or I could brew coffee. That is, if I can find the coffeemaker."

"Let's keep it simple with a cola. Can I get them?"

"Sure. Pull two from the fridge while I spray some cleaner over the glass top on the table."

He returned with two colas and sat on the floor across from her at the low coffee table.

"Why don't you say the blessing?" she suggested.

He bowed his head, feeling a bit out of touch. Hopefully his sister's insistence that the Lord was a God of forgiveness was legit.

"Dear God," he prayed. "We thank You for the arrival of Becca's shipment. Help her bring order to the chaos and allow this BOQ to be a good home during her assignment to Fort Rickman. Help both of us with this investigation, and thank You for those who prepared the food we are about to eat. May it nourish our bodies, and may You find us open to Your promptings as we face the rest of the day together."

"Amen," they said in unison, and then both laughed.

"I'm not used to extemporaneous prayer," he confessed.

"Really? You fooled me. If I prayed, I'd be afraid of a lightning strike."

He dug in the bag and pulled out two containers. "There's white rice and condiments. Also egg rolls."

She placed one of the egg rolls on her plate and then reached for the rice and spooned out a large portion. "I'll take a little of each dish, if that's okay with you." She arranged both over rice, and he followed suit.

Colby hadn't realized how hungry he'd been.

Before he finished, his phone chirped. "Which reminds me," he said as he pulled it from his pocket, "I tried to call you today."

"Yikes. I left my cell in my purse." She got up and headed into her bedroom and returned seconds later with her phone in hand. "Sorry. I turned down the volume on the ring."

He smiled as he glanced at his sister's name on his own phone screen and raised the cell to his ear. "Hey, Gloria. What's up?"

"Just wondering how my brother's doing."

"Eating Chinese and welcoming a new neighbor to post. Can I call you back?"

"Sure, but I hear something in your voice that hasn't

been there since you redeployed home. What's her name?"

"You're jumping to conclusions."

"Don't keep secrets, Colby."

"Are Mom and Dad okay?"

"Busy and content. So are the rest of the clan. We miss you, Colby. You need to come home for a visit."

"I'd like that. Now what about you?"

"I'm okay."

"Anyone new in your life?"

"I'll be the first to let you know."

"It's time, Gloria."

"That's what I told you, my dear brother, four months ago. At least you sound happy."

He looked across the table at Becca and smiled. "I am happy. Talk to you soon."

"You and your sister must be close," Becca said when he disconnected.

"We are, but she insists on checking up on me. She's older, by fourteen months, and thinks that gives her control over her baby brother."

"You're lucky to have her."

"I know that. Plus, I've got four more that are just like her although not quite as interested in my well-being. Probably because they're younger and focused on their own lives."

"I'm jealous," she joked, but he knew there was an element of truth to her statement.

"I can loan you Gloria."

"She's the one who was stood up at the altar?"

He nodded. "She says she's okay, but I know better."

"Maybe she needs more time to work through the rejection."

Colby took a swig of his cola and then hesitated, wondering if he should ask the question that continued to circle through his mind. "We didn't talk about the note last night, Becca. Was there something between you and Jacob?"

Her cheeks flushed, and she dropped her gaze. "I don't want to discuss it, Colby"

"It might help if you could—"

"—talk about it?" She bristled. "There's nothing to talk about. Besides, I'm not your sister."

"I wasn't implying you were. It's just I could tell how upset you were last night."

"I was upset going back into the house where my father and sister were murdered."

"I know." He patted his chest. "Remember, I'm on your side. We're in this together, Becca."

She shook her head. "That's not true. We're investigating together because that's the way Wilson wants it, but you don't have anything to do with Jacob's murders. You weren't the one responsible for what he did."

"Why do you feel responsible?"

She shook her head as if realizing she'd said too much. "I don't."

"It's because of Katie, isn't it?"

He saw the hurt in her eyes and knew he'd found the sweet spot of her pain.

"You're not at fault, Becca."

"You don't know what happened, Colby."

"Then tell me."

"It doesn't have any bearing on the investigation. Besides, some things are personal and don't need to be shared. Can you live with that?"

He nodded. "I'll have to. You pretend to be hard as

steel, but there's always a part you keep hidden. That's the part I want to know more about."

"It's the part I'll never share, Colby."

"You were so young. Jacob Yoder was a man who thought only of himself. Whatever happened, you weren't to blame. He's the one who forced his way into your life and then later into your home."

She glanced at her watch. "I'm too tired to discuss this any further. Why don't you take your Chinese food and go home?"

"Becca, please."

"Please, what? Please, tell me more about how you fell in love with a madman?" She shook her head and stood. "I'll see you at the office in the morning, but right now, I want to be alone."

"We don't have to talk about Jacob."

"We don't have to talk about anything." She pointed to the door. "Do I need to see you out?"

He threw down his napkin and huffed. "I know the way."

Colby left, frustrated more with himself than with Becca, and headed back to his own apartment. He shouldn't have pressed her for information, but they had an investigation to solve, and Becca might have some of the answers. Why wouldn't she let him into her secret past?

Chapter 17

Becca shoved the rest of the Chinese food in the fridge. The rather heated discussion she'd had with Colby had dampened her enthusiasm for food. Nor did she feel like unpacking another box, but she had a houseful of items that needed to be arranged, and if she didn't do the work, no one would.

Certainly not Colby. She couldn't rely on him to help. He would broach questions that upset her and would force her to raise her voice and ask him to leave again.

What was wrong with her? She should have tried to change the subject. Instead, she had gotten hot under the collar, as the guys at work often said.

She ran water in the sink and began to wash the dishes she had unpacked earlier. Once they were put away, she glanced out the back door window, noting the dark skyline. Night had come too early. Either that or the afternoon had passed too quickly.

The uncovered window made her feel vulnerable, which she didn't like. She'd hang curtains tomorrow or call post maintenance about installing blinds.

Jacob Yoder was still alive and out there some place, although she doubted he would try to come on post since the military police had enhanced security. She should feel secure, but after the tiff with Colby, all she felt was confusion.

Glancing at her phone, she considered calling him and apologizing for her sharp words. Whenever she was afraid, she tended to lash out too quickly, just as she had done this evening. The look on Colby's face told her he hadn't expected her affront.

Nor did he deserve her wrath. Not Colby with his compassionate eyes and strong arms, which made her feel special in their embrace.

Convinced she needed to apologize, Becca grabbed her purse, flicked off the lights and hurried to the front door. Before she turned the knob, a sound caused her to look through the house to the backyard. Something or someone moved in the shadows outside.

She stepped into the living area and peeked from the window. Her new place sat at the far end of the row of town-house apartments, and a thick wooded area surrounded her on two sides. The leaves in the trees swayed in the wind. Surely that was what had drawn her attention.

The tension in her chest eased. She rolled her shoulders, relaxing her muscles. Letting out a deep breath, she started to turn away from the window.

Then something caught her eye. Something or someone.

She backed into the corner and narrowed her gaze.

Tension pounded up her spine. The muscles in her back tightened again. Blood rushed to her head.

A man stood at the edge of the undergrowth. Tall, perhaps Jacob's height, dressed in black.

She glanced at the overstuffed chair sitting near the window and thought of a box she had unpacked earlier. She hurried to her bedroom. Digging through a pile of clothing, she found the costume she had worn for the German-American Club's on-post carnival celebration. Along with the outfit was a curly wig, the color of her own hair. She grabbed a bathrobe and pillows off the bed.

Returning to the hall, she dropped to the floor and duck crawled across the living area, holding the items she had collected in her arms.

With swift, sure movements, she wrapped the robe around the pillows and arranged them in the chair. She placed the wig on a smaller throw pillow that she positioned on top of the large, bed pillows. If someone looked in the window, they'd see the back of the chair and hopefully mistake the wig and arrangement of pillows for a person. Namely her.

Crawling out of the room, she turned on the small lamp in the entryway. Diffuse light angled toward the living area. The stuffed dummy was visible but not distinguishable to someone peering through the window.

She opened her purse and drew out her gun and cell phone and keys. No matter who was outside, she needed backup. More than that, she needed Colby.

Becca pushed the preset button for his cell. Before it rang, she opened the front door and stepped onto the sidewalk.

The call went to voice mail. Why wouldn't he answer? Was he angry because of her earlier outburst? She'd try again when she had a clearer view of the back-yard Peeping Tom.

She rounded the BOQ and slowly inched her way through the undergrowth, taking care not to make a sound. The snap of a twig or the crunch of dried leaves could cause him to flee.

Thirty feet from the perp, she halted.

Tree frogs and cicadas filled the night. A cool breeze blew through her clothing.

Ever so slowly, the man in black approached the lighted window.

She held her breath. Just a few more feet and she'd be able to see his face.

A door closed.

The man startled at the sound.

A cold chill wrapped around Becca's heart.

Colby hurried down his back steps, carrying something in his hand, and walked across the common rear area heading for her BOQ.

The man moved away from the window.

"Stop." She stepped from the shadows, her gun raised. "CID."

He flicked a glance over his shoulder and ran into the darkness.

Becca raced after him.

The prowler ducked into the thick, wooded area. She followed. Brambles caught at her legs, and twigs slapped her face, but she kept pushing forward.

Behind her came the sound of footfalls and the pull of air, just as she had heard in her dreams. Only this time Jacob wasn't chasing her, it was Colby.

She dashed on to where the trees parted. To one side

was a drop off to a creek bed that led to the river. On the other was a series of military buildings, each providing shadowed areas where the assailant could hide.

Colby caught up with her. "Where'd he go?"

She shook her head. "I lost him."

"Did he hurt you?" Colby reached for her arm.

She shrugged away from him, angry that her attempt to identify the guy had failed. "You scared him away, Colby. He was walking into the light. I needed to see his face. Two more seconds and I would have known if it was Jacob."

"What were you doing outside?"

"I set up a decoy and then circled around the house to wait him out," she explained.

"You didn't call me."

"I tried." She held up her phone as if to confirm the call.

Colby's face twisted with frustration. "My phone never rang."

Had she made a mistake and called the wrong number? She shook her head, unwilling to back down. "Once I was outside, I didn't want to make any noise that might startle him so I couldn't call you again."

"You could have gotten killed."

"I had the upper hand, Colby. Until—"

"Until I walked outside? What if one of the other neighbors had emptied their trash or had gone for an evening stroll? If the perp had a weapon, the neighbors could have been caught in the cross fire. Did you think about that?"

She hadn't. She'd only been thinking of identifying the perp. Squaring her shoulders, she turned to retrace her steps. Behind her, she heard Colby call in a report to CID Headquarters.

"Notify the military police. Close off post. Check every car that leaves Fort Rickman. Cordon off the area around Sheridan Road. Set up roadblocks and have the military police patrol the area on foot. We need to find this guy."

He hesitated for a moment.

"Yes, notify Chief Wilson and General Cameron."

With a huff, Becca shoved a branch aside and walked through the woods back to her BOQ. Colby was right. She shouldn't have tackled the problem alone, but she had tried to call him, even if he didn't believe her.

Sirens sounded, and a swarm of military police spilled from their patrol cars and quickly fanned out to search the area.

She knew the main gate was locked down and each car leaving post was being searched, all because she hadn't been able to stop Jacob.

Using large battery-operated spotlights, the crime-scene team searched the wooded area where the prowler had been hunkered down.

"The perp didn't leave much to go on," one of the men told Becca.

A soldier approached her, holding something in his hand. "These were on the grass, ma'am. Special Agent Voss said they belong to you."

She took the bouquet of flowers, yellow roses, each flower a perfect bud almost ready to open. The flowers Colby had probably purchased at the Shopette on post and planned to give her as he walked toward her BOQ. Had they been a way to make right their earlier disagreement? Now there was no hope of rectifying the situation.

A lump filled Becca's throat. She was tired and cold and upset that she hadn't handled the situation correctly. Once again, she'd tried to do everything herself instead of calling in backup.

With a heavy heart, she walked into her apartment. The military police and crime-scene techs could continue to work outside, but she wanted to put the flowers in water and then sit by herself in the dark.

She never should have come to Fort Rickman. She had allowed her attraction for Colby to get in the way of the investigation, and that could prove deadly.

Chapter 18

Colby arrived at work early the next morning, hoping to talk to Becca before he briefed Wilson on what had happened. She wasn't in her cubicle, and Wilson saw him in the hallway and motioned Colby into his office.

"Tell me about last night," Wilson said as he slipped into the chair behind his desk.

"Agent Miller noticed someone outside her BOQ, sir. She rigged a dummy in a chair in her living room, left her apartment through the front door and circled around trying to spot the perp when he approached her window."

"Seems her plan backfired."

"I'm probably to blame for that, sir. He saw me exit my BOQ and fled. Agent Miller followed in pursuit. I did, as well. We lost him in the training area."

"Did Agent Miller call you for help?"

"Yes, sir, she did. Unfortunately, I didn't hear my phone."

"What about the military police?"

"I don't believe she contacted them."

"So she attempted to capture the assailant without calling for backup?" Wilson's tone was stern.

"In all fairness, sir, Agent Miller was hoping to get a positive ID on the prowler. The Harmony, Alabama, sheriff still hasn't gotten a court order to exhume the body in Jacob Yoder's grave. Becca needs proof he's alive, which is only complicated by the Amish avoidance of photos. As you know, we don't have a snapshot of the guy."

"Do you think Yoder is alive?"

"I'm not sure, sir, but someone is out to do her harm."

"I told Becca to remain at her desk. That means she shouldn't be staging booby traps in her backyard."

"Yes, sir. But she probably didn't want the opportunity to pass her by."

"Hauling an Amish man in for murder before the first farmers' market and craft fair on Fort Rickman could put a damper on the festivities."

"I understand your concern, sir."

"Which has no bearing on us bringing him in, no matter what activity the commanding general's wife has planned."

"Yes, sir."

"I'll call the Harmony sheriff and see if I can't encourage them to exhume the body. You mentioned having a DNA specimen that can be traced to Yoder?"

"Yes, sir. An envelope he sealed."

"Someone was lucky. Any idea how they uncovered the envelope?"

"Ah...." Colby wanted to tell Wilson the truth, but he also wanted to protect Becca. "I believe it was retrieved in one of the old Amish homes."

"Someone was saying their prayers."

"I'm sure they were, sir."

Wilson pursed his lips and lowered his gaze, signaling the meeting was over.

"Thank you, sir." Before Colby could do an about-face, a tap sounded at the door.

The chief glanced up. "Enter."

Becca stepped into the office. Her eyes widened when she saw Colby.

"I was just leaving," he assured her.

"Hold up, Colby," Wilson said. "You and Becca have been working together. You need to stay."

"Uh, sir, I've got some calls to make."

"This shouldn't take long," Wilson insisted.

Inwardly, Colby groaned. Last night, his relationship with Becca had hit rock bottom. Being present when she faced the boss would only do more harm.

Becca didn't want to believe him or trust him. She had her own ideas about how an investigation should be run, and Colby wasn't the top man on her go-to list. As far as he knew, she probably wanted to team up with one of the other agents.

Becca was a problem.

Not to the investigation but to his heart.

Finding Colby in the chief's office made Becca's day go from bad to worse, and it was only 7:00 a.m.

"Ray said you wanted to see me, sir."

"A lot happened last night."

"A prowler, sir, outside my BOQ."

"You think it's the same man who caused the explosion?"

She glanced at Colby who stood to the side, hands clasped behind his back in a typical army, parade-rest stance with his eyes lowered.

"That might be putting too many pieces together and getting the wrong picture, sir. I didn't get close enough to ID the Peeping Tom."

"But it could have been Jacob Yoder?"

"That's a possibility."

"What did I tell you about this case, Becca?"

She swallowed. "That I should handle things from my desk and let Special Agent Voss do the legwork."

Wilson nodded. "Did you comply with my request?"

"As best I could, sir."

"Did that include setting a decoy to catch the man last night?"

Evidently Colby had been very forthright with the chief. "I merely wanted to distract him. The danger to me was minimal."

Colby cleared his throat.

Even more anxiety bubbled up within her.

Wilson steepled his fingers. "I hardly think going outside to surprise an assailant is a protective measure. In my mind, you were putting yourself in danger."

"I planned to call law enforcement."

"But did you?" His brow arched.

She hesitated. "I tried to contact Agent Voss. The call went to voice mail."

"Did you leave a message?"

"I—I, uh, ran out of time."

Again the raised brow. "What does that mean?"

"It means I needed to move closer to the prowler while his attention was focused on my back door."

"Actually, his focus was trained on the dummy inside that he thought was you."

Another detail Colby had shared with Wilson. "Yes, sir."

"You drew your weapon?"

"When he started to flee."

"Yet you weren't in danger?"

Heat warmed her neck. "I had hoped to apprehend him before any exchange of gunfire."

"Therefore the situation you walked into could have been life threatening."

"In hindsight, that might be the case."

Wilson cleared his throat and adjusted himself in his chair as he seemingly mulled over his next comment. "You were fortunate this time, Becca. But I don't like agents who strike out on their own. Everyone in this organization needs to follow the rules and my directions. Is that understood?"

"Yes, sir."

"I want you to work on the security plans for the farmers' market and craft fair. Nothing else. Is that understood?"

"Yes, sir."

"Under no circumstances are you to knowingly put yourself or anyone else in danger."

"Sir, I didn't think—"

Wilson held up his hand to cut her off. "That's it exactly, Becca. You didn't think."

He handed her a piece of paper containing a phone number. "Call the general's wife. Mrs. Cameron had a request to make concerning the market."

She took the paper and nodded. "Thank you, sir."

Unwilling to even glance in Colby's direction, she hurried from the office and let out a lungful of air she had been holding too long. Her cheeks burned as she recalled the scoldings her father had given her of old. Today, she felt like a wayward child who had done something wrong. Colby's presence only compounded her humiliation.

She should have contacted law enforcement immediately after seeing the man in her backyard. Of course, she'd thought she could take care of it herself.

Why did she always have to be so headstrong and self-sufficient? Maybe because no one had ever been there for her in the past.

She hurried along the hallway to her cubicle, dropped the message from Mrs. Cameron on her desk and grabbed her purse. Tension pounded through her head, and she blinked back tears. The last thing she wanted to do was cry or let anyone in the office see her agitation. Especially not Colby.

She raced out the back door and ran to her car, not sure where she was headed until she turned onto Eisenhower Drive. Pulling to a stop, she stared at the burned wreckage of her BOQ.

Looking back, she wished she had handled things differently. But what was done, was done.

Sitting in her parked car with no one around, she started to cry, feeling the entire struggle from the last week well up within her. She'd tried to keep her secrets buried, but Colby had pushed his way into her life, and now he knew too much about the mistakes she had made.

All she'd ever wanted in life was to be loved, but it

always cluded her. Maybe she didn't know how to accept love, and if she couldn't accept love how could she return it to someone else? Today, she realized "that someone else" had a name.

Colby.

Colby sat in his cubicle, wondering when Becca would return to CID Headquarters. She'd been away from her desk a long time, and that worried him. He wanted her to know they were in this together.

In hindsight, Colby should have run after her when she left Wilson's office. Instead, he had tried to ease Wilson's frustration by mentioning his own regret at walking headlong into a situation Becca seemed to have had under control. Whether Wilson bought into what Colby shared was debatable, and by the time he left the chief, Becca was nowhere to be found.

Surely she wouldn't be gone long.

To kill time, he pulled the list of Amish communities from the folder on his desk and did a computer search, working his way into Ohio.

None of the police departments he called had information about any violent crimes in their local areas. He was relieved as well as discouraged. Everything was still so nebulous when it came to Jacob Yoder. They weren't even sure he was alive.

Going back and forth between search engines, he tried various key words and finally pulled up information about a small Amish community just across the Ohio River from Kentucky. He called the closest police department in Ohio, found nothing of interest and, on a whim, contacted law enforcement on the Kentucky side. Although Colby doubted the call would be productive, the name of the town was Harmony, and the coincidence of two towns with the same name wasn't lost on him.

He tapped in the digits for the local sheriff.

"Harmony Sheriff's Office. This is Deputy Oaks."

Colby quickly introduced himself and asked about any nearby Amish communities.

"Not on this side of the Ohio. Cross over the bridge and you'll find a number of Amish farms."

"I'm looking for an Amish drifter who preys on lonely widows. He helps with handy work and farm chores and often ends up moving in with them."

"What's the bottom line?"

"A string of older women who become ill or infirmed and die within a year or two of meeting him."

"Nice guy, eh?"

"You got that right." Colby pushed back in his chair, ready to disconnect. "Just wanted to check. Thanks for your time."

"What about non-Amish?" the deputy asked.

"Pardon?"

"We had a widow by the name of Lucy Reynolds who took up with a drifter. She needed help. He was a willing worker. Six months later, she ends up dead."

Colby straightened in his chair. "I'm listening."

"The widow told a friend he'd asked her to marry him but she refused. Still she kept him on as a hired hand. He stayed in a room in the back of the garage until he eventually left town."

"What happened to Mrs. Reynolds?"

"She died two weeks later. Fell down an old well on her property. A friend of hers said she'd taken money out of her savings account a few days earlier. The cash was never found. Plus, her car was gone."

"What make and model?"

"A 2005 Crown Vic, metallic blue in color."

The car they'd seen in the barn. "Are you sure the guy wasn't Amish?"

"He wasn't dressed like the Amish and he drove a car, although he did have a beard."

"Do you have a description?"

"I can do better than that. I've got a picture. That friend of the widow's was an amateur photographer. She snapped a photograph of Lucy and captured the drifter in the background of the shot. I can fax a copy to you. It's attached to a rundown of the widow's estate, which I'll include, as well."

"Perfect. Thanks." Colby relayed the CID fax number.

"I've got a city council meeting that will tie me up for the next few hours," Deputy Oaks continued. "I'll try to send the fax before I leave the office. Otherwise, it'll get to you by the end of the day."

Colby disconnected, feeling that the tide was changing. Hopefully, the photo would confirm the drifter was Jacob Yoder.

His phone rang and he heard the Alabama sheriff's voice on the other end of the line. "Hey, Lewis, what can I do for you?"

"Just wanted you to know we're expecting to get the go-ahead for exhuming Jacob Yoder's body. Also his wife's. The DNA from the envelope is being tested. Two exhumed bodies might speed the process and ensure everyone knows this case has priority."

Colby appreciated the chief's interest in getting to the bottom of the investigation.

"I thought you might want to be here when we open the graves," Lewis added.

"Looks like the investigation is taking a turn in the right direction. I may have a photograph of Jacob Yoder, although it won't get to my desk until later today. I'd like you to see the picture and then distribute it to your folks so they can be on the lookout for him. I'll have someone from here scan it and send it to me."

Colby looked at his watch. He was still worried about Becca, but he had to get to Harmony as soon as possible. "I'll meet you at the gravesite in two hours."

"Sounds good. The Amish cemetery sits back from the main road, on the right, not far from Hershberger's farm and Yoder's old property. You should be able to spot us from the road."

Despite Becca's hasty departure, Colby wanted her to know about the exhumation. He peered into her cubicle, surprised she hadn't returned.

He found Ray Otis at his desk. "Any idea where Special Agent Miller went?"

"I'm not sure, sir. Maybe Quarters One. Mrs. Cameron called earlier and left a message. She wanted Becca to pick up some papers concerning the farmers' market."

"Do you know when she plans to be back in the office?"

"Negative, sir."

"I'm expecting a fax, Ray, sometime in the next few hours. It's from a sheriff's office in Kentucky. When it arrives, scan a copy and send it to my email."

"Will do, sir."

Colby hurried outside. Becca had pushed for the disinterment and would, no doubt, be relieved to know it was in the works. Maybe the news would help soften the struggle between them.

On the way to his car, he tried her cell, but she didn't answer. No reason to leave a voice mail. If she wanted to talk to him, she'd return his call. Otherwise, he'd see her when he returned later this afternoon. He wanted to discuss everything that had happened and ensure she knew nothing had changed in their relationship, at least as far as he was concerned.

Maybe he'd invite her over for dinner tonight so they could get back on better footing. On his return from Alabama, he'd stop at the commissary for a couple steaks to grill.

Things would be better by evening.

At least that's what he hoped.

Becca hoped no one noticed her blotched cheeks or puffy eyes when she returned to CID Headquarters through the rear entrance. She walked the long way around the office skirting Colby's cubicle only to run into Sergeant Otis standing near the fax machine.

"I have to make a phone call, and then I'll stop by Quarters One, Ray, in case anyone asks."

"Anyone like Special Agent Voss, ma'am?"

The sergeant had a knack for putting things together.

"In case you're interested, ma'am, he's driving to Alabama."

"What?"

"Yes, ma'am. Two bodies are being exhumed. He wanted to be there."

Of course he did, without her.

She pushed past Ray, her eyes burning almost as much as her anger.

"Wait up, ma'am. I know you and Agent Voss were working on the explosion investigation. He probably wants you to see this photograph he received from up north. I made a copy for you."

Becca took the file and opened it at her desk. Her heart stopped for a long moment when she looked at the photo. Not of the older woman with the short gray hair and a wide smile, but the man standing behind her.

All the memories came back to haunt her.

She closed the folder and threw it aside, unable to look at the deceitful face that sprouted lies and hate.

A photo she never thought she'd see.

A photo of evil itself.

A photo of Jacob Yoder.

Chapter 19

Becca had to get a grip on herself. She was feeling emotional and needy, which wasn't like her at all. Maybe it was lack of sleep or concern about the investigation or her standing with Chief Wilson. Although more than likely, it was her relationship with Colby.

She's spent too much time this morning stewing over her own mistakes. She needed to buck up and move on. Plus, she needed to contact Mrs. Cameron.

"How can I help you, ma'am?" she asked once the general's wife answered her call.

"I need someone to take the layout of the market stalls to Bishop Zimmerman. Unfortunately, I'm tied up with a Thrift Shop board meeting. The bishop enjoyed talking to you, and I thought you might be able to help me out."

Becca reached for the discarded folder containing Jacob's photo, feeling a sudden burst of energy.

"Yes, ma'am. I'll be glad to deliver the market overview to the bishop."

Hurrying to the copy machine, Becca reproduced Jacob's likeness and dropped a stack of print outs on Sergeant Otis's desk.

"These photos need to be distributed to the military police on post, Ray. Can you let them know Jacob Yoder is a possible suspect in the BOQ explosion?"

"No problem, ma'am, except Special Agent Voss had me email that very same photo to the provost marshal's office so the MPs already have it."

"You talked to Colby?"

"Yes, ma'am. He's still on the road heading to Harmony, Alabama, but he had me notify on-post law enforcement as well the Freemont police who also have the photo. Plus Special Agent Voss put in a be-on-the-lookout order to the Georgia Highway Patrol."

"There's a BOLO out on Jacob Yoder?"

"Yes, ma'am. Anything else you need me to do?"

"No. Thank you, Ray." She turned and headed for the door. "It's seems Special Agent Voss has thought of everything,"

Everything except including her in the investigation.

Becca was mad enough to cry, but she'd already shed too many tears today. Instead, she'd focus on the Amish community and the widow who could be in danger.

Stopping at Quarters One, she picked up the packet containing the plans and layout for the marketplace, and hurried off post. The bishop was cordial when she arrived at his farmhouse. Mrs. Zimmerman invited her inside for a cup of coffee and a piece of pound cake. The offer was tempting, but Becca declined, wanting to talk privately to the bishop.

He walked her to her car and stared into the distance for a long moment before he spoke.

"I talked to Fannie Lehman," he finally said. "The widow had someone helping her. An Amish man from up north. He stayed in her barn for only a few days and is gone now."

"Along with his car?"

The bishop nodded. "That is what she told me."

"Did the widow provide a name?"

"Ezekiel Lapp."

Jacob was using his brother's first name and the new last name he had chosen in Ohio.

"And the dogs?"

"They left with him."

"Was she telling the truth, Bishop?"

"I did not question her honesty. That is something *Gott* will decide."

"She's in danger."

"The widow does not believe he will hurt her."

"You need to warn her. Jacob Yoder is an evil man. He knows how to tempt women. He's killed before. He will kill again."

Becca pulled out a number of copies of Jacob's picture from a folder in her car. "This is his photo. He preys on unsuspecting women, but he has killed others. I suggest you distribute these copies to the Amish families. Make sure Mrs. Lehman sees it as well. I have a strong suspicion this is the man who helped her."

"I do not want violence to upset our way of life. Keep your pictures, Becca. I will pray for God to protect us."

"You'll need more than prayers," Becca insisted. "You need to warn the Amish community, and especially Mrs. Lehman, about Jacob Yoder."

Becca felt a sense of foreboding as she drove away from the bishop's farm. Fannie Lehman was in danger. The bishop, as well as the widow, needed to realize that having a relationship with Jacob Yoder could be deadly.

Becca knew that only too well.

The drive to Harmony seemed especially long and boring. Maybe it was because Colby kept thinking about Becca and wondering how he could mend their broken relationship. He had called her a number of times, but her cell kept going to voice mail.

At least now they had a photo of Jacob Yoder. With a BOLO order in effect, law enforcement across the state would be on high alert for the Amish man and his Crown Vic. Hopefully, he'd be tracked down and brought to justice. That is, if he wasn't buried in the Amish cemetery. There were still too many unanswered questions.

On a whim, Colby had hooked up his GPS, which directed him a new way. He skirted Harmony and drove into a rather expansive subdivision of three-and four-bedroom homes. The community looked comfortable and family friendly and, from the sign on the side of the road, claimed to be a Tucker Reynolds development. Whoever Tucker was, he seemed to be succeeding in this otherwise stagnant economy.

The far end of the housing complex butted up against the Amish community. Colby turned left out of the subdivision and soon spied Lewis and his backhoe. The sheriff's car was parked on the side of the hill along with three other vehicles.

A gathering of men stood watching nearby.

Colby parked and greeted the sheriff.

"There's been a delay with the court order," Lewis said as they shook hands.

"I thought you had the go-ahead."

"The mayor claims exhuming the bodies is a waste of taxpayer money. He's talking to the judge as we speak."

Colby looked around the pristine landscape and the rows of graves, each with a small cement marker. The one near where they stood bore the name Yoder.

"Is there something going on I don't know about? Something more than revenue?"

"The mayor's got his own way of doing things in this town. We've clashed on more than one occasion. In my opinion, he's not interested in what's best for Harmony. His focus is on his construction company and the huge track of homes he's developed and expanded over the years." Lewis pointed in the direction Colby had come.

"I just drove through one of his subdivisions."

Lewis nodded. "His property runs right up against some of the Amish farms. When they go to foreclosure, he makes a phone call to the bank manager, who happens to be a good friend."

"I thought the Amish hold on to their land and pass the farms on to their children," Colby said.

"They try to, but taxes have gone up significantly, and we had some years of drought. A bad crop can make all the difference for a farmer these days. Plus McDougal's his right-hand man. He likes to threaten the Amish with what could happen."

"McDougal? You mean the former sheriff?"

"One and the same. He started working for Tucker shortly after he retired."

"How does the mayor's interest in real estate have anything to do with the court order?"

"I'm not sure, but if we don't hear from the judge soon, I'll head back to town and talk to him myself."

He looked at Colby. "I could use some backup and would appreciate your support. Having the military involved gives more weight to the situation."

"You've got it."

Lewis pulled out his phone and hit one of the prompts. "Helene, see when I can get in to talk to Judge Clark." He nodded. "Call me back."

A buggy clip-clopped along the nearby road. Colby recognized the woman sitting next to the blond, muscular man leading the horses. Sarah Hershberger. She averted her gaze. Evidently she still hadn't told her husband about Jacob's brother or Colby and Becca's visit.

"Excuse me for a moment." Lewis hustled to where the buggy had stopped on the side of the road. He and the blond man spoke for a few minutes.

"It's Samuel Hershberger," Lewis said when he returned to the gravesite. "You know his wife, Sarah."

Colby nodded. "Did you ever question her about Jacob's brother?"

"Once when she was in town to buy fabric. Samuel wasn't with her, which was fortunate. He might not appreciate a wife who wasn't completely forthright with her husband."

"What did he want today?"

"He asked why we were disturbing the dead."

"Did you tell him?"

Lewis nodded. "He wasn't happy, but then he's carrying a lot of worry, trying to keep afloat and concerned he'll lose the farm."

"More property for the mayor?" Colby asked.

"I hope not. Samuel works as one of our local volunteer firemen to help pay his bills. He's a good man and an asset to the community."

Samuel flicked the reins, and the buggy continued along the road. Sarah glanced back at Colby and nodded her head ever so slightly as if to thank him for keeping her secret.

Lewis's phone rang again. "What'd you find out?" A scowl covered his face. "Not until then?"

He let out a stiff breath. "Okay. Confirm that I'll be there."

He disconnected and turned to Colby. "The judge can't see me until late afternoon. Can you stick around?"

"I'll have to."

But Colby didn't like killing time in Harmony, when he needed to talk to Becca. He tried her cell again and sighed with frustration when she didn't answer.

He'd get back to post too late to see her tonight. Tomorrow was the farmers' market. He would seek her out first thing in the morning, but she'd be busy with security issues. The longer he waited the more likely she wouldn't be interested in listening to what he had to say.

The court order was important, and he'd have to bide his time. Would Becca talk to him when he returned to post? Or was their relationship over before it had even gotten started?

Becca parked in front of Fannie Lehman's house and checked her phone, noticing the missed calls from Colby. As much as she wanted to talk to him, she couldn't. Not now, not until they were face-to-face. She needed to be able to gauge his reaction when she apologized for her actions the other night. She also wanted to question him about leaving her out of the investigation.

Of course, Colby was just following Wilson's orders, yet she still felt the sting of humiliation, especially because Colby had been in the chief's office when she'd been counseled on her inappropriate actions. They'd have an opportunity to talk after the investigation was closed and Jacob was brought to justice. Until then, Becca needed to stay away from Colby to protect herself and her heart.

Glancing at the farmhouse, she eased her car door open and listened for the dogs. All she heard was the rustle of the wind in the trees and a few birds who chirped a greeting.

Grabbing one of the printouts from her folder, she stepped to the roadway and flicked her gaze to the barn. Just as before, the door hung open.

No car. No dogs. Hopefully no Jacob Yoder, either.

She climbed the rickety stairs to the front porch and knocked. Once. Twice. Three times.

"Mrs. Lehman, I just came from seeing Bishop Zimmerman. There's something I need to show you."

Evidently the bishop's name pulled weight. The door creaked open. Becca recognized Fannie Lehman as the same woman who had stared at her from the barn raising.

She flashed her identification, introduced herself and shoved the printout in Mrs. Lehman's face before the widow had a chance to reconsider and retreat back into her house.

"Is this the man who was staying here?" Becca asked.

The widow's gaze narrowed. Her hands shook ever so slightly as she stared down at the photo.

"He's dangerous, Mrs. Lehman, and he preys on women living alone."

"Ezekiel is a good man," the widow finally said.

"He's fooling you and trying to win your trust. Then he'll take your valuables and leave you with nothing."

"I do not think this is true."

"You don't have to think, Mrs. Lehman. I know for sure. He's killed women. You are in grave danger. Is there someone you can move in with? Do you have family in the area?"

"I am alone."

"Come with me then. I'll find someplace safe for you to stay?"

The widow shook her head and gave the paper back to Becca. "You must leave now."

"Please listen to me, Mrs. Lehman."

"I have heard you. Now I must prepare my needlework for the market tomorrow."

"You'll be at Fort Rickman in the morning? We can talk more then." Hopefully, the widow would change her mind about accepting help. "I'll contact the Freemont police and ask them to keep your house under surveillance tonight."

If only the widow had a phone or a gun.

"Lock your doors, ma'am, and don't let Jacob—or Ezekiel—in. If you see him, hide until he leaves, then hurry to the bishop's house. He and his wife will help you."

"Do not worry about me, Special Agent Miller. Worry about yourself."

The widow closed the door.

Becca returned to her car, thinking of how easily someone like Jacob could prey upon the Amish. Fannie Lehman wasn't willing to accept help. That self-sufficiently had probably been drummed into her since she was a little girl.

Glancing back, she saw the curtain move ever so slightly and knew the widow was watching.

The older woman had a mind of her own.

Independence or stupidity?

Becca wasn't sure, but one thing was certain. She and Fannie were a lot alike.

Chapter 20

Saturday dawned cold and damp, not the ideal setting for the first farmers' market and craft fair. Mrs. Cameron had hoped for blue skies and sunshine, but even the general's wife couldn't control the weather.

Becca's mood matched the gray sky. She had slept little if at all. Her thoughts had been on Colby and the way she felt wrapped in his embrace. Not that she would ever know that feeling again. Anything that might have developed was over between them, no matter how much she wished otherwise.

Her heart was heavy when she arrived at the grassy knoll ahead of schedule. Located near the Fort Rickman Museum and nearby river, the expansive area was filled with newly erected booths, all painted white.

Many of the Amish families had already arrived in their buggies. The horses and rigs were in a special spot behind the cordoned-off site reserved for automobile parking.

The military had provided trucks and transported the larger items for sale. Finely designed tables and benches stood near dollhouses and rocking chairs. The Amish men had arranged the pieces for display while the women hung beautiful quilts and crocheted lap blankets in the various stalls.

In other booths, spring cuttings and winter vegetables sat next to Mason jars filled with colorful jams and jellies.

An assortment of homemade breads and cakes and pies made Becca's mouth water as she walked around the perimeter of the market and examined the wares. She bought a cinnamon roll that melted in her mouth and washed it down with a cup of coffee the Army Community Services was selling to raise money for some of their on-post programs.

Slowly the area started to come alive as more people from both the *English* and Amish communities arrived. From what Becca could tell, the committee members spearheading the event handled their jobs with great attention to detail, and the day promised to be a success in spite of the less than perfect weather.

Becca briefed the military police she had requested to help with security and passed out copies of Jacob's photograph. Although she wanted everyone to know who to be watching for in the crowd, she also stressed the importance of maintaining good relationships with the Amish. Her final instruction was to check with her before confronting anyone who might fit Jacob's description.

Glancing at her watch, she stamped her feet against

the chill. The earth was damp with dew, and a breeze tugged at her jacket. At least she had donned slacks and a heavy sweater.

Colby was probably still in his BOQ, catching a few extra winks of shut-eye this Saturday morning. Maybe he would appear later, although she almost hoped he wouldn't. She had a job to do and didn't want to be distracted by the handsome agent who had woven his way into her heart.

As much as Becca wanted to apologize for her actions, she knew the night before last had been a turning point. Maybe a stopping point would be a better term to use. Colby had been perfectly clear that he wanted to keep everything professional. He was right, of course, yet she still regretted what had happened. Even more than that, she regretted losing Colby.

Mrs. Cameron approached her. "Everything seems to be going as planned, Becca. The security team has been most helpful, and I'm sure we won't have any problems today."

"That's my hope, ma'am. What time is General Cameron planning to arrive?"

"His opening remarks are scheduled for nine. He had some papers to sign at his office, but I'm sure he'll be here soon. The band's getting ready to warm up, and the children's choir from the Main Post Chapel is on its way."

"You've done a great job with all the details, ma'am."

The senior wife smiled. "It was everyone coming together to help make it happen. I'm so glad you could be part of the committee."

"Thank you, ma'am. We'll keep our eyes open and wait until the day's over before we let down our guard."

"I'm relieved to know you're here, Becca. Now, if you'll excuse me, I want to buy a quilt for the guest bedroom. Bishop Zimmerman said his wife had some lovely patterns that I might like."

Mrs. Cameron hurried to a booth where a number of bedcoverings hung over the wooden frame. The bishop stood nearby and watched the two women examine the various quilts, all colorful patterns Becca knew so well.

The band started to play a jaunty march, and soon people were tapping their feet or clapping their hands to the music.

As if with new eyes, Becca saw the beauty of the Amish way of accepting each day as a gift from God. In her youth, she had wanted to control her own life, something with which she still struggled, but as she glanced around the marketplace, she was overcome with a renewed appreciation for these good people who put God first. If only she could share this bit from her past with Colby.

She circled through the area and was relieved to see Fannie Lehman arranging handmade aprons and crocheted shawls in one of the rear stalls. Noticing the woman's furtive glance over her shoulder and the dark lines that circled her eyes, Becca hurried forward.

"Is something wrong?" she asked, her own gaze flicking to the nearby parking area. "Did Jacob Yoder come back?"

The widow hung her head.

Becca reached out to touch her hand. Fannie glanced up. The look on her face spoke volumes about her struggle.

"Is he here?" Becca asked again.

The older woman pursed her lips as if annoyed. "I told you he left the area."

"You don't have to be afraid," Becca insisted. "I'll be close by. If you see him, let me know. A number of military police are in the crowd. We won't let him hurt you."

"I do not fear for myself."

"Is there someone else he wants to harm?"

The woman looked into Becca's eyes. "I thought you knew. He wants to hurt you."

General Cameron arrived at the fair shortly before nine. The two stars on the general's flag flying from the front bumper of his sedan looked impressive, and many of the shoppers turned to stare as he climbed from the car.

His aide rode with the general and escorted him to the stage area. Mrs. Cameron met him there. Together they walked to where the bishop stood. The men shook hands and chatted amicably before the general nodded and pointed to the stage. He and Mrs. Cameron climbed the raised platform and approached the podium.

Becca glanced back at the widow's stall to ensure Fannie Lehman was all right.

Her heart jerked in her chest.

The booth was empty.

She circled through the crowd. The general's voice boomed over the loudspeaker.

"Welcome to the first annual farmers' market and craft fair hosted by Fort Rickman and our new Freemont neighbors in the Amish community."

Becca flicked her gaze to the surrounding stalls. Surely the widow was talking to a friend. Perhaps she had gone for a cup of coffee.

Glancing at the beverage stand, Becca's optimism plummeted. A young woman and her two little ones were the only customers in line.

To the right of the stage, the bishop and his wife stood. Just like many of the other people, their attention was focused on the general.

Becca's neck tensed. Where was Fannie Lehman?

She raised her cell and called the head MP onsite. "I'm looking for the Amish woman who was in stall seventeen. Gray hair, about 145 pounds, five feet four inches. She was wearing a blue dress, apron and a short black jacket."

"Ah, we've got a problem, ma'am. I see a number of Amish women who fit that description."

"Jacob Yoder might be in the crowd. Inform your men. Let's search the area. If you see anything, call me."

She disconnected, wishing Colby were here. He would understand the urgency in finding the widow and ensuring she was okay.

Becca hurried to the widow's stall and peered behind the counter. Seeing nothing out of order, she checked the surrounding booths.

Cars filled the designated parking area. The horses and rigs were lined up in the distance. Perhaps Fannie had gone back to her buggy. Becca double-timed across the field.

Behind her, the general continued to talk about how the military and civilians in Freemont had come together on a number of projects. Both he and Mrs. Cameron hoped today's market would grow into a bimonthly event that would draw people from the outlining areas.

Cheers from the crowd punctuated his pauses as he introduced the Freemont mayor and city council.

Becca neared the first buggy and gazed into the carriage, seeing nothing except a lap blanket neatly folded on the seat.

A horse neighed. She turned at the sound and saw something on the grass. A quilt or—

The widow.

She raced to where Fannie lay. Becca felt her neck relieved to find a pulse.

A bulging welt on the woman's forehead and scratches to her throat confirmed the foul play Becca suspected. Raising her cell, she called the MP with whom she had just spoken.

Before she could say anything, a rag covered her nose and mouth. "No," she tried to scream, inhaling a sickening sweet smell that affected her equilibrium. She fought against the cloying scent and the hands and the body that overpowered her.

Her strength ebbed. The scream died in her throat, and slowly the world turned dark as she pitched forward onto the cold, damp grass.

Colby pulled into the parking lot of the farmers' market much later than he had hoped after being tied up at CID Headquarters with Chief Wilson. The general had concluded his remarks and a group of schoolchildren were taking the stage.

Exiting his car, Colby's gut tightened as he spied four MPs gathered in the rear of the whitewashed stalls. He glanced around the area, looking for Becca. Fear settled along his spine. Something had happened and it wasn't good.

Racing toward the men, he held up his identification. "CID. Where's Special Agent Miller?"

A corporal, tall and beefy, shook his head. "That's what we want to know. I got a call from her, but she didn't say anything. I only heard a gasp."

Colby's heart lurched. "How long ago?"

The corporal raised his cell. "The call came in ten minutes ago."

"Fan out. Check the parking area." Colby pointed to a second MP. "Call your headquarters for backup."

"Over here." A young Amish woman waved frantically from where the buggies were parked. "Fannie's hurt. I need help."

Colby called CID Headquarters as he raced forward. Ray Otis answered. "I need an ambulance and every available CID agent at the market area. Agent Miller is missing. Lock down the post. Set up roadblocks. We could be looking for a 2005 Crown Vic, metallic blue, or an Amish buggy. Search each car leaving post."

"Roger that. I'm on it."

"She's hurt her head," the young woman told Colby as he approached, noting the angry lump on the older woman's forehead and the marks on her neck.

He knelt and felt for a pulse. "An ambulance is on the way." He turned to glance at the nearby road. "Did you see anyone leaving the area?"

She shook her head. "No."

One of the MPs approached.

"Stay here until the EMTs arrive," Colby ordered.

He raised his cell again. "Ray, have the river path checked. Someone could have escaped along that route unnoticed."

"Will do, sir. I contacted the guardhouse at the main gate. An Amish buggy passed through not more than two minutes ago."

"Call the Freemont police. Have them set up road-blocks. We need to stop that buggy."

Hearing the sirens approach, Colby left the MP in charge of the widow's care and hurried back to his car.

He pulled onto the main road and accelerated, stopping only briefly at the Main Gate.

"Which direction did the buggy go?" he asked the guard on duty.

"North, sir, toward Freemont."

A horse-drawn carriage could never outrun a motorized vehicle. Colby pressed down on the accelerator. Fear tangled through his gut.

Jacob Yoder was on the loose and he had Becca.

Colby had to find her before it was too late.

Chapter 21

Becca's head throbbed, and her muscles ached as if she had the flu. Blinking her eyes open, she knew any illness would have been better than what she faced.

Her hands and legs were tied, and she was lying on a dirty mattress, wedged against the wall. She raised her head and stared around the small, bare room. A jackhammer of pain stuttered through her skull.

She moaned.

As if in response, a dog growled. His paws tap-danced across the wooden floor. She smelled the animal before she saw him. A huge, black beast with pointed ears and large jowls.

The Doberman she had seen at the widow's house.

A second dog trotted forward, larger than the first. A female. She barked twice.

A door creaked. Afraid to turn, Becca kept her gaze

on the animals. The shuffle of footsteps approached the bed.

"You're awake." Jacob's voice.

"Call off the dogs." Becca tried to sound assertive.

"You're frightened by them?"

He knew she was.

"Because of your father's threats about the neighbor's dog. Is that not right?"

She refused to respond.

"All right, Rebecca. Hearing your voice after all these years has softened my heart. I will do as you ask." He snapped his fingers and the dogs backed off.

Becca let out the breath she had been holding and dropped her head onto the thin mattress. The musty smell filled her nostrils and sickened her stomach.

Jacob peered down into her line of view.

Again her stomach rolled.

His eyes were wide and a smirk covered his mouth. "You haven't changed, Rebecca."

"I've gotten smarter."

He sneered. "Not smart enough to run from me."

She didn't answer. He was right. She'd allowed herself to get caught.

"I've missed you." His voice had a seductive pull that sent another volley of fear to weave around her spine.

"You've been busy, Jacob, wooing unsuspecting older women. You used them and killed them and ran off with their money and their treasures." She steeled herself to act defiant.

"You don't know where I've been or what I've done."

"I know you killed your mother."

His face twisted with rage. He raised his hand and

slapped her face. Her head crashed against the wall. Pain like white lightning shot through her.

"No," she cried, unable to control herself.

"Did you like that? Because that's what my mother used to do to me. My brother, Ezekiel, and I tried to run away from her, but she always found us. I never complained and suffered in silence. Do you know about that, Rebecca? Do you know how to suffer in silence?"

"You killed your brother and your wife and then burned down the house around them."

He shook his head. "Ezekiel died so that I might live."

"Are you parsing words, Jacob. Do you even understand what that means?"

"If you think I am *doppick,* dumb, why did you fall in love with me?"

The question Becca had struggled with for so long. Coming face-to-face with him after all this time allowed her to see more clearly. She hadn't been at fault. Jacob had wooed her just as he wooed the widows.

"I was young and foolish and taken by an older man who promised to show me the world."

"Yet you changed, Rebecca."

"You mean after you married Mary and still tried to have your way with me."

He laughed. His hand touched a lock of her hair. "You fought so hard, even when I surprised you in the barn. I knew your father would not believe you. He thought you tried to seduce me, didn't he?" Jacob chuckled. "Your father loved you, but he loved money more."

"My father saw what he wanted to see. He thought you were a good man. How completely you fooled him, Jacob."

"I told you not to run from me, Rebecca. I said how mad I got when people left me. Katie promised not to leave me, but she went home to pack a bag just as you had done the night I said I'd meet you at the covered bridge."

"Thankfully you never showed up because you were already laying claim to the widow Mary."

"Merely investing in our future. The farm was worth saving, which you didn't understand."

"I understood about Mary's failing health. You poisoned her."

He shook his head and laughed. "I provided relief from her aches and pains. She was old and infirmed when I married her. Since I couldn't have you, I wanted Katie, but she rejected me just as you had done."

"You killed her because she tried to escape." Anger mixed with Becca's fear. "Katie called me from Elizabeth's house and said she needed help. I didn't want Elizabeth to get hurt so I told Katie to go home, thinking my father would protect her until I arrived. Only you got there first."

Overcome with the guilt she still carried because she had sent Katie home to her death, Becca moaned.

"You're an animal, Jacob." She glanced at his dogs. "Although that's an insult to your pups."

He put his hands over his ears like a child. The sleeve of his shirt slipped down, exposing red welts on his arms.

"Does it bother you to hear the truth?" she pressed, thinking of Elizabeth and how she had fought to save herself.

He backed from the bed and pulled a bottle from a shelf in the corner, but she continued on.

"You killed Katie and my father and Elizabeth Konig and your wife and brother and mother. An Amish woman died in Tennessee and an *English* widow in Kentucky. You're planning to kill Fannie Lehman and me and probably more people until someone stops you."

She saw the rag in his hand and scooted closer to the wall, trying to distance herself from Jacob and the chloroform.

"No." She shook her head.

He glanced at the animals lying in the corner and nodded. Both dogs trotted to where he stood.

"The dogs won't hurt unless you try to escape. In that case, they will attack you. The last person they stopped did not survive." He leaned closer. She smelled his stale breath and saw the evil in his eyes. "You won't be able to run ever again."

He lowered the cloth to her face. She struggled, trying to free herself from the restraints and from the saturated rag that covered her nose. She held her breath far too long and gasped when her lungs were ready to burst.

Instead of air, she inhaled the chloroform that took her to another place far from Jacob Yoder and his dogs.

Colby raced along the Georgia back roads that skirted Freemont and led to the Amish community. He passed a number of farms and turned onto the narrow path that ran through the forested area.

At the clearing, he pulled to the side of the road, drew his weapon and ran toward the Lehman widow's house. He pushed through the door, surprised to find it unlocked, and moved stealthily from room to room.

Finding nothing that had bearing on where Jacob had taken Becca, he climbed the stairs, his senses on high alert and his weapon raised to fend off any attack. At the second-floor landing, he turned into the long hallway and made his way from room to room.

Once outside, he hurried to the barn and pulled the door open. Empty.

He studied the landscape. Even the dogs were gone. The widow was in the hospital. A phone call from Ray said she had revealed nothing they didn't already know.

Colby hurried back to his car.

Where was Becca and how would he find her?

The door creaked open. Becca kept her eyes shut, hoping Jacob would think she was still drugged.

"Hey, pups."

She was sickened by the irony of a man who killed in cold blood yet cared so lovingly for his dogs. Their paws brushed against the floor as they danced around their master.

Footsteps approached the bed. She could feel his presence and knew he was peering down at her.

Don't move.

Don't react to his nearness.

Think of better days.

A mental image came to mind. Colby standing next to her. His hand on her arm.

The thought soothed her fear and brought comfort.

"Rebecca?" Jacob touched her cheek. She struggled not to recoil. "You are still asleep?"

He turned and called the dogs. They scurried forward.

Their cool, moist snouts nuzzled her face, sending waves of repulsion rippling through her.

She fisted her hands tied behind her. Her nails dug into her flesh.

"Come, pups."

Evidently satisfied she was still drugged, Jacob's footsteps moved toward the door. The dogs whined.

"Yes, yes. We will take a walk while Rebecca sleeps."

The door opened, then closed. Silence filled the void.

Becca's eyes popped open. Her gaze flitted around the room. The bottle of chloroform sat on a wall shelf. No pictures. No curtain at the small window above the bed.

She strained against the ropes binding her hands and feet. Scooting to the side of the mattress, she forced her legs over the edge and pulled herself upright.

Her head pounded in protest, and she closed her eyes to the kaleidoscope of light exploding through her brain. Her stomach rumbled, and a wave of nausea forced her to drop her head and take deep breaths.

Something sharp jabbed the back of her leg.

She shifted to see more clearly. A raw edge extended from the bedframe.

She shimmied closer and twisted her hands until they touched the exposed metal. Would the edge be sharp enough?

Slowly, deliberately, she rubbed the rope against the roughness. Concentrating, she added force to each thrust. A portion of the thick hemp frayed loose. She groaned and tugged at the restraints, unable to break free.

She expected to hear Jacob's voice or the barking dogs.

Silence.

Returning to the task, she continued to saw the rope. Back and forth. Back and forth.

The metal nicked her hand. She grimaced but refused to stop. Every second was precious. She had to keep working to free herself.

Over and over again, she sliced at the remaining portion of cord. With one last thrust, the rope gave way.

Gasping with relief, she rubbed her wrists. Her shoulders ached. Leaning forward, she untied her legs and wobbled as she tried to stand. The room shifted. She hesitated and then stumbled to the door.

Opening it ever so slowly, she peered into the living area of the small cabin. Couch, card table and folding chair. Frayed, braided rug lay in front of the fireplace. Small kitchen area to the left.

Two doors. One beside the front window, the other next to the kitchen stove.

Gathering her courage, she lifted up a silent prayer. *Please, Lord, keep me safe.*

She hurried across the room and cracked the back door, seeing low hills and the end of a gravel driveway.

Stepping onto the small stoop, she breathed in the cool, fresh air. Her gaze flicked right, left.

A thick wooded area sat forty feet behind the cabin. She ran. Her legs ached and her head pounded. She tripped over a mound of dirt and nearly toppled forward.

Still sluggish from the chloroform, she stumbled again but pushed on. She had to keep moving. Eventually she would come to a road or a house or someone who could help her.

Ten feet farther and she'd disappear into the thick underbrush. Jacob would never find her there.

The sound came with the wind and sent terror through her veins.

"No, please."

Her blood chilled.

She glanced over her shoulder, knowing what was behind her.

Gaining...

Closing in...

She heard them...

The dogs.

Chapter 22

Colby joined Wilson in the CID Headquarters conference room where special agents and staff personnel were studying maps, plugging coordinates into laptops and relaying information to other law enforcement agencies around the state.

Wilson looked as worried as Colby felt.

"Don Palmer from the Freemont PD is compiling information on any abandoned cabins, caves, anyplace Yoder might be hiding," the chief said. "We've been doing a similar search with maps and satellite images of the surrounding areas. The Highway Patrol in Georgia and all neighboring states have photos of Yoder and Becca and are on the lookout for a blue Crown Vic. All county sheriff offices and police departments have also been notified."

Which still wasn't enough.

Colby checked his watch. Time was passing too quickly, and they were no closer to finding Becca.

Glancing at the maps strewn over the conference table, Colby tried to concentrate on what he knew about Jacob and his past. Amish communities. Rural locales. Isolated farms.

Something niggled in the back of his mind. What was it? If only he could remember.

Frustrated, Colby stepped into the hallway and headed to his cubicle. He glanced at the list of Amish communities and police departments still on his desk. A list Becca had compiled.

Rubbing his hand across his forehead, he groaned. *Please, Lord. Lead me to her.*

What had he heard or seen recently about a remote hunting cabin?

Rifling through the papers on his desk, he stumbled on the photo of Jacob Yoder attached to the printout of the Kentucky widow's property. Scanning the items from her estate, he felt a surge of euphoria and tapped in the number for the sheriff's office.

"I need Stan Oaks," he said after hastily stating his name and affiliation.

"He's not here, sir."

"Where is he?"

"In the hospital. Possible appendectomy."

Colby's stomach tightened and not with sympathy. "He mentioned a widow who died some months ago. Lucy Reynolds. She owned a cabin in Alabama."

"I can check on that, sir."

Colby shoved the phone closer to his ear.

He needed to get in his car and drive. He didn't know where. Staying in the office made him want to scream.

"Sir." The deputy came back on the line.

"Did you find the cabin's location?"

"I'm not sure, sir. There's mention of a place over the state line from Georgia. I checked the map. It's north of Dothan and west of Eufaula."

Colby raced back to the conference room. Wilson looked up when he reached for the Alabama map and spread it over the table.

"Where's the cabin in relation to Harmony, Alabama?" Colby asked the deputy, the phone still at his ear.

"It on a rural route, sir. Looks to be southeast of Harmony by about thirty or forty miles." He provided the address. Colby wrote it on a scrap of paper and handed it to Wilson.

The chief plugged the address into the satellite search. A shabby cabin came into view.

Colby went with his gut and his gut screamed Becca.

"I need a chopper."

"You've got it." Wilson picked up his own phone and contacted the aviation unit on post.

"They'll be ready to lift off as soon as you arrive at the airfield."

"Call Alabama Highway Patrol," Colby ordered. "I'll contact Lewis Stone in Harmony. We'll rendezvous at the cabin. Whoever gets there first needs to call me."

He left without uttering another word. Time was running out. He had to find Becca.

Becca woke and blinked her eyes. Her head throbbed. She moaned, remembering the dogs that had surrounded her and Jacob's hand crashing against her ear.

He'd dragged her screaming and kicking to the cabin

for another dose of chloroform that sent her into a chilling darkness where she'd confronted killer canines that attacked without mercy.

Hallucinations from the drug, no doubt, yet the attacks had seemed so real. She shivered at the memory and opened her eyes, needing to ground herself in reality. Four bare walls. Two Dobermans by the door. The chloroform cloth, near the bed, as if Jacob had dropped it on his way out the door.

"Give yourself up, Yoder."

The blare of a bullhorn sounded through the stillness. A similar voice had bellowed in her dreams. The warnings hadn't been her imagination.

She wanted to rejoice, but everything could go south fast, especially with a volatile psychopath like Jacob calling the shots.

Becca moved her legs and arms. She wasn't bound. Had law enforcement arrived before Jacob could tie her up again?

Overhead the *whomp, whomp, whomp* of the rotor blades of a helicopter cut through the air. The roar of the craft grew more intense. Wind blew the trees. Somewhere close by, the chopper touched down.

The dogs clawed at the door and whined.

In one swift move, she reached for the dropped rag and jammed it in her pocket. Having to search for a new cloth would cause Jacob aggravation and buy her time.

Another volley of pain. She clamped down on her jaw, unwilling to distract the dogs and draw attention to herself.

The door creaked open. She shut her eyes and inwardly groaned, expecting Jacob to approach the bed. She'd fight him to the death this time. Although weak as she was and still reeling from the effects of the chloroform, the odds would be overwhelmingly in his favor. Even without adding the Dobermans to the mix.

The door closed.

She raised her head.

No dogs.

She dropped her feet to the ground and stood. The room went black. Lowering her head, she grimaced until the vertigo passed.

Twilight was falling outside, and long shadows filled the narrow room.

Hurry, an inner voice warned.

She stumbled to the window. Small though it was, she unlatched the lock and pushed on the glass that refused to budge. Drawing on her reserves, she tried again with the same result. Breaking the window would alert Jacob. Still, it was an option, and she didn't have many at this point.

She glanced around the barren room and reached for the chloroform bottle on the shelf, unsure if it be heavy enough to break the glass.

"We know you're holding Special Agent Miller." The bullhorn again. "Let her go, Yoder."

The shuffle of feet.

The dogs barked just outside the door. Jacob was coming.

Think. Think.

She dumped chloroform on the rag and backed against the wall. If only he wouldn't see her there.

The door opened. Jacob stepped into the room.

Becca jumped him from behind and jammed the rag against his nose.

His elbow jabbed her gut. Air wheezed from her

lungs. He grabbed her wrist and turned until he had her in a rear choke hold with her right arm angled up against her spine. Pain radiated across her shoulder.

The dogs growled.

She kicked her foot back, hoping to make contact with Jacob's shin. He sidestepped. His hold around on her neck tightened.

He forced her forward. "You're coming with me."

She shook her head. "Let me go, Jacob. You can't escape now."

Half pushing, half dragging, he shoved her into the main room.

She kicked again, then locked her knees.

Enraged, he increased the tension on her wrist. Tears stung her eye. Sure that he'd rip her arm from its socket, she arched her back and moved forward.

He pushed her toward the window by the front door and smashed her face against the cool glass. Patrol cars from every agency—local police, county sheriff's office, state highway patrol—were parked along the dirt road.

Crushing her with his weight, he raised a gun to her head, cracked the front door and screamed through the opening. "You shoot and Rebecca dies."

She tried to fight him, but he was too big and too powerful. She needed help.

Glancing into the falling darkness, she searched for a face she knew. Someone she had pushed away forty-eight hours earlier because of her own fear. She hadn't wanted to expose the past, but it had found her just as Jacob had.

She saw him in the sea of uniforms.

Colby.

* * *

Colby's heart lurched. He couldn't take his eyes off Becca's twisted face shoved against the windowpane. Jacob was a killer and a maniac. At least she was alive, although Colby could only imagine what she'd endured.

He fisted his hands and swallowed the angry bile that filled his throat. From the beginning, Becca had insisted Jacob was seeking revenge. She'd been right. Now she was paying for law enforcement's inability to accept what she had told them all along.

A county deputy had been first on the scene. He'd called Lewis Stone who had driven here from Harmony. Thankfully, the sheriff had contacted Colby, although getting confirmation Jacob had captured Becca felt like a sucker punch to his gut. He'd wanted to double over in pain. Instead he formed a plan, seeing the layout of the cabin in his mind from the satellite imaging.

Jacob wanted freedom and a safe passage out of the country. Lewis had been negotiating with him over the phone. They'd switched to the bullhorn to let Becca know she wasn't alone.

As soon as the military chopper had touched down, Colby assessed the situation and looked for a way to get inside the cabin. The side window was too small, leaving the back door as the best option.

"I'm going in," Colby told the Harmony sheriff.

"Wait until dark."

"There's no time. Jacob's irrational and escalating."

"We'll go in together," Lewis insisted.

Colby held up his hand. "Stay on the bullhorn. He knows your voice. Keep him calm and agree to anything he wants."

"He wants a new car and a new life in Canada."

"Convince him everything will be forgiven if he doesn't harm Becca."

"That's what I keep promising him."

Would it be enough?

The sound of an approaching car caused both men to glance over their shoulders. Frank McDougal, the former county sheriff, sat behind the wheel.

Riding shotgun was a man Colby had met last night—and instantly disliked—when he and Lewis had tried unsuccessfully to convince the judge to sign the exhumation order.

Tucker Reynolds. Harmony's mayor was as pompous as he was large and flaunted his wealth along with his ego.

Colby's stomach soured. "What's Tucker doing here?" Lewis shook his head. "Probably another attempt to shove his weight around. Don't let him throw you. I'll handle the mayor and McDougal."

Colby nodded. "Give me three minutes to get in place." They both glanced at their watches.

"Where's that new car you promised me?" Jacob shouted from inside the house.

Lewis grabbed Colby's arm. "You need a vest."

Even at this distance, he saw the fear in Becca's eyes. "There's no time. Remember three minutes. Keep Jacob occupied."

Colby disappeared into the nearby stand of trees and made his way to the side of the cabin. He peered through the small window and saw the empty room. Continuing around the house, he approached the back door.

"Lord, let it be unlocked."

"The car's on the way." Lewis's voice over the bullhorn. "How much cash will you need, Yoder?"

Colby hesitated. Would Jacob take the bait or realize he was being set up?

"Five thousand," he called back.

Colby nodded. A small, but significant step in the right direction.

Lewis had been confident he could negotiate Becca's freedom. Colby wanted a more hands-on approach. He didn't trust Jacob, and waiting until nightfall would provide an opportunity for him to slip away under the cover of darkness.

"What denomination of bills?" Lewis again.

Colby glanced at his watch and counted down the remaining seconds. Three. Two. One.

Pulling in a deep breath, he turned the doorknob ever so slowly.

Chapter 23

Becca had felt a surge of relief when she first saw Colby outside the cabin. Now she couldn't find him in the crowd of uniformed personnel.

Hopefully he wasn't doing something foolish like trying to be a hero. *Please, Lord, keep him safe.*

She saw Frank McDougal raise the trunk of his car. Strange for him to be on-site.

An overweight guy in a coat and tie slouched against the hood of the same car, looking somewhat bored.

Another blast from the bullhorn. "We'll stock the car with food and water, Yoder."

"You'll be free, Jacob." She tried to sound confident and keep the fear from her voice.

"I do not trust them," he grumbled. "They will kill me if I let you go."

"That's not true."

"I told you before, Rebecca. You will never run from me again."

Lewis raised the bullhorn. "Is there anything else you need, Yoder?"

Jacob lowered his mouth to her ear. His stale breath fanned her cheek. "I need you."

She had to let Jacob think he was in control.

"I'll go with you willingly." She softened her voice and relaxed against him. "I was wrong before. Now I see more clearly. You had to endure so much. I ran away. No wonder you were angry with me."

He eased his hold on her ever so slightly. "I cannot forgive you, Rebecca."

"Of course not. I hurt you just as Katie did, but I can make it up to you."

"You are lying. My mother told me I was bad when I ran away, like my father had done. She said no one would love me or want to be with me."

"That's not true."

Becca glanced behind her, searching for the dogs. Jacob had let down his guard. She needed to act.

Seeing movement out of the corner of her eye, Becca peered into the shadows, knowing instinctively she had seen something.

She had seen Colby.

Standing in the open doorway, Colby quickly assessed his options. None of them was good with Becca in the line of fire.

Jacob stood behind her, a .38 special jammed against her head. The only hope was to provide a distraction.

As if sensing his presence, Becca nodded almost imperceptibly then jammed her heel onto Jacob's instep.

He cursed and lifted his injured foot.

She dropped like a dead weight, forcing him off balance. Twisting out of his grasp, she fell to the floor and rolled.

Colby raised his gun. Before he could fire, a dog lunged from out of nowhere. Razor-sharp teeth sank into his arm.

"Aah!" He fought to free himself.

Another dog grabbed his leg.

Becca screamed.

The gun slipped from Colby's hand.

Two tear-gas canisters sailed through the front door, landing on the frayed rug.

Smoke and flame billowed from the incendiary devices.

The weight of the dogs knocked Colby to the floor. He fought to free his arms, his legs. They were on him, over him, growling, biting, tearing at his flesh.

His only thought was Becca.

The threadbare rug caught fire. Smoke and tear gas mixed into a deadly combination.

Becca's heart stopped.

Colby lay on the floor, overpowered by the savage Dobermans. His gun out of reach.

One of the dogs backed into the fire and yelped.

He threw his weight and flipped the other Doberman onto his back. The dog pawed the air. Colby righted himself, and both animals ran yipping out the back door.

Jacob coughed and rubbed his eyes. Then, as if in slow motion, he raised his gun and took aim.

In half a heartbeat Colby would be dead, killed by the man who had taken everyone Becca had ever loved.

Ignoring the caustic tear gas that burned her throat, she groped along the floor, unable to find Colby's gun. *Please, God!*

Her fingers wrapped around the grip. Using two hands, she raised the weapon and squeezed the trigger.

Jacob gasped as the bullet pierced his chest. His eyes widened. He stared at her through the smoky haze. Disbelief washed over his face. He fell to his knees and crumbled chest-first onto the floor.

His blood, dark and thick, spilled across the hardwood planks just as her father's blood had done so long ago.

Before she could process what had happened, Colby was lifting her, holding her, running with her to safety.

Chapter 24

Colby ushered Becca from the smoke-filled cabin into the still-remaining daylight. He pulled her close and stared into her eyes, needing to ensure she was all right. "Did he hurt you?"

She shook her head and nestled against his chest. "I'm okay."

All around them cops raced into the cabin. Jacob was dragged outside. He was alive, but only barely. EMTs worked to save him.

Firemen poured water on the blaze. The smell of smoke and tear gas filled the air.

The dogs were found and tranquilized then carted off to the pound.

Additional medical personnel approached Colby. "We'll need to treat those bites, sir."

He held up his hand, unwilling to move away from Becca. "Give me a minute."

Lewis raced forward. "You two okay?"

Colby nodded. "Who tossed the gas?"

"McDougal. I thought you made the request."

"No, but it may have saved our lives."

"You should thank him," Becca suggested, easing from his arms.

"Good idea." Colby spied the former sheriff heading to his car and hustled toward him.

"Wait up, McDougal."

"Nice job, Colby." He laughed nervously. A muscle twitched in his neck. "That's one dude who needed to be taken down."

Confused by the former sheriff's comment as well as his unease, Colby thought back to what he knew about the case. Slowly one of the missing pieces fell into place.

"Funny," Colby said, sauntering closer, "that you didn't ask who was in the cabin since you buried Jacob eight years ago."

McDougal quickly shooed off the remark. "The body was badly burned. Of course, I thought it was Jacob back then. Who else would have been in Yoder's house?"

"His brother, Ezekiel, was visiting. What a shame you jumped to the wrong conclusion. Or was there a reason you said Jacob had died in the fire?"

Colby spied the mayor backtracking into the crowd. "Where're you going, Tucker? Back to Harmony to buy more land?"

The mayor grumbled. "What are you talking about?"

"I'm talking about the Yoder property. You needed another entrance into your mega subdivision. The widow Mary's farm was headed for foreclosure until Jacob took up with her. He turned the farm around, but you still wanted the land. That's why McDougal had to claim Jacob's body was recovered in the fire, so you could buy the property after the estate went to probate."

The mayor's eyes widened. "That's preposterous."

Samuel Hershberger, wearing his volunteer fire-fighter shirt open over his black pants and suspenders, stepped from the crowd of law enforcement personnel and first responders. "Jacob Yoder was my neighbor. His was not the body I pulled from the fire that night long ago."

Lewis patted McDougal's shoulder. "You knew the body you uncovered wasn't Jacob's, which means you falsified official documents. We need to have a talk."

On the way to the squad car, the sheriff pointed to the mayor. "I know where to find you, Tucker. Don't leave town."

Colby glanced at the ambulance. EMTs were still hovering over the stretcher where Jacob lay.

One of the paramedics approached Becca. "Yod-er's calling for you, ma'am. He's agitated. Might calm him a bit if you'd talk to him. He keeps saying *Mamm, Mamm.*"

"That's Pennsylvania Dutch. He's calling for his mother." She glanced at Colby.

"I'll go with you," he assured her.

She hesitated a moment and then nodded. Together they walked to the stretcher.

Jacob raised his head. His eyes were wild with fear, his lips dry and caked with blood.

"I… I'm sorry." He grabbed Becca's arm. "For… give…me, *Mamm.*"

Jacob thought she was his mother. He was dying and

wanted forgiveness, yet he had killed everyone Becca loved. How could she forgive him?

She stared down at Jacob for a long moment then her gaze softened as if the weight that she had carried for too long had eased.

She pulled in a deep breath and patted Jacob's hand. "I… I forgive you, Jacob."

"It's over." Becca stepped into Colby's arms as the ambulance pulled away.

Law enforcement still had more to do at the crime scene, and cops hustled back and forth between their squad cars and the cabin.

Looking up at him, she sighed. "I need to apologize for Thursday night. I gave my heart too readily when Jacob first came into my life and carried that burden, along with feeling responsible for Katie's death. I told her to wait for me at home that night, otherwise she might have been safe staying with Elizabeth. I was afraid your questions would force me to reveal my own guilt."

"Oh, honey, it wasn't your fault that Katie died. You're not to blame," he insisted.

Becca nodded ever so slightly. "I'm beginning to realize that you're right, but I still shouldn't have gotten upset with you."

He touched her chin and tilted her head back so he could see into her beautiful eyes that made him forget about killers and attack dogs.

"I thought I'd lost you that night, Becca, in one way, and then today I thought I'd lost you for good."

"Oh, Colby, I tried to take care of myself—only I

needed you. Just as I needed God when I shut Him out. My *datt* said I had a problem with pride."

"Your father had the problem. How could he not be proud of you, Becca? You're the most wonderful person I've ever met. You're beautiful and determined and strong and committed to doing what's right. I grew up surrounded by love and you had no one. Yet what you did for Jacob taught me about forgiveness and compassion. Jacob took everything from you. I don't know how you could forgive him."

"I had to or my heart would have turned as dark as his. I thought about the lessons I heard each Sunday as a child, about God's forgiveness and His love, about everlasting life and salvation. I now see the goodness of the Amish way that I turned my back on years ago."

He pulled her closer. "I love you, Rebecca Meuller and Becca Miller, whichever name you choose."

His smile faded replaced with an intensity he hadn't expected. "I'd like you to take my name someday."

"Oh, Colby."

He touched his finger to her lips. "Shh. Don't answer me now. We need more time. We need to heal. We need to laugh together and play together and work together. Then, I promise, we'll discuss the future, a future together."

She lifted her lips to his. "I love you, Colby Voss, and—"

Whatever else she was going to say would have to wait for another time because, at that moment, he lowered his lips to hers.

As they kissed, she snuggled into his embrace and Colby realized what the Amish had always known. Simple pleasures were the best. Having Becca, sharing their love, becoming a family someday soon, those were the God-given blessings that would last forever.

Epilogue

Four months later

Becca reached for Colby's hand as they walked along the beach. The waves lapped at their feet, and the sun hung low in the evening sky.

"Your family's Virginia Beach home is beautiful, Colby."

Breathing in the salty air, she turned to see their footprints in the sand. Becca remembered a scripture reflection about Jesus carrying a person along the shore during troubled times so that instead of two footprints there was only one.

"I told you my father talked about having to carry such a heavy cross," she said. "As much as he talked about God, he never knew how much he was loved by the Lord. If my *datt* had worried less about himself and more about others, he might have felt his load ease."

Colby squeezed her hand. "You and Katie were a help to him, I know."

"I was too headstrong."

He laughed. "I call that determination, which saved you when you were being held captive by Jacob."

She nodded. "He was a twisted soul who manipulated women for his own desires, including me. But I was young and didn't see who he really was until I took care of his wife."

"At least he lived long enough to confess everything to the sheriff, including that he had started the fire that killed his wife and brother."

"The last I heard," Becca said, "McDougal still claimed he had thought the body recovered from the fire was Jacob's."

Colby nodded. "At least the good folks of Harmony forced the mayor out of office. Tucker sold his real estate holdings and moved north, which left McDougal without a job. His house is in foreclosure, and his trial is still pending for falsifying documents."

"I'm sure justice will be served," Becca said as she sidled closer to Colby. He put his arm around her shoulder as they walked on, both lost in thought.

"My parents like you," Colby finally said.

"Are you sure?"

"Absolutely. They show their love with food. Mom made her special homemade carrot cake for dessert. Dad had the butcher cut extra-thick steaks that he'll grill tonight. You've definitely stolen their hearts."

She laughed. "If we stay too long, I'll gain weight."

"Gloria gave you a thumbs-up."

"She's darling and seems to adore her brother. As do

all the girls. I told them they had trained you well since you're such a gentleman."

He playfully splashed water on her legs. "Now you're making fun."

She stopped and looked into his eyes. "Actually I love having a man take care of me."

"You do." He gazed at her, his brown eyes reflecting the love she felt for him.

"Colby, I never thought I'd find a man to love. Not a man who made me feel so special."

"You are special, Becca."

He kissed her long and hard until their toes were buried in the wet sand.

Then turning her around, he pointed to the shoreline. "Someday, I'd like to have a home on the water. Maybe a beach house."

"You mean after the military?"

He nodded. "Although by that time, the kids will be in college, and I'll need two jobs to foot the bills."

"Maybe your wife will work."

"Whatever she wants to do."

Becca pretended to walk again. "I'm sure you'll be happy."

"Hey." He touched her arm. "Where are you going?"

"Don't you need to find a wife before you plan your future?"

"You're right."

He reached into his pocket and pulled out a small box, his expression suddenly serious. "Becca, would you marry me and be my wife?"

"Oh, Colby." She held out her hand and he slipped the ring on her finger.

She nestled closer, feeling his strong embrace. All

the love she had for him welled up within her. She'd found the perfect man, a wonderful, righteous man to walk with her into the future.

"Yes," she said, "I'll be your wife, and we'll have lots of babies, if God wills it, and a house on the beach and a lifetime of love."

Later they drove back to the Voss home. A huge sign hung over the door. "Welcome to the family, Becca! We love you!"

She smiled, wrapping her arm around Colby as they climbed the front steps. After all this time, Becca had a home and a family that cared for her. But more important, she had Colby, the man of her dreams, who would love her and cherish her forever.

Pulling her close, he lowered his lips to hers and kissed her once, twice, three times before he opened the door. She felt a sense of homecoming and knew that the rest of their lives would be as special as today had been with the sunshine and the warm water and blue sky.

With Colby at her side, their life together would be simply wonderful.

* * * * *

"It looks delicious," a male voice murmured in her ear.

"Eli!" she gasped and turned, her heart beating wildly. "You startled me."

His eyes twinkled. "I couldn't resist taking a look."

"And now you want a piece," she guessed.

His handsome mouth curved into a grin. *"Ja."*

"I shouldn't give you one, but…" She sighed dramatically, but she was pleased that he was eager to try it.

Eli looked delighted. "Then I may have a piece now?"

Martha chuckled as she picked up the cake and carried it into the other room. "One. You may have one slice." She sliced a piece, set it on a plate and gave it to him.

"Danki," he whispered, beaming. He dipped his fork into the cake, brought it to his lips.

Martha couldn't seem to take her eyes off him. "I should have brought two cakes."

"Eli? Are you coming outside?" a young voice called into the house.

Eli continued to eat his cake. "That was delicious," he declared after he'd eaten his last bite.

"I'm glad you enjoyed it," she said.

"I wouldn't mind a second helping, but I won't ask," he added quickly when he saw her disapproval.

"Gut," she replied, trying hard not to be charmed by his smile.

"I should go." He paused to study her a long moment. *"Danki* for the cake."

"You're welcome."

Martha continued to feel his gaze on her as she crossed the yard to join the other women who had gathered on the back lawn.

She knew the exact moment when Eli had rejoined his friends. The girlish laughter grated in her ears. Martha frowned. Why would she care who he spent his time with?

Suddenly, Eli locked gazes with her. A small teasing smile played about his lips, making her heart race.

You can bring chocolate cake anytime, he mouthed. Martha looked away.

She had to admit that Eli was both handsome and kind, and if she'd been younger, never married and had never suffered a broken heart, she might have felt differently. Like the giggling girls, she might have welcomed the man's attention. But she wasn't young and she wasn't looking for another husband.

Twice men had disappointed her. She wouldn't allow one to disappoint her a third time. Especially a man like Elijah Lapp.

Don't miss
ELIJAH AND THE WIDOW by Rebecca Kertz,
available April 2016 wherever
Love Inspired® books and ebooks are sold.

www.LoveInspired.com

SPECIAL EXCERPT FROM

Love Inspired
SUSPENSE

*His first case as a rookie K-9 unit officer is to protect
Gina Perry from the danger that is stalking her, and for
Shane Weston and his dog Bella, failure is not an option.*

*Read on for an excerpt from
PROTECT AND SERVE, the first book in a brand-new
K-9 cop miniseries, **ROOKIE K-9 UNIT**,
available April 2016 from Love Inspired Suspense.*

"Georgiiiinnnaaa!"

Gina Perry froze midstride in the middle of her bedroom. An explosion of panic detonated in her chest. She recognized the unmistakable singsong tone of her brother.

Oh, no. No, no, no. Tim had tracked her to Desert Valley, Arizona.

Frantic with alarm, she whirled around to search the confines of her upstairs bedroom. The sliding glass door to the terrace stood open, allowing the dark March night air to fill her house.

Where was he? How had he discovered where she'd been hiding? Had she made a fatal error that brought him to her door?

She stumbled backward on shaky legs just as her brother stepped from the shadows of her bedroom closet.

Light from the bedside table lamp glinted off the steel blade of a large knife held high in his hand. His face was covered by a thick beard, his hair stuck out in a wild frenzy and the mania gleaming in his hazel eyes slammed a fist of fear into her gut.

Choking with terror, she turned and fled down the stairs.

She couldn't let him catch her or he'd make good on his threat to kill her. Just as he had their father two years ago.

Her bare feet slid on the hardwood steps. She used the handrail to keep her balance.

Tim pounded down the stairs behind her. The sound hammered into her like nails on a coffin.

Her breathing came out in harsh rasps, filling her head with the maddening noise. She made a grab for her phone on the charger in the foyer but missed. Abandoning the device, she lurched for the front door and managed to get the lock undone and the door open.

Without a backward glance, she sprinted into the night, across the small yard to the road. Rocks and debris bit into her bare feet, but she ignored the pain. *Faster!*

Dear God, help me!

The Desert Valley police station was only a half mile down the quiet residential road on the west side of town. Street lamps provided pools of light that threatened to expose her. She ducked behind the few cars parked along the curb for cover and moved rapidly through the shadows.

She had to reach the police station. Only there would she be safe.

Don't miss
PROTECT AND SERVE by Terri Reed,
available wherever
Love Inspired® Suspense books and ebooks are sold.

www.LoveInspired.com

Turn your love of reading into rewards you'll love with
Harlequin My Rewards

**Join for FREE today at
www.HarlequinMyRewards.com**

Earn **FREE BOOKS** of your choice.

Experience **EXCLUSIVE OFFERS** and contests.

Enjoy **BOOK RECOMMENDATIONS**
selected just for you.

PLUS! Sign up now
and get **500** points
right away!

Earn
**FREE
REWARDS**
Join
Today!
HarlequinMyRewards.com

MYR16R

Love Inspired®

Love the Love Inspired book you just read?

Your opinion matters.

Review this book on your favorite book site, review site, blog or your own social media properties and share your opinion with other readers!